Eneit, Simon had called her in the old language.
Eneit—*his soul, his inner life*. And as he said the
ancient word, his green eyes were clear, hiding
nothing.

Rhiannon very nearly cried out that she would
finally yield and be Simon's wife, but she could not
say the words—for thus far she had won. Simon was
her lover, and she had promised no more than she
ever intended.

But to be his wife...A wife swore faith no matter
what her husband did—and Rhiannon knew she
could be destroyed if she paid back his false coin
with false coin of her own.

is the fifth book of the magnificent romantic saga,
THE ROSELYNDE CHRONICLES. *Once
again, Roberta Gellis weaves a colorful medieval
tapestry of power and passion, and now introduces
her most fascinating heroine, Rhiannon.*

*Roberta Gellis's historical romances are "care-
fully researched costume dramas that never fail
to bring a long-ago time wonderfully to life....
Her description of high romance is as successful
as her depiction of battle scenes....Delightful."*
—Publishers Weekly

Rhiannon

Roberta Gellis

PLAYBOY
PAPERBACKS

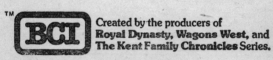

TM

Created by the producers of
Royal Dynasty, Wagons West, and
The Kent Family Chronicles Series.

Executive Producer: Lyle Kenyon Engel

RHIANNON

Published simultaneously in the United States and Canada by Playboy
Paperbacks, New York, New York. Printed in the United States of
America. Library of Congress Catalog Card Number: 81-82368. First
edition.

Books are available at quantity discounts for promotional and industrial
use. For further information, write to Premium Sales, Playboy Paperbacks, 1633 Broadway, New York, New York 10019.

ISBN: 0-872-16933-2

First printing January 1982.

This book is dedicated to the many faithful readers who wrote the publisher and me requesting a continuation of the Roselynde Chronicles. I wish here to thank them for their interest and the trouble they have taken.

PREFACE

In 1233 Richard, the Earl Marshal, raised rebellion against King Henry III because of the intolerable behavior of two ministers the king had appointed, Peter des Roches, Bishop of Winchester, and Peter of Rivaulx. These men advised the king to turn out nearly all his past officials and appoint new ones, thereby concentrating power completely into his own hands. Whether or not their advice was given for the king's benefit (it probably was), it was very bad advice for England, which had a long tradition of shared power between the king and his barons. In addition, the barons had a written guarantee of the power of the barony in the Magna Carta—to which the king had sworn when he was crowned.

For the family of Roselynde this problem raised dangerous strains. The older members, Ian and Alinor and Geoffrey and Joanna, remain faithful to Henry—Ian out of honor, Geoffrey because he is the king's cousin. Geoffrey has been greatly favored by Henry, and feels he cannot "bite the hand that has fed him." When we first meet them, Simon, Alinor and Ian's son (now twenty-two), and Adam, Alinor's son by her first marriage (now thirty-five), lean strongly in the other direction, and they are joined by Sybelle, Joanna's eldest daughter.

CAST OF CHARACTERS

❖•❖•❖•❖•❖•❖•❖•❖•❖•❖•❖•❖•❖•❖•❖•❖•❖•❖•

THE LORDS AND LADIES OF ROSELYNDE KEEP
Alinor de Vipont, Lady of Roselynde
Ian de Vipont, Alinor's husband
Adam Lemagne, Alinor's son by her first marriage
Joanna FitzWilliam, Alinor's daughter by her first marriage
Simon de Vipont, Alinor and Ian's son
Gilliane Lemagne, Adam's wife
Geoffrey FitzWilliam, Joanna's husband
Sybelle FitzWilliam, Joanna and Geoffrey's eldest daughter

THE COURT AND BARONAGE OF ENGLAND
Henry III, King of England
Peter des Roches, Bishop of Winchester, Henry's primary adviser
Peter of Rivaulx, Winchester's nephew
Richard of Cornwall, Henry's brother and husband of Isabella, Earl of Pembroke's sister
Richard Marshal, Earl of Pembroke
Seagrave ⎫
Ferrars ⎬ barons torn between their loyalty to the king and the terms of the Magna Carta
Norfolk ⎭

THE CHURCH
Roger of London, Bishop of London
Robert of Salisbury, Bishop of Salisbury

THE OUTLAWRY AS DETERMINED BY THE KING
Hubert de Burgh, Earl of Kent, Henry's former tutor and adviser
Gilbert Bassett
Richard Siward

THE WELSH

Llewelyn ap Iowerth, Prince of Gwynedd, Rhiannon's father

Rhiannon uerch Llewelyn

Kicva, Rhiannon's mother

Gruffydd, Rhiannon's bastard half-brother

David, Rhiannon's legitimate half-brother

Gwydyon, Rhiannon's grandfather

Angharad, Rhiannon's grandmother

NOTE: There is a glossary of feudal terminology provided at the end of the book.

Irish Sea

River Mersey

Chester

CLWYD ← River Dee

Aber
Bangor • • Krogen Keep

Angharad's Hall

Caernavon

Dines Emrys

GWYNEDD

Powys

POWYS

River Severn

River Wye

Hereford

Builth Gloucester

Grosmount

Monmouth

DYFED Usk

GWENT

Bristol Channel

AN ENLARGEMENT
OF
WALES

© BOOK CREATIONS 1981

RON TOELKE 1981

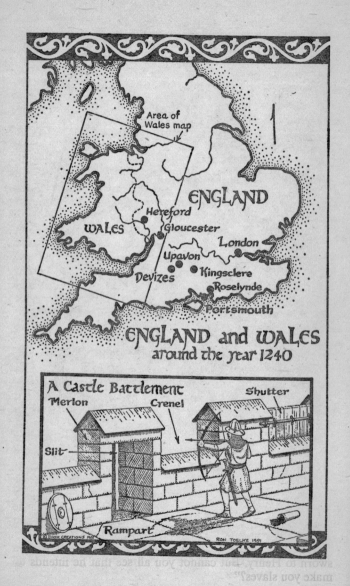

Area of Wales map

ENGLAND

WALES

Hereford
Gloucester
London
Upavon
Devizes   Kingsclere
Roselynde
Portsmouth

ENGLAND and WALES
around the year 1240

A Castle Battlement

Merlon   Crenel   Shutter

Slit

Rampart

© BOOK CREATIONS 1991   RON TOELKE 1991

CHAPTER 1

❖•❖•❖•❖•❖•❖•❖•❖•❖•❖•❖•❖•❖•❖•❖•❖•❖•❖•❖•❖

"You will kill Papa!" Joanna hissed, holding Simon, her half-brother, by the wrist as hard as she could.

"And I will die of frustration myself if I do not speak my piece. The barons must not tolerate King Henry's behavior," Simon snarled, but his voice was low, and he cast a glance over his shoulder toward the stairwell where his father and mother might appear at any moment. He looked in vain for a sympathetic face among his gathered relatives.

Restraining Simon was like clinging to a living version of the black leopard painted on his shield. Joanna could feel the ripple of steel-hard sinews under the skin and sense the quivering tension in his whole body, but he did not pull loose. His eyes were full of flickering green and gold light, and his beauty could have stopped a woman's heart. He had Ian's face and Alinor's eyes, Joanna thought, and until this visit, Joanna would have said he had the best of both their natures.

"Ian is not so frail as that," Adam rumbled. There was a defensive note in his voice, however, and his eyes, too, went to the stairwell. He adored his stepfather and, simultaneously, resented the implication that Ian was aging and secretly feared that any exertion might in fact be a strain for him.

"That is not what Joanna means," Gilliane said. Her voice had none of Joanna's whiplash quality, but there was a silken strength in it. Fourteen years of happy marriage to Adam had changed her from a fearful, anxious girl to a very strong, though quiet, woman. "You know what kind Ian is," she continued. "What he has sworn, he will abide by. You will break his heart, Simon, if you openly defy the king."

"Why?" Simon asked passionately. "I have not even sworn to Henry. But cannot you all see that he intends to make you slaves?"

Gilliane, too, was wondering what was wrong with Simon. Not only was his disposition usually very sweet, but he had never cared a bit about politics. There was a wild streak in him—not in the usual sense of drinking and gambling, but in disregarding practical matters. Unlike the rest of his family, he was totally uninterested in land and had little sense of possession. He did not wish to be encumbered by the management of property. So, usually, he did not care what the king did, but after Henry had dismissed the Earl of Pembroke's deputy from office—which he had no right to do—Simon had come roaring out of Wales to demand that his family defy the king.

"I have sworn to him, and I am still of your mind, Simon," Adam growled. "There can be no question of oath-breaking if we refuse to go to this summoning. The king has broken *his* oath first. Does he hold by the great charter that he has sworn to more than once? Well, Geoffrey, what have you to say?"

Geoffrey, Joanna's husband, had been sitting in one of the deep window embrasures, staring out into the beautiful garden of Roselynde keep. Roses made a blaze of color against the wall, and their perfume, mixed with the sweeter, stronger scent of the lilies that edged the beds, came up to him on the soft, sun-warmed breeze of June. He was only six years older than Adam, but his face was graven with deep lines of worry, and his eyes, golden in laughter or rage or passion, were dull mud-brown.

"What can I say?" he replied to Adam's prodding. "The king has broken that oath and others, yes. . . . But he is no John, Adam. There is no *evil* in Henry. He wishes to be loved. He desires to do good—"

Simon made a strangled, furious sound and Geoffrey's eyes moved to him.

"I cannot blame you for your anger," Geoffrey admitted, "but what can I do? There is a close blood tie between us—he is my cousin—and he has cherished me and mine. William and Ian are in his household, and he is as kind and indulgent to my sons as a fond uncle. Can I turn on him like a mangy cur and bite the hand that has fed me?"

"And what will you do when he bites you?" Simon challenged. "Has he not turned on those closest to him already? Did he not call Hubert de Burgh 'father' on one day and imprison him in chains in a deep vault the next?"

"Henry will not turn on Geoffrey." Ian's voice, deep and slightly hoarse, came across to them from the entryway.

Everyone tensed a trifle. Gilliane rose from the window seat opposite Geoffrey and drew Alinor forward to sit with her, while Geoffrey smiled a similar invitation to Ian. Now Ian looked around at the assembled faces. The profusion of black curls was gone and his olive skin was sagging somewhat over his jowls and throat, but the luminous dark eyes were as warm and bright as ever and the good bones beneath the aging flesh showed where Simon had inherited his looks.

"Blood is a sacred tie to Henry," Ian reiterated. "He will never strike at Geoffrey, just as he has never acted vengefully toward Richard of Cornwall."

"Sit down, Papa," Simon urged.

"Do you think I am exhausted from walking down the stairs," Ian teased, "or do you want me to sit so I will not collapse with shock when you tell me you want all of us to join Richard Marshal's party?"

Joanna frowned furiously at her half-brother, and Ian smiled at her, slipped an arm around her waist, and kissed her brow. Alinor laughed. She had grown somewhat heavier with the years and her black hair was now iron gray, but her acerbic personality had not changed and her eyes snapped and sparkled as clearly as Simon's.

"Perhaps it is time you presented your lord with a new young one, Joanna, and stopped trying to be a mother to Ian and to me," Alinor remarked, smiling. "We are neither blind nor stupid. We hear quite well—even what is not said aloud."

"Then I assume you have heard that Henry is become insufferable," Simon snarled.

"It is not so much Henry himself as the Bishop of Winchester and that bastard of his," Adam said, trying to smooth over the vicious tone in Simon's voice.

"Peter of Rivaulx is said to be Winchester's nephew," Ian corrected absently, while his mind was obviously elsewhere. Then he sighed and went to join Geoffrey.

"Winchester has been too long out of this country. He seems to have forgotten everything he once knew about the English."

"No," Geoffrey said softly, "no. He has not forgotten. He remembers very well. He always hated the fact that power in this realm was divided by right between the barons and the king. He was as strong for the king's uncontested right in John's day as now, but John was so hated that Winchester realized any effort to curb the barons would bring war. In the end John tried it, of course, and it did bring war."

"You would have thought Winchester would have learned something from that," Simon remarked caustically.

"Yes. I am disappointed in him. We were good friends once," Ian mused.

"Oh, he loved you well. You were always faithful. Why should he not love you? And you always see the best in everyone, my love," Alinor said. "Those who desire power seldom see the truth and never learn."

"That is true and not true," Geoffrey amended. "Winchester assigned the wrong reasons to the resistance toward John. He thought it was because John was hated for himself."

"Well, he was," Adam put in, his mouth set in grim lines.

"Yes, which made men spring to arms faster," Simon cried passionately, "but even had they loved him, they would not have permitted the king to trample on their rights, seize their property without reason or justice, and set himself above the law. Nor will they endure it now."

"Nor should they," Ian agreed, "but Henry is *not* John, and there is no reason to fly to arms. I did not take up arms against John, and I certainly will not offer violence to the king who trusts me and to whom I swore when he was a child."

"There is no question of taking up arms," Joanna said quickly. "Even Richard Marshal has no intention of taking up arms. We are only discussing what to do about this summons to a council on the eleventh of July."

"What is there to discuss about that?" Ian asked.

"Whether to go or not—that is what there is to discuss," Simon snapped.

"Do not be a fool!" Ian responded sharply.

"Are you afraid to defy him?" Simon taunted.

"Simon!" Alinor exclaimed. "You shame me! I knew your father should have used his belt on you more often, and if he did not, I should have. Thus are we justly rewarded for our indulgence."

Simon had crimsoned so much that tears came to his eyes, and he knelt down before his father. "I am sorry, Papa. You know I did not mean that—not that *you* are afraid for yourself."

Ian touched the unruly black curls of the bent head. "I know what you meant, and I am not ashamed that I fear for my loved ones. When you have what I have in this family, you will also be less daring. But that is not why I said you were a fool, Simon."

"What your father meant," Geoffrey remarked dryly, "was that absenting ourselves from the council can accomplish no purpose beyond angering the king. We have already used that method to no purpose. Now, since Henry will be enraged in any case, it is reasonable to tell him what we think in plain language and anger him that way. If there is to be a measure of bravery, Ian's way is more courageous than sulking from a distance."

"You are right about that," Adam put in, his eyes brightening. "I was half-minded to go back to Tarring and tell my vassals to close themselves into their keeps, but I like Geoffrey's notion much better. First I will tell the king what I think of him, his ways, and his new favorites, and *then* I will seal my keeps."

"You will need to seal them if that is the way you go about it," Gilliane pointed out tartly.

Alinor laughed. "Sometimes you remind me very much of your father, Adam. He could be horribly honest at just the wrong time, so that he ended by running his head into a stone wall."

"But not about managing a king, beloved," Ian reproved.

"Oh, yes," Alinor insisted. "He crossed the last Henry so unwisely that he was told to go sit on his lands and not stir lest worse befall him."

"That Henry and this are not to be compared—unfortunately." Geoffrey sighed. "The one was a man—sometimes overhasty, greedy, and unjust, from what I have heard, but a real man in every sense. This one is a spoiled child who never grew up."

"Such a man is not fit to be king," Simon said, lifting his head. "Richard of Cornwall, however—"

"Do not let Cornwall hear you say that," Ian ordered sharply, "or he will kill you where you stand. Henry has many faults, but lack of love for his brother and sisters is not one of them, and they return that love full measure. Richard of Cornwall may stand up in full council and roar at the top of his lungs that his brother is a coward and a fool, but he loves Henry dear, very dear. He will never rebel against him. That door is closed, Simon."

"Yes, it is," Geoffrey agreed forcibly. "I tell you that if Henry died in battle against rebels, Richard would pursue them until the last man was dead. He will not take the throne while Henry lives, and he would never forget or pardon any man who had even the remotest connection with those who caused his brother's death."

"I know it," Simon said ruefully. "I do not know why my tongue is running at odds with my head today. I just feel that if I cannot do *something*, I will burst."

"The only thing you could do in the mood you are in is harm," Ian remarked wryly. "Why do you not go back to Wales? This is a most beautiful season in the hills. No doubt Llewelyn can find a nice little war for you if you feel you must break heads."

"No!" Simon exclaimed, and stood up abruptly.

Ian looked very much surprised. He had, with his overlord's approval, ceded the Welsh lands Llewelyn had bestowed upon him to his son as soon as Simon had won his spurs. It was a happy arrangement for everyone. The Welsh lands needed closer attention than Ian had been able to give them since he had married Alinor and taken up the responsibility of defending her huge estate. Simon was so wild that he would have made endless trouble for his parents idling about the rich, smooth-functioning estates in England. Llewelyn was glad to have a strong, eager fighter to lead Ian's men. Alinor and Ian, although they worried about him a little, were delighted to have their son usefully occupied instead of making mischief.

Wales and Simon suited each other as a hand fits a glove. There was something feral and untamed about

Simon that was more at home in the untouched forest and precipitous mountains of northern Wales than in the tilled fields and softly rolling hills of Sussex. The young man had always loved the Welsh estates passionately—which was why Ian gave those to him rather than the northern lands—and Simon was always happier there and in Llewelyn's court with its barbaric undertones than in England. Thus, Ian was startled when his suggestion was rejected so violently. In the past Simon had been delighted to be sent to Wales.

"Joanna, have you been advertising my imminent demise again?" Ian asked his daughter-by-marriage, half-exasperated, half-laughing. Nothing Joanna did was ever really wrong in his eyes, especially not the anxious care of him that so clearly demonstrated her love. "I know my lungs were affected again last winter," he complained, "but I am hale and hearty now. There is no reason for Simon to hang over me, expecting me to fall on my deathbed at any moment."

"No, I did not 'advertise your imminent demise'!" Joanna protested indignantly. "Anyway, the way Simon has been acting, he is more likely to throw you into your deathbed than help you out by his presence."

"I simply do not wish to go to Wales now," Simon said in a more controlled voice. "I have been thinking it over and I, too, believe that Geoffrey is right. We should go to the council, and we should make clear our displeasure at the king's behavior."

"Yes, but not in that tone of voice if you wish Henry to moderate his actions," Geoffrey pointed out. "I do not say that Henry cannot be forced, but if he is, he will remember and hold a spite. On the other hand, if he can be convinced by soft words, the same end can be achieved without making him hate us."

A chorus of women's voices agreed and went on to suggest methods of leading the king away from his folly, but Simon did not hear. When his father said the word *Wales*, a face had risen into his mind's eye, a voice had sounded, not in his ear but on his heartstrings. Rhiannon! *Rhiannon of the Birds*—she whose bare feet twinkled like silver in the dew-starred, moonlit grass of a high valley, whose silvery white hands drew silver songs from the silver strings of her harp, whose streaming hair was perfumed with the wild flowers and mosses and rich earth, whose lips tasted of wild strawberries from the high pastures warmed with the spring sun. Rhiannon! The only woman he had ever loved—and she would not have him.

Simon could not remember a time when he had not tumbled females. Even before puberty, he had wielded his tool with great satisfaction to himself and his partners, if with little effect in the procreative sense—and never had he been refused. In fact, it was rare indeed that he needed to ask. The girls and women had always come after him. Nor did he refuse any—young and old, pretty and ugly— Simon gave them the best his magnificent body could produce. But he did not offer, did not even think or speak of love—and he warned all his lovers that he would be inconstant.

The permanence of marriage held no appeal for Simon. His need for gentle warmth, for steadfast, unwavering affection was well supplied by his parents, his half-sister and half-brother, and their spouses. The unquestioning adoration of children, the need for heirs to the land that would be his when his father died, was also provided by his nieces and nephews. Simon already had his eye on one of Adam's younger sons who seemed to him to have the temperament to deal with the northern barons.

Yet, when he had first seen Rhiannon singing to her harp in her father's hall, before he had even exchanged a word with her, he had been conquered. It was not her beauty, although she was beautiful; many more beautiful women had lain in his arms without touching his heart. Perhaps it was the wild tale she sang, full of enchantments and tragedy, that had sent love's dart into him. She looked a part of that ancient tale herself. Her gown, heavy with gold and jewels, was a hundred years out of date; her hair, black and shining as the sleek feathers of a raven, flowed unconfined by veil or net or wimple down to her knees. Jewels hung in her ears and bound her brows. Simon had never seen a woman who appeared so wild and free.

"Who is she?" Simon had asked Prince Llewelyn when Rhiannon's song had ended.

"My daughter," the Lord of Gwynedd had answered, smiling, "or so I believe. Her mother is not a woman with whom a man would argue—or trifle—not even I. I say I do not believe in such things, but Kicva is a 'wise woman.' Kicva's father, Gwydyon, was bard to my court in those years, and she came to me and said she wished me to sire a daughter on her. It was no burden; she was a lovely thing. Later she brought Rhiannon to me from time to time that I should know her and she me, but she never asked for anything nor would even take what I offered freely. Of course, they were not in need. Gwydyon was a real power in the hills and Kicva also. Rhiannon . . . I do not know. She is stranger than her mother in some ways."

"Is she married?" Even as he asked, Simon wondered why he had done so. It had never mattered to him before whether an attractive woman was married or not. Those who were ready to betray their husbands, Simon took without a thought; those who loved their men, he did not pursue. But in the infinitesimal pause before Llewelyn answered, Simon knew it was of great importance to him, and his breath sighed out in relief when Llewelyn shook his head.

"God knows I have presented enough men to her," Llewelyn said, "and I am willing to dower her with lands as well as what she will have from her mother. Rhiannon will have none of it. They are not marrying women. Gwydyon did not marry Angharad, Kicva's mother—or, more like, she would not marry him."

"That is very strange," Simon said. The ruses his unmarried mistresses had used to attempt to trap him into marriage were myriad. He had not thought the single state was ever a woman's choice, except those who professed the celibacy of a religious life. "Did they have many lovers?" he asked.

Llewelyn laughed. "I never had the courage to ask Kicva, to tell the truth, and Rhiannon just laughs at me and says it is not my business when I ask her why she will not take a husband."

"But as her father it is your right—"

"With Rhiannon it is easier to name a right than to enforce it. I do not provide for her. I cannot even command her comings and goings." Suddenly Llewelyn shook his head. "Do not reach for Rhiannon, Simon; you will get your fingers burnt."

"Do you forbid me, my lord?" Simon asked, his breath catching again with a strange anxiety. "I mean you no dishonor." His eyes wandered to Rhiannon where she stood talking to her half-brother Gruffydd.

Llewelyn's eyes followed Simon's and then moved back to the dark, incredibly handsome face. "That is something new in you," he said thoughtfully. There was a pause while Llewelyn considered what Simon had proposed half-unconsciously. "Certainly I would not oppose such a marriage," he went on, "but your father and mother might not welcome it."

"My father would not object, my lord," Simon said eagerly. "He loves you well and would be glad of another bond with your house. My mother, I think, would welcome any marriage I was willing to make and—" his eyes wandered to Rhiannon again, "—and she would understand Lady Rhiannon better than most other women. She is old now, but her spirit is still strong."

Llewelyn smiled reminiscently. He knew Alinor well. "That is true, but I fear they will never meet despite the ease with which *we* seem to have decided this matter. I do not believe you will ever get Rhiannon so far from her hills. You may try for her with my blessing, but remember I have no power to give you more. Rhiannon is a law unto herself. I fear you will have only grief from her."

Simon had not believed him, nor had he noticed the sly glance that touched him and moved away. It would serve his purposes very well, Llewelyn thought, if Simon married Rhiannon; he should have thought of it himself, but at least he had applied the right spurs now that his brain had been jogged. He watched with mild amusement the confident carriage as Simon crossed the hall. This would be a struggle worth witnessing.

There was no reason for Simon to lack confidence. No woman except those whose hearts were already given had ever refused him. When he approached Rhiannon he was more concerned that he would be disappointed by her on closer acquaintance than that she would not welcome his attentions. At first, indeed, it seemed as if he would succeed with her as easily as he expected. When he came near, Gruffydd looked up from his half-sister's face and said rather nastily, "Here is our tame Saeson."

It was a remark calculated to raise animosity in both Simon and any full-blooded Welshwoman, but Rhiannon knew her half-brother and turned to look at Simon without apparent reluctance. A slow, appreciative smile dawned on her face.

"Heavens, how beautiful you are," she said. "A veritable work of Danu."

"I might say that as well for you, Lady Rhiannon," Simon rejoined, but his voice did not hold the light laughter with which he usually addressed and flattered women.

Close up she was even more impressive, although actually less lovely. Her nose was a trifle too long, her mouth too full and wide for absolute beauty; however, it was not possible for Simon to think of such things. Her eyes did not drop as a modest maiden's should; they seized him and held him boldly. They were large, almond shaped, tipped upward at the outer corners, and of a clear green—a color Simon had never seen except on a cat. More intriguing still, she examined him with the frank, slightly contemptuous appraisal that a feline bestows upon humans. No blush mantled her cheeks, although her skin, denied the sun which tanned it in milder weather, was white as snow.

"Oh, you might say that and any number of other pretty things, I should think," she answered, laughing. "I imagine you are a great master at saying sweet things to women."

"I tell them what they wish to hear," Simon said, stung by her amusement. "What do you wish to hear? That your singing still sounds within me? That the bright glance of your eyes has blinded me to all other beauty? I will say it, and it is true. I am no liar—even to women."

"How can you tell a woman what she wishes to hear and yet be no liar?" Rhiannon asked. There was no sneer in her voice. She sounded genuinely interested in the solution to such a paradox.

"Deep within, each woman knows her own beauty. There is always something lovely in a woman, unless her soul is corroded beyond hope with evil. The ugliest may have a sweet smile or a soft skin or a warm, gracious voice. Women are not fools. They may seem to desire and to accept untrue flattery, but if you praise what is truly beautiful in them, you will strike them to the heart."

The laughter vanished from Rhiannon's face and the contempt from her eyes. She stared unwinking at Simon, then shuddered slightly. "You are a very dangerous man, very. It would behoove me to have no more to say to you."

"Are you afraid?" Simon's eyes sparkled with challenge. "Yes."

Simon laughed. "Your father has just told me that I should not reach for you lest my fingers be burnt. In response to that, I asked for your hand in marriage."

"No!" Gruffydd spat. He had been listening to them with a steadily blackening scowl, and now he exploded. "My sister will not be sold to a Saeson. I will bestow her on a suitable man in Wales when I—"

"I will be sold to no one," Rhiannon interrupted sharply. "I will marry where I choose, when I choose, and not at all if I choose. You have no right to bestow me any more than does Lord Llewelyn. Do not be a worse fool than you can help, Gruffydd. You are allowing this Norman-English-Welsh matter to unsettle your thinking. Not all Cymry are paragons of virtue and not all Saeson are evil."

"Perhaps not all Welshmen are perfect," Gruffydd snarled, "but I still prefer to live and breed within my own kind. I say my sister will not go to a stranger—"

"What a fool you are!" Rhiannon repeated in an exasperated voice and, in defiance, placed her fingers on Simon's wrist. "Let us go," she urged.

"I am sorry," Simon said as he led her away. "I did not mean to make a quarrel with your brother. Nor, I hope, will you misunderstand me. Your father neither sold nor bestowed you. What he said was that I might try for you with his blessing, but that you were a law unto yourself and he had no power over you."

A faint blush of pleasure tinted Rhiannon's translucent skin, but it receded at once. The green eyes lifted to Simon's. "Oh, you are clever," she exclaimed. "You are a very devil for seeing into my heart."

"I have seen nothing," Simon denied, but that was not really true. Unlike most other men, Simon was intimately acquainted with passionately independent women, and he understood a great deal. "I have only repeated to you your father's words to me," he went on. "He also said you would bring me only grief. But I am not afraid. It is not possible to know joy without daring sorrow—and I see in you a hope of joy such as I have never known."

"No doubt you see that same hope in each woman you pursue," Rhiannon remarked, the laughter coming back into her eyes. "To say that you hope would be no lie. Each time you would only need to confess that your hope had not been fulfilled."

"I see someone has been warning you against me," Simon sighed. "The half of it is not true at all, the other half much exaggerated. Were I what is said of me, I would need seven of everything a man uses to make love *and* the ability to send each to a different place at one time."

Rhiannon burst out laughing at the mock plaintiveness in Simon's voice and the spurious, outraged innocence of his expression. "You are wrong," she told him. "I have read what you are in your face. I do not even know your name."

"I beg your pardon, Lady Rhiannon. My name is Simon de Vipont, and I am son to Lord Ian and Lady Alinor of Roselynde. I was knighted by King Henry last Christmas and did fealty to your father for the keep at Llyn Helfyg, Crogen keep, Caerhun, and Dinas Emrys at the May Day festival. How is it that you were not there, my lady?"

She did not answer him at once, but stood staring. "*You* hold Dinas Emrys that looks over the Vale of Waters?"

"Yes. It is the most beautiful place in the world, is it not? From the keep I can look down Nant Gwynant until I feel the soul drawn out of me into the blue distance."

"You love it," Rhiannon said. It was a statement, not a question.

"The best of all my holds," Simon confirmed. "Although each is dear to me in a special way."

"Do you hear nothing in the winds that play around Emrys rock?" Rhiannon asked, her eyes fathomless.

"Perhaps, but nothing that I need fear," Simon replied. "I am no unwelcome conqueror to this land—in spite of what Gruffydd said. Llewelyn gave the lands to my father out of love and trust. I was squire to William Marshal, Earl of Pembroke, and served in south Wales, but my heart has always been here—which is why my father ceded the lands to me while he yet lives. But you did not answer me, Lady Rhiannon. Why have I never seen you in your father's court before?"

"Because, I suppose, you came in spring or summer. I am seldom at any keep then. I go to my mother's place, Angharad's Hall, in the hills, after the New Year's festival in March. Why are *you* here in the dead of winter, Sir Simon?"

"The lands are mine now, and I must oversee them in all seasons. I will be here in Wales always—except at such short times as I visit my family."

There was an odd expression in Rhiannon's face, approval mingled with apprehension; however, all she said was, "You say so, but you will soon tire of our barbaric ways and hie you back to the softer air of England."

Simon laughed. "No one can know the future, but it is very amusing that it is foretold so differently for me on each side of the border. My family sent me here because they believed I could not be content with the tame ways of Sussex. Now you tell me I will soon tire of the wild ways of Wales. I do not think so. I do not think I will ever wish to leave my lands, except for some small times to be with those I love."

"You are too young to know what you believe," Rhiannon said sharply, as if she were trying to convince herself.

"Ah, grandmother," Simon teased, "your gray hair and wrinkles make me sure the wisdom of great age infuses the words you speak. How old are you, Rhiannon? Sixteen? Seventeen?"

"I am one and twenty, and women are always older than men." She paused, bit her lip, and said even more sharply, "And when did I so shame myself that I have descended from Lady Rhiannon to Rhiannon alone?"

"I beg your pardon, my lady." Simon bowed deeply and without mockery, but his eyes still twinkled with mischief. "No affront was intended. You so enchanted me with your time-won knowledge of men that for a moment I lost my sense of propriety and spoke as a man to his loved one, without formality."

"You never had a grain of propriety to lose," Rhiannon snapped, but the corners of her mouth turned upward. "Do you not know it is highly improper to ask a woman's age? And do not bother to find another smooth reply. I am not your beloved—"

"Yes, you are," Simon interrupted. "You may refuse to love me, but you cannot stop me from loving you."

At which point, Rhiannon gave in and began to laugh again. She put out her hand. "Come, let us be friends. I would like to be the friend of a man who does not fear the voices in the winds around Dinas Emrys, and who has firmly decided he is in love with me after half an hour's acquaintance."

But Simon would not take her hand. "I do not wish to be your friend," he said seriously. "I want to be your husband. This is not the time or place for passionate declarations, so I speak lightly, but I have never said those words to any woman and I have—as you said— known many."

"In the names of Danu and Anu, if this is not a jest— why?"

"I do not know," Simon replied with perfect honesty. "I only know that I felt for you, while you were singing, and feel now, what I have never felt before."

Rhiannon took his hand and held it between hers. "Today, you feel; tomorrow, you will forget. It was the strangeness of my song and my dress, perhaps. Love comes and goes, but friendship endures."

"Both endure when they are true. It is an easy enough matter to prove. Let me attend you. If I weary of your company, I will soon drift away from it."

There was a silence while Rhiannon seemed to consider this proposition. Simon could not read her expression; her green eyes were empty as clear water. After a moment she smiled very slightly and said, "Very well, since that is your desire, and because you amuse me. But I warn you now that I do not believe I will ever marry any man. To give my heart and soul into another's keeping—no! Now I have warned you. If you wish to play with fire, do not cry when you are burnt."

There was neither winner nor loser of the challenges exchanged—or, rather, both lost and won equally. Simon attended Rhiannon at court and escorted her to Angharad's Hall, her mother's home, which left him open-mouthed in surprise. It was just as Rhiannon had named it, a hall, built of wood, much like a large barn but with windows and hearths, hard to find but otherwise indefensible. Later, in the early spring, Simon took her to Dinas Emrys.

That she should come alone to his keep, without a maid or any other protection, shocked Simon a little. Even his mother was not so bold and free. Yet he found it was impossible for him to take advantage of the situation. At court he had pursued her with words of love and glances of longing. Under her mother's roof, he had made open declarations of his honorable intent to Rhiannon and to Kicva, whom he found not at all fearful, but worthy of respect. At Dinas Emrys, where Rhiannon was utterly in his power, he could find neither words nor looks to express the desire that burned ever more fiercely within him.

Yet it was there that trouble crept into Rhiannon's eyes. At court she had fenced with him, laughed at him, and teased him with love songs. At her mother's house, she treated him as if he were a companion of the same sex— not that she expected him to weave and sew, but that she seemed to lose awareness of his maleness. Loose in the hills, Rhiannon was more man than woman. Barefoot, she coursed the deer with her mother's hounds, as sure a shot with the longbow as any huntsman; she tickled fish in the streams, and snared hares in the brush. She butchered and skinned her prey, cached what was too heavy to carry, and even cooked over an open fire and slept rolled in her cloak on the ground if they were too far from home.

At Dinas Emrys, however, for the first time since their initial meeting, Rhiannon looked more often at Simon than he looked at her. She stood long on the walls gazing out over the Vale of Waters during the day. At night she climbed up again to listen to the wind as it whispered and moaned and howled. The men of Simon's guard, Welsh born and bred in that country, wild as the rocky crags, lowered their eyes and bowed to her when she passed, and there were both fear and admiration on their faces when Simon stood by her on the walls as she sang—and the wind answered.

Here again she wore the barbarically rich gowns and hung her neck and ears and hair with gems. Here she sang for the first time in Simon's hearing of Rhiannon of the Birds and her sorrow and her joys—how she married Pwyll, Prince of Dyfedd, and how she was accused of murdering her son Pryderi. And when she sang of the love between Pwyll and Rhiannon, how he stood by her even when she was accused of murdering her own babe, she looked at Simon—and there was trouble in her clear eyes. But later, when the song was done, she told Simon she wished to leave the next day.

Although he was bitterly disappointed, he could not urge her to stay where he was master, and he bowed and asked, "Where shall I take you, my lady?"

"I will go alone or with what escort you care to send with me, but not with you," Rhiannon answered, and for the first time since they met, her eyes were lowered before him. "You have won the contest, my lord, and I must seek safety from you in flight."

"That is a bitter winning to me, Lady Rhiannon," Simon said. "You know I have not grown weary of you. I cannot urge my suit here where you have no recourse, no protector, but you *must* know that you have become more precious, more desirable, not less. The more I have of you, the more I crave."

"You are stubborn; you have recently seen no others. Go back to England, my lord. I will play this game no longer. So much comfort I will give you as this—you are dangerous to me. If I have the power to hurt you, as you have to hurt me, you are better off in England. I will not marry you. Remember, I bade you not cry if you were burnt. Now let me go and do not pursue me."

CHAPTER 2

❖❖❖❖❖❖❖❖❖❖❖❖❖❖❖❖❖❖❖❖❖❖❖❖❖❖❖❖❖❖

"Simon."

There was an urgent tug at his sleeve, and Simon was shaken out of his unhappy memories. He turned from them gladly, however, a smile replacing the rather grim set of his mouth when he saw that it was Sybelle, Joanna's eldest daughter, who was demanding his attention. Simon loved all his family, but Sybelle was someone special. She was only six years younger than he, and he had played with her in her cradle and been her closest friend and confidant all her life.

"Where have you been?" Simon asked.

"Keeping the children away from Grandpapa and Grandmama or they would never have been ready. You know what he is—always willing to listen or to play or to tell another story. Tostig has young Adam now, and the girls are at their weaving. What are you looking so black about?"

"Rhiannon," Simon replied shortly.

Sybelle was Simon's confidante as he was hers. It was a great relief to him to have a woman friend. He had mothers and lovers in abundance; Alinor and Joanna were forever giving him well-meant and acerbic advice, and, although Gilliane was never sharp, she, too, offered advice and gentle reproof rather than simple attention. All other women seemed to regard him as a sexual object. Simon had not the least objection to this, but, of course, he could not speak of other women to a woman who wanted him for herself. Sybelle alone never seemed to notice his appearance, except in an impersonal way—for example, to say his face was dirty or his hair needed combing—and she listened to his adventures with amusement and interest.

"But I did not mean you in particular," Sybelle said, not commenting on Simon's answer directly. There was nothing more she could say about Rhiannon. "Everyone looks as if we have suffered a death in the family."

"Oh, that." The frown returned to Simon's face. "It is this summons to the council sent out by the king. Council! Either he wishes to squeeze more money from us, or he wishes us to confirm his tyrannies by our attendance. Certainly he has no desire for advice."

"From what Walter said the last time he came to visit Papa—"

"I do not think Walter de Clare comes to visit your father." Simon laughed.

Sybelle made a face at him but continued as if he had not interrupted her: "—there will be little meekness in the attendance." Then she shrugged. "But I think you are all mad. Two years ago you were all reviling Hubert de Burgh, calling him a power-mad upstart and urging the king to curb him. Now, all of a sudden, he is a holy martyr."

"No, Sybelle, you exaggerate. Naturally it was necessary to curb de Burgh. Through Henry's indifference, the chancellor was growing more powerful than the king. He was trying to drive a wedge between Henry and his brother Richard also, taking young Gloucester into his own care instead of letting him go with his mother when she married Cornwall. And too much of the kingdom's money was finding its way into de Burgh's coffers instead of Henry's —which made the king cry poverty and squeeze us."

"I know that. So then why is there now such a great outcry on de Burgh's behalf?"

"Because the king has gone too far. It was reasonable to deprive de Burgh of his power and of his ill-gotten gains. I suppose it was even necessary to keep him under control. There were so many who regarded him as a benefactor or who feared him, that he might have regained his power if he were at large. We all agreed to that, and Ferrars, Cornwall, Warrene, and Richard Marshal went surety for him to place him in honorable confinement."

"So that was what Walter meant when he started to rave about Henry not trusting to the honor of the two men dearest to him. He meant Cornwall and Richard Marshal! Walter was so angry that I could hardly make head or tail of what he said, but I gathered that the king dismissed the guards assigned by de Burgh's wardens and set others in their place."

"Walter told you that?" Simon remarked, grinning. Until he had met the women of Roselynde, Walter had been prone to say women had no room for anything but the roots of their hair inside their heads. Now he was discussing politics with Sybelle.

"Never mind Walter," Sybelle insisted. "Why did the king change de Burgh's guards?"

"It is beyond me," Simon admitted. "God knows Richard Marshal and Richard of Cornwall had no love for de Burgh. They were at his throat all along. Warrene and Ferrars were less opposed, perhaps, but their first loyalty is to Henry and certainly neither of them would have countenanced de Burgh's escape or his meddling in the realm's governance again."

"Then it was spite," Sybelle said distastefully. "The king was not satisfied that de Burgh should be comfortable in his imprisonment. He wished him to suffer."

"No," Simon contradicted slowly. "I do not like Henry, but he is not a man to be cruel for the sake of cruelty alone. It is true that he has increased the severity of the conditions under which de Burgh is held—I have even heard that the old man is kept manacled—but there is some other reason, not simply a desire to be cruel."

"Why not?"

"Henry does not enjoy making others suffer—that much I know of him. Besides, if cruelty was the purpose, Henry would have gone to gloat over de Burgh, to relish his tears and groans. That he has never done."

"No, that is true. In fact, Papa was saying that the king cannot bear to listen to a report on de Burgh's condition. But why—"

"I think Henry is still afraid of the man," Simon said slowly, frowning in thought rather than anger or distaste. It was always good for him to talk to Sybelle because while explaining to her he straightened out matters in his own mind. "Papa once said that when Henry was a boy, he was always a little afraid of de Burgh. He loved the old Earl of Pembroke, you can tell that when he talks of him to this day, and the Bishop of Winchester fascinated him—and still does—but it seems to me that Papa must be right. When Henry speaks of de Burgh it is almost like a boy who has escaped from a harsh tutor and cannot really believe he *has* escaped."

"But surely the king must have got over that feeling. It is more than a year—"

"I hope you are wrong," Simon interrupted, his frown deepening. "If it is not for that reason, then the king has done what Walter believes—that is, changed the guards as a deliberate affront to Richard Marshal."

"But why, Simon? I cannot get any sense out of Walter when I ask. He gets so angry he sputters and chokes. And I do not like to ask Papa. He is so unhappy about the king's behavior."

"Are you sure it is the king's behavior that makes Walter sputter and choke?" Simon teased. "You grow more beautiful every day, Sybelle."

That was not a fond uncle's flattery. Sybelle was as beautiful as her mother, if less flamboyant. In Sybelle, Joanna's flame-red hair was muted to a deep golden bronze, and she had her father's changeable light-brown eyes, bright as new-minted gold when she was happy. Her skin was also a blend of her mother's milk-white and Geoffrey's warmer complexion. Altogether, Sybelle was a golden girl, warm and rich as honey in the sun.

"Never mind that," Sybelle said dismissively.

She liked to be flattered as well as the next girl, and she enjoyed Simon's frank approval, but at the moment she did not want Simon to be diverted from the political subject to teasing her about Walter de Clare's interest and the possibility that he would offer for her.

Agreeably, Simon returned to the original subject. "You mean why the king wishes to affront Richard Marshal? I am not sure. There is a rumor that Richard stood against him when the king wanted Margery of Scotland, but I cannot really believe Richard would interfere in such a matter. Then there was the crazy rumor that de Burgh had poisoned William Marshal so that Richard could inherit. The idea was that William had too much influence with the king. Supposedly, de Burgh *would* be able to control Richard. But I know that was not true. William was my lord, and I was with him when he died." Simon's eyes clouded with remembered pain. He had loved the man he had served as page and squire almost as dearly as he loved his father, and he had grieved bitterly for him.

Sybelle patted his hand. "I know, Simon," she said softly. "But it is mad! Why should Henry dislike the younger brother if he liked the eldest? You loved William, but you do not hate Richard."

"I told you I did not know. Perhaps it is the association with the French. Richard took over his father's French lands and had not been much in England until he inherited. Henry is not the most reasonable of men. But the business of changing de Burgh's guards may be another case of the king wishing to prove he is the master of us all."

"Well, but—but he *is*," Sybelle said uncertainly.

"In a way, yes. His vassals are sworn to uphold him and their vassals to uphold him through their overlords. But—and this is a most important but—the king is bound by certain oaths and laws and customs. The king may not break these any more than a vassal may break his oath. One of the oaths he has sworn is to uphold Magna Carta, which his father signed, and one provision of that charter —to call a council with his barons and consider their wills—he has broken most often."

"I say again you are all mad." Sybelle sighed. "If you *wish* the king to take counsel, why such long faces when he has *called* a council?"

"Because Henry has no intention of asking for or listening to advice," Simon replied angrily. "He has called a council so that his barons should approve what he has already done."

"Then I must suppose he is mad also," Sybelle remarked in an exasperated voice. "Surely the king must know that Richard Marshal is not tamely going to swallow the dismissal of William de Rodune. After all, he was Richard's own deputy to the court. The king had no right to dismiss him. If he wanted him gone, he should have told Richard. Only Richard could take his office from him."

Simon grinned at her. "How do you know that? Since when have you become an expert on feudal rights?"

"Since I have been considering marriage. All men these days seem to become incoherent when they speak of the king. I have no desire to say the wrong thing. It is because

I must often stand in Mama's place at Hemel or in London."

Her voice faltered a little and her eyes moved to Ian, who was laughing heartily at something Gilliane had said. He looked well now, but he had been very ill twice during the winter, and Joanna had taken over her mother's duties while Alinor nursed her husband. This had left Sybelle to act as her father's hostess and sometimes even as chatelaine all alone. Simon's glance followed hers. It was clear he understood her concern, but neither of them spoke of it.

"Everyone is so touchy these days," Sybelle went on. "I do not wish to add a woodenheaded remark as fuel to the flames."

"No, you are quite right. Sometimes I feel that I will burst myself—and I am not even deeply involved, since my lands are in Wales. It is Winchester, all Winchester, I think."

"My father thinks so too, although he does not say too much because there was an old friendship between Grandpapa and the bishop."

Simon nodded. He had been wrong to oppose attending the council. Really, there was no other way to determine who pulled the strings causing this unhappy dance. He found, however, when he and Sybelle joined the larger group, that they were discussing a danger he had never considered. The council might be a trap for those who opposed the king's—or Winchester's—will. Since there were many ways to spring such a trap, the family's forces were divided. Alinor, Joanna, and Gilliane would remain in Roselynde to rally their husbands' vassals should the need arise. Sybelle alone would accompany the men of the family to run Alinor's house on the northwest bank of the Thames and see to their comfort.

They had barely settled into the house on the ninth of July when Walter de Clare rode in. He had had a man watching to notify him of Geoffrey's arrival, and it was clear that he was surprised to see the male contingent in full force. He was even more surprised to see Sybelle, and after his first sensation of pleasure, he was not pleased.

"I do not know whether it is wise for you to be here,

any of you—except Lord Geoffrey," Walter said, "and especially not you, Lady Sybelle."

Sybelle started to ask why not her especially, but her father gestured abruptly for her to be silent and she acquiesced, realizing this was no time to discuss the right of a woman to share her menfolk's danger.

"What do you mean?" Ian asked. "We were summoned to the council for July eleventh. Is it not to be?"

"Most likely not," Walter replied. "Had you not heard that nearly all the lords have refused to come unless Henry dismisses the Bishop of Winchester and Peter of Rivaulx?"

"Again?" Geoffrey asked. "But this was the same message they sent on the Feast of Saint John, when they refused to come to Oxford. All that happened was that the king grew so furious he was about to issue a decree compelling attendance and cry outlawry on those who failed to comply. Who *is* here?"

"Cornwall, Norfolk, Ferrars. . . . It is said Pembroke is on his way."

"Fools!" Geoffrey exclaimed. "If they are to be declared outlaw, at least they should have their say for it. Henry will—"

"I told you I should have sent word to my vassals to shut themselves into their keeps," Adam growled.

"Gilliane will see to it if it is necessary," Sybelle soothed.

Walter looked at the most attractive woman he knew as if she had sprouted a second head, then glanced at Adam to see whether he would laugh at the joke. Adam, however, merely nodded acknowledgment. He knew Gilliane would do what was necessary. His statement had been a mark of irritation, not an expression of a real anxiety. Before Walter could remark on so startling an idea, he was diverted by Ian.

"Men do vent their rage when they can," Ian remarked. "Thus, if they have not come, it is fear, not rage, that restrains them. I have heard the lesser men say that there is a plan to seize those without strong overlords, to disseisin them, and to send Poitevins or other foreigners to take their lands."

"That is ridiculous," Geoffrey said.

Walter nodded. "Cornwall and Ferrars are worried, but not about such a thing as that. They talk to Henry and he wavers toward giving assurances that he will proceed only according to strict law. Then the Bishop of Winchester gets at him and tells him that he will be a laughingstock, forever shamed as a weakling, if he yields. But there is this shadow of a substance to the fear you mentioned, Lord Ian. Isabella tells me that there *are* foreigners in court—men with considerable retinues, although what they live on is a puzzle—and they flatter Henry and tell him that they would not so defy him if they were his vassals."

"This is madness," Ian sighed. "Henry is behaving like a child—"

"Which is not exactly unusual," Sybelle snapped, thrusting a goblet of wine into Walter's hand.

Walter was so surprised by her interposition into the conversation that his hand almost failed to close, but Geoffrey and Ian, the two who had the most right to correct her, merely shrugged in a jaundiced way in agreement with what she had said.

"It is not Henry I blame," Ian went on. "Peter des Roches *must* know that he is pushing the king down a dangerous path. What is wrong with the man? Tomorrow I will go and talk to him."

"Ian—" Geoffrey and Adam said together, and Simon cried simultaneously, "No, Papa."

"Winchester may have forgotten much, but I do not think he has forgotten me," Ian said grimly, ignoring the protests. "My very presence here is a testimony to my loyalty. Moreover, what can he do to me when all of you are here waiting for my return?"

"And what can we do if he holds you and threatens you?" Adam asked angrily.

"He will do no such thing," Ian said calmly, and would not be moved from his decision.

He did not have it all his own way, however. Adam and Simon conspicuously escorted him to the Bishop of Winchester's lodging, fully armed and with a large troop of men. More ostentatiously still, they would not go in but sat on their horses a bowshot from the gates. Simon's Welsh archers unlimbered their bows and strung them, although they did not pull any arrows from the long quivers slung across their backs.

In spite of this, Ian was not denied access to the bishop, which many claimed was hard to obtain these days. Peter des Roches's black eyes narrowed as Ian bowed to kiss his ring. Unlike many churchmen, he had not become portly with age. He had dried until he looked as hard as the rocks for which he was named. Yet he was no ascetic; his intensity and activity burned away what he ate and drank.

"Why do you come here with such an escort, Lord Ian?" he asked.

He could not have seen or heard the troop, but Ian was not surprised that he knew. Winchester had not reached his past and present eminence by having stupid servants or by being uninformed.

"My sons," Ian said quietly, "think I am too old to defend myself. And it is true that London is overfull of roistering men who take what they want when they think they have a sufficiently weak victim."

Winchester's lips tightened, but he did not answer directly. "What brings you here?" he repeated, but the emphasis was different. There was almost relief in his voice because he thought Ian had some specific complaint about the lawlessness in the city.

"Memories," Ian replied. "When John was king, you and I thought much alike. We desired a peaceful realm where king and barons both knew their roles and carried them out with honesty."

"I desired peace, yes," Winchester responded, but his mouth and eyes had gone hard. "And I still do, but neither this realm nor any other will ever be at peace when authority is torn and divided. It is the role of the king to command, that of his vassals to obey."

"In war, perhaps, but for day-to-day life, my lord, that would make all except the king slaves. Even the serfs have their small rights. There is the law—"

"The king makes the law," Winchester interrupted sharply.

"Only in council with the approval of his barons," Ian said. "That was signed and sealed at Runnymede, and Henry swore to the charter both when he was crowned and again when, no longer a child, he took the reins of government into his own hands."

"Ridiculous! A charter extorted by force from the father,

and pushed upon a child who knew no better until the man was made to believe—"

"You were beside him then and beside the father when he first swore!" Ian exclaimed, his voice rising as his temper erupted.

"Both oaths were under compulsion, and you know it, Lord Ian," Winchester said more calmly. He realized it would do no good to make Ian angry. "And you also know the Holy Father absolved both John and Henry of that pernicious oath."

"It was *not* pernicious. It was necessary so that the barons would know what was their right and what belonged to the king to decide as he willed. My lord, I beg you to reconsider. You know I am no rebel. You know that I held by my fealty to King John when others did not. You see I am here, in answer to the king's summons—"

"Indeed, I know you to be a true man," Winchester agreed, smiling, "which is why I care nothing if your sons sit outside and glower." The smile faded. "True men have naught to fear, but too many are unlike you, Lord Ian. Bethink you, as an example, how the French lands were lost because of the narrow vision of the English lords. When the king called for men and money for war, all he received was argument—how it was no man's duty to serve outside the realm; how foreign wars were not to be laid on the backs of the English vassals. If the king had been obeyed, half of France would still be in Henry's hands."

"Perhaps. Or perhaps there would have been more money and more blood lost and the result would have been the same. God knows, John was no soldier, and. . . ." Ian paused, then shrugged. "Henry is no better."

"That is not true—or, at least, it was not the cause of the defeats. They were largely owing to the need for dependence on the disloyal vassals of Anjou and Poitou. It was treachery, not lack of military skill, that lost the French lands."

There was more than enough truth in that to make Ian abandon that line of reasoning. He sighed. "You may well be right, my lord, but I still beg you to think again and to urge the king to moderate his ways. There is long custom in this land supporting the right of the barons to take part in the king's decisions. I believe this to be just, but I did not come to contest with you over our differing opinions of absolute right or wrong. All I wish to tell you is that— right or wrong—the lords of England will not endure the abrogation of Magna Carta. They will fight."

"Are you threatening me?" Winchester asked softly.

"You know I am not," Ian said. "I have given my fealty, and I will support the king in all that is just. I am trying to explain how the barons think—for I am one of them and you, forgive me, my lord, are not. Moreover, you have been long away and you may not understand how things are. You think you achieved a great victory when you overthrew Hubert de Burgh, but that was accomplished because he was grown too powerful, and the lords would not lift a finger to support him or even give him a refuge."

"Yet he had been benefactor to many," Winchester remarked cynically. "Does this not prove that it is unwise for the king to trust in love and favor? It is strength he needs."

"There is not so much strength to be had in the whole world as to tame this baronage while they believe they are wronged. My lord, can you not see that the king's strength lies in the habit of the lords of snapping and snarling at each other so that he must settle their quarrels? Thus if a few cry out unfairly that they are oppressed, all the others support the king. Believe me, my lord, I am not threatening. I am warning you that what you are doing is causing the barons to forget their private quarrels."

Winchester laughed. "Oh, they will all curse and rage, but the moment it comes to acting. . . . They are all so swollen with pride that they will fall to fighting over who should lead. Unless Pembroke—" He stopped suddenly, having said more than he had intended, even to an old friend.

Ian pretended he had not heard the last words. "Do not press them too far," he urged. "Show only a little yielding. Say a few sweet words. You are wise and subtle, my lord. These men can be led little by little to where you want them to go, but if you try to drive them by force, you will drive them instead to unite."

"They will never unite." Winchester sneered, misunder-

standing why Ian had ignored his reference to Richard
Marshal. "If they could not unite against John, who had
such faults of person that he was hated, they surely will
not unite against Henry, who is not flawed as his father
was. Now you listen to *my* warning, Lord Ian. Henry will
rule this land of himself, without let or hindrance from
his vassals, who, by God's will, derive all their power only
from the king."

"And where will the king's strength come from, if not
from the support of his vassals?" Ian asked, lifting his
brows.

"From those who are paid to obey, who understand that
the king made them and can unmake them."

"From where will the money come to pay them?" Ian
asked sardonically. Taxation was *not* in the king's hands
and Winchester knew that. In the end it was that power
which had to be seized, of course, but the country would
need to be reduced to abject surrender first and, for that,
money would be needed *before* the surrender.

"From the dues owing to the king, which will come to
him instead of slipping into this sheriff's coffers and that
bailiff's purse—or not being paid at all through the taking
of bribes or giving of favors." This time it was Winchester's
voice that rose in passion.

Ian did not reply. Again there was enough truth in the
claim to preclude a simple denial, and this was not the
time for explanations and qualifications that Winchester
knew perfectly well.

"You will not achieve it." Ian sighed. "You will bring
us to war—brother against brother, father against son."

"If it must be, it must be," Winchester said, his face set
like flint. "Lord Ian, we have known each other long, and
I see that you mean well. I am not blind to the selfish
anger of the barons. It is they who are blind. When all are
obedient, the king will be a mild and just master. His word
will be law, and the whole land will obey and be at peace.
If a brief war must be fought to lesson those who will not
accept that this is the Divine Will, that one alone should
rule, so it must be. Thus, there is only one God, one Holy
Father, and there must be one king for each realm."

Ian stood up. "God gives man free will."

Winchester raised his eyes to Ian's face. "But those who

use this free will to transgress are cast into everlasting torment. On earth also. Those who obey will flourish; those who transgress will be cast out."

Once more Ian bowed and kissed the bishop's ring. There was no purpose in further talk. He had not had much hope when he came, for he knew that Winchester was an astute man. However, Ian had not wished to ignore the small chance that the bishop had failed to gauge the depth of feeling against him and the strong possibility of a civil war. Even that faint hope was gone. Plainly, Winchester saw the situation quite clearly and was convinced that the rebellion could be put down both quickly and firmly enough to end resistance once and for all.

When he came out, Ian's face told the story to Adam and Simon. They hardly had patience to listen to the report Ian gave Geoffrey, crying out that they should go home and stuff and garnish their keeps for war.

"No, you will not!" Ian exclaimed. "This is all talk. So far the king has done nothing—except for the dismissal of Rodune—that is not within his right. That dismissal is a little thing, no cause for war. You must not act in such a way as to give Henry an excuse to punish you. For God's sake, do you want to find yourselves opposed to me on a field of battle?"

"This is no time for hasty action of any kind," Geoffrey interposed quickly, seeing that Adam was about to point out that even Henry would not be so foolish as to summon a man to attack his own sons, particularly Ian, who was well known to be a doting father. "All is not yet lost. You should have known, Ian, that Winchester could not be bent, but the king is not so inflexible."

"Not so inflexible, but more dangerous," Adam pointed out. "Winchester might have decided to hold Ian or may act against him in some other way for political reasons, but he is not likely to fly into a fit of rage and say or do something out of spite which, later, he cannot back away from."

"I did not intend to go to the king—not at first," Geoffrey said. "If we have any hope, it will come from Richard of Cornwall."

"But Cornwall has already done and said everything," Simon protested in disgust.

"He has done and said too much," Geoffrey admitted wryly. "You know his temper. He called Henry an ungrateful cur for being so harsh with de Burgh and a long-eared ass when he dismissed the officers of the court. He has bellowed like a mad bull in council, threatened violence, stormed out of Westminster, and ridden back to Wallingford, refusing to speak to Henry at all. . . . No, I do not need to urge Richard to say more, but perhaps I can convince him to say the same words in a manner that will not make the king too angry to listen."

Geoffrey went out in midafternoon, soon after dinner, but returned almost at once accompanied by Walter, who had been staying with Cornwall, whose wife, Isabella, was his brother's widow. The earl, Walter reported, had ridden away to attend the funeral of the father of a very close friend.

"Is it an excuse?" Simon asked, his eyes glinting with interest. "I thought he intended to attend the council."

"The council is canceled," Walter told them. "The earls —Cornwall, Norfolk, and Ferrars, who are the only ones who have come—refused to hold a meeting when nearly no one else is here and, in particular, when Richard Marshal is not here. It is mainly his complaint that was to be heard. But that is just an excuse because Isabella is sure Richard is on the way and would be here in time. As to the funeral, that is no excuse. Richard was in this man's keeping for some years, just before and after King John died, and he has remained closely tied to the son. Even if the council had been held, he would have gone."

"Then it is just as well that it is canceled," Ian remarked. "But what the devil are we to do now? Stay here? Go home?" He was frowning, and there was anxiety in his eyes. "Does Cornwall know what his brother plans to do next?"

"I do not think so," Walter replied. "At present they are not speaking to each other, and Isabella tells me that Henry is so furious that he will lash out at *someone*."

There was a brief silence while everyone considered this statement. Then Geoffrey put his hand on Ian's arm. "There is something else. What is it?"

Ian stared at nothing, then said slowly, "A slip of the tongue—if it was a slip—during my talk with Winchester.

He said that instead of uniting, the barons would fall to fighting over who should lead 'unless Pembroke—' and he stopped. I do not like it. There was no *real* reason to call this council, and Winchester and the king must have known there was little likelihood that many would come. Yet . . ."

"Yet the king dismissed Rodune, which must infuriate Richard Marshal, and offered this council to discuss the matter—which meant that Richard would probably be here nearly alone." Simon's voice was too loud in the quiet that had followed Ian's unhappy remarks.

Geoffrey covered his face with his hand momentarily. "Your questions are answered, Ian. We must stay. Norfolk and Ferrars and Cornwall have delayed matters by gaining this cancellation, but that has only increased Henry's anger. Walter is right. Henry will lash out at someone."

CHAPTER 3

Rhiannon lay in the long grass of the high meadow and watched the clouds drift across the sky forming and re-forming, building keeps and beasts, men and monsters, mountains and rivers. Always the high meadows had brought her the peace of absolute freedom, but she found no peace there now—not in the soft, warm air of a sunny day, nor by moonlight, nor in mist or rain.

She found no peace anywhere. In the flames that burned in her mother's hearth, a dark face formed and flickered. When she hunted, she found herself turning to look for the astonished and delighted expression of a laughing companion who had kept pace and had not outrun her—although he could have. And when she sang, she felt the draw of the longing in the green-gold-flecked eyes that had added a meaning to the words describing the love of the heroes for their ladies.

It was not only when she sang that Rhiannon felt the pull of Simon's desire. Often she woke in the night with the feeling that someone had whispered her name, and now, lying on the sun-warmed earth, she found her head turning toward the east, where Rhuddlan keep lay, or to where Dinas Emrys towered above the Vale of Waters. She told herself that one naturally chose a southern meadow because there the sun felt warmest and the mornings in the hills were chilly even in the end of July on the fairest day. But when the wind murmured *Simon seeks* across the tall grass, Rhiannon rose and fled.

"I am not happy," she cried to her mother, whom she found seated before her loom.

Kicva lifted her head from the intricate pattern she was weaving and looked steadily at her daughter. They were alike to an unusual degree, except that the mother's hair was lighter and streaked with gray; Rhiannon's thick black mane came from her father.

"I have noticed," she said, and looked back at her weaving to hide the amusement in her eyes.

It was a wool as fine as silk with which Kicva worked, dyed just the leaf-green color of Rhiannon's eyes, and the pattern in gleaming gold was of interlaced branches upon which many birds perched. Rhiannon did not look at her mother's work; Kicva was always about some household task. The daughter's sensitive nostrils flared with irritation.

"Am I such a fool as to be ensorceled by a handsome face?" Rhiannon asked furiously.

"I did not think so," Kicva replied, "but you must know yourself better than I can. What you say, I must accept."

"What?" Rhiannon cried, stamping her foot. "You say I am like all those others, creeping after him to beg for a kiss for the sake of his beauty."

"I did not say that at all." Kicva's voice was perfectly grave, and her eyes did not lift from her weaving. "I have no idea what you will do. You heard what I said. If you want to know more certainly what I mean, you must ask me. If you want to decide for yourself what I mean—that is your right."

"Why am I so uneasy?" Rhiannon asked plaintively.

"Because you desire Simon de Vipont," Kicva replied, and this time her lips did twitch with amusement.

Rhiannon, who had turned a little away, whirled back so violently that her swirling skirt flashed into the face of an abnormally large cat, which leapt backward hissing.

"So you *do* think I have been entrapped by a handsome face."

"I saw a great deal more in Simon de Vipont than his handsome face and magnificent body," Kicva said calmly. "However, if you can find no more in him than his beauty, and if that has the power to destroy your peace, then I suppose what you say of yourself is true."

"But I am *not* a fool, Mother. I am not. What is wrong with me?"

"I have told you that already."

"But *why* should I desire him? I have known handsome men before."

"Perhaps because Simon is *more* than just a magnificent male animal."

"Are you pleading his cause?" Rhiannon stooped and

lifted the cat, who had come and rubbed his head forgivingly on her ankle.

"Not at all." Kicva laid down her shuttle and looked up. "I do not usually need to explain you to yourself, Rhiannon. I thought I had taught you that lying to yourself is the most dangerous lie of all. Why do you do it now?"

"Because I am afraid. Did you ever love a man, Mother?"

"You mean aside from Gwydyon? No. I have not that nature. I have been fond of many, but love . . . I think not."

"Was that all you felt for my father? Only fondness?"

Kicva smiled. "For Llewelyn? Not even that—no. Llewelyn is not a man of whom a woman can be only fond. One can only love him to madness and self-exclusion —or not love him at all."

"Then why is he my father?" Rhiannon asked, obviously surprised.

This time Kicva laughed aloud. "Did you think he had cast me out? Or that I nursed a wounded heart? You know I would have told you. You wished to believe me tender— and so I am, but not in that way. Llewelyn and I were good friends. We still are. Why I chose him to father you? I admired him, and my body craved his."

"As you say mine craves Simon's?"

"That I do not know. I did not wish to be Llewelyn's woman as my mother Angharad was my father's woman, only to take pleasure of him, to give him pleasure, and to beget a daughter. I wanted him to father my child, not to be mine—well, I knew that was impossible."

"You said you did not want him because you could not have him," Rhiannon said angrily. "Who is lying to herself now?"

Kicva's clear eyes met her daughter's. "I could have had him and held him—but what I held would not have been Llewelyn. Your father is more prince than man. To hold him to me, I would have had to turn his nature inside out and tear him from his first love—the glory and power of Gwynedd. Besides . . ." Kicva left that unfinished and began again. "You and I are much alike in looks, my daughter, but not in our hearts. Believe me, I never longed to bind any soul to mine, nor have my soul bound to another's."

"Yet you desired a daughter."

"Our line breeds one daughter, at least, in each generation. And the tie between parent and child is a bond that does not tether, or should not. You are free to go and never return, if that is your need. It is different between a man and a woman."

Rhiannon sighed and sat down. The cat was heavy, and she knew it was useless to try to bait her mother, who really did have a calm of spirit that surpassed Rhiannon's understanding.

"Very well, let us say I *do* desire Simon—what am I to do?"

"How should I know?" Kicva asked. "It is your desire. Only you can know how to satisfy it. All I can tell you is to make sure *what* you desire before you grasp for it. Is it only your body de Vipont has wakened? You have been very long about growing into a woman, Rhiannon."

The cat was purring in a steady roar so loud that Rhiannon had to raise her voice a trifle. "I began my flux at the usual time. What do you mean?"

"The flux does not make a woman. At ten or twelve, a girl with her flux is still a child; at forty or fifty, a woman without her flux is still a woman—in every way. All I meant is that until now you have shown no sign of interest either in bedding or begetting."

"It is not a child I want," Rhiannon said quickly, and then wondered if that was true. Simon's child? That was a pleasant thought.

"Probably not," her mother agreed.

"Perhaps I merely wish to couple?"

"That might be so. All beasts have their seasons," Kicva said judicially.

"And am I no more than a beast?" Rhiannon cried.

"Your body is no different from the body of a beast—it is a body. *You* are not a beast because you can rule your body. A heifer couples when she is in season. If the bull is not there, she bellows for him; when he comes, she yields—any bull, any time. You can choose your time, your bull, or not to couple at all according to the dictates of your soul. Thus, you are Rhiannon, and a heifer is a heifer. But the desire is the same."

Rhiannon knew all that. Kicva might not have been so

explicit in the past—she never offered more than her daughter asked for—but the body/soul dichotomy in humankind had been discussed thoroughly in other than sexual aspects. Suddenly Rhiannon began to laugh. The big cat rose, stretched himself, leapt down to the floor, and stalked away.

"Math knows," Rhiannon said, looking fondly at the tiger-striped animal she had named for the high king of ancient Wales. "He senses that I do not need comfort any longer. I think you are right, Mother. I think this heifer has been wandering the fields bawling for a bull. And all my bad temper has been owing to lying to myself about it."

"And so what will you do now that you have decided this?" Kicva asked.

"Go to my father and look around him for a bull, of course," Rhiannon said lightly.

Kicva smiled slowly and swung herself back to her loom. Her eyes clouded for a moment as she looked at her weaving. Then she nodded. "Yes," she said, "if that is what you want, do that."

She began to weave again without watching as her daughter got to her feet and walked away, presumably to begin examining her clothing to see what she had to take to court with her. Kicva would not argue with a decision Rhiannon had made, nor would she offer her any except the most general advice. In the past Rhiannon had always made the correct decision, but Kicva had never seen her daughter so much disturbed. Would the fear she recognized and admitted distort her reasoning and drive her into the arms of a man she did not want, just to avoid one she wanted too much?

The cloth in the loom might then never be used for the purpose Kicva had in mind when she began it. She had strung the loom the day after Simon brought Rhiannon to Angharad's Hall in the end of March. At first she had wondered whether she could finish the cloth in time; now she wondered whether she should finish it at all. If Rhiannon chose a bull at random, de Vipont might be unwilling. . . . That was ridiculous. If he was of the kind that cared so much for a maidenhead, or could not see that such an act of desperation had nothing to do with true feeling, then Rhiannon was far better off without him.

When that thought had been formed and absorbed, Kicva smiled again and her shuttle flew faster. It was not likely she was so wrong about Simon—or about Rhiannon either.

The blow that Walter and Geoffrey predicted the king would deliver fell on Sir Gilbert Bassett before Richard of Cornwall returned from the funeral in Oxfordshire. Without apparent cause, Henry disseisined Bassett of Upavon, a manor in Wiltshire, and gave it to Peter de Maulay. Ian blamed himself for what had happened. He felt that his conversation with Winchester had confirmed the inevitability of war in the bishop's mind. Thus, Winchester had urged Henry to disseisin Gilbert Bassett to start the conflict before his opponents could be ready.

Simon and Adam told him in one breath not to be ridiculous. Certainly, they pointed out, he was not the only one who had warned Winchester that the path the king was treading would lead to violence. Geoffrey agreed with them.

"This action cannot be a wild start on the part of the king. It is too clever, too apposite to the purpose. It must have been planned in June, after the first summons to council was so ill-answered," he said bleakly. He was heavy-eyed and drawn, and his brothers-by-marriage looked at him with concern. "Henry might act out of furious impulse, but Winchester would have restrained him if he had not approved—and Winchester does not act on impulse. It has nothing to do with you, Ian. The fact that it is Upavon and Bassett shows planning."

"Why?" Simon asked.

"Firstly, Bassett has a connection with Pembroke. They know each other and have lands in the same area—the southwest. However, the connection is not close enough that Richard should be obliged to support Bassett. If he does so, the king could say he is interfering without cause. Secondly, Upavon was the property of the Maulay family— to whom Henry has returned it—in the past. It was taken from them and given to Bassett's father by King John. I do not know what the reason for the transfer was—"

"Sometimes John had perfectly just reasons for what he did," Ian remarked.

"Quite true. In any case, that is not the problem. Perhaps the property *should* go back to Maulay. In truth, I suspect it was chosen because Maulay had a good claim. What is wrong is not the transfer; it is the way it was done. There are courts and judges to deal with such matters. If the king did not trust the judges, he could have heard the case himself. That is the point—there was no case, no judgment, only the king's will."

Adam mouthed an obscenity, adding, more practically, "I had not thought of that. It is a pretty trap. Say justice is on Maulay's side. If we do not protest, we have agreed that the king's will is law. If we do protest, we are unjust in backing Bassett's desire to keep the land."

"There is a middle path," Geoffrey offered. "We can demand that Bassett's claim be brought before the king's court—but I greatly fear all will forget that and remember only that Gilbert Bassett was deprived of his land by the king's will."

"I do not care what they remember, so long as we do not have to bow down like Moslem slaves," Simon exclaimed hotly.

Ian looked at him and sighed. He wished Simon would go back to Wales. Sooner or later his tongue would wag at the wrong moment, and he would be in real trouble. However, Ian remembered the expression of unspoken pain in his son's face, and he suspected that a private hurt of which Simon would not speak kept his son in England.

"One thing I do not see," Adam said suddenly. "How can the king be sure Pembroke will hear of this—oh, of course, Isabella will write to him, I suppose. She is his sister, after all."

"Well, I will write to him whether Isabella does so or not," Ian said. "Do you think I want to take the chance that he will be surprised by such news when he comes to court?"

"Why should he come? Possibly he will think this summons will be canceled as the last was," Sybelle pointed out.

"Do not be such a goose," Geoffrey replied. "This is the third summoning. If he does not come, that will be considered open defiance."

"But I thought he had already defied the king last winter when he convinced so many not to come to the first council," Simon said.

"That was a warning, not defiance," Ian stated. "Richard—all old William Marshal's sons are honorable men. I know Richard does not wish to come to blows with the king. This was one way, after his protests and explanations did not move Henry, to show the king how many men agreed with him. I did not go to the first summoning, nor did Norfolk, nor Ferrars, nor even Geoffrey."

"Then why—"

"Simon, I have shown our disapproval by silence. At the second council I wished to speak it aloud. I suppose Richard did also, but the council was canceled. This time, he has no choice. You know as well as I that a man may be outlawed without trial if he does not come to a third summoning."

"Yes, but does he know it is a third summoning?" Adam asked, his mouth grim. "If the second was canceled by the king, Richard might think this is only the second summoning and decide to try passive resistance again."

Geoffrey shuddered suddenly. "No, I do not think that device will be used. I fear more and more that what you said the other day, Ian, is true. I fear Winchester has seen too clearly. If Pembroke is removed, there will be no man strong enough around whom the barons could rally."

"Then it is not war, but an end to Richard Marshal's meddling that is desired," Adam growled.

"What do you mean?" Simon asked.

"If Richard cries out against this—would that not be a reason to seize him? If Richard were kept prisoner like de Burgh, is there another of sufficient courage and stature to oppose Winchester?"

There was an appalled silence. Geoffrey's lips moved as if to protest that Henry was not as treacherous as his father, but he did not say the words. Henry had gone to pray with Hubert de Burgh, had kissed his lips and said he was all his strength and only on him could reliance be placed—and a week later de Burgh was a prisoner. It would not be *open* treachery to take Richard prisoner if a shadow of a reason could be presented, and, in the heat

of argument about the "wrong" done Bassett, no doubt
more than a shadow of defiance and rage would be shown.

"He must be warned," Simon cried, leaping to his feet.

His own ties with the Marshal family were closest since
Lady Pembroke had died, ending Alinor's friendship of
many years. Simon did not know Richard very well because
the Earl of Pembroke's second son had spent most of his
life in France; the French estates were to be his. Nonetheless, Simon could not ignore the possibility that his former
master's brother would fall into a trap.

"Yes, he must be warned," Ian agreed, "but I have not
the faintest idea of where he is. I had intended to write to
Pembroke keep, from where my letter would be sent on,
but this is more urgent than mere news."

"Perhaps Isabella will know," Simon suggested.

"Ride over and ask," Geoffrey said, "and do not be
afraid to tell Isabella everything. She will not fall into a fit."

This second daughter of Isobel of Clare was very like
her mother, soft of voice and manner, gentle, but not weak.
She listened to Simon quietly, and, although her voice
trembled, she wasted no time on useless cries nor did she
exaggerate or belittle what was a real possibility but not
a fact. Still, she could not be of help. All she knew was
that her brother was definitely expected in London by the
end of July.

"He will be on the road by now," Isabella said, "but I
have no idea which way he intended to come. He might
even stop at Wallingford to talk to Richard—my husband,
I mean. It is so confusing to have a brother and husband
both named Richard. And then they might come by river.
But, Simon, I think he would come anyway, even if you
warned him."

Since Simon himself would have come anyway, he did
not contest this conclusion. He accepted Isabella's assurance that she would tell her husband of Adam's
suspicion as soon as he arrived home and would let Ian
know as soon as either Richard—Cornwall or Pembroke—
came. But he was dissatisfied and restless, and, at last, Ian
suggested that it would do no harm if he and Walter rode
out toward Wales for a few days. Nothing more could
happen, Ian said, until August first when the third summoning must be answered.

CHAPTER 4

❖❖❖❖❖❖❖❖❖❖❖❖❖❖❖❖❖❖❖❖❖❖❖❖❖❖❖❖

Ian was wrong in his belief that nothing more would happen until the council began, but he was glad to have Simon out of the way when Gilbert Bassett arrived to complain at court the following week. Gilbert maintained stoutly that the escheat of Upavon was settled on his father for service to King John and that he had done nothing to merit being deprived of it. He would plead his right and show that Maulay had not been unjustly deprived. Gilbert offered to take his case before a judge, before the king, or before God in judicial combat.

Instead of agreeing to any of the offers made, Henry called Bassett a traitor and threatened that if he did not leave his court forthwith he should be hanged like a dog. Not satisfied, the king also ordered that Richard Siward, who had married Gilbert's sister, should be imprisoned. The crime was that the marriage had not been approved by the king. If true, Siward and Bassett had committed an offense, but not the kind that merited imprisonment. Failure to get royal permission to marry was a common occurrence, to be satisfied with a fine—small or large according to the king's temper and the wealth of the perpetrator.

It was now obvious that Henry intended to use Bassett as an object lesson. Richard of Cornwall had arrived, but he and Geoffrey could not move Henry. The king had the bit well between his teeth. He cried furiously that he was not a babe to be governed always by other men, that he would rule as a king or not rule at all. If Cornwall's and Geoffrey's remonstrance had any effect upon him, it was a bad one. The next move Henry made was to send more messengers hastening out with a demand that hostages for the good behavior of his barons be brought to him before the first of August.

Hard on the heels of this news, Richard Marshal arrived at his sister's house. He had come by the main road with only a few men-at-arms. The small troop served the double purpose of making him inconspicuous and of marking his "trust" in the king's goodwill. Simon had missed him on the road, but by chance they rode into London the same day and Simon arrived at Cornwall's house to ask whether Richard was there only an hour after he had come.

Isabella had already told her brother of Adam's suspicions, but Richard only laughed and kissed her and called her a nervous goose. Thus, when Simon's name was brought to her, she bade her maidservant bring him into Richard's bedchamber, where he was soaking off the dirt and sweat of travel in a tub.

"Tell him I am not making it up," she cried, as Simon stepped in and the servant closed the door behind him.

Simon bowed, a little embarrassed by the look of surprise on Richard's face. The Earl of Pembroke was a big man, as tall as Simon but broader and heavier, his shoulders and arms seamed with the scars of combat. The room was warm, redolent with the scent of the herbs Isabella had strewn in the bath water. Somehow a sense of urgency and discussion of plots seemed out of place. Although Simon was sure that danger existed and that Isabella's nervousness was justified, he felt his warning would sound ridiculous.

"My lord," he said uneasily, "I am Simon de Vipont—"

"William's squire! I remember you."

"Simon, tell him! Make him believe it is dangerous to stay," Isabella repeated urgently.

"It is also dangerous to go," Richard said, a little more sharply. "Have sense, Isabella. If I am not here to answer this third summons, Henry will have the right to call me a traitor. And I am not! I only want the laws to be observed."

"Then you want more than any man is likely to have, my lord," Simon said.

"That is a hard thing you have said," Richard rejoined cautiously. "I hope the bad response the king has had to his summonses may have given him food for thought—"

"The wrong kind of thought," Simon interrupted.

Richard sat more upright in the bath. "What are you talking about?"

"You have not heard about Bassett's land?"

"I know the king seized the manor at Compton on the excuse that Bassett was de Burgh's man and Compton was too close to Devizes where de Burgh is imprisoned—"

"No. This is a new thing. Bassett was disseisined of Upavon—"

"What? When?" Richard rose from the tub, splashing water in all directions. Isabella hurried forward with a drying cloth, which he seized from her and began to ply about his body hurriedly. "Why did you not tell me this," he said to her, "instead of that farrago about—" He stopped abruptly and looked away from Isabella toward Simon.

"I thought you knew," Isabella said, but Richard did not look back at her.

"Tell me the whole," he said to Simon.

By the time the story had been related, including Henry's reaction to Bassett's attempt to obtain justice and the demand for hostages, Richard was dressed and seated beside the empty hearth reflectively sipping a cup of wine. Simon had remembered Geoffrey's oft-repeated advice that too much passion made the most solid fact sound suspect, so he had described the situation more calmly than those who knew him would have expected. It was clear that his temperate manner had convinced Pembroke.

"I am caught in a cleft stick," Richard said bitterly, his fine eyes bleak. "If I do not cry out against the king's action and uphold Bassett, I will not only violate what I believe to be right, but I will seem to break faith with a long-time friend of our family. And if I do protest, I will be playing into Henry's hand, offering him an excuse to—"

"If you will give me leave, my lord, to say what I think —and what Sir Adam, my brother, thinks—it is that it does not matter what you do unless it be to yield entirely. Even then I am not sure the king will be content. What he did to de Burgh seems to have given him an appetite for subduing to utter helplessness every man in the land."

"I told you, Richard—" Isabella interrupted.

"Hush, Isabella," Richard said absently, his eyes fixed on Simon. "What do Lord Ian and Lord Geoffrey say?" he asked slowly.

"My father says nothing, except that Henry does not

mean evil. He remembers a golden-haired child bereft of a father and with a mother who had no soul. Lord Geoffrey says nothing also, but—but he looks like death. What *can* he say, my lord? Henry is his cousin and—and I cannot deny has always behaved most lovingly to him. Even this spring when he dismissed all his castellans and put his castles into the hands of those two—"

"Mind your tongue before my sister," Richard said, half jesting, but with the jest covering a warning as servants entered the room to empty the bath water. Simon drew a breath; the servants belonged to the brother of the king.

"My brother-by-marriage is tied with bond upon bond," Simon said. "He could no more fail to support the king than my Lord of Cornwall."

Reminded of something that had been overwhelmed in his sister's excited greeting and then in Simon's news, Richard asked, "Where is Cornwall?"

"He had business with the king," Isabella said, staring hard at her brother and then letting her eyes slip to the servants and back again. "I sent word that you had come. He will be here as soon as he can."

Simon's breath drew in again, but Richard's eyes flicked to him and he said nothing. As if the preceding question and answer were of no importance, Richard said, "You were knighted before my brother died, were you not?"

"Yes, my lord."

"Do you now hold, or have you taken over your father's meinie?"

"Papa is not so old as that," Simon said. "In any case, the lands are mostly my mother's. They will be Geoffrey's to worry about when—but that will be many, many years."

"Lord Geoffrey's?" Richard asked, actually interested as well as relieved to have an unexceptional subject to discuss while the servants tidied the room. "How does that come about? Is not Adam your mother's eldest son?"

"Yes, but Adam inherited his father's lands. My mother has full power over her own, and chooses to leave them in the female line. My sister Joanna will hold Roselynde and my mother's other honors, and it is already settled that the bulk of the lands will go after her to Sybelle, and then to Sybelle's eldest daughter."

"You do not mind?" Richard asked curiously.

"God, no!" Simon exclaimed. "That is not to my taste at all, to be tied to a seat of justice and an account book. My father has already given me what I most desired. With Prince Llewelyn's permission, he has ceded to me his Welsh properties."

"Welsh? You are vassal to Lord Llewelyn?" Richard asked, leaning forward with sudden alertness.

"Yes, my lord."

"Are you in good repute with him?"

"Very good," Simon replied, and then, seeing it was important for some reason, he added, "He has given me permission to seek the hand of his natural daughter, Lady Rhiannon, in marriage."

"Seek? If he desires you for a son—"

"Lady Rhiannon is not that kind of woman," Simon said stiffly. "She cannot be given away like a horse or a parcel of land."

"Well, as soon as she sees your face, she will be lost." Richard laughed. "We can consider that bond as good as made."

He leaned back in the chair, his eyes fixed on nothing while he considered certain possibilities uncovered by Simon's willingness to save him and the connection with Llewelyn. Thus, he missed Simon's expression. Isabella did not, and she bit her lip, hoping her brother would say no more on the subject of marriage. She held her breath as Richard turned to look intently at Simon again. The servants were leaving. When the last two were gone, staggering slightly under the weight of the tub, which was still a third full of water and would be tipped empty in the yard, he signed to Isabella, who went and closed the door.

"Did you love William?" Richard asked unexpectedly.

"Yes," Simon replied shortly, but his bright eyes misted, and Richard was more assured of the depth of his feeling than if he had made a passionate avowal.

"Then—" Richard began.

"Richard," Isabella interrupted, "the reason my husband is not here to greet you is that he does not wish to lie to his brother. If he does not *know* you are here, he does not have to tell Henry. Will you not take warning and go, dearling?"

Distracted from what he had been about to say to Simon, Richard frowned. "But you just said you sent him word that I had come."

"The servants! I sent him word not to come home," Isabella said with tears in her eyes. "Oh, Richard, it hurts me how much he suffers. In his heart he agrees with you. He has done everything from pleading on his knees to threatening to turn rebel himself—but he cannot do that, no matter how wrong—"

"I am no rebel!" Richard thundered. "That I am here in answer to Henry's summons is proof I am a loyal vassal. I have a right, even a duty, to complain of a breach of law and custom."

"If you do, you will be taken prisoner," Simon warned.

"And if I do not, outlawry will be cried on me," Richard responded angrily.

"It is better to be a free outlaw than an unoutlawed prisoner," Simon remarked cynically. "Think what has befallen de Burgh, who yielded and threw himself upon the king's mercy. My lord, I am young, and you doubtless think I see all things as black or white. Let me ask Geoffrey and my father to speak to you. You know both are loyal to the king, but—but neither would betray you."

"Yes, yes, please, Richard," Isabella pleaded.

There was a little silence while Richard considered Simon's remark, the offer that followed, and the result of the action he would have to take if Geoffrey and Ian confirmed that the situation was really desperate. Then he said, "Very well, I would be glad and grateful. Before you go, however—Isabella, will you go and tell someone to ready Simon's horse?"

Her face whitened. "Do you no longer trust me, Richard?"

"With my own life, to the uttermost, sweet sister, but—but if I leave this house without attending the council, as you have urged me so strongly to do, it is most likely that, within days, your husband and I will be enemies—"

"No, Richard, no!"

"Did you not just say he would support his brother? Now, now, Isabella, do not weep: I know you will not do me, nor anyone else, hurt apurpose, but there are questions I wish to ask that—well, if you never heard either question or answer, no blush or look could give a hint to Richard that you knew more than you were willing to tell him. There will be strains enough between you and your husband if he and I . . . I do not wish to add to that. Go, my dear."

"It is monstrous," Isabella whispered, but she was a sensible woman and understood her brother was right. Her husband had enough problems without adding the knowledge that his wife was concealing information from him. She wiped her eyes and left the room.

Simon was puzzled. "I will tell you anything I can, my lord," he said, "but I do not know anything more than I have already said."

"I do not want information. That was just for Isabella's ears. I do not distrust her purposes, but she might say something thoughtlessly. . . . She is only a woman, after all. I wish to ask you where you stand in this."

"With you," Simon responded at once, his lips tightening. "Somehow the king must be constrained to obey the law."

"Do you understand what you are saying, Simon? To stand with me, if worse comes to worst, may set your hand against your own father and brothers."

"Not Adam," Simon said, and then swallowed. Geoffrey would certainly respond to Henry's call to arms if one should be issued. Then relief brightened his eyes. "And not Papa either. If I am with you, he will take the excuse of his age to send his men out in Geoffrey's care. I do not need to worry about Geoffrey coming to blows with me. Wherever I am, he will not be. Papa always said Geoffrey was too clever by half. He will manage to avoid me somehow—if I cannot avoid him."

"And you may be sure that I will do my uttermost that you avoid each other. But this is going too far. I have no intention of making war on the king. God forbid! He is my lord. I have given my oath to support him—"

"In all that is right," Simon inserted quickly. "Not in oppressing his people, robbing them, imprisoning them—"

"That is true, but still I would not wage war against my overlord if any other path is open to making him mend his ways. Let us not talk of such extreme measures. Perhaps I am too much moved by what you have told me.

What I should have asked is whether you would be willing —should it become necessary—to be an emissary for me to Lord Llewelyn."

"Of course," Simon answered, almost too quickly, then flushed.

A violent joy suffused him. When Rhiannon had bid him go at the end of May, he had done so, telling himself furiously that she was quite right. No doubt he was ensorceled by her presence. If he returned to the civilized and elegant women of England, he would soon grow disdainful of her wild, primitive charm. Only he had not been able even to try. Such a sense of disgust filled him each time he began a flirtation that he fled away. He could not even take joy in those old partners he did not need to woo, who did not demand sweet words but only desired the sensual pleasure his strong, skilled body could provide. He could ease his body, just as he could use a chamber pot, but there was no pleasure in it. He desired only Rhiannon.

By June, Simon would have been on his way back to Wales, ready, like the courtly lovers in romances whom he had always ridiculed, to plead for a smile, a look, a single word—except that he knew Rhiannon would say he had not been away long enough. Pride, too, warred with love and might have lost if he had not been caught up in the political problems the king was creating. Still, Simon was not yet directly concerned with the actions of the English king. He would not be directly affected by Henry's lunacies until Ian died and Simon did homage for the northern lands. However, what happened in England always affected Wales. Besides, Simon knew it was useful to have firsthand knowledge of what was going on, rather than garbled rumors or the sometimes deliberately slanted news in his mother's letters. Alinor was a great one for bending the truth a little this way or that to forward her own purposes.

This, coupled with the fact that Simon knew he could not say to Rhiannon *I have been constant* without sounding ridiculous when he had been away for less than three months, kept him from returning to her. Now, however, Richard was offering him the perfect excuse to do what he ached to do. Even if he were not sent back to Wales at once, there would be high excitement in being with Richard Marshal and—whatever the earl said about not wanting to oppose the king—Simon was sure there would be fighting. That would at least serve to take his mind off Rhiannon.

"If you will give me leave, my lord," Simon said quickly, "I will bring back my men with me when I bring Geoffrey and my father. Then I can accompany you when you go."

"I will be happy to have you, having come with only four men, but do you think it wise to associate yourself with me so openly? Will Lord Ian be willing?"

"He will be so glad to be rid of me," Simon said merrily, "that he would welcome it if I accompanied the Devil himself. He thinks me too outspoken." Then he added more soberly, "If you would consent to a small subterfuge, my lord, and play the part of one of my men-at-arms until we are clear of the gates, you would be safer, and the question of my being in your company would never arise."

Simon was a little afraid Richard would be insulted by the notion that he should conceal himself, but Richard was too practical to allow false pride to endanger him. "Good!" Richard exclaimed, "Excellent! I do not believe I was noticed coming in, and if I am not remarked leaving, it will be less trouble all around. Also, it will be better if you are not known by the court to be my man. If I wish to reach the king's ear, I will be able to do so through you and Lord Geoffrey. By all means, I will be your man-at-arms, with a heavy cloak to cover my mail—you can say I have a fever, if asked."

It was obvious that Richard had become convinced by Simon's warning and had accepted the necessity of flight. His later conversation with Ian and Geoffrey confirmed that beyond doubt. Geoffrey had heard enough to be sure and make Richard sure that there was a definite plan afoot now to seize him, which would make him an even more powerful object lesson and would destroy the focal point of all opposition to the king. Geoffrey looked haggard as he related what he knew.

"It is a sickness," Ian said, his voice shaking a little. "This is not Henry—I swear it is not. He looks and talks like a man raving with fever. I have known Henry all his life, from a babe, and he is a loving person who greatly desires to do good."

"I cannot understand it," Richard agreed. "It is not as if Henry even *enjoyed* the business of ruling. You know he was happy to leave that in de Burgh's hands. William wrote me often enough to complain that whenever he brought a matter to the king's notice he would be told to ask the Earl of Kent."

"No, Henry does not enjoy the business of ruling—but Winchester does," Geoffrey said tiredly.

"That is silly," Simon remarked. "If the king does not wish to hold the reins in his own hands, why should he go to the trouble of casting out de Burgh only to put Winchester in his place?"

"There were reasons enough," Geoffrey replied. "For one thing, the barons were all crying that de Burgh had grown too great. There was some truth in it, but there was also considerable ill will because Hubert was foolish in one thing only. He believed that if he were truly devoted to the interests of the king and the kingdom, he did not need to use smooth words to explain what he did."

Richard Marshal snorted. "I know that, too. He set up William's back, and you know William was not one to seek a quarrel. There was a matter of a parcel of land that he settled in William's favor, but he was so coarse that William was more affronted than if he had settled it against William's right."

Geoffrey sighed. "That was what really ruined the chancellor—that manner. It was not only the barons that he treated without proper dignity—it was the king also. He acted always as if Henry were an ignorant child."

That time Simon snorted, and Geoffrey looked at him reprovingly.

"The king is no fool," he said sharply, "and do not ever think he is. Unfortunately, he is not interested, really, in governing. He loves other things better—beautiful churches, music, books, fine clothes, merriment—but his mind is very good. De Burgh fell because when Henry said he wanted something, the chancellor replied, 'No, do not be a fool.' De Burgh should have sought a way to satisfy the king's desires or distract him from them, although usually they were not bad in themselves. But

de Burgh was too busy governing. Henry was only a figure
to mouth his words and sign his decrees—and Henry
felt it."

"Yes," Ian agreed, "you are right. I think Henry tried
to win Hubert's love. I suppose in his own style Hubert *did*
love him, but he did not show it in the right way. Henry
needs to be loved—needs it. That father and mother . . ."

He closed his eyes and shuddered. Richard nodded in
sympathy. He had spent some years in John's court as a
hostage for his father's behavior. He was somewhat surprised at the violence of Ian's reaction because he did not
know that Ian understood that part of Henry all too well.
Ian had himself been cruelly mistreated as a child.
Geoffrey's lips twisted. There was nothing anyone could
say about Henry's mother that was too bad as far as he
was concerned. That vain and heartless woman had made
four years of Geoffrey's life a hell of misery. Nonetheless,
he did not lose track of the point he was trying to make.

"Winchester is more clever. He does not offend the king
in the same way. He treats him with great deference, and
even allows him to work at kingship until he begins to be
bored. Most of all, he does not tell Henry that the beautiful things he loves are a waste. It is *most* unfortunate that
Winchester does not understand this realm. He could
manage the king very well, if only he could be brought to
see that absolute power will never be accepted by the
lords."

"Yes, and he has even infected Henry with the idea that
he is 'divinely' king," Ian said. "Winchester seems to
forget that the oaths we swear work both ways. The king
has duties and obligations to us just as we have to him."

"True enough," Richard agreed. "Moreover, there are
laws and customs that no king can ignore. If those are not
held by king and man alike, there can be no order, no
security in the realm. No man could trust the king or any
other man. The law must be upheld by all."

"And Henry knows this," Ian insisted. "Your father
taught him and de Burgh also—he abode by the law,
however unfortunate his manner of doing it. I say again
that what Henry has is a sickness, a fever roused in him
by Winchester's mistaken ideas. There is no deep, basic
fault in the king as there was in his father."

Richard did not answer directly. He agreed with Ian only to a certain extent. He had been a child in court when Henry was a younger child, and he knew the king's capacity for spite and deceit. However, he also knew Henry's capacity for loving and giving. Richard agreed that the king was acting out of character in this current violent severity. Henry did not enjoy severity. The king was very generous; he liked to give and to be thanked for it. He did not like to face anxiety and animosity and criticism and could not bear to be blamed for any fault.

"Well and so, but what do you recommend that I do?" Richard asked.

"Go back to your own lands, my lord," Geoffrey replied promptly.

"Even if I be outlawed?"

Geoffrey was silent for a moment; he hated to say what he must say, for loyalty conflicted with justice. "Yes," he got out at last. "Hold your lands, my lord, with force if you must, although I hope it will not come to that. It would be harder to regain what had fallen into the king's hands—and your efforts to regain your own would wake new anger and resentment. If Henry holds nothing of yours, which he might be tempted to give another—"

There was a multiple, inarticulate sound. Every man there knew of Henry's predilection to giving away what was not his—particularly to foreign relatives and suppliants.

Geoffrey glanced around but did not comment directly. "It will be much easier to forgive and forget," he continued. "If the king must disgorge what is bringing money into his purse or, perhaps, deprive a favorite of what he has gifted to him, there would be a temptation to maintain the state of enmity. You know how he has stripped de Burgh, little by little, of everything he could."

"I agree," Ian said emphatically. "Only stay out of his hands until he has recovered from this fever, and all will be well. The words of outlawry are easily revoked when no other real amends must be made."

CHAPTER 5

By the end of the first week of August, the doubts Kicva had felt about the need for a wedding dress for Rhiannon were dissipated. Rhiannon was ready to leave for her father's court, and Math had chosen to go with her. Growling with rage, but not attempting to tear his way out, which he could do and would do if he did not wish to go, Math sat in his traveling basket on the croup of Rhiannon's palfrey. If Math was going, there was no chance that Rhiannon would make any serious mistake.

Kicva was highly amused by the relationship between her daughter and the big cat; obviously Math believed he owned Rhiannon rather than the other way around. And Rhiannon seemed to accept it. However, the fondness Kicva had for Math was not shared by Llewelyn, who kissed his daughter warmly enough in greeting but groaned when a bedlam of barking from the dogs was followed by yelps of pain and fear.

"Have you brought that monster with you again?" he cried. "Do you not know a cat is no fit pet for a gentlewoman?"

"Math is not my pet," Rhiannon replied, laughing. "I am his—or, perhaps, we are friends, although he may not regard me highly enough for that honor."

"I hoped he was dead when you did not bring him last winter," Llewelyn said sourly.

The dogs having been routed, Math stalked solemnly up the hall, stopping before Llewelyn's chair to regard him with an unwinking stare. The ruler of many counties sighed. Math flitted his tail, seemingly contemptuous of what he saw, and walked on past Llewelyn toward the door that led to the hall of women. Rhiannon burst out laughing again at the look on her father's face and embraced and kissed him warmly. Llewelyn looked almost as surprised as if the cat had done it, but very pleased.

"Now, what has won me such a rare display of affection?" he asked fondly.

"Your own love for me, of course," Rhiannon replied. "Greater love no man can show than to endure Math for my sake."

That restored Llewelyn's good humor completely, and he asked pleasantly for news of Kicva and the homestead. He did not ask why Rhiannon had come, assuming it was the usual combination of affection for him and a need for more varied company and conversation than could be obtained in Angharad's Hall.

After a week, however, he began to wonder. Rhiannon was inviting attention from the young bucks of the court in a way she never had before. Llewelyn was not too pleased; he had hoped she would take Simon, if she took anyone. When the second week had passed, Llewelyn was even less pleased. He began to fear that Rhiannon planned to choose her man in the ancient way: whoever survived the combat over her would take her. He could have stopped it, of course, by sending her away, but in a way it was useful. It was grossly inhibiting the favorite summer sport of raiding English strongholds in Wales and on the border. At the moment, Llewelyn did not want any action of his men to divert the attention of the English from the iniquities of their king and his ministers.

After the drubbing Henry had taken in 1231 and the rebuilding of the keep called Mold, Llewelyn had expected a massive retaliatory invasion. Henry had been so busy destroying de Burgh, however, that he had not called up an army. Llewelyn knew that one was summoned now, to gather at Gloucester on the Assumption of Saint Mary, but what Henry planned to do with it was very doubtful. The stated purpose of the summons, Llewelyn's informants told him, was to attack the vassals of Hubert de Burgh in Ireland. Llewelyn could not believe this. Not even Henry, much less that clever fox Winchester, would sail off to Ireland with an army when half the men in the southwest were openly in rebellion and many barons throughout the rest of the country were on the brink of following that lead.

Most likely the army was being readied to curb Gilbert Bassett and his brothers and henchmen. If so, the rest of the baronage might rise against Henry. Nothing could please Llewelyn better than a long, bloody civil war in England. It was greatly to his advantage, and he would do whatever he could to encourage it. However, it was also possible that the army was being gathered to attack Wales. A war with Llewelyn was one of the devices a clever minister or king might use to divert animosity from himself.

Thus, Llewelyn had absolutely forbidden his major vassals to engage in even the smallest raid against English property. In fact, he had sworn that he would roast alive any man who dared steal a pig, a cow, even a chicken, and send him to the victim of the theft to replace the animal.

It was easy enough to control the older, propertied men, but the younger ones, who depended for their livelihood on what they could steal in raids, were less amenable to reasons of a political nature. The hungriest of all for loot and glory were in his own court, Llewelyn knew, and the greediest and most ambitious of those hung around Rhiannon, eying each other hotly and watching lest one or another be favored. So long as they did that, held by the lure of the dower that could be expected from Llewelyn and the advantages of a blood bond with him as well as by Rhiannon's beauty, they would not form a raiding band.

Ordinarily Llewelyn preferred that the hungry young men prey on the border holdings or even raid into England than kill each other. He had good use for every fighting cock in his court. Just now, however, he would rather they kill each other over Rhiannon than that they disturb the precarious balance of politics with England. It was all the more amusing in that none of those who pursued his daughter had the least chance of success. And that brought Llewelyn back to wondering what Rhiannon thought she was doing.

By that time Rhiannon herself could not have told him. When she first came to Aber, she had expected to look around for a day or two, choose the man who appealed to her most, and couple with him. That was simple enough in theory; in practice it seemed impossible. There were attractive men in plenty, and all were sufficiently eager to please her—and all were pleasing until Rhiannon brought her mind to the final stage of her plan. The truth was that she had not the slightest inclination to yield her body to any of them. The inescapable conclusion was that it was not a generalized desire that tormented her. She had not, as a heifer did, come into season. It was one single man her body craved.

While Rhiannon wrestled with the new problem this revelation produced, she continued—because she could think of no way abruptly to terminate them—the flirtations she had begun. She did, of course, act with greater coolness, but this only produced still greater difficulties. Now that her mind was free of the preoccupation of which man to choose, she saw the animosity she had raised among her suitors. This sent her, filled with remorse, to her father, but he only laughed heartily and begged her not to leave or turn her pursuers away just yet.

The explanation of his reasons for this request relieved Rhiannon's mind but created a problem. She had intended to write to Simon and ask him to return. When she thought matters through, however, Rhiannon realized that the last person she wanted at court just now was Simon. Whether or not he was in sympathy with her father's purpose of keeping his wild bucks from raiding, Simon was not likely to consent to being one suitor in a crowd of others. Besides, if she showed him favor, all the others might turn on him. Although in a general way Simon was well liked, it would be a far different matter to see a suitor from England run off with a Welsh prize even though Rhiannon had no intention of marrying. The satisfaction of her desire was reasonable, but she was strongly opposed to submitting her body or soul to the tether that marriage oaths would impose.

Thus it was with more horror than pleasure that Rhiannon saw Simon ride into Aber on a fine afternoon in mid-August. Instinct conquered reason: Rhiannon fled —across the bailey, out the rear postern, down the precipitous slope that led up to the walls, and into the woods. Like a wild thing, she cowered behind a tangle of brush until the quiet of the afternoon wood brought her some calm. Even then, flight seemed the only answer.

To return meant that her cheap device to escape her need for Simon would be exposed. Shame did not often touch Rhiannon. Fearlessness and honesty had protected her from the kind of actions that engendered shame. She had known that ugly emotion only as a result of a certain heedlessness that sometimes made her careless of the needs and feelings of others. Now that carelessness plus the fears that Simon had awakened in her had driven her into behavior she considered shameful.

There was no way to hide what she had done—or was there? Rhiannon sat up straighter, and two squirrels that had been gathering food within feet of her, taking her for inanimate because of her stillness, chattered angrily and sprang for the nearest tree. She could say, truthfully, that she was following her father's orders. And add spoken lies to the shame she felt already? No. It would be better to go secretly, before Simon knew she was at court.

And not see him? There was a sickening sinking in Rhiannon, followed by a strange ache. Neither sensation could be real, she knew. Nor would seeing Simon do her the least good, she told herself bitterly. When he knew what she had been about, it was highly unlikely he would be willing to have anything to do with her. That decision did not produce an even greater depression as it should, perhaps, have done. Rhiannon knew that love prompted forgiveness. Let Simon hear the worst from others. If he came to her after that . . .

In calculating her plans, Rhiannon had not included Math—a factor that could not, she soon found, be ignored. She had forgotten Math's unusual fondness for Simon's company. When she returned to Aber, warned the two men who had accompanied her, and packed her belongings, she found Math was missing. Calling him in the women's quarters and in the stables, storage huts, and outdoor areas produced no result.

Rhiannon was surprised. Although Math often ignored her when she called him at home, he was usually eager to go back to the hall in the hills and would stay close to her heels or come running when she began to pack. There was only one place he could be where he would not have heard her—in the great hall. She could only hope that Simon had left there already, and she peered in cautiously from a doorway not far from the dais where her father's chair of state stood. The sight that met her eyes drew a gasp of combined amazement and fury and precluded any stealthy retreat from court.

Simon and her father were talking very earnestly in low voices, Simon sitting on a stool drawn near Llewelyn's chair. However, Rhiannon hardly noticed her father or his attitude. What had caused her gasp and the accompanying emotions was the sight of Math. sitting in Simon's lap and purring away as Simon absently stroked his head and gently scratched under his chin. Escape was no longer possible.

Stormily, Rhiannon went to tell her men she had changed her mind. They would stay at Aber. Then she stamped out to the women's hall and unpacked. Finally, eyes gleaming with defiance, she came to the great hall. There she met only more frustration. Simon and her father had disappeared. Math, however, came to her at once, his tail high, purring, looking, to Rhiannon's jaundiced eyes, inordinately pleased with himself.

"Traitor!" she exclaimed bitterly. "Is this how you reward me for all my devoted service to you?"

A low exclamation of fear close by made Rhiannon turn swiftly. She was about to say it was only a jest, but Mallt uerch Arnallt and Catrin uerch Pawl. the two ladies who had been nearest, were hurrying away, doubtless making signs against the evil eye. Now those two would probably spread the word that she had confirmed herself a witch and Math her familiar. She wished briefly that she was and that she could bespell their silly tongues to restrain their chatter, but she had not that kind of power.

At odds with herself and knowing she would probably only make matters worse by trying to explain or, indeed, speaking to anyone before she had calmed herself, Rhiannon went out to walk. This time Math followed, which drew from his mistress several even less favorable remarks on his character. She returned only when the light started to fail, not actually at peace with herself but determined to speak the plain truth to Simon and cleanse thoroughly the wound of shame.

She found that Math was not the only traitor whom she had unwisely trusted. Simon darted forward as soon as she came in, his eyes glittering with excitement.

"Your father tells me you have changed your mind," he said, seizing her hand and kissing it.

"Changed my mind about what?" Rhiannon countered coldly, infuriated all over again.

About me, Simon nearly said, but he swallowed the impulse, realizing that he had been incredibly gauche. In his eagerness to commit himself to her immediately and irrevocably, he had said what must be wounding to the pride of any woman and, worse, made himself sound like a cocksure fool. What Rhiannon might confide in her father and what Llewelyn might pass on in a spirit of helpful mischief could not be wantonly exposed.

"About being involved in your father's political doings," he said, eying the gentlemen who were converging on them with an unholy light in his eyes.

Rhiannon looked over her shoulder and withdrew her hand hurriedly from Simon's. He might have thought the glares directed at them were funny, but she did not. "I am glad to see you again, Sir Simon," she said with reserve, "but I am not dressed for an evening in company."

"You are beautiful in any dress, Lady Rhiannon, even with cockleburs in your hair instead of pearls," Simon remarked sententiously. As Rhiannon wrinkled her nose disdainfully and began to turn away, he continued with spurious gravity, "I think I like the cockleburs better, in fact. They are less expensive to gather, which must be a point to consider for a husband who is not rich."

She could not help laughing. Simon knew she had gems enough not to need more from a husband and that she cared very little whether she wore rubies or polished stones which could be had for the simple labor of picking them up from the ground and rolling them in a mill. Even so, in Welsh terms, Simon *was* rich.

"Do you delay me hoping that these gentlemen"— Rhiannon nodded at the four men who now stood close— "will be discouraged by my appearance? I assure you they will not. They, too, prefer cockleburs. Then the dower my father gives with me could be spent on objects worthier than my adornment."

"You need no adornment," one said.

"There is naught worthier than your adornment," another exclaimed.

The other two, keener witted, said nothing, seeing the trap. Rhiannon raised her fine-arched brows, preparing to impale the unwise flatterers on their own lances of wit. But, before she could praise the economy of one, who would offer fine words in the place of rich gifts, or complain that the other thought her so ugly that any sum expended on baubles to hide her true appearance would be worthwhile, Simon deflected her aim.

"We may all soon be rich enough not to care for your dower or the price of rich gifts," he suggested provocatively.

Instantly the attention of the four young men shifted. The eldest of them, Owain Brogynton, had not fallen into Rhiannon's snare, but greed drew him headlong into Simon's.

"How so, when Prince Llewelyn has forbidden raiding? Do you think yourself safe from his command because of your Saeseneg relations?"

"Not at all," Simon replied blandly, ignoring the insult implied by *Saeseneg*—English-speaking—*relations*. "I am Prince Llewelyn's man and have neither intention nor desire to disobey any command he may give, but I have news. . . ." He allowed that to drift off temptingly.

"From so noteworthy a source, I am sure your news will be the mainspring of all Prince Llewelyn's future decisions," another sneered. He was the youngest of the group and the first to leap into Rhiannon's pitfall.

Antwn ap Madog, the second man who had been clever enough to hold his tongue, put his hand on the speaker's arm. His father held lands in Powys and was one of Llewelyn's bulwarks against the Marcher lords. Thus, he was better acquainted than the others with the nobility and politics of England and knew to whom Simon was related.

"His source may well be noteworthy," Antwn said. "His brother-by-marriage is cousin to King Henry. What is your news, Simon?"

"You know, I suppose, that King Henry has summoned an army to gather at Gloucester on the Assumption and that many Flemish mercenaries have been brought in also."

"Of course we know," Madog ap Sior snapped. He was the second to fall into Rhiannon's trap and still did not realize she had laid a snare. He was less quick-witted than the others, more stubborn also, prone to cling to opinions he had made on the basis of superficial evidence. "That is why we are forbidden to raid. The king will soon take his army to Ireland, however, and we will be free of him. This is no news."

"I do not think the king will take his army to Ireland—and neither does Prince Llewelyn," Simon said, smiling.

"You dare to say our prince fears the stupid, slow-footed Saeson?" Madog snarled, thrusting forward.

Antwn grabbed him. "Do not be a fool, Madog. I am sure Simon would not insult Prince Llewelyn. Go on, Simon."

"I do not intend insult to Prince Llewelyn by calling him a coward. but I will not insult him by saying he is fool enough to desire that an army of that size fall upon Wales either."

"What if they did?" the youngster sneered. "They would starve as others have done before them."

"Yes, and then we would starve all winter also, since the crops are not yet in nor the herds fully fattened," Owain remarked, his eyes narrowed. "If we must starve, we can. But I agree with Simon that Prince Llewelyn would not invite the Saeson in at this time."

"Unfortunately, it is not a question of not inviting them in but of keeping them out—if they are not going to Ireland," Antwn said. "The message with the summons said to 'bring to obedience the Earl of Kent's men in Ireland.' This much I know for certain. Do you think this is a ruse to befool us? If so—"

"That was not the intent," Simon said quickly. The English were enough hated; he did not wish to add fuel to that fire. "Likely the summons was honestly intended when it went out, but matters have changed. Gilbert Bassett is now in open rebellion. He has sent a defiance to the king, and the Earl of Pembroke knows that justice is on Bassett's side. He does not wish to fight King Henry, but the earl will do nothing to curb Bassett. If Henry uses this as an excuse to attack Pembroke's keeps in the south—"

"Who cares what Pembroke or the Saeson king does in the south?" Madog growled. "You may keep your news to yourself; we—"

"But Madog," the youngster interrupted, having noticed the expressions of glee on the faces of Owain and Antwn and put two and two together, "if Henry's army is busy in the south—"

"We may all grow rich raiding the baggage trains," Simon put in smoothly. "Prince Llewelyn would never forbid the raiding of an invading army, even if he does not want attacks to be made on English lands just now."

The four huddled closer to discuss this splendid possibility, not realizing that Rhiannon had slipped away and that, a few moments later, Simon had followed. He caught her just outside the hall of women, where she had stopped to say some reproachful things to Math, who merely stared at her enigmatically.

"Lady Rhiannon," Simon said, "do forgive me for foiling your intention of pricking those conceits, but I was most eager to drop my burden of news where it would do the most good."

"I am happy you found me so useful," she retorted coldly, "but I cannot say I think much of your discretion. My father does not love men with wagging tongues."

"Neither do I. It was Prince Llewelyn who bade me start the gossip. No, forget that for now. I could not believe my good fortune when I saw Math and so knew you were here. I have been racking my brains all the way from Clifford to think of a reason to go to Angharad's Hall—and here you are."

"Do you think I came to seek you?"

"No! My lady, do not quarrel with me without cause, I beg you. I wish only to please you."

"Like those others?"

Several pat answers sprang to Simon's tongue, but he swallowed them. "How can I answer that?" he asked slowly. "I do not know what they feel. You said they desired your dower, but that might have been a jest. I certainly do not—you know that. I will be glad to have a blood bond with your father, but that is because I love him well, not because I hope to gain by it."

The door of the hall opened, yellow light from the torches spilling from it along the ground. It did not touch Simon or Rhiannon where they stood, but she took Simon by the wrist and drew him around the building to the garden at the back. She was ashamed of her sharp retorts, aware they were the product of her anger with herself and that Simon had done nothing to deserve them She knew it was time to unburden herself before shame bred more anger, which would breed more shame, and round and round until the walls of self-hatred had grown too high and too hard to be breached.

Simon had been surprised into silence by Rhiannon's sudden move. When he saw where she was leading him, he maintained silence, afraid he would go too far or not far enough and irritate her again. It was a wise move, giving Rhiannon time to drop her defenses When they reached a bench set at a crossways amid the beds of herbs and flowers she stopped and looked up. It was very dark, the moon not having yet risen, but that was all to the good. Rhiannon preferred to get through her confession without either seeing Simon's expression or having him read hers.

"Simon." she said quickly, "the question I asked—did I come to seek you—held a falsehood in it because it implied I did not."

"But— oh, my lady, did you send me a message and think I had not come? I never received it, I swear. You see, I left London suddenly and I have been with the Earl of Pembroke, moving from one keep to another because—"

"No, I did not send any message, nor did I expect to find you here. I came to see if any other man would content me—"

"What!"

"You heard me," Rhiannon said sharply. "I came to see if—like a heifer—any bull could service me."

It was most fortunate that Simon's mother was given to crude and forthright language when it served her purpose and that Llewelyn had told him already that Rhiannon had found all the young bucks at court insufficient The combination of experience and private knowledge saved him from losing his temper. As soon as the initial shock of Rhiannon saying such a thing of herself had passed. Simon was touched by her desperate honesty —and was amused.

"There are more delicate ways to say you are now

ready to consider marriage, my lady," he said gravely, determined not to make another mistake.

"But I am *not* ready to consider marriage," Rhiannon snapped. "And there is *no* delicate way to say that I desire you."

Simon gulped. He had been invited by many women in many ways, but never like this. He stared helplessly down, but it was too dark to see anything except the faint gleam of Rhiannon's luminous eyes. There was no way to make out her expression.

"Rhiannon," he stammered, "my lady—"

"You have now the right to call me Rhiannon, nor need you add 'my lady.' We are done with honorifics."

She put out her hand, and Simon saw the flash of her teeth as she smiled at him. There was no implication in what she said of shame or of being made less than she was. Rhiannon was merely admitting him to an intimacy she had previously withheld by insisting on formality in his address.

"But if you love me—" Simon began to protest.

"I never said I loved you." Rhiannon cut him off, her voice sharp again. "I said I desired you. Do you not know the difference?"

"Indeed I do!" Simon responded furiously. "Which is why I asked your father formally for permission to address you and asked you for the honor of becoming your husband. I love you! If you do not love me, you do not. There is no need to insult me!"

Whereupon he stalked away, leaving Rhiannon somewhat stunned.

CHAPTER 6

Neither Simon nor Rhiannon spent a very pleasant night. Five minutes after he left her, Simon hurried back, but she was gone. He regretted what he had said and done, not because he was willing to take Rhiannon on her terms but because of the way he had rejected them. Too late he had remembered Llewelyn telling him that Rhiannon's mother and grandmother had also been unwilling to marry. He had reacted as if Rhiannon's offer was one of contempt for him, as if she thought he was not worth marrying, and that was probably not true.

Simon stood in the garden awhile, hoping Rhiannon would guess he would return, but she did not come back and he could have torn out his hair with frustration. It would not be easy, he realized, to find a time alone with her again to explain himself. He stood irresolute, thinking that it might not be easy even to be alone with himself in Llewelyn's court after the news he had dropped, and he had to be alone to think. It might not be difficult—once he found a time and place—to explain away his anger. However, changing Rhiannon's mind about marriage would be another matter entirely.

Rhiannon had regretted her own blunt words as soon and as deeply as Simon regretted his outburst of temper. She had hurried after him—or so she thought—as soon as she recovered from the surprise of having made him so very angry. But she had assumed that he would have gone back to the hall, and, once inside, she had been snatched up into the group from which she had previously escaped. She had little choice but to stay with them and then excuse herself after a decent interval and go back to the women's hall. This she did, making a detour into the garden, but Simon was long gone by then.

It had been stupid and unkind, Rhiannon thought, to state her purpose so crudely. There were gentler ways to say that one does not wish to marry. And Simon did not carry, as she did, a leavening of the old religion. Doubtless he thought a union without marriage sinful. At that point Rhiannon paused in removing her clothes and chuckled softly. If so, he had managed to bear up very well under the burden of sin he had accumulated so far. No, it was not his faith to God that had been offended. What then?

Only when she rethought the scene between them carefully did it come to her that she had said she did not love him, whereas he claimed to love her. So it was his pride that had been hurt—too bad. Her eyes sparked angrily, but then the expression in them softened. Perhaps he did love her right now. Perhaps he even lied to himself that he would love her forever. Rhiannon stood staring at the tall night candle considering that possibility. If it was no lie, if Simon did love her and could be faithful, would she wish to bind *herself* forever?

A response began to build up in her and Rhiannon shook herself sharply, but she felt a greater sympathy for Simon. No doubt he did not lie consciously; no doubt he felt the same urge, the same sneaking conviction that he would love forever as she had begun to feel. Nonetheless, no man was ever faithful, and one like Simon least of all. Too many women followed him, called to him, offered themselves to him. And she was not sure *she* would love him forever, no matter what she felt right now.

At first, sleep would not come, and when it did it brought such dreams of mingled ecstasy and terror all dappled with blood that Rhiannon started awake sweating. Math leapt onto the bed and walked up her chest, purring loudly. She stroked him, and the soft sleekness of his vibrating body assured her of reality. Yet the dream shadowed her waking, and it was not, as her dreams usually were, clear in memory. She tried to pick it apart, to determine whether the joy had engendered the terror or whether they were two separate things, but even that she could not do.

To Rhiannon, dreams were not to be ignored. They were true foreshadowings—if properly interpreted. But the maelstrom of joy and fear she had experienced could not be disentangled for interpretation. However, as she lay sleepless in the dim light of the night candle, the pleasure took a greater hold on her mind, and that was most unusual. Mostly, with dreams, it was the terror that grew until all else shrank into insignificance. Without clear memory, however, there could be no true guidance. She tried to blank her mind and concentrate wholly on Math's rhythmic purring on which she could float into sleep.

Simon had no bad dreams, but he had found sleep equally elusive. In England he had not been celibate. It had never entered his mind that when Rhiannon spoke of keeping to one love she could include the casual use of a whore now and then to relieve his body. Nonetheless, he had taken no woman since he had left London with Richard. They had been moving too quickly, and he had been so busy, he had scarcely felt the lack, except for a little while when he had wakened in the morning.

The contact with Rhiannon and her offer had roused desire. To satisfy it would have been no trouble—there were several women in the court who had given Simon solace before he had fixed his heart on Rhiannon. All of their eyes said they would welcome him back, and Mallt uerch Arnallt had even begun to follow him across the hall when he had rushed forward to speak to Rhiannon. That was out of the question, however. Even to look in Mallt's direction would be the end of any hope he had of convincing Rhiannon to be his wife. Besides, he did not want Mallt.

When the hall was dark and silent, Simon found his way among the other men to his pallet. Not far away Madog ap Sior's eyes opened. He had been the most annoyed when the four men discussing raids on the baggage train of Henry's army discovered that Rhiannon was gone, because he was the most convinced that a woman should wait patiently until a man had time to attend to her. He had been even more annoyed when it seemed that Simon had gone with her. That Simon should now steal in so late and so silently infuriated him even further. Naturally, he assumed Simon had been with Rhiannon.

Worst of all, Antwn had made it clear to him that it was not possible simply to find a dark corner and stick a knife between Simon's ribs. Simon was the only son of Prince Llewelyn's dear friend and clan brother Ian de

Vipont. More important, he was personally a great favorite with the prince. And, at the moment, most important of all, he was an envoy from the Earl of Pembroke. Thus, if any harm should come to Simon, Llewelyn would harrow the court so effectively that Christ's Harrowing of Hell would seem a jest in comparison.

Madog was not quick of mind, but the pressure of rage and the need for secrecy jolted him into an unusual mental agility. He put together Simon's English connections and Prince Llewelyn's affection for him with the fact that Llewelyn's illegitimate son Gruffydd loathed the English and was jealous of anyone his father preferred. Madog did not mind if Gruffydd got into trouble. He would watch Simon, he thought, and when he caught him with Rhiannon he would report the matter to Gruffydd. Then Gruffydd would take care of the elimination of Simon, one way or another.

The absolute stillness of Simon's body on his pallet further infuriated Madog, who thought Simon had dropped asleep instantly and associated that with sexual satisfaction. However, it was discipline rather than satisfaction that kept Simon so quiet. He had more or less decided what he would say to Rhiannon, but he was quite unable to think of a way to convince her to listen to him. He had assumed she was so furious at the crude way he had rejected her offer of herself that she would not even permit him to approach her.

To add to the difficulty, Simon did not dare leave it to time to appease her anger while he furthered his cause by looking depressed and lonely—a ruse he had found very efficacious when a lady in one place finally heard of his exploits in another. Time, usually so much a lover's friend, had turned on him. Simon did not know whether he would have a day, a week, or a month or more before Llewelyn came to a decision as to what he would do, when he would do it, or whether he wished to ally himself to Pembroke at all. He was pretty sure of a day or two while Llewelyn consulted the major clan leaders who were beholden to him. After that, Simon knew he might be sent back to Richard at any time, and then he did not know when he would be able to return. Once the fighting started, it might be many months before his time was again his own.

By morning Simon was convinced that the only certain method was to lay violent hands on Rhiannon, carry her away into the woods, and try to excuse both offenses at once. It was, however, easier to make this decision than to carry it out, he feared. How was he going to find her in a place where he could seize her without interference? If she screamed and resisted, doubtless every man in Aber would pursue them. Nonetheless, after breaking his fast and idling about the hall, hoping Rhiannon would come in, Simon began to make plans to forward this purpose. He told his grooms to saddle Ymlladd and stood watching their struggles with the evil-tempered gray stallion, while trying to formulate a message that would bring Rhiannon out into the bailey. He was so absorbed in his thoughts that he did not notice the prize he so ardently desired approaching him. In fact, he reached automatically for the horse's bridle when it was led toward him.

From Rhiannon's viewpoint, Simon seemed first to be looking right through her, as if she did not exist, and then to be intending to ride quickly away. Ordinarily she would have been very angry, but her sense of being at fault, together with the fear that he had been so hurt he was leaving for good, drove her to call his name and run forward. A number of heads turned in the direction of the sound. One of them was Mallt's, another was Madog's. He had followed Simon out of the hall, suspicious of the fact that de Vipont seemed to be avoiding his usual cronies. Now Madog's suspicions were confirmed.

Simon's hand jerked on Ymlladd's bridle, and the horse reared. Knowing that swift movement or loud sounds could set the battle-trained animal into a frenzy, Simon vaulted into the saddle and curbed the horse fiercely. Rhiannon realized at once what she had done and stopped abruptly. She understood animals, and it was also too late to do anything about Simon. If he did not wish to speak to her, he would ride away; there was no use in running after him. Since her dignity would be rather damaged if he rode away, Rhiannon turned, as if she were about to return to the hall.

Simon brought his horse under control just in time to see Rhiannon's move. He spurred the beast forward, bent from the saddle, and pulled her up in front of him. Madog sprang forward, but the cry of alarm on his lips changed to a low curse as he saw Rhiannon turn toward her abductor, laughing, and throw her arms around his neck.

Although he was delighted with this reaction, Simon did not curb the speed of his destrier, but merely directed him toward the gate. They galloped through and away, then turned north where, after a quarter of a mile of forested land, a series of coves broke the headlands fronting the ocean.

"You must listen, Rhiannon," Simon began.

Simultaneously, Rhiannon said, "Simon, try to understand—"

Laughter followed naturally and the destrier stumbled, which was not surprising at the pace he was going with the weight so oddly distributed. Relieved of his fear that Rhiannon was unwilling to talk to him, Simon gave his attention to his horse. Equally reassured, Rhiannon relaxed and allowed Simon to go where he wanted while he slowed the animal to a trot and then to a walk. At last she asked curiously where Simon was taking her.

"I have not the faintest idea," he responded cheerfully. "Anywhere, so long as we are not likely to be interrupted." He paused and then added seriously, "We really must come to an understanding. I do not know how much longer I will be permitted to stay. You know I am only serving as a messenger, Rhiannon. My coming and going are not at my own discretion."

"Then you came to my father as an emissary, not of your own will?" she asked.

Simon tried to judge her expression, but it was difficult. Even with her head turned as much as possible toward him, he was so close that he saw her from a strange angle. Nor could he trust himself to interpret her voice. It sounded good-humored and curious, but Rhiannon had a tendency to set traps for unwary tongues and Simon was determined not to fall in.

"Do you know where we can be private and comfortable?" That was a safe question, and it saved him from the need for answering her immediately. "I am not very familiar with Aber."

Rhiannon looked up through the trees at the sun. "That way," she pointed. "We will come out above the water, and we can find a cove. If it gets hot enough, we can swim. Oh, can you swim, Simon?"

"Of course I can. Roselynde lies on the narrow sea."

He touched Ymlladd with his spur to pick up the pace, not because he wished to arrive sooner, but because he wanted to forestall conversation under what he considered adverse conditions. In fact, it was extremely pleasant to hold Rhiannon clutched against him. He had never had so prolonged a contact with her before and found it so stimulating that the real purpose of this ride began to become obscured. By the time they had reached the shore and picked their way down along a stream that had cut a path to the narrow, rocky beach, Simon was beginning to reconsider Rhiannon's offer and to wonder whether it could make any difference if they married before or after they became lovers.

Still in the grip of this emotion, Simon slid from his horse, carrying Rhiannon with him. It was not completely safe to leave Ymlladd loose while he was saddled and bridled. An empty saddle and a loose rein were battle signals to the war-trained stallion that could set him to attack anyone who moved except Simon, whose scent he knew. That would put Rhiannon in danger if she were alone, but Simon had no intention of releasing her. As long as they were locked together, the horse would not attack.

In fact, Ymlladd gave no signs of restlessness or bad temper when Simon released him. Instead, he wandered a few steps away to suck water from the stream and then lip at leaves on the bushes that grew on the bank. Had Simon been less preoccupied with his own feelings, he would have noted this behavior as being very strange. As it was, he merely lowered his head and fastened his mouth to Rhiannon's.

She had been about to say something, but the feel of Simon's lips put it right out of her head. This was not the first time he had kissed her; there had been formal exchanges in greeting and parting, but this was very different. There was a physical urgency in the force of his kiss and in the quivering intensity of his arms around her, although he was not holding her tight. Rhiannon was in no condition at the moment to analyze anything, but later she understood just how skillful Simon's "assault" on her was. To other women, a crushing grip would signify passion, but Simon knew it would mean restraint and compulsion to her. So he held her close enough that their bodies touched and she could feel his tense eagerness, but loosely enough that she could break away if she chose.

Thus, it was Rhiannon who pressed closer, one arm around Simon's neck and the other around his hard-muscled back. This encouragement and the deep, sighing breath she took led Simon to experiment further. His left arm still encircled her shoulders, but his right hand began rhythmically to stroke her back, dropping lower and then lower until he was caressing her buttocks—caressing and pulling her closer. Simon knew what Rhiannon must feel each time he drew her tightly against him. Since he was dressed for the heat of August, only in a silk tunic and thin woolen chausses, his engorged manhood must be clearly apparent to her.

It was, and her perception of his violent desire heightened her own. Behind her dammed lips, Rhiannon uttered soft excited cries while she pressed forward on her own. However, like his father, Simon was an unusually tall man. Simple forward pressure merely pushed Simon's shaft into her abdomen, and that excited her further without giving her the smallest relief.

Rhiannon had always been a creature who responded to physical sensations. She was extremely sensitive to all such stimuli—the warmth of the sun, the feel of wet grass beneath her bare feet, the kiss of the wind, and the damp caress of the rain. She knew, also, all the facts concerning sexual union. However, the intimate connection between the senses and the act had only been known to her through assumption—by the reminiscent pleasure in her mother's eyes and by deduction from what others had said. Her own experience was limited to the restless uneasiness she had felt from the time she sent Simon away in the spring.

Now her body knew. Sensation flowed over and through her, spreading from wherever Simon had intimate contact with her—from her lips, from the skin and muscle where his hands held and stroked her body, most poignantly from the mute messenger of his own desire. Passion warmed, then burned, hot and urgent, centering in her own loins, which demanded further sensation that was denied by her position.

Instinctively Rhiannon pushed up as well as forward, wrapping both arms around Simon's neck and rising on her toes in her attempt to satisfy her need. Failing, she sank back momentarily to a less strained position, but the urge was irresistible and she pushed upward again. Simon groaned softly, and that excited Rhiannon even further. She let herself drop again, preparing for an even more strenuous effort.

Although Simon was also extremely excited, there was little new in the physical sensations for him. His thinking processes were somewhat blurred but were by no means extinguished. He had, after all, considerable experience keeping his wits about him while making love. Rhiannon's innocent abandon was making this more difficult than usual by the moment, but the more difficult it became to think and the more violent his desire, the more determined Simon became that this was the woman he wanted as a life companion. Through the pulsing pleasure that racked him with every movement Rhiannon made, one conviction held firm. Somehow he had to convince Rhiannon to marry him.

Equally urgent was the satisfaction of his desire. Yet, if he satisfied himself by coupling with Rhiannon, he would be confirming a liaison on her terms—and he was not at all sure what those terms were. He could not take the chance that he would truly be playing bull to her heifer, that she would feel free to go after another bull any time she wished. There was, however, an easy solution to this problem. Simon pulled Rhiannon even closer, both hands on her buttocks now, and assisted her rising and falling motion, twisting her a shade to one side so that he could thrust a thigh between her legs.

At this application of pressure where she most desired it, Rhiannon made a low sound that was a cross between a moan and a purr of pleasure. She clung tighter, twisting and shifting and, with each movement of her body, rubbing against Simon's swollen shaft. Normally he would have distracted himself from that sensation as best he could to ensure the satisfaction of his partner, but he was not sure he could content Rhiannon in this strange way, and he was not even sure he wanted her content. Thus, he let his body have its way and he came to climax in moments.

Finished, he pulled his mouth free, automatically straightening his leg and gripping Rhiannon harder, flat against him to stop her motion. She protested with wordless sounds and struggled to move, seeking to regain the pressure she desired, but Simon's strength was too great for her and she cried his name, sobbing with frustration.

"Hush, love, hush," Simon soothed, shifting her gently so that she was not pressed so hard against him.

This was by no means what Rhiannon wanted, but Simon persisted, kissing her forehead and cheeks, patting her back, and murmuring soothingly. Soon she calmed. Her arms loosened and slipped down from his neck; she sighed deeply and then stood away from him.

"Why?" she faltered. "Why did you not take me? I am willing."

"Because I love you," Simon replied. "A man does not *take* a woman he loves. You know without my telling you that I have taken many women—all willing. I do not need to force a woman. But I did not love any of them—nor did I say to them that I did. I will not despoil you, Rhiannon —no matter what you think you want."

She stood looking at him, puzzled still but with a trace of suspicion in her clear eyes. "Then why did you begin to make love to me—to whet my appetite?" The last words held a dangerous sharpness.

"No," Simon protested, and began to laugh. "Did you think I did that apurpose? Rhiannon, I have said more than once that I love you. You are very beautiful. I have been a long time without a woman. All the way here I held you close in my arms. I am afraid I was not thinking at all when we came down from Ymlladd."

"Then what started you thinking again?" she persisted.

Simon could not tell her of his satisfaction or she would become too furious to listen to anything else he had to say. Besides, he had decided not to consummate their lovemaking before that had happened; he would not be lying, then, if he did not mention it.

Still smiling, he replied, "Two things. One is this cove

you chose. Is there a place where we could lie down?
Sharp rocks are no good bed for a maiden to bear her first
man."

That made Rhiannon smile also as she looked around.
Then she glanced sidelong at Simon, suspicious again.
"How is it that you noticed the rocks? I did not."

"It is not my first time of desiring," Simon pointed out
with candor. He would never have said such a thing to
another woman, but Rhiannon's honesty demanded honesty in return, when the truth would not lead to so false
an impression as to amount to a lie.

Rhiannon considered that answer and nodded acceptance, beginning to smile again. "And your second reason?"

"Your very great willingness. No, do not grow angry
before you hear the rest. I was *not* disgusted by your
forwardness. It was a delight to me. I very nearly forgot
the rocks and everything else; otherwise I would have
stopped sooner." He stepped back a little so he could take
her hands and raise them to his lips, after which he held
them against his breast. "My love, my love, you are as
innocent as a young doe, knowing the need of your body
but not considering anything beyond it. I cannot grasp at
that and forget all else. If you do not think of your own
good, I must."

The rigidity that had come over Rhiannon at Simon's
first words passed. She bent forward and kissed his hands,
which were holding hers, then lifted her head and smiled
at him. "You are very dear and very kind—but very
wrong. I do, indeed, desire the satisfaction of my body. . . ."
Her voice faltered slightly over the words as they brought
back the throbbing excitement she had felt. "But I assure
you, I have given the matter much thought. Truly I have,
Simon."

"Rhiannon—"

"No, you must listen. I have gone wrong about this
matter with you. I knew you would not understand, and—
and I misjudged you also, thinking you would take eagerly
what you desired and what I offered freely."

"But I do not *only* desire you, Rhiannon," Simon
interjected.

A slight shadow passed over her face, but she shook her

head. "I do not understand you. All else of me you may have as freely as any other person. What is it you want?"

"What I want, you do not offer to any person, except, perhaps, Kicva. Give me your inmost thoughts, your willingness to lay your life in my hands as I willingly lay mine in yours for all eternity. No, I do not mean you should never think a private thought, only that when you wish to share a thing you would not dare tell another person, you will tell it to me. This is what—" He stopped because Rhiannon was shaking her head.

"Eternity is a very long time," she said. "Especially long to a young man of two and twenty—"

"And very short to an ancient grandmother one year younger?" Simon interrupted teasingly.

"No. It is even longer to me. How long is your eternity, Simon? Until you return to Pembroke? A month longer? A year? Beautiful one, let us both take joy of each other in this brief eternity—and when it is over, let us part with fondness and liking, never having promised each other more."

"No." Simon's bright eyes were almost black with pain, but his voice was steady. "That is all I ever had with any woman and all I ever wanted until I saw you. I tell you, I love you, Rhiannon. I do not want a little easy pleasure. I want you for a life companion."

"*Now* you do," she sighed.

"But Rhiannon," Simon said, brightening as he realized that all her objections seemed to center on the fact that he would not be steadfast, "if you wish to hold me, all you need to do is agree to marry me. Then I will be stuck fast, will I, nill I."

"Are you mad?" she cried, recoiling and pulling her hands free with a shudder. "Such a life is an abomination! Do you think I could endure to hold a man on such terms? Am I so poor a thing—"

"Rhiannon, Rhiannon," Simon exclaimed, following her and repossessing her hands, "I was only jesting. How could you think otherwise? You will need no bonds and no lures to keep me faithful. That you are Rhiannon is enough. My love, you have set a *geas* upon me that I will never break."

"No! I did not 'call' you! I—I do not think I did."

"Call me? What do you mean?"

For answer, Rhiannon took her hands from Simon gently and turned toward where his stallion still stood quietly lipping at the sparse grass. "Ymlladd," she called in a peculiar soft, singing tone, "Come, Ymlladd. Come. Come. Come to me."

The animal raised his head and snorted softly. Simon tensed, preparing to jump in front of Rhiannon if the warhorse decided she was a threat and charged.

"Come, Ymlladd," she called again, her voice hypnotic with its singing croon.

And the horse came! Simon held his breath as the stallion dropped his head to nuzzle Rhiannon's hand and butted gently against her to demand attention when the hand with which she stroked him paused. Simon blinked and blinked again. Was this Ymlladd, who for years tried to savage the grooms who had tended him? True, Ymlladd never tried to kill Simon himself and would accept tokens of affection from him with grave dignity—but the stallion was acting like a colt!

"Enough," Rhiannon said softly, and pushed the horse away.

She turned to Simon, smiling at his stunned expression but with worry deep in her eyes. "That is calling. I was told it was Angharad's skill. My mother does not have it. She—she reads people. I can call almost any animal—but it does not work with people. Men and women have minds and wills—"

"So do horses, and I never met one with a stronger will than Ymlladd," Simon said, but his eyes were glittering with mischief and laughter. "So you *did* set a *geas* on me!"

"No!"

"Yes you did. As soon as I saw you—you were singing to Prince Llewelyn—I was called and held."

Rhiannon laughed. "You devil! You are trying to make me feel guilty. I did not even notice you."

"Nonetheless," Simon teased, "you have ensorceled me. See how I returned resistless, even after you yourself sent me away. I am enchanted."

"You are enchanted with your desire to have your own way," Rhiannon replied tartly. "Do you think I am an idiot and do not remember that you just told me you were Pembroke's messenger?"

But she was not angry, and Simon laughed with her. "How inconveniently honest you are," he complained. "Any sensible woman would be delighted with the idea that she could bewitch a man—"

"And especially you!" Rhiannon exclaimed.

"Do not offend my modesty," Simon retorted, grinning, then sobered. "But it is true nonetheless—oh, not that you bewitched me but that I loved you from my first seeing and that each time I see and speak with you that love grows. Rhiannon, you say you do not love me. . . . Do you love any other man?"

"No! Nor will I ever."

"I do not believe you."

She shrugged. "Nor do I believe that you will love me long. No, do not protest. How can you say what will be a year hence?"

"I do not know that I will be alive a year hence—or a month, for that matter, but while I live I will love you."

"Simon, I do not dare. You do not really know me or my kind. I am a whole being. If I give you the heart out of my body and you lose it, I will die."

He began to say that no one died of a broken heart, but he was looking into her strange, clear eyes. Quite suddenly Simon realized that Rhiannon could, just as certain hawks could die when captured although most of their kind were readily tamed, will herself to death. This put a new light on Rhiannon's resistance. Simon was in no doubt about his own feelings. This was the first woman he had ever loved, and he was sure he would love her forever. *He* knew she was in no danger from a change in his heart, but how to convince her—not to love him but to trust him —was different. Time could convince her, but he had no time. She was very lovely, and it was very hard to wait.

CHAPTER 7

∻∻∻∻∻∻∻∻∻∻∻∻∻∻∻∻∻∻∻∻∻∻∻∻∻∻

If it had not been for the jagged rocks on that shore, Rhiannon might have achieved her purpose. Since it was barely possible for Simon to find two stones large enough and flat enough to sit on, he did not long consider an immediate coupling. To remount and to look deliberately for a place was a crudity Simon did not contemplate in connection with the woman he loved. One sought the nearest hedge or ditch with a whore or a serf girl off the land. With a lady, time and place must flow together with feeling—and more especially with Rhiannon, who was so sensitive.

When they were seated, Simon opened his mouth to ask Rhiannon how she thought their problem could be resolved, but she beat him with a question about his errand from Pembroke to her father. Simon obliged with the very shortest précis he could give of the situation and tried to switch the talk back to private matters.

"No," Rhiannon said. "I do not wish to talk about us, Simon. I am too overwrought still. I must think while you are not near."

"I do not trust such thoughts. You will make me into a monster and break my heart. You are no coward, Rhiannon. Will you not dare a little to have a life of joy?"

"If you mean I do not fear the death of the body, you are right. But I will not give you my soul to play with, Simon."

"Play with? I said you would make me into a monster. Listen—"

"No. You are trying to trap me in a net of words. I do not wish to talk of this now. Simon, do you not realize that it is important to me whether or not my father goes to war?"

"But Rhiannon, he will not go himself," Simon soothed.

His own father still did go to war, and Ian and Llewelyn were about the same age. But the type of war usually waged by the Welsh was much more of an individual effort, and Simon did not think it practical for an older man to be involved. He did not believe Llewelyn was capable any longer of flitting through the forests or climbing the precipitous mountains. It was different for Ian, who rode to war surrounded by his vassals and, of recent years, with Adam on his right and Geoffrey on his left. Between the iron mountain that was Adam in battle and the swift, ravening flame that was Geoffrey—not to mention his own efforts—Ian could come to little harm even if he should become exhausted.

"I was not concerned for Llewelyn's person," Rhiannon pointed out patiently, not understanding why Simon should raise such an idea. "It is the homestead I must warn."

"Angharad's Hall—I never thought! But, Rhiannon, I do not believe the king intends to attack North Wales. He will have troubles enough with Pembroke. And the hall is —well, it is not easily accessible. Do you really think there is danger?"

"Of the king's army coming there? Very little. But if Pembroke should fail and the king should turn on my father, our men will flee into the hills. Llewelyn has come to us in the past—" She stopped abruptly and looked at Simon.

"Do not insult me by wondering whether I will betray him," Simon said softly.

His voice made Rhiannon shudder. She had a glimpse of a cold, hard core inside the man, something that would not bend or break and could be destroyed only by Simon's death. That was his honor. If only love could be . . . Rhiannon thrust out that thought and bowed her head.

"Forgive me. I know your father is clan-brother to mine and that you love him."

"I have also given Prince Llewelyn my fealty," Simon said in the same soft voice, "and I have no divided oath of homage. No wonder you do not trust me. You think me a Judas who would sell my lord for thirty pieces of silver."

"No! Simon, I did not think that at all. You must know it was trust that caused me to say such a thing in the first place. I have never told another person—never! I would not even tell Llewelyn's vassals."

Simon sighed and Rhiannon saw the tenseness go out of him. Then he smiled at her. What she had said of Llewelyn's vassals brought sharp remembrance of how often Llewelyn had been betrayed by those he should have been able to trust.

"I do not think you need worry about Pembroke failing your father. He is a man of high honor. If he says he will not make peace without Prince Llewelyn's agreement, he will not."

"That is no warranty of safety. In war many things can happen. Pembroke could die—"

"That would not matter. His brother Gilbert will carry on. Gilbert will abide by any oaths Richard swore."

"Where is Gilbert?" Rhiannon asked pointedly.

"In Ireland," Simon replied, then frowned. "Yes, I see what you mean. Until the time Gilbert had word and came here, your father would bear the whole weight of the conflict. But I still do not think the king's forces will drive him so far as Angharad's Hall."

"We must be ready, nonetheless. Food must be stocked. We have enough for ourselves, but not much extra. What is not used may be returned to those who gave if there is no need for it. But if we do not gather what we need before danger comes, there will be no getting it later. It will be burnt or scattered. Also, once the people are fled from the lower lands, they will not return until the danger passes."

Simon was silent for a moment. Then he asked slowly, "Will you leave at once to warn Kicva?" He could not help wondering if this was only an excuse to escape him.

"No," she replied to his relief. "How can I go before I know what my father decides? Do you know how he leans, Simon?"

"He leans toward Pembroke, but in the spring the Prince of Powys and several others received substantial gifts from Henry to win their friendship. Prince Llewelyn must be sure they are willing to forget those gifts and will side with him or, at least, not attack his lands if he joins Pembroke."

"That will take time."

"Yes, but he is willing that his young men go off on their own and make what profit they can on Henry's baggage trains. That was why I was so loose-lipped last

night. I do not doubt that today word is passing from
mouth to mouth that, although Prince Llewelyn has pro-
hibited the raiding of English lands and holdings, he
will not frown on those who harass invaders of Welsh
territory."

Rhiannon smiled impishly and Simon's grin mirrored
hers. Both appreciated the subtlety. It would permit
Llewelyn to bewail the wildness of younger sons and
promise punishment, which would never be meted out, in
case it was necessary to pacify the English instead of
attacking them. However, in the next moment Simon was
shaking his head.

"It must come to war, Rhiannon. If Prince Llewelyn
does not stand with Pembroke now, he will need to stand
alone later. The Bishop of Winchester and his accursed
spawn are not like other men. They do not value the laws
and customs of our people. They talk of one man ruling
alone, holding all power and right as a Divine gift, above
and apart from all others. They will not be content with
subduing the English. Next they will be here, claiming
that, because your father has done fealty for one or two
holdings to Henry, he is no prince with a right to rule his
people as he sees fit. He, too, will be required to submit
utterly without recourse to law or custom."

"Others have tried to make the Welsh submit,"
Rhiannon said. "We often find their bones when we till
the soil."

"Yes, but . . . Rhiannon, your father is not a young
man. Do you see in either of your half-brothers another
Owain or Llewelyn?"

Rhiannon's eyes fell, and she sighed. "They are more
like to fly at each other than to unify or overawe the other
princes."

"And do you think Prince Llewelyn does not know this?
I believe—"

Simon's voice cut off abruptly as Ymlladd whinnied,
stamped, and pawed the earth. Simon rose to his feet, his
hand dropping to the hilt of his sword. Rhiannon rose also.

"Do not dare," she cried loudly, fearing a flight of
arrows from so stealthy a watcher. "Or by Danu and Anu,
I will curse you!"

Before her voice died away, the horse had dropped his

head to the grass again. Simon looked at her. "Did you know who that was?"

She shook her head. "I am not even sure anyone was there. It might have been an animal that startled Ymlladd, but I think we had better go back. I was a fool to leave so openly with you, Simon. I may have stirred up envy among the young men for which you will suffer." Her eyes were wide with fright.

Simon knew that Ymlladd would not react that way to an animal, but he was not going to say that to Rhiannon. He put an arm around her and drew her close, smiling down at her. "Do not worry. Have you not already covered me with a broad shield by cursing any who try to harm me?" he teased.

"I have no power to curse," Rhiannon confessed anxiously. "I only said the first thing that came into my head that might frighten anyone—if anyone was there."

"Likely not," Simon soothed. "Who knows what Ymlladd thought he saw or heard. These high-bred animals are half-mad."

Still, he did not argue when Rhiannon again asked to return to Aber. He caught his horse, swung up on it, and reached down to draw Rhiannon up. She did not raise her hands to be lifted but backed away.

"Let me walk back alone, Simon," she suggested.

"Do not be ridiculous!" Simon exclaimed. "I do not mind if a few idiots are jealous, but I do not want your father furious with me. The whole court will know that I seized you and rode off with you. I do not dare come back without you."

"My father will not care. He knows I go my own way. He will think I made you angry—"

"And so I left you!" Simon did not know whether to fly into a rage or laugh. "Even if I were so angry I murdered you—which will soon come about if you do not mount at once—I would not leave you. I assure you I would bring your corpse home for decent burial."

Rhiannon had to laugh. Realizing it was useless to argue because Simon would never agree, no matter what she said, she held up her hands, put her foot on his, and was lifted. When he had her safely settled, Simon turned and kissed her throat.

"If you would agree to marry me at once, there would be no reason for any man to try to eliminate me," he murmured slyly against her skin.

"Why not?" Rhiannon snapped, even while she arched her neck to facilitate his kiss. "There is no betrothal to a corpse, nor wife to a dead man. A widow is as good as a maid."

"But at least I would be rewarded for my early demise," Simon said plaintively, kissing between words. "I would enjoy my last few days of life."

"You may enjoy them without betrothal or marriage," Rhiannon reminded him, "any time you wish."

There was a silence. Simon withdrew his lips; Rhiannon sighed regretfully. Ymlladd picked his way carefully up the steep slope of the stream's course. Simon might have been more troubled by Rhiannon's seemingly lighthearted refusal if half his mind had not been wondering whether his unarmed back would be pierced by an arrow. However, nothing stirred in the wood and Ymlladd reached level ground Simon touched him with the spur and they went through the wooded area at a speed that would leave any footman far behind. A master archer might have succeeded in pinning Simon even at speed, but there was no one in the wood when Simon passed.

Earlier. Madog had seen the direction Simon took and had followed. It had taken him some time to find the correct cove, and he had actually seen nothing more revealing than Simon and Rhiannon sitting decorously side by side and talking. He could not hear what they were saying, but their placid manner did not soothe him in the least. Disregarding the practical fact that it would have been extremely painful to try to couple on that rocky beach, Madog decided that they were finished and were planning their next assignation.

He had not stopped to think that he might as well have accused them without trying to follow, but now he decided that if he could hear what they planned, he could bring Gruffydd with him next time. But he was too intent on his purpose, and did not stop to realize that the wind was blowing from the shore toward the sea so that the horse sensed him. As soon as Simon rose ready to draw his sword, Madog had begun to back away. He was not looking for a fight; he had taken Antwn's warnings to heart and realized they would plan no further now that they had been disturbed.

Rhiannon's threat thus offended and terrified Madog all the more because it seemed prescient. She had not said *Do not shoot* or *Go away*. She seemed to have read his heart, for it was a daring notion to involve Gruffydd in removing the cursed Saeson. But Rhiannon had cursed him! Only witches could curse. Then Rhiannon was a witch. Of course she was! She had always been very strange, not like any other woman. That monstrous cat that spat and hissed at him every time he sought to have a few private words with her must be her familiar.

Sweating with fear, Madog had withdrawn and hurried directly back to Aber. The distance was not great. Running as fast as he could, Madog reached the gate while Ymlladd was still setting one foot cautiously after another on the steep rise from the cove. Inside the gate he felt terribly weak and sick, which added greatly to his terror. He sank into the shade at the side of a building to rest. After a while, when he had caught his breath, he felt better and began to wonder what he should do instead of expecting to be struck dead any instant. He did not know whether forswearing his plans would automatically lift the curse; he did not know how swiftly or by what mechanism the curse would work. In fact, when he tried to think it out, he had no idea exactly what limits the *Do not dare* had.

He was just about to find a crony with whom to discuss the matter, when his throat tightened with a new terror. Surely the *Do not dare* forbade him to accuse the witch. Besides, to whom could he carry this tale? Even Gruffydd was not likely to listen with sympathy. She was his half-sister, after all. And Prince Llewelyn fairly doted on her. And, now Madog remembered, it was said her mother was also a witch and had ensorceled Llewelyn so that he coupled with her and bred a witch-daughter.

Hearing hooves, Madog scurried away toward the first area that offered better concealment from the main gate. This was where the bulk of the women's hall protruded toward the main hall. His head was turned apprehensively over his shoulder so that he did not see what was ahead of him, and before he could round the building his arm was caught.

"Is your interest in Rhiannon uerch Llewelyn so great that you must tread down every other woman?" a spiteful voice demanded.

Madog started to wrench himself free but then stopped. Even Rhiannon would not dare hurl curses when there were others than her ensorceled lover to hear. "I have no interest in her. I hate her," he stated, with such passionate sincerity and malevolent expression that Mallt was convinced.

"Then why—" she began, but Math streaked out of the women's hall and dashed by them heading for Rhiannon as she came down from Simon's horse. Mallt and Madog shuddered simultaneously, and Mallt hissed venomously, "Cursed witch."

"You know!" Madog exclaimed.

Mallt stared at him and then nodded slowly. "Catrin and I heard her talking to her familiar when she did not know we were nigh. He had not done something she desired. I suppose, because she called him 'traitor' and asked if that was the way he 'rewarded devoted service.' When she saw us, she was angry."

"Did she curse you?" Madog asked anxiously.

"She would not do that in the hall," Mallt replied. "Prince Llewelyn may cherish her, but even he could not protect her if too many knew of her evil."

Her eyes, however, were not on Madog. They followed Simon, who, after watching Rhiannon walk away, was leading Ymlladd toward the stable. Had Madog not been so preoccupied with his own fears, he might have realized that Mallt's conviction that Rhiannon was a witch was based upon jealousy. However, he was too relieved to have a safe confidante to examine her motives.

"Can she curse when her familiar is not by?" Madog asked.

Simon had disappeared, and Mallt's eyes returned to Madog. "How should I know?" she retorted. "I am no witch."

"Who would know?" Madog persisted.

"A priest—I suppose," Mallt answered, but her expression was interested, calculating, now that the distraction of Simon's presence was gone. "I do not think it would be wise to ask too many questions of a priest here in Aber," she said. "It would come to Prince Llewelyn's ears —and that would not be good for you."

"I—" His voice strangled in his throat as Rhiannon appeared in the doorway of the main hall.

Madog was frozen, not knowing whether to run, but before he could move Rhiannon nodded pleasantly, wished him and Mallt a good day, and passed by them into the women's hall. Math, a little way behind her, paused and hissed before he, too, entered the doorway and disappeared from sight. Madog choked. Was it possible that Rhiannon did not know it had been he in the wood by the cove? Did that mean she was not a very powerful witch? If she did not know who had been there, would the curse take effect?

Mallt had returned Rhiannon's greeting coldly if civilly. Madog could not, but it was quite apparent that she had not noticed. Her face had a closed, withdrawn look that implied her mind was elsewhere than on casual civilities. That caused a reversal of Madog's initial sense of relief. Did she know after all and merely make a pretense of civility because Mallt was there? The familiar certainly had displayed animosity. But did that mean anything? The cat had hissed and spat at him even while Rhiannon was inviting his attentions when she had first arrived at court.

"What is wrong with you?" Mallt asked.

Madog realized that he had stopped midsentence. He felt a need to explain himself, but could not admit he was afraid of Rhiannon. "I—I only learned today what she is," he confessed. "It is horrible to think that I once considered her for a wife."

"Oh, she has bewitched half the men in the court," Mallt said bitterly.

Then she drew her breath in sharply. What a fool she had been! She had not thought of it before, but doubtless that was what had happened to Simon. He was bewitched. That was why he would not even look or smile at her any longer. It must be true, Mallt thought, remembering that Math had not spat at Simon yesterday but followed him about, weaving between his footsteps, and even sitting in his lap. This cast a new light on Mallt's jealousy, and she needed a little time and privacy to think it over.

"I think you must be right," Madog replied, but there was a marked lack of interest in his voice.

Madog knew there was no need of witchcraft to attract men to Rhiannon. Even if they thought her a little strange and too willful, the advantages of a blood bond with the ruling house of Gwynedd—for her half-brothers David and Gruffydd were both fond of her—plus a handsome dower were quite enough to draw suitors. But even that subject, which had been so enthralling to him before the encounter at the cove, could not hold his interest. He felt Rhiannon staring at him from somewhere inside the women's hall. The fact that he knew it would be impossible for Rhiannon to see him and Mallt from almost any angle could not relieve his anxiety.

Since both Mallt and Madog urgently desired to be away from that spot—she to think and he to take refuge— they soon drifted apart. However, a sense of sympathy had been generated between them, and each thought that the other might well be useful. Madog could not bear to be alone, and he headed for the great hall where he could be likely to find company and would also be able to conceal himself from Rhiannon. At first it did not help much; Madog felt dreadfully sick, hollow, and shaky, but as the hours passed, his symptoms abated—no one can remain at a peak of terror for very long.

With the remission of fear Madog's confidence rose a little, but neither remission nor budding hope outlasted Madog's next sight of Rhiannon, which was at dinner. She came in a little late, after they had started eating; however, a place had been saved for her and she was seated beside her father, as she often was when there were no important guests. Llewelyn very much enjoyed his daughter's conversation. As she took her seat, Rhiannon's eyes flicked over the seated gentlemen at the lower tables. She was looking for Simon, but because Madog was staring at her, her eyes caught his and she nodded a courteous greeting. Madog felt a cold shiver pass over him and found that he could scarcely chew and swallow his food. In a few minutes, he had to leave the hall. He barely made it out to the latrine area before he vomited everything he had eaten, and he felt so weak that he was convinced for a few minutes that he would die right there.

Now he knew, for certain, that he had been cursed and that the curse had taken hold. His first notion was to flee the court, but his strength started to return. Perhaps the curse only worked in Rhiannon's presence. However, he did not feel well enough to ride away just then. Through the rest of the afternoon he had no serious attack, but to his horror, he still felt the curse working in him. His mouth was dry and his heart frequently pounded hard. Periodically, too, he broke out into a cold sweat.

During the remainder of the day his terror and his symptoms—a direct result of that terror, had he only stopped to think about the sensations of fear—continued. Half-believing that death was imminent, Madog found a priest and confessed his sins. Then, although he was still afraid that he would die instantly if he named Rhiannon, he told the priest there was a witch in the village near his father's estate and asked, in general, what could be done to save a man from a cursing.

Various remedies were suggested, but Madog quickly realized that the answer was to get rid of the curse—or the witch. He did not long consider appealing to Rhiannon to convince her he had meant no harm so that she would withdraw the curse. Spiteful bitch that she was, she might take against him in the future for some imagined slight. It would be better, far better and more permanent, if he eliminated the witch. But how? Having cursed him, surely she would not trust herself alone to him. Even if she would, he did not dare be seen with her shortly before she disappeared. To wake Llewelyn's enmity would be as bad as being cursed.

Then he remembered the venom in Mallt's voice, and he considered the consequences of enlisting her help. He found Mallt without difficulty and made his proposal— not mentioning what he intended after she brought Rhiannon to a private meeting with him. Mallt opened her mouth to refuse, but she knew Madog had been sincere when he said he hated Rhiannon, and, from his looks now, he feared her, too. Suddenly, Mallt realized Madog meant murder!

A very brief sense of shock passed into heartfelt enthusiasm. Yes, she would help, Mallt agreed. She looked at Madog speculatively. He was no Simon, but he would do for a husband. Once Rhiannon was dead, Madog would have to marry her to keep her mouth shut. Or, if he would not agree to marriage, likely Llewelyn would be glad to dower richly the woman who told him who had killed his daughter.

CHAPTER 8

❖·❖

Simon did not speak to Rhiannon again that day. He was
kept busy, first by Llewelyn and then by David, Llewelyn's
legitimate son. David liked Simon. Being half-English
himself—his mother had been King John's natural daughter—David could not afford Gruffydd's prejudices. He
was several years younger than his half-brother and was
both pleased and excited by the possibility of a war. He
was eager to discuss politics and strategies, and Simon was
very willing, although he would rather have discussed other
matters with David's half-sister.

All in all Simon was not ill-pleased with his progress
with Rhiannon. When she came in to dinner, her eyes
sought him out, and she smiled at him. And, although
she talked to her father and half-brothers as freely as
usual, Simon noticed that her glances flicked toward him
more than once. He did not think, however, that it would
be politic to pursue her after dinner. Let her think, as she
had said she must.

Thus when David came to him and suggested riding out
to hunt with a group of young men, Simon agreed without
hesitation. They all enjoyed themselves, bringing down
a handsome buck after a long chase. By the time the dogs
were rewarded and the buck prepared, it was near dark,
and they arrived too late for the evening meal. Rhiannon
was not in the hall, but Simon was not really disappointed.
He was quite happy to discuss the future raiding of King
Henry's supply trains, even though it was highly unlikely
that he would be free to participate in that profitable
amusement. Several more men joined them, and altogether
they had a most convivial evening, staggering off to bed
very late, singing or giggling or cursing as drunkenness
took them.

Several hours earlier, just before the women had gone to
bed, Mallt approached Rhiannon and drew her aside. She

whispered to Rhiannon her need for certain herbs which grew in the forest and needed to be plucked just as the sun rose for greatest efficacy. She did not know where they grew, Mallt said, but doubtless Rhiannon did. Rhiannon was tempted to laugh at her, but she restrained the impulse. She used herbs for healing, but she did not believe in their effectiveness to generate love. That, Kicva had taught her, came only from within the person. If it should be constrained by potions or magical practices, it was only a compulsion akin to hate, and was not love at all.

Still, Rhiannon knew Mallt was both jealous and a little fearful of her. If she laughed or refused, Mallt would never believe that it was because the herbs would be ineffective. She would only be convinced that Rhiannon was selfishly keeping her knowledge to herself. Rhiannon agreed, after only the smallest hesitation, to take Mallt into the forest to gather what she needed. And, not many hours after Simon had reeled into his bed, Rhiannon and Mallt rose from theirs to dress in the dim light of the night candles, wrap themselves in warm cloaks, and make their way out of the keep. Just before they reached the postern, Mallt exclaimed that the lacings on her shoe had broken. She urged Rhiannon to go ahead and she would catch up. Rhiannon offered to wait, but Mallt said it was silly to stand still in the chill morning. She would have no trouble catching up if Rhiannon went slowly.

This seemed a little odd to Rhiannon, but the predawn air was sharp and much of the behavior of the women of the court seemed odd to her—as hers did to them—so she simply did what Mallt suggested without thinking any more about it. The guards at the postern let her out without comment. The sun had not risen, but the sky was light with coming dawn. There was nothing uncommon in women going out to gather berries or herbs in the dawn and, anyway, Lady Rhiannon did as she pleased.

Mallt walked a few steps slowly, sliding the foot with the loosened laces so that the shoe would not come off. As soon as she was hidden from Rhiannon's sight, she bent and tied the unbroken lace securely. Then she ran swiftly to the western gate and told the guard that she wanted to gather fresh seaweed at the shore. There was nothing strange in this either. When she was out, she angled north toward the shore until the curve of the stockade hid her. Then she ran as fast as she could around to the east.

Mallt soon caught up to Rhiannon, who was walking slowly, watching the patterns the light and trees made, and was so enraptured by their beauty that she had almost forgotten why she was out in the dawn. When Mallt spoke her name, she started and sighed at the interruption, but she went forward cheerfully to fulfill her promise.

In Rhiannon's bed, Math curled tighter together. He was thickly furred and cuddled into the blankets so that he could not have been cold. Nonetheless, he was discontent. Now he missed the warmth of her body, the vibration of her breathing—something. Grumbling deep in his throat, Math leapt from the bed and stalked toward the door. Here he let out one raucous howl and then another. In the next moment an irritated woman hurried to open the door. She cursed, but she did not kick; Math retaliated sharply with claws and teeth against those who were not properly respectful.

Yowling outside the hall door did not produce the same effect, but it was dawn and men were coming out to piss and, for those who did it, to wash. It was not long before the door opened and Math slipped inside. He picked his way with delicate care among those who were still sleeping, weaving a path, sniffing inquisitively at hands that hung over or rising on his hind legs to examine a shoulder, neck, or face. Eventually he found what he wanted—Simon's long-fingered hand, the part of Simon he knew best. With a deep-throated rumble of satisfaction, Math leapt up and settled himself comfortably on Simon's broad chest. In a little while, his eyes half-closed, and he began to purr.

Convivial evenings are a pleasure that must be paid for with bleak mornings. In his half-sleep, the heavy weight that had settled on Simon's chest seemed connected with his general misery. It was not until after Math's roaring purr began that Simon realized what had happened. Math's purring rasped into Simon's aching head like a file across his brain. He mumbled a protest and extended a hand to push Math off. Math dug his claws firmly into the blanket and clung. In several places the claws, long, strong, and sharp, pierced through the blanket into Simon's skin. All the while purring to show that he was disciplining a servant and not really angry, Math bit Simon's hand. The combined sharp pains overrode Simon's other miseries and brought him fully awake.

He did not dare lift his head for fear it would explode like a barrel of burning pitch, but he did get his eyes open and moaned, "Math, get off. Shut up!"

The results were not in the least what Simon desired. Math did rise to a standing position, but he did not stop purring, and rather than jump down, he walked with slow dignity further up Simon's body so that he could peer down into his victim's face. Moreover, since Simon was neither perfectly firm nor perfectly flat, for security Math inserted his claws well into the surface he was walking on with each step.

Simon howled—but he did not make the mistake of trying to push Math off. His agonized gaze met Math's enigmatic green eyes. The cat stared. Simon shut his eyes again, moaning softly at the burst of agony the light caused in his brain. His stomach heaved. Math sat down heavily right over the uproar in Simon's midsection and began to knead Simon's chest with his claws. Surprisingly, instead of adding to Simon's misery, these actions were helpful. The sudden weight on Simon's churning stomach quieted it, and the rhythmic pricking in his chest steadied the whirling in his head. He reopened his eyes.

"What the devil are you doing here?" he asked the cat.

Naturally the question answered itself. Rhiannon must have gone out. Simon knew she took no part in the early-morning household chores, and he realized the sun had not quite risen, although it would at any moment. Simon was not troubled by Rhiannon's leaving Aber so early. She took great pleasure in seeing the sun rise out in the open. Actually, it was not Rhiannon but Math who occupied his thoughts.

"You cannot sit or lie on top of me," he said severely. "You are too heavy. You know Lady Rhiannon does not permit that. Now get off." Very gently he exerted pressure on one side of Math. "I will make room for you," he promised, turning sideways as he spoke.

Simon was never sure whether Math really understood

what was said to him or reacted to some combination of tone, expression, and movement. In any case, his behavior this time was typical of Simon's previous experience with addressing him directly. The cat stopped purring and moved with slow dignity to the hollow Simon was creating by lying on his side and bending his knees. Simon sighed with relief and shut his eyes. At the moment he cared not a whit why Math did what he desired. All he knew was that peace was restored. Gratefully, he sank back to sleep.

At the edge of the wood, Mallt suddenly began to tell Rhiannon the sad tale of her life. She was a fourth daughter in a purse-pinched household, and there was no money to dower her. She might have been forced into a religious life, but fortunately the position in Llewelyn's household had opened and she had been chosen. But it was not fair, she complained to Rhiannon. Her blood was every bit as good as that of the others, but she was looked down upon because she had no fine clothing and no dower. Was it not reasonable, she said, that she should seek any method to win a husband and a settled, honorable place in life?

Because Rhiannon was very sure the herb preparation Mallt would make would have no effect on any man, she muttered some ambiguous answer. She was regretting bitterly that she had ever agreed to this expedition. Mallt's loud chatter broke the peace of the forest and drove away the birds and little animals that gave Rhiannon so much pleasure. Twice Rhiannon had tried to hush the continuous stream of Mallt's loud complaints. Mallt had looked at her in simulated surprise, protesting that there was no one to hear her in the woods, and even if there were, she was not ashamed of her condition or purpose.

In desperation Rhiannon had tried to hurry Mallt along so that she could be sooner rid of her. This had drawn even louder complaints, of fatigue, of being out of breath, and at last a stumble—only partly contrived—which left Mallt weeping and rubbing an ankle. Rhiannon had sighed, partly with irritation and partly with relief, and suggested that they should return to Aber since Mallt could hardly walk further. This Mallt refused to do, weeping even louder and reminding Rhiannon that she had *promised* to find the herbs.

"I can walk, if only you will help me and not go so fast," Mallt cried.

Patience was not one of Rhiannon's strong points, but she was not one to break her word either. If she went back now, she would have to go out with Mallt another time. She helped her companion to her feet and assisted her onward, doing her best to close her ears to the continuing spate of talk that poured from Mallt's lips. This effort not to hear was all too successful. Rhiannon did not notice the sharp snap of a twig behind instead of beside her, nor the fact that Mallt's words flowed even faster and louder for a moment. She had withdrawn into herself so successfully that she was totally unaware of anything unusual—until a heavy, evil-smelling cloth was flung over her head and pressed hard into her mouth.

The method of attack, which effectively muted and blinded Rhiannon, had been the result of considerable frightened planning on Madog's part. When he initially made the plan, he had intended to sneak up behind Rhiannon and strike her on the head. Then he realized this would not do at all. If he did not strike her quite hard enough, she would surely realize who had attacked her, and she might have time to make her curses last after death. Madog had no idea how long the formulae were; it might take only one word. On the other hand, if he hit her too hard, she might die of the blow. To kill a witch directly, Madog knew, made her curses more virulent.

All night Madog had pondered the question of how without killing Rhiannon he could keep her from uttering the formulae that would perpetuate the curse or freeze and bewitch him with a potent glance of her eyes—some witches could do that, he had heard. The stealthy practices of sneak attacks answered both questions. To silence a guard, one crept up from behind and cast a heavy cloth over his head, pressing it against his mouth. One could then slip a knife between his ribs or even cut his throat under the cloth in complete silence.

The thought of cutting Rhiannon's throat sent a thrill of pleasure through Madog, but he soon felt a renewal of the terrible symptoms of the curse—the sickness in his belly, the difficulty in breathing that made him sweat and pant, the pounding heart and growing vertigo. Madog nearly began to weep. If the thought of harming her could do this to him what would happen when he actually laid hands on her? Trembling, he reached under his bed and drew out the small horn of holy water he had bought from a priest and took a sip. At once he felt much better. Perhaps he would not need to . . . no, he could not go on buying and drinking holy water all his life. He must do something about Rhiannon.

Then he realized he would not need to harm her. All he had to do was blindfold and gag Rhiannon, tie her securely and hide her well in the forest. What happened after that would be up to God. No palpitations or dizziness or sickness followed that thought, and Madog sighed with relief. It would be God's Will that would make Rhiannon die of hunger and thirst or be eaten by wild beasts or be wetted and chilled and die of fever and affliction of the lungs *He* would not have done anything to harm the witch and her curse would die with her.

Before dawn while he waited for the women to come out of Aber the curse struck Madog again This onslaught was so fierce that his shaking hands could barely unstopper the horn that held his remedy. When he did manage to swallow some, however, it fortified him so well that he was not stricken with sickness and trembling even when Rhiannon passed into the forest no more than a spear's throw from him. He followed, closing the distance slowly but steadily until he was sure that no sound would be heard back in Aber. Then he struck.

Rhiannon's reaction was so violent that, in spite of his greater strength Madog could barely hold her. Too late he realized that to muffle a man's mouth and stick a knife in him is one thing—a knifing is swift, usually finished before the shock of being seized is over. It is quite another thing to hold, gag, and subdue a strong woman fighting with the ferocity of a wildcat. Madog could do no more than keep his hold on Rhiannon's mouth and around her waist It was Rhiannon's own struggle that defeated her.

Twisting and turning and lunging ahead to free herself while totally blinded, Rhiannon slipped on the uneven floor of the forest and her foot struck a rock with great force. The pain was so excruciating that her knees buckled. Her final convulsive effort to save herself only resulted in twisting severely the ankle of the foot she had already hurt. Rhiannon fell forward heavily with Madog atop her.

The impact of Madog's weight upon her knocked the breath out of Rhiannon and rendered her nearly unconscious. The heavy cloth covering her head and mouth prevented her from drawing in air freely. Rhiannon swirled down into a smothering blackness in which nothing was of importance except expanding her lungs. She was no longer aware of Madog's grip, and although she twisted her head feebly in an attempt to free her mouth, she could make no other effort.

The fall had not been completely an accident. Madog was quite strong enough to hold Rhiannon upright when she stumbled, but he was also experienced enough as a fighter to know what would happen if she fell. Thus, he thrust her forward and threw his full weight upon her while bracing himself for the impact. Her limpness worried him a little. If she had taken serious hurt, would that mean he had caused her death? The curse, however, did not strike and Madog took heart. He drew a thong out of his belt where several hung ready and drew it around her head between her teeth in no time. This gagged her even more effectively than Madog's hand and fixed the cloth immovably.

The rest was easy. There was no way Rhiannon could do anything at all while Madog was kneeling with his full weight on her back. As it was, the pain and pressure, which further impeded her breathing, rendered her totally unconscious. Madog wrenched her arms behind her, bound them, and then bound her feet. Assured that Rhiannon was now helpless, he looked around for Mallt and ground his teeth in fury when he realized she had escaped him. Mallt had to die, too, since she could connect him with Rhiannon's disappearance. She might not intend to betray him, but when the questions started, her courage might easily fail. Madog had intended to thrust a knife into Mallt right here and leave her. If she were found stabbed after Rhiannon was missed, some enemy or band of outlaws skulking in the woods would be blamed for the crimes.

Then he remembered that Mallt had not come out of Aber with Rhiannon. That had puzzled him, but he could not worry about it. He would get to Mallt later in the day.

As he swung Rhiannon over his shoulder, however, he
realized he really did not have much time to attend to
Mallt. He would have to get to her as soon as he returned.
Once a hue and cry was raised about Rhiannon, all the
women would stay close inside Aber for many days. This
meant he would have to dispose of Rhiannon quickly, and
he reconsidered a possible hiding place, several miles
farther into the forest.

Madog cursed Mallt viciously while his eyes searched
the area immediately around him. There was no hiding
place worth the name—only a few stands of bracken
where the trees thinned and where one tree had fallen.
Muttering angrily, he started off in the direction of the
safe hide he knew, but now he kept looking for a suitable
spot, and before he had gone a quarter of a mile, he was
rewarded.

Off to the right was a tiny stream. Beside it, a giant tree
had fallen many years before. The combination of extra
water and light had encouraged the growth of a dense
thicket. Madog wormed his way in with great caution,
treading on moss which would spring back without record-
ing his footsteps for longer than a few minutes and lifting
branches out of the way so that they would not break and
mark his trail. Sure enough, on the stream side of the
long-dead tree, the earth had been hollowed out.

Madog set Rhiannon down and began to increase the
size of the hollow and deepen it. When he was satisfied
with what he had done, he thrust Rhiannon into the space.
Then he packed over her the earth and debris he had
scraped out of the hollow. Madog took considerable care
that she should not smother, for that would be killing her
directly. Finally, he restored the outer area as well as he
could to its original condition. When he was sure no casual
search would detect his work, he eased himself backward
out of the thicket, cautiously, erasing the few footprints
he had made.

It was only with difficulty that Madog restrained himself
from jumping and skipping with joy on his way back to
Aber. As soon as he had had Rhiannon gagged and helpless, perhaps unconscious, he had felt the curse lift away
from him. He was sure now that he had done the right
thing, sure that as soon as Rhiannon was dead he would

be permanently free of her evil influence. He knew she was not dead yet, for he had felt her breathing while he carried her and while he was hiding her away. However, he was reasonably sure she had been severely injured when he fell on her and would die soon; her breathing had been deep at first but had grown shallower and shallower. Now all he had to do was find Mallt, lure her back into the woods, and kill her. Then he would be safe.

As soon as Madog had enveloped Rhiannon's head, Mallt had fled away as fast as her feet could carry her. She did not fear Madog, and she would have liked to see him kill Rhiannon, but her own safety was more important. She wanted to be sure that Madog could not counter any threat to betray him she might make—or the actual betrayal, if that became necessary—by involving her. She had already established the first half of her excuse for being out that morning. Now she needed to complete it.

She ran back down the path Rhiannon and she had followed earlier until she came to the edge of the forest. Following this northward, Mallt came out on a headland above the ocean. When she found a way down to the rocky beach, she grabbed hastily at whatever seaweed came to hand and quickly filled the basket she had brought. At the end of the cove, Mallt discovered she had chosen luckily. She found a broad, easy path to the top of the headland and a well-defined road leading first to a small village of fishermen and from there to Aber. She sang aloud as she walked along, swinging her basket of seaweed. Everything was going just as she had planned, even better than she had planned. The fisherwomen looking out of their huts and working around them would remember her and back up her story.

Moved by her general good spirits, Mallt resolved to see if she could win Madog more gently than by threats. She could begin easily and in a very flattering way by pretending she admired his courage and resolution in dealing so promptly with Rhiannon. After all, she would have to live with the man after she married him. It would be more comfortable if he accepted the marriage relatively willingly Also, that would permit her to save her whip for other occasions.

CHAPTER 9

❖•❖

In a hall used for all the activities of a household, a man cannot sleep very long no matter how great his need. All too soon after Simon and Math had adjusted their individual needs into a harmonious whole, the servants were routed from their pallets to begin the duties of the day. They did not actually demand that the gentlemen on their cots wake, but there was sufficient noise made in rolling and storing the pallets, setting up the trestle tables, and moving benches and other gear that it was soon impossible to sleep. Groaning and cursing, Simon sat up. This disturbed Math, who protested raucously but eventually accepted the situation as inevitable and stalked away to find a quieter place to finish his morning slumbers.

After a cursory washing, made horrible by having to bend over, Simon slowly put on his clothing and blearily examined the breakfast set out on the tables. His reaction to the coarse bread and redolent goat cheese—which he usually enjoyed heartily—made him seize a cup of wine and go as far from the tables as he could. By accident rather than design, although he was already beginning to feel less like a corpse animated by magic, Simon found himself near the door opposite the women's hall. Memory of the previous morning hastened his recovery. He leaned against the door frame, sipping his wine slowly and wondering whether Rhiannon would return from whatever outing she had taken while he was there.

Before he tired of waiting, a page summoned him to Llewelyn. By the time their talk was finished, Simon found he had recovered from his overindulgence and he was hungry. There was virtually nothing left on the tables, but Simon grabbed a heel of bread and some cheese right out of the hands of a maidservant. He asked if she had seen Rhiannon, but she said she did not think the lady had returned. This disturbed Simon slightly. Rhiannon had a good appetite and seldom missed a meal.

Simon grew more and more uneasy as the morning passed. In the hills, Rhiannon would stay out all day, but she did not do that at court. If he had known where to look, Simon would have sought her, even though he knew she hated to be followed and watched over. As it was, all he could do was idle around near where he could see the entrance to the women's hall and yet not be seen himself. When Rhiannon returned and he was sure she was safe, he could just slip away before she saw him. Then, at least, his mind would be at ease.

There was no sign of Rhiannon, but Simon noticed that Madog ap Sior was also idling around the women's hall. That was a nuisance. Simon tried to think of some way to be rid of the man, who, he was sure, was also waiting for Rhiannon. Before he became desperate, however, Mallt came out of the door. Simon tensed to withdraw. She had made several attempts to approach him previously, but he had avoided her adroitly enough that Rhiannon had not noticed The last thing he needed was to have Madog telling Rhiannon that he was pursuing Mallt.

To Simon's intense relief, Madog approached Mallt and asked her why she had run away. She smiled up at him provocatively and replied, "I had to gather seaweed this morning. And I knew a man as strong and clever as you are would have no trouble dealing with the witch."

Dealing with the witch? What witch. Simon wondered? A wave of uneasiness passed through him He had not intended to listen, since he did not care what Mallt did or to whom she attached herself, but he strained his ears as Madog hushed her sharply and looked over his shoulder to see whether anyone had heard her remarks. That gesture worried Simon deeply because it implied that "the witch" was known and recognized in Llewelyn's household. Yet there was no such person.

At that moment Math came out of the women's hall and hissed at Madog. Instantly, the man launched a terrific kick at the animal. Simon was so amazed that he neither spoke nor moved. Math, no matter how annoying, was a privileged creature because he was Rhiannon's. Although Math avoided the kick with contemptuous ease, ran in and clawed Madog so that he howled with pain, and was away again before Madog could strike, kick, or grasp him,

Simon was puzzled. The attack on Math seemed in some way connected with "dealing with the witch"—but if that was so, the witch must be Rhiannon.

Ridiculous, Simon told himself. No one would dare. It must be some old crone in the fishing village or among the farming folk in the vicinity. The kick at Math could not mean anything more than that an unpleasant person had tried to hurt the cat while his mistress was absent and could not protect him. But Simon did not believe his own reasoning because too many coincidences were piling up: Rhiannon's extended absence, Mallt's involvement, and the sudden contempt for Math.

With some difficulty Simon restrained himself from leaping out and grabbing Madog by the throat. He and Mallt would deny what they had said, and there was no way inside Aber that Simon could squeeze information out of either of them—no, it was Madog alone he needed. Mallt had run away before. . . . Simon swallowed and ground his teeth. Before what? How had Madog "dealt with" the witch? Was Rhiannon dead? Simon put a hand against the wall to steady himself.

Madog had stopped cursing and rubbing his leg, which showed spots and streaks of blood where Math's claws had gone in. Mallt had pressed her hand over her mouth to keep from laughing at Math's revenge, but she was sober when Madog looked at her. She knew a woman did not endear herself to a man by laughing at him, particularly when he had made a fool of himself.

"I will have to get rid of the familiar, too," Madog said, looking after Math.

For an instant the proof that Rhiannon was "the witch" to whom Mallt had referred—a thing Simon had not completely believed despite his instinctive fear—froze him. He would have attacked Madog then, except that Madog said to Mallt that he needed to talk with her privately. Simon stood still and listened. In a private place, he could seize Madog and wring the truth from him where no one would ask questions.

Mallt nodded and smiled. She expected that Madog wanted to warn her to say nothing or perhaps tell her what he had done, and she agreed wholeheartedly that it would be wise to go where they could both speak freely without fear of being overheard. Madog was not too clever, and she wished to make her terms quite clear. Hints and circumlocutions might go right over his thick head or be too easily misinterpreted.

"I will meet you inside the trees just opposite the eastern postern," Madog said and, ignoring Mallt's angry surprise, walked quickly away toward the front gate. Since no alarm had been raised about Rhiannon, he still had the chance to kill her and leave her where the ground had been disturbed by his capture of Rhiannon, and he had no intention of needing to carry her body farther than necessary.

Simon cursed under his breath. He could not dash out and follow Madog directly. Mallt would certainly see him and call to him, which would warn Madog. He hated to lose sight of the man, but was reasonably sure Madog would arrive at the place he said he would meet Mallt. Simon glanced at her and noticed that she seemed both surprised and offended, presumably at Madog's sudden departure. She took a few steps toward the eastern postern, hesitated, and then with a thoughtful expression turned back and went into the women's hall.

With a sigh of thanksgiving, Simon took off to the gate as fast as he could walk. Once through it, he ran like the devil over the cleared land, praying that Madog would not round the stockade until he was out of sight. He hoped Mallt had been so offended that she would not come at all. It would be much easier to deal with Madog if she were not there to screech and run back to Aber to report what was happening.

In fact, Simon need not have run himself breathless. Mallt was not yet really afraid of Madog, but she had decided she needed an additional weapon against him. After all, she believed he had already killed one woman who threatened him. Admittedly that woman was a witch and to kill her was no crime; the Bible itself said: *Thou shalt not suffer a witch to live*. Still, just to be sure that Madog would not think he could remove her from his path also, Mallt had stopped to give her friend Catrin a précis of what had happened and tell her she was meeting Madog in the forest. If she did not return soon, Catrin should raise an alarm.

Madog was not hurrying to the meeting spot either. He was more interested in covering his tracks than in arriving early, although he moved swiftly for fear Mallt would get tired of waiting. For the sake of the guard at the gate, he walked down the road until the first curve hid him before he stepped into the trees. As soon as he was out of sight of the road altogether, he began to run, keeping within the wooded area but heading for the meeting place as directly as he could.

The caution of both parties gave Simon more than enough time to find an adequate hiding place in a clump of trees back from the edge of the woods but near enough to see a broad area that could be considered opposite the east postern. It was heavily shadowed among the close-growing trunks, and Simon hoped he would be able either to surprise Madog or, if he were too far away, to challenge him.

It was disappointing when Mallt appeared outside the stockade and walked quickly toward the wood. Her presence would complicate matters. Simon wanted no witnesses to what he would do to Madog, but as his fear and anger grew, he cared less and less about anything except laying his hands on the man. Then for a few minutes he thought he would need to silence Mallt before he could get at Madog. She seemed to be coming directly toward him; however, she stopped just inside the trees and looked around.

At the edge of the clearing the trees were widely spaced and the brush had been cut away by Llewelyn's order to prevent men from concealing themselves there for a surprise attack. Farther back there was no need to remove the brush. Little grew where the treetops met, and the ground was deeply shaded.

Mallt idled on the periphery, watching for Madog across the open field while Simon tried to decide whether to seize and silence her or not. Either way she was a nuisance. If he grabbed her, she might cry out and warn Madog; or if Madog did not see her waiting, he might not come to where Simon could spot him. If he let her be, she would doubtless run back to Aber screaming for help, but the latter seemed the least serious. Simon was sure he could subdue Madog and drag him away somewhere more private before Mallt could bring assistance.

Because he could not permit himself to think of Rhiannon, Simon fixed his attention on Mallt and on the southern edge of the stockade where he expected to see Madog appear at any moment. He had not stopped to put on his armor, but Madog was not—or had not been— wearing armor either, and he probably did not own a hauberk of steel. Simon drew his sword and held it naked in one hand, his knife in the other. Madog would not escape him, armed or not.

Simon's fixity of purpose nearly undid him. While he stared in one direction, Madog appeared from the west with the silent stealth of the Welsh hunter-warrior. In a flash, he seized Mallt by the arm and drew her backward a few feet. As she began to protest, he stabbed her in the heart.

Simon gasped with outrage and sprang from his concealment. In any other circumstances his sense of honor would have demanded that he give Madog a chance to draw his own weapons and defend himself, but a woman-killer did not merit such courtesy. In fact, if Simon had not needed to learn what Madog had done with Rhiannon, he would have grabbed him by the hair and cut his throat, as one slaughters a noxious animal. Besides, a cut throat was too sweet and easy a death. Simon was sure now that Madog had killed Rhiannon. He planned a long, very long and painful, excruciatingly painful death for Madog.

When Simon leapt out from behind the trees and charged at him, Madog was so startled that he screamed like a woman and turned to run. He was not usually a greater coward than any other man, although he was certainly no hero, but too many incomprehensible things had happened to him over the past two days. Terror so unhinged him, however, that he forgot the dead woman at his feet, and he stumbled over her body and fell. That was the stroke that finished him. He lay on his face, screaming and whimpering and begging for mercy.

More because he was nauseated by Madog's behavior than because he feared the man would try to resist, Simon brought the hilt of his knife down sharply on Madog's head. The whimpers and cries stopped abruptly. Simon pulled Madog's sword from its sheath and tossed it well away. Then, since he had not expected to need to restrain anyone, he pulled off Madog's cross garters and used one to tie his hands firmly behind his back and the other to form a noose around his neck. As long as Madog was quiet, the noose would lie open. The moment he tried to run or resist, it would tighten and choke him.

Simon then stood and began to slap Madog's face with the flat of his sword. He was not overcareful of just how he held the weapon, so now and again the edge cut. However, he had not hit Madog very hard and a few strokes were enough to bring him fully conscious.

"Where is Lady Rhiannon?" Simon asked quietly.

"I do not know!" Madog wailed, shaking with fear.

Simon smiled. "Would you prefer to lose your right ear or your left ear first?" he inquired.

"You would not dare," Madog quavered.

For answer, Simon swiftly put his heel on Madog's throat, pinning his chin with the ball of his foot, and in one swift motion sliced off his right ear. Madog's first scream was so loud that Simon began to fear a guard at Aber would hear him, but the solution was simple. Simon merely pulled the noose so tight that Madog's screams were strangled. He then tucked his sword under one arm, grasped the man's sword belt, and began to drag him behind the thick clump of trees in which he had hidden, where the sound would be muffled and distorted. Then he dropped him, inserted his sword under the knot, and loosened the noose.

Before Madog could get enough breath to begin to scream again, Simon said pleasantly, "Now you know I am in earnest. I will ask you again what you have done with Lady Rhiannon. I will take your left ear next, then your balls, then a finger at a time. You do not need to worry about bleeding to death, you know. I will make a fire and heat my knife and sear your wounds so that you will live." He paused a moment and then added bleakly, "I will be very, very careful that you live."

Tears ran down Madog's face mingling with the blood, and he shook his head mutely from side to side. In his first shock and terror he had not believed Simon could know he had anything to do with Rhiannon, and for a moment more he believed that if he still claimed ignorance after losing an ear, Simon would believe him. However, when he saw Simon lift his foot to secure his head for the removal of his other ear, he understood that Simon knew for certain what he had done. The "witch" or her familiar had somehow informed against him.

"I will show you," he screamed. "I did not kill her. I did not even hurt her."

In that moment Simon almost lost his prisoner. Relief at hearing that Rhiannon was still alive struck him like a physical blow. He turned pale and his hand loosened on the noose that held Madog. Utter desperation lent the man more swiftness and perception than was natural to him. He rolled over, stumbled to his feet, jerking the noose out of Simon's lax fingers, and started to run. The attempt did not succeed. In ten strides Simon had caught up with him and put his foot on the trailing noose, throwing him to the ground.

Madog screamed again and lashed out with his feet as Simon bent to retrieve the noose, but Simon merely grabbed the cross garter higher up and pressed the point of his sword into Madog's neck—but not hard enough to draw blood. The unspoken threat turned Madog's screams into whimpers mixed with assurances that Rhiannon was unharmed.

"If I find her alive and unhurt," Simon said, "I will do no worse to you."

"Will you let me go?" Madog pleaded.

"I cannot do that," Simon replied. "Do you think I have forgotten that you murdered Mallt? However, that is no affair of mine. Whether you are punished at all and what your punishment will be is Lord Llewelyn's business. Now get to your feet and take me to Lady Rhiannon without more talk, or I will begin again where I left off with you."

"I will die anyway," Madog wept. "She is a witch. She cursed me."

"You are an idiot," Simon responded in a disgusted voice, prodding Madog ahead with his sword. "Lady Rhiannon is no witch. She has no power of cursing. Now bring me to her at once. And do not think to lead me around in circles. Whatever happened to my lady took no more than the time from early dawn to breakfast—where I saw you. If you do not find her in half that time, I will have your manhood off instead of your ear. You deserve it for laying a hand upon her."

Madog plunged ahead, knowing that Simon would not repeat his threat but would carry it out. Simon's face was as rigid as that of a corpse and his eyes were terrible. That, Madog thought, was the will of the witch. For that reason he made no attempt to delay but found the path Mallt and Rhiannon had taken that morning. They went much more quickly than the women had because Mallt had slowed progress as much as she could. A few minutes' swift walking brought them to the place where Madog had attacked Rhiannon—a patch where the earth, twigs, and dry leaves were scuffed and disturbed.

Here Madog hesitated and turned his maimed head toward Simon. "You are ensorceled," he whispered. "That is how you know what I did and why you did not hear her curse me. You were right there beside her in the cove. Do you not remember?"

Simon burst into bitter laughter. "Idiot! Dolt! How could she curse you even if she was a witch? Neither of us knew who was there. My horse scented you. I tell you Lady Rhiannon has no power of cursing. She was afraid, that was all, and cried out what she thought would protect us. And I knew what you had done because I heard you talking with Mallt. Now go ahead."

Madog did not dare disobey and started to move off the path in the direction he had carried Rhiannon, but he whimpered, "She did curse me. I felt it. I could not eat and my breath choked in my throat. . . ."

"You are twenty times a fool," Simon raged. "You feared the effect of a curse and felt the effect of your fear." He prodded Madog harder. "Quick, before I lose my patience and give you a reason to move more swiftly."

The grimness of Simon's voice warned Madog to hesitate no longer, and Simon's conviction made Madog begin to wonder whether he had not jumped too fast to a conclusion about Rhiannon, misled by Mallt. He was not sure; he still *felt* Rhiannon was a witch—she was so strange—but perhaps she had not cursed him. In any case, his fate at

Simon's hands seemed far more certain than his fate at Rhiannon's, and he hurried along the way he had carried her. He was terrified that he would lose his way, for he had been careful not to break branches or step on soft ground, but his hunter's eye had unconsciously marked a lightning-riven tree here and a dead, oddly gnarled one there, as when he cached a kill too heavy to carry back alone. Spurred by panic, he found his way almost without a single hesitation to the great fallen log.

"There on the other side," he gasped, shaking with terror because he did not know whether to hope or to fear that Rhiannon was dead. Either way, Madog knew he would suffer.

Simon could not endure to waste even the few moments it would take to tie Madog securely, and he did not dare try to control him at the same time that he released Rhiannon. Madog had not said how he had secured her, but Simon did not need to be told that she was bound or chained. If she had not somehow been imprisoned, she would have made her way back to Aber. Perhaps there were even others in the plot. They might have been warned by Madog's voice and their incautious approach and be hidden, ready to attack.

"Go around," Simon urged, and when Madog bent to climb over the trunk, he hit him good and hard on the head with the flat of his sword.

As Madog fell, Simon dropped the noose and leapt over the log. He let out a roar of rage when he did not see Rhiannon, and turned toward the unconscious man. Even as he did so, his eye caught the disturbed earth around the hollow under the fallen tree. A less cursory glance showed the trail where Rhiannon had pushed herself along the ground. For a minute or two Simon could not see any more. Tears of relief had flooded his eyes. Despite Madog's assurances that he had not harmed Rhiannon, Simon feared he would find her dead, that the man had only been buying a few minutes more of life with his lies. The fact that there was a trail, that Rhiannon was not immediately to be seen in the vicinity, was proof that she had strength enough to escape.

Shakily, Simon knelt to examine the ground with care. Then he sighed with relief again. There was no sign of blood. Probably Rhiannon had not been stabbed. The exertion of getting out of the hollow and humping herself along the ground was considerable. Any wound would have bled. Simon glanced toward Madog, but the man had not moved at all. Then Simon realized Rhiannon could not have escaped in that slow, painful manner if anyone had been guarding her.

Simon knew quite well that he should now bind Madog's feet and secure him to a tree, but he could not bear to waste the time. If he did not find Rhiannon in the next few minutes, he told himself, he would return. Just now, finding her was more important.

"Rhiannon," he shouted, "it is Simon. Where are you? Can you hear me? It is Simon."

CHAPTER 10

When Rhiannon dropped into the black pool of unconsciousness, her body reacted automatically to satisfy its
needs. Relieved of the panic of her conscious mind, she
began to breathe more easily. By the time Madog spotted
the fallen tree, she was conscious. Fortunately, the first
thing of which she became aware, after her realization that
she was not smothering, was the jolting discomfort of
being carried. Full memory of what had happened and that
she was tied hand and foot followed. Rhiannon realized
she was being abducted.

As far as Rhiannon knew, she had not an enemy in the
world; the only reason she could grasp at was that she
might have been taken for ransom. Her father was fond
of her, and her mother loved her dearly. Either one would
pay ransom for her. However, if she had been abducted
for ransom, Rhiannon knew she would not be harmed.

Soon after this hopeful idea took hold of her, Rhiannon
felt herself set down on the ground. She listened intently
but could make little of what she heard because the cloth
over her head muffled the sounds around her. One thing
became relatively sure, however. She had been taken by
only one person. At this moment, Rhiannon was convulsed
by a combination of rage and embarrassment. She, to be
taken in so obvious a snare. No, Mallt and her partner
would make no profit. Rhiannon resolved she would
escape if it was the last thing she did.

When Madog tumbled Rhiannon into the hollow under
the log, she was briefly frightened until she realized it was
not deep enough to be a grave. She managed to roll onto
her stomach with her face inward, and it was soon clear
that her abductor was taking great care not to pack dirt
over her face. Striving for patience, in case the man was
waiting to see whether she would try to escape, Rhiannon
counted to one thousand slowly. Then she could wait no
longer. She had to rid herself of the discomfort of the gag.

Rhiannon dropped her chin as far as she could and pushed with her tongue. At last she slid the thong over her lower lip. Setting her teeth so that it could not slip back into her mouth, she began to rub her cheek against the ground to push the thong over her chin. As she worked, Rhiannon began to feel cool, damp earth on the back of her neck. That meant that she had managed to lift the cloth as well as push down the thong that tied it around her head. With renewed vigor she began to scrape the cloth downward and forward. Finally, when she lifted her head the cloth fell away completely.

Although Rhiannon's neck and back ached from the peculiar, confined movements, she was so thrilled by her success that she did not pause a moment before turning as much as she could to her side bending her knees, and feeling with her feet for a solid surface This was not far to seek, for the trunk of the tree curved into the ground immediately adjacent to the hollow in which she lay. Bracing her feet, she straightened her knees. There was resistance at her back where Madog had packed earth and dead leaves around her, but several strong pushes with legs made very powerful by years of coursing game forced the blockage aside. Rhiannon's head and shoulders emerged from the hollow.

It was extremely difficult, Rhiannon found, to balance when one's feet were tied together and one's hands were bound. She had discovered this while she was levering herself upright against a tree. Having spared a moment to listen and be assured that no one had noticed her partial escape, she chose a level spot and jumped. Landing safely but painfully on her turned ankle she balanced herself, looked for another spot, and jumped again.

At first her eagerness and anxiety grew with each foot of progress. Because success seemed within her grasp, she feared more acutely that her abductor would return to snatch it away from her. She began to choose landing places farther and farther apart. At last she overestimated her ability and fell. The bruises were painful, the disappointment and effort needed to regain her feet more so. It was clearly impossible for her to get far enough away to elude pursuers in this manner. Moreover, she was leaving a trail that a blind man could follow. Thus, it would be better to find a sharp or rough enough rock on which she could rub her hands free.

This was less easily done than said. The soil of the forest was rocky enough, but years of blown soil and fallen leaves obscured any but the largest stones. These, moreover, were smoothed by millennia of wind and rain. The only place a sharp-edged rock might be found was in a stream, where the freshets of spring tumbled stones over each other so hard that they cracked or tore rough rocks from the earth of the banks.

Biting her lips to keep back useless tears of frustration, Rhiannon turned back toward the tiny stream that ran by the fallen tree where she had been concealed. Painfully, carefully, she hopped along on her bound feet, feeling them grow deader and deader as time passed. Her heart sank with each moment. The movement was keeping some life in her feet, but her hands were dead already. Even if she found a stone, how would she be able to draw her arms across it when she could not feel where her hands were?

Panic seized Rhiannon. Frantically she hopped back toward the stream she had—just as frantically—hopped away from half an hour previously. Panic then engendered carelessness, and she fell again. This time she lay weeping for some time, too hurt and too frightened to struggle further. Her head ached, her whole body ached, as much with fatigue as with her bruises. Hopeless, weeping, Rhiannon slipped where she lay into the deep sleep of physical exhaustion.

Dimly, after a long time, a dream voice called to her, *It is Simon. Can you hear me?* but her dream was of captivity and pursuit and treachery, and she whimpered softly, afraid even in her sleep to respond to that seductive hope of safety.

When Simon had no answer to his call, fear for Rhiannon gripped him again. It did not seem possible to him that, bound as she must be, Rhiannon could have gone farther than his voice would carry. A hundred deaths, each more horrible than the last, flashed through his mind. Without another look in Madog's direction, he set off to follow Rhiannon's trail. However, he was hardly out of sight of the fallen tree when he saw her lying on the ground.

"Rhiannon!" he cried. "Beloved!"

So close as he was, his voice was too loud to be mixed into a dream. Rhiannon's eyes opened. "Simon," she breathed, "oh, Simon! How did you find me?"

He did not bother to answer that, turning his attention first to cutting the thongs that bound her hands and feet, then to taking her in his arms and holding her so tight that she gasped in pain. Indeed, although her arms were too numb to move, Rhiannon pressed herself as tight as she could into his broad chest. After a little while, however, she lifted her head and smiled. Simon was shaking. Apparently he had been more frightened than she.

"Simon, I am all right," she assured him. "I was not much hurt, except for a few bruises from falling. But how did you find me?"

He began to tell her how Math had wakened him and he had grown uneasy, thinking she was away too long.

"You were right. Mallt asked me to take her into the forest to gather herbs. I should have been back soon after sunrise." Her eyes flashed. "Wait until I get back to Aber. I will teach that Mallt to connive with ransom-seeking abductors. I—"

"She is dead," Simon said, "and Madog . . . oh, good God, I forgot the man completely."

He got to his feet, lifting Rhiannon in his arms as he rose, but when he got back to the fallen tree, Madog was nowhere to be seen. On the way he had told Rhiannon briefly what had happened.

"But why?" she asked as he set her down. "It is quite mad. Surely he did not think he could force me to marry him—"

"He did not want marriage," Simon said, examining the ground near where Madog had been lying. "He believed you had cursed him. He was the one who made Ymlladd uneasy when we were at the cove yesterday."

"Oh, dear Lord," Rhiannon sighed, "it is all my fault! How sorry I am, and how useless it is to be sorry. Mallt also thought I was a witch because of my stupid habit of talking to Math. She heard some silly words I said in jest. . . . And now she is dead, poor foolish woman."

"And just as well, too," Simon retorted in a hard voice. "You are a fool if you waste any grief over her. She knew what Madog intended, and if she really thought you a witch, it was her right to accuse you—"

"Do not be silly, Simon," Rhiannon said softly and sadly. "How could a nobody like Mallt find the courage to accuse Prince Llewelyn's daughter of being a witch? It cannot be unknown that the same kind of rumors were afoot about my mother—and Llewelyn lay with her notwithstanding. I am a favorite, too. . . ."

"Mallt was a mean, vicious bitch, and the world is none the worse for her loss," Simon said comfortingly, but his voice was absent. He had found Madog's trail.

The question occupying his mind while he comforted Rhiannon was whether it was worth pursuing Madog. Simon was not sure he could catch up to him if he carried Rhiannon, and he would not consider leaving her alone even for a minute, much less for the time it would take to pursue Madog and drag him back. Nor could Rhiannon come with him under her own power. He knew that feeling was returning to her hands and feet because he had noticed she was moving her arms and legs uneasily as she sought to relieve the pain of the blood returning. Still, it would be some time before she could walk.

Rhiannon realized what must be going through Simon's mind. "Go after him," she urged, "not for me, but because a man who would murder his own partner in crime is an evil thing. Poor Mallt. I am not afraid to stay here. Leave me your knife. I will soon be able to use it."

"Oh, no! You will not go out from under my eye until I have you back safe under your father's."

"You will not tell him! No, Simon! No!"

Simon swung her up into his arms. "What do you mean 'no'? Do you think I intend to allow Madog to get away with trying to leave you alone to die of suffocation or starvation, not to mention his outright murder of Mallt? Even if I were so soft-headed as to agree to that, how do you suggest I explain your condition? If you think I can smuggle you into Aber without anyone seeing you, you are mad."

Rhiannon thought that over and sighed. "Could you not?" she begged. "I do not mean not to tell my father about Madog. He must know that Mallt was killed. But . . ."

"Rhiannon, do not be an idiot," Simon said. "What do you want me to do, stuff you under my tunic and say I am a pregnant woman?"

She laughed at that, but persisted. "I will soon be able to walk. All you have to do is go back and report Mallt's murder. Just do not mention me at all. I can say I had a fall."

"Of course," he replied sardonically, "and in the ravine —or whatever you fell into—the roots of the trees tangled themselves around your wrists and ankles. Rhiannon, you will bear the marks of that binding for a week or more. You may be able to hide the bruises from Prince Llewelyn himself, but one of the women will see. It will come to his ears—everything does. Can you imagine how angry—and hurt—he will be?" Simon paused and then said, "Do not be so selfish, Rhiannon. You may be indifferent to the danger to you, but Llewelyn and I are not."

"Selfish!" Rhiannon exclaimed. "Man! How dare you! So that you may be easy in your mind, you will bind me faster than Madog did. You would chain me hand and foot and mind to a bower. But when the trumpets blow for war, you will run to them. What woman dares to say, 'There is danger; do not go to it'? 'Duty,' you answer, but—"

"It is not true," Simon interrupted.

"What? That you run to war as to a festal merry-making?"

"That I wish to chain you," Simon rejoined hotly, setting Rhiannon down on a convenient rock so he could look at her while they argued. "I do not go to war alone against all my enemies. That is all I ask of you."

Rhiannon looked so stricken at these words that Simon paused. "Have I so many enemies?" she asked softly. "I have never intended harm to any man or woman."

"Perhaps enemies is the wrong word," Simon allowed, and he could not help smiling as he added, "especially among the men. But—"

"You need not fear that I will be taken by surprise again," Rhiannon said with a touch of bitterness. "I will not easily forget this, and I will be on my guard."

That was true. The frown of worry on Simon's face disappeared. He knew Rhiannon's woodcraft to be the equal of any Welsh huntsman's, which was to say a miracle of perceptiveness. There was always the danger of an arrow shot from concealment, but a whole army surrounding her could not really protect her from that kind of attack. Then his eyes narrowed.

"If you desire, I will say nothing to Prince Llewelyn," he agreed, "but neither will I lie to my overlord. If he questions me, I will tell him you bade me not to answer. Will this content you? However, I will not leave you alone. If you wish to walk into Aber on your own feet, I will wait with you until you are able. Of course, that means that Madog will most likely escape. He need only find a woodsman's hut and say he was set upon by outlaws."

Rhiannon could see the wicked gleam between Simon's narrowed lids. Her own eyes glittered with rage for a moment, and then she burst out laughing. "Devil! Clever devil! You know I could not lie to my father any more than you could. And he *will* ask. You are quite right. Someone will tell him I am all bruised." She flexed her fingers weakly and set a foot to the ground, but the ankle turned and she winced with pain. "Very well," she said, "I am ready to be carried home, but—but do we have to tell Llewelyn about the idea that I am a witch?"

"No," Simon replied instantly, all concern for "lying" to his overlord passing from his mind.

In Wales such a reputation might not be too dangerous. Wise women versed in herb lore and the old religion were usually respected and allowed to live in peace, although it was clear from what had happened that some danger was involved. However, if an aroma of witchcraft tainted Rhiannon, it would be worse for her in England, where the old faith was equated with Devil worship. That would mean that Simon might not be able to bring her to Roselynde. Even without any accusations, Rhiannon was so strange in her ways that she was looked at askance. To raise the subject of witchery, even to deny it, would be a mistake.

"What will you say?" Rhiannon asked.

"The truth—that I never asked Madog why he had attacked you. That I assumed he wished to force marriage on you, and I was too busy finding out what he had done with you—and to you—to worry about why he had done it."

"But he told you unasked . . ."

Rhiannon fell silent and shrugged. She had no right to complain about Simon's duplicity in clinging to the literal truth. She intended to use the same device herself to avoid the subject of whether or not she was a witch. Nonetheless, Simon's rapid perception of how the truth could be used as a direct lie distressed her. How many times had he done it already? How often would she herself be a victim of that kind of "truth-telling" if she weakened and linked her life to his?

When Simon had found her, if he had asked her to marry him, Rhiannon would have agreed, so overwhelming was her joy and relief. It was not only important that he had found her but that he was so aware of her that her absence had made him uneasy enough to seek her. Now she was armored again. She did not blame Simon or dislike or despise what he was going to do. In fact, she admired the quick intelligence, the flexibility, and the adroitness that permitted him to find such an escape from the problem. Unfortunately, she also feared those aspects of his personality.

Her resolution came just in time to save her from a new assault. As he came forward to lift her again, Simon said, "I can see no reason to start a stupid rumor about you which, the more it is denied, the more those who wish to believe will believe it. Prince Llewelyn will take no chances that another man will conceive the notion of abducting you and forcing you into marriage. Like it or not, Rhiannon, you will have to be accompanied when you run loose in the woods. Of course," he added after a thoughtful hesitation, his eyes gleaming with mischief, "you could agree to marry *me*. It would not be worthwhile seizing you after that because your father would not yield the promised dower to any other man."

Although what he said was true and Rhiannon knew he would gladly accept her agreement, his expression did not seem serious. Nor was there the slightest implication that Simon felt she should accept him out of gratitude because he had saved her life. He was only teasing her to

sweeten the bitterness he knew she must feel, for he was
aware how precious her freedom was to her.

"I think it would do less permanent damage if I simply
went home," Rhiannon replied, placing her arms around
Simon's neck and resting her head on his shoulder as he
carried her. "I will be safe enough there. There is no
reason for me to stay here any longer. I have found the
answer to the question I brought with me."

"What was that?" he asked, sounding surprised.

"I told you the first night, and you did not like my
answer. Put that question aside, and I will give you an
answer you will like. Now I desire only you, Simon—but
not for marriage. If I cannot have you without that bond,
there is nothing to hold me here. I will go back to
Angharad's Hall where, if any do think of me as a witch,
they do not hate me for it. And no man aspires to marry
me. They know there that the women of Angharad's line
do not marry."

Simon's step hesitated. "Rhiannon," he said uncertainly, "is that why you will not have me as a husband? Is
it the tradition of your people? Something could be worked
out—"

Rhiannon wondered whether she should allow him to
believe that, but it was not true. Some of the things Kicva
had said implied that she expected her daughter to marry
in the usual way. At last she did not answer him directly
and only said, "Please, Simon, can you not accept me as
I am? It is not owing to any fault in you that I refuse. I
must be free. I cannot be bound to any man."

"I can leave you free, Rhiannon," he said slowly. "Indeed, I know no way to hold you against your will, nor
would I wish to do so. But I do not understand what you
mean by not being bound to any man."

"You understand it well enough. Until you decided for
some reason known only to yourself and God that you
had fixed upon me for a wife, you desired many women
but never wished to be bound to any one. So why—"

"Men are different," Simon interrupted sharply.

"Perhaps," Rhiannon agreed. "I have discovered I
desire only you—but that is now, this day, this week,
perhaps this year, or even for ten years. Simon, I wish you
would listen to reason. I cannot give you more than I

have. I offer my body and my friendship. Will you not take them?"

There was a long silence while Simon strode steadily back along the trail. His arms were growing weary. Slender as she was, Rhiannon was hard-muscled, and her wiry strength weighed more than another maiden's soft plumpness. After a time he had to stop to rest, and he put her down on a fallen log. He still had not answered her question when he sat down beside her and took her hand.

"I cannot take just your body and your friendship," he said. "God knows, you burn in me like a branding iron, so hot is my desire, but that is not all. I need more than your body to slake my heat."

"Let it be, then," Rhiannon urged hastily. She could neither hurt Simon nor expose herself to the disaster that would overtake her if she permitted herself to love him. "I will go home tomorrow if I can, or the next day at the latest. You know where to find me if you should change your mind."

Simon hated the thought of her going, but it would not have mattered if she remained. When he finally carried her through the gate of Aber, he was greeted with cries of relief—but not for Rhiannon's sake. No one had missed her at all; however, a message had come for Simon from Richard Marshal and Simon could not be found. Since age had not dulled Prince Llewelyn's perceptions, he was not unaware of the envy Simon had aroused because of Rhiannon's favor. Llewelyn had said nothing, convinced that Simon was also aware and could take care of himself. However, the news that Simon had left Aber alone, unarmed, and clearly for some urgent purpose—the guard had seen him running like a wild thing toward the forest —worried the prince.

After Llewelyn found out what had happened in the forest, he sent a party to retrieve Mallt's body and messengers flying in every direction to order the apprehension of Madog ap Sior. Beyond that, Llewelyn could do little and did not allow himself to waste time and energy on the subject. He greeted with relief the news that Rhiannon intended to go home to her mother. She would be unhappy if it was necessary to keep a watch on her. Now that Llewelyn expected to send out raiding parties any day, he did not want his young men distracted by the possibility of a rich dower and a beautiful wife, particularly when it was clear to him that Simon would have her eventually.

Truly, Llewelyn was far more interested in what was in Richard's letter than in his daughter's future. He kissed her absently and waved her away into the care of one of the healing women, his eyes fixed on Simon, who was reading the letter at his insistence. Having perused it, Simon simply handed it over.

"It is mostly for you, my lord," he said. "Richard sent it in my name so that you would not be compromised if you did not wish to be connected with his doings."

Llewelyn's lips twitched. "I see that your delicacy is less than Pembroke's."

Simon grinned at him. "Much less." Then he shrugged. "My lord, if Henry wishes to believe you guilty, he will find fault no matter how careful you are. I am your vassal, and you have a perfect right to receive me, no matter who are my friends. However, Henry might well claim that you have offended him by giving me countenance. You also have a right to see a letter your vassal receives from a man who might be your enemy."

"But if I am to believe you, other men's rights have short shrift at King Henry's hands." Llewelyn nodded. "Then I need not worry. If my rights are respected, I am doing no wrong. Otherwise, I might as well be hanged for a sheep as a lamb."

Llewelyn turned his eyes to the letter he held, and the smile fixed on his face for a moment. Then his expression eased. "How sure would Pembroke be of this information?" he asked Simon. "Can I trust in it?"

Simon shook his head. "You see what he says. It comes from those who 'wish him well' in Henry's own camp. I *think* they are to be believed. There are few except the foreign mercenaries who favor this attempt to crush Richard. He has friends, I am sure, who would be glad to warn him of a move by the king to entrap him. However, the Bishop of Winchester is a most subtle man. He knows all this as well as you and I. It is possible that he would send out false information in this guise—only I cannot see how it would benefit him."

"In that he may hope my eyes will be fixed so firmly in the south that I will not notice Henry's army slipping through the passes northward," Llewelyn pointed out.

Simon looked startled and then laughed. "They would not be such fools, not after you stopped Henry dead and starving only two years ago."

"Men sometimes do not wish to remember events just as they were, and Henry is notoriously given to blaming others for failure, rather than looking at facts clearly. I have heard he says it was de Burgh's fault, not Welsh skill, that turned back the army."

"That is true," Simon agreed, "but the king's spite is very strong and he is bitterly angry with Richard—Pembroke, I mean." A shadow passed over Simon's face. "I cannot seem to become accustomed to the fact that my own Earl of Pembroke, Lord William, is dead and his brother is now earl. Yet Richard is a fine man."

"One's heart clings to the most familiar. You will grow into acceptance," Llewelyn comforted, but he was obviously thinking of something else. After a short silence he brought his eyes into sharp focus on Simon again. "You had better go to him as soon as may be. Do not take too many men, only as many as might be reasonable when traveling across country in which a war is brewing."

Simon's eyes glittered. "If I should be caught by the king's attack in Richard's company, I hope you will not be angry with me if I lend him my aid."

"One must support one's host," Llewelyn replied with spurious gravity. "I will no doubt remonstrate with you for your thoughtlessness in visiting your old lord's brother at such an unsettled time, but I imagine I will forgive you. The young are thoughtless, and one cannot expect too much foresight or self-control from them."

"Perhaps, my lord, knowing that Richard's brother was my old master and that I would be interested in the subject, you might have commented to me on the situation, especially as it affects Gwynedd?"

At that innocent question, Llewelyn laughed aloud. "If I had, I would have remarked that it is very unwise for foreign troops to come into Wales—north or south. It excites the rapacity of a people who are very poor, especially young men who see a chance to enrich themselves with goods that are not under their lord's protection. Unless that lord's protection should be sought specifically, there is little to hold them back. More than that, I cannot say at this time."

Although he was somewhat disappointed not to have a clearer commitment to bring to Richard, Simon had to accept that. He was, after all, only a messenger. He was neither of an age nor of sufficient rank to offer counsel to Prince Llewelyn, and he did not allow his head to be swelled by the fact that Llewelyn sometimes seemed to ask for his advice. It was more likely that his lord was testing his wisdom and loyalty than that he needed or wanted advice. Therefore, Simon accepted the dismissal inherent in Llewelyn's words.

"I will take my leave then, my lord. I must first ride to Krogen for men. You will find me there this night if you wish to give me further orders."

"Do not raise expectations I cannot fulfill," Llewelyn said with a sharp, admonitory glance.

"No, my lord, I will not," Simon promised, and bowed and strode away.

He stopped briefly to tell a manservant to warn Siorl, his headman, to be ready to ride out in an hour, and then went to the women's hall where he asked for Rhiannon. She came out to him herself, walking carefully, the protests of the healing woman who had been tending her drifting behind her. Simon swept her up into his arms and carried her into the garden where they could have a little privacy.

"Simon," she protested, "you will make more enemies than you need."

"I will not be here to face them," he remarked indifferently, "and I cannot believe anyone has not heard of how I brought you home. Does that not give me the right to bid you farewell when I must go?"

"You are going to Pembroke?"

"To Krogen for men."

"Then it is to be war?"

"Not for certain," he soothed, setting her down on a bench near the herb beds. "I am only taking a meinie large enough to be safe when traveling through an area likely to be infested with hostile bands snatching up whatever they can find. Foreign mercenaries are not overscrupulous in whom or what they seize."

Rhiannon's green eyes observed him with grave disbelief. Her lips curved with amusement, but worry wrinkled her brow. "That sounds very much like something my father would say when he wished to explain a war party where no war was yet declared."

Simon could not help laughing at her perception. "It may smack of that, indeed, but I know Richard does not desire a war against King Henry. He is not a rebel, he swears, and only desires justice. He will not attack the king's forces—"

"But he will defend himself, I suppose," Rhiannon interrupted, "and you will help him." She shook her head and sighed. "Never mind, I have heard all the words already. It is far to Krogen, and I must not keep you. Go with God, and with the blessings of Anu and Danu also, Simon. I will pray for your safety."

"And I for yours, my lady. Rhiannon, you *will* go home to Kicva, will you not?"

"Yes, as soon as I can ride with comfort." She gave him her hand. "When you can come, you will find a welcome there."

Holding her hand, Simon bent forward and kissed her. After a moment, he pulled back with a sigh. Without saying any more, he lifted her again and carried her back to the entrance of the women's hall, setting her carefully on her feet.

"Fare thee well, Simon," she said softly, using the tender, intimate pronoun she had never offered him before.

"And thou also, my lady. Take care of thy well being. Thou hast in thy keeping my heart, and ill will befall me if it be lost."

"Simon—" she cried, but he had turned and walked quickly away. "I do not desire that burden," Rhiannon whispered, but there was no one to hear and she knew the protest was useless.

She had spoken without thinking and had given him by her use of *thee* a hope she should not have offered. It did not matter, she told herself. There was no way to prevent Simon from loving her except by making herself too foul for him to love. That was not a path she contemplated. Fiercely she reminded herself that she had warned him repeatedly that she was not responsible for either what he wanted or how he felt. Nonetheless, Mallt's dead body and Madog's outlawry reproached her for carelessness and thoughtlessness. It was useless to say that she had meant no harm or that Mallt and Madog were worthless. She had been thoughtless and careless with Simon, too, and he certainly was not worthless.

Rhiannon sighed, hobbling cautiously back to her bed to rest. For the meantime, Simon's heart would be quite safe with her, and she would be firmer and more careful when he came to the hall—if indeed he came to the hall. Rhiannon wished she could be as certain of his body's safety as she could be of his heart's.

CHAPTER 11

✥•✥

Simon and his few archers had no trouble reaching Krogen keep. Llewelyn's men were out in the woods watching, but they recognized Simon's colors during the day. In the night, the calls and countercalls, which unknowing persons would take for those of night birds, marked the travelers as friends. Krogen keep was the best-manned of Simon's holds, and was managed by Bifan ap Arnalt, who was fanatically faithful to Simon. When Simon had gone for fostering to William, Earl of Pembroke, Bifan went as his servant-guardian, and a powerful bond had been forged between them. Now he held Krogen, the most sensitively placed and strongest of Simon's properties, and Simon never needed to give a thought to its security.

When Simon left the next morning, fifty men-at-arms followed him. They were the best in the keep, expert trackers, able to fade into virtual invisibility in the thinnest cover, skilled with the longbow, and in addition, unlike many Welshmen, trained to fight on horseback and armed for defending the walls of a keep. Simon was not concerned about stripping so many from Krogen's roster. Bifan would call in some veterans who had been settled on the land around Krogen if he needed them; meanwhile, he would choose and train some new young men.

The news Simon had from Richard included the information that the king had moved his army northwest from Gloucester to Hereford. Simon had debated taking the most direct route from Krogen to Usk, hoping he would have the satisfaction of encountering some of Henry's patrols and foreriders. Bifan eyed him coldly and remarked on how pleased Henry would be to hear of one of Llewelyn's men carrying messages to Pembroke. There was, of course, no certainty that such a deduction could be made from the mere facts of recognizing Simon and knowing he was riding south, but the remark was enough to remind Simon that he was not about his own business but on a mission for his overlord.

They took the slower route, west along the valley of the Ceiriog River, then climbed the goat trails over the mountains to the Iwrch, which they followed southeast until it joined the Tanai. They had to backtrack along the Tanai to the long vale that led to Llanfyllin and then eastward to the Vrynwy. Here, although they had come only about twenty-five miles from Krogen, they stopped and camped. The terrain was so rugged that, even in the river valleys, they had more often led their horses than ridden them. And, with backing and winding around obstacles, the real distance was nearly doubled.

It was, for a wonder, a lovely night, clear and with just a bare hint of the coming chill of autumn. Usually, Simon thought, staring contentedly up at the stars, if there was no shelter to be had and sleeping out was a necessity, it poured rain for spite. Tonight, however, was like a benison, a peaceful promise of a good future. He had been too much on the alert on the way to Krogen and too busy while there to permit himself to think of Rhiannon, but now he reviewed their parting and was well satisfied.

It had come just at the right time. If he had remained in Aber and Rhiannon had remained also, he would not have dared let her out of his sight. In that case, he knew quite well that she would have won the contest of wills. Unable to work off his lust elsewhere and with Rhiannon only too eager to satisfy him, he could not have resisted her for long.

Simon chuckled softly. He would win her yet. Her softness to him in parting was no result of any desire of the body. That was her heart speaking. And he had done well to resist his own wish to linger near her and see her once more before he rode away. Wild as she was, she would have seen the pit into which she was slipping and hardened her heart to escape it.

Rhiannon o yr adar, Rhiannon of the Birds—had Kicva known when the child was born what she would be? Simon did not fear Kicva, although he realized she was worth fearing and that some might have good reason to fear her. Her eyes were always kind when they rested on him, but he was sure they could read the soul within. Kicva, he thought, knew him better than his father or mother. Yet she was willing for him to have Rhiannon. She knew, if Rhiannon did not, that he would never try to tame or cage that wild bird. No, Rhiannon must tame herself, must come to rest willingly on the strong tree of his love.

He smiled into the darkness. Blessed Richard, blessed messenger, who arrived at so perfect a moment. Fear would tame his wild bird. She would worry and wonder and that would keep her thinking about him. And thinking about him would increase her desire. Simon chuckled again, then sighed. It would have been even better if she was promised to him. Then he could have written to her to tell her he was safe and well and she would not have worried. Simon did not relish the thought of any shadow on Rhiannon's happiness, not even if the shadow was fear for him. Of course, from a different viewpoint, Simon was amused by the idea that Rhiannon should fear for him. He could not see that there was anything to fear in a pleasant little war.

At dawn he was rousing the men, urging them into the saddle. Breakfast—hard cheese and wine from the small skins each man carried—could be eaten while riding. Simon was eager to bring the news of Llewelyn's sympathy to Richard, though he was sorry he could not say Llewelyn was willing to call up men and join him. But Richard probably had never hoped for that. He would be much cheered, Simon knew, by the one guarantee Llewelyn was willing to give—he had promised not to join with or aid the king in any way. And as a tender of his good faith in that direction, he had loosed his raiding parties to prey on Henry's army.

The land was gentler and they made better time down one river valley and into another until they came to the Wye. Then overland to Aberhanddu and southeast along to Usk to Pembroke's keep. That took only three days more, although it was nearly dawn when they finally came to the castle overlooking the river. Naturally enough, the guards would not open the gates at that time of night, and there was a shouting match. Simon won it, but only at the cost of having the earl himself dragged from his bed.

"God in heaven," Richard growled, "could you not wait two hours? Is your news so urgent?"

"I am very sorry," Simon said meekly. "No, it is not. I just lost my temper. We have been riding all night, and I am tired."

"So am I," Richard said pointedly, and then, "If your news is not urgent, why the haste?"

"I wanted to be sure to be here before any attack, in case the king should, for once, move faster than a snail."

"Attack? What the devil do you mean? Henry is as far north as Hereford—" Richard's voice checked as he saw Simon's expression. "Do you know different?"

"I heard . . . we came across a huntsman of Rhys Ievanc, who told us that the king was moving south again, but—"

"You did not think that urgent news?" Richard snapped.

"I did not know it would be news to you, my lord," Simon exclaimed.

"What else did he say?"

"No more than that. I asked, but he had little interest in the matter since his home lies north and well west. He had followed a boar too far and come upon a hunting party that had also been led too far by their quarry. Naturally he listened around their camp when he saw they were English, but as soon as he was sure there was no danger to his own people, he left. Do you want me to send out a few of my men?"

"No, we are ready for anything. I was only surprised that . . . never mind."

Simon did not need an explanation. Richard was surprised and disturbed by the fact that whoever had been sending him information about the king's movements had failed to transmit this very essential news. There might be many reasons, only one of which was a deliberate betrayal, and obviously Richard did not wish to taint his informer's name before he was sure of the cause of the failure.

They had been walking from the gate toward the inner keep. Richard had stopped when Simon mentioned the king's movement but now he went on, silent and frowning until they climbed the stairs and came into the hall. Here, picking his way carefully among the sleeping bodies, the earl gestured Simon toward the hearth, where the banked embers gave a gentle warmth that was pleasant in the damp chill generated by the thick stone walls.

"You may as well empty the budget now, since I am awake already," Richard said.

"Yes, my lord. This news is good, although not the best." Simon went on to state Llewelyn's promise not to oppose Richard and to describe his interest in an active alliance— eventually. His reluctance had nothing to do with the cause or any doubt of Richard, Simon pointed out, but he could not commit himself until he could make at least a temporary truce with his neighbors. "I do not think that will be difficult," Simon concluded. "They will wish to hold aloof until they see which side is the more powerful. Then they will leap on the weaker to share the spoils."

Richard shuddered slightly. "Truce or no truce?" he asked.

"Certainly," Simon said cheerfully. "A truce with *estraid* —I beg your pardon, I have been speaking only Welsh for some days to my men. A truce with foreigners has no validity to begin with, and even with other Cymry . . . they can always find an old feud—or two or three or more— that had been forgotten and precluded in making the truce in the first place."

"You think that is funny?" Richard asked, amazed at the tone of Simon's voice. "How can you trust such people?"

"But everyone knows the rules of the game," Simon protested, somewhat surprised by the earl's distress. "I do not know how to explain," he continued earnestly. "They are *not* dishonorable. They simply have a code that is different from ours. There are ways to bind them to each other with words—if they really wish—and such bonds will be kept with no regard for cost. If you—an *estraid*— need to be sure of good faith, you must take a hostage, and you must treat that hostage with honor. If you do not—"

"God forbid that I should have so great a need of Welsh support," Richard exclaimed. "And what the devil does your message from Llewelyn mean, if—"

"No, no," Simon hastened to say. "I did not mean you to include Prince Llewelyn. He has had long experience with your father and your brother and my father, of course. He will fulfill with exactness any agreement he makes with you because he knows a failure will prohibit any future agreement at all. Indeed, my lord, that is why he has been so chary of making any promise of assistance to you at this time."

"You are his vassal and love him, and you wish to marry his daughter," Richard said, frowning in perplexity.

"I am also my father's son," Simon pointed out, his voice suddenly cold. "If you do not trust me, I will call my men and go, having delivered my message."

Richard raised a hand and covered his eyes. "Sorry, Simon, that was not meant for you. I am sick at heart, that is all. I know I am doing wrong, and yet to do otherwise would be an even greater wrong. The world is black to me now, and everyone I look upon is smirched with my own dishonor."

"You have done no wrong," Simon cried. "My lord, you must stand fast or we will all be slaves."

"Yet I gave fealty to Henry. How am I better than those—"

"My father says King Henry is possessed, is sick," Simon interrupted. "He has known the king from a babe and says this is not his will or his spirit, that the Bishop of Winchester has infected him with evil notions. It is Winchester and Seagrave and those evil councillors you are standing against. Freed of them, King Henry will return to reason and you may return to your duty."

"That is what I tell myself." Richard sighed, dropping his hand. "Well," he went on, "so you advise me to trust in Lord Llewelyn's promises."

"Yes, and even without an alliance he will be of great service to you. Until now he has forbidden his men to raid English land because he did not wish to give Winchester an enemy to point at so that men's eyes would be turned away from his iniquities. Now he has lifted that prohibition with regard to foreigners on Welsh soil."

"Would that not apply to me as well as to Henry in the opinion of most of Llewelyn's men?" Richard asked wryly.

Simon grinned. "Perhaps, but you need not worry about it. They will not assault your keeps. They have not the means and they are not fools. Why should they try to crack a nut they know will break their teeth when plenty of sweet meat is lying about loose? They will prey on Henry's baggage trains." He paused and frowned. "I do

not say any of them—not even Prince Llewelyn—loves
you. They do not wish to do you good, only to enrich or
protect themselves. Why should you care? If Henry's army
begins to starve and the men are too busy watching over
their shoulders for raids to give full attention to Usk keep,
Llewelyn and his men will have served you as well as if
they were your devoted servants."

Richard did not like what he said. Simon could see that
in his face. He was accustomed to spoken and sworn
alliances, not to these negative, roundabout benefits. Sometimes sworn partners were no more reliable than the
ephemeral Welsh, but you could curse them with a clean
heart. The only safe path, to Richard's mind, was to
assume they would give no help at all. Still, Simon knew
them well and, although young, had shown more than once
that he was no fool. He said Llewelyn would act.

"When would such help as Llewelyn's men will give me
begin?"

"I should imagine Henry's army has already been well
stung. Ievanc's man said they were over the border, and,
anyway, the raiding parties often claim more land for
Wales than was ever truly ruled by the Cymry. The
raiding parties would have reached the army before I came
here. They are on foot and able to travel quicker."

"On foot? Quicker than riding?" Disbelief was clear in
Richard's voice. "And what could they do against armed
and mounted knights?"

Simon opened his mouth to laugh, then reminded himself
that Richard was not being stupid. Because he had spent
nearly all of his adult life in France, Richard really did not
know.

"They run up the mountains and across the ridges where
no horse can go," Simon said patiently. "My men and I
came down the river valleys, more than two hundred miles,
perhaps nearer to three hundred. For them it will be little
over one hundred. As to what they can do against knights,
it is more a question of what the knights can do against
them. This is no formal, open challenge on a clear plain.
The attacks will be made when a group passes through a
heavily wooded area or through a narrow ravine. They
will cut off the guards with a hail of arrows, drive away

the horses, carts, and oxen, and disappear into the hills or woods again." Simon sighed. "I wish I could be with them."

"You have been too long among the Welsh," Richard growled, appalled by such tactics and Simon's approval of them.

Simon shrugged. He knew that many knights thought Welsh-type war dishonorable. But any other kind would be suicide for the numerically weaker and infinitely poorer Welsh. However, it did not seem worthwhile to argue the question, so all Simon said was "Perhaps, but I never loved to be pent up within walls."

Nonetheless, Simon had little choice in the matter. In private Llewelyn had given him specific orders in addition to the oblique promises to Richard, and the oblique permission to take part in the war. Before he allied himself, Llewelyn wished to be sure that Richard was really committed to this war and would not yield at the first offer of compromise. Now Simon was not at all sure that this was true. Richard's distress over the broken vow of fealty was very great. Simon understood; he would have felt the same and could only be grateful that his homage had been given to Llewelyn, so he had no vows to break.

This, however, made very strong the possibility that Richard would compound with the king. Undoubtedly the earl was an honorable man and would not make any truce in which Llewelyn was not included once Llewelyn was his ally. But this was not sufficient. Llewelyn did desire the overthrow of ministers who fed Henry ideas of grandeur and absolutism, because such ideas might engulf Wales, but his nation was too poor to engage in a war that would bring no real profit and might bring a massive and disastrous retaliation. Simon was sure that the Bishop of Winchester was every bit as skillful as any Welsh princeling at finding "honorable" reasons why a truce should not be kept. Unless Richard was ready to fight until Winchester was dismissed from office, Llewelyn could not afford any formal alliance. It was thus imperative that Simon stay in Usk until Henry made his move and Richard responded to it.

Two days later Simon's doubt of Richard's willingness to fight was confirmed. Word was brought to Pembroke that King Henry and his army had paused in an open valley some three miles north of Usk. Plainly they were inviting attack. Philip Bassett, a keen soldier who knew the area and was very hot against the king because of his brother's Gilbert's injuries, pointed out that there were several approaches to that valley. He was sure the king's men did not know all of them, and Richard would have an advantage in both attack and, if necessary, retreat, despite the fact that he had fewer men.

Richard listened but shook his head. "I do not know why the king is doing this. He is no soldier, I know, but he has with him men who know war as well as or better than I do."

"I and my men can scout the routes," Simon offered. "We can make sure there is no trap set there now, or"—he smiled grimly—"remove the trap so that it turns to our benefit."

"No," Richard said. "I do not fear a trap." His lips twisted. "I will not raise my hand against my overlord. If he attacks me—well, then, I must defend myself, but I will commit no act of aggression against him."

Simon was quietly thoughtful after that. Usk was a strong keep and very well stocked for war. Around it, for miles, was only forest and barren fields from which all produce had been harvested. Nonetheless, all the people of the area were also in the keep. If Henry was ready to sit in front of Usk for six or eight months, Usk would be starved out. Simon did not think the king had that kind of patience or the money to pay mercenaries for so long, but it was possible. In any case, Simon did not want to be trapped with no chance of action—and that would be just what he would face if Richard refused to act and Henry determined to carry out a siege.

Later in the day, he requested permission to take his men out to scout Henry's army. Richard gave permission, but Simon could see he was not happy with even so minor an initiative against the king's forces. To ease his mind, Simon promised that his party would not raid, would only mark the size of the army, what engines of war they carried, and other such matters.

"That is not really fair to your men, is it?" Richard sighed. "They are accustomed to raiding."

"There will be opportunity enough for them later," Simon said, eager to get away before Richard changed his mind altogether.

He was not concerned for his men, who were most accomplished thieves and would doubtless collect enough loot without actually raiding to make the little excursion profitable. What Simon wanted to know was whether Henry intended assault or siege, and he knew just how to get the most accurate report of Henry's state of mind.

Probably Richard would have had a fit if he had seen Simon when he and his men left Usk just after dark. They went afoot, and there was nothing at all to mark the knight as different from his base-born followers. All wore knee-length tunics of deerhide mottled dark and light, with chausses and shoes deliberately splotched and streaked with dirt. All had short swords—or very long hunting knives—that were meant for stabbing and slitting throats rather than for formal combat. All carried long-bows and quivers filled with yardshafts and a long dark cloak rolled tight across their shoulders, and all had well-blackened faces and hands.

One by one they slipped through the postern. The guard saw them cross the small footbridge that spanned the moat and, before his unbelieving eyes, seemingly disappear, even though there was a well-cleared area for several hundred yards surrounding the keep. Once or twice the guard caught a flicker of movement across the open area, but he was sure that if he had not known there were fifty-one men out there, he would have assumed it was a hare or a cat or some other small animal.

Simon's bent body moved automatically in the slow steps and quick rushes that carried him from one shadow to another. Bifan had taught him the art when he was a child. He was not quite as proficient as his men—it was Simon whom the guard saw—but he was good enough not to endanger them, and they were as proud of him as they would have been critical of one of their own. For a Saeson he was a miracle, and they believed that only the greatest devotion to their ways and people could have permitted him to learn so well.

Although Simon was aware of what the men thought,

he no longer worried about the fond condescension with which they regarded him. Tonight in particular the silent slipping through the darkness released a well of joy in his soul. Richard's depression was oppressive and made the crowded conditions and restricted activities inside Usk even less palatable than usual.

They had reached the forested stretch now and could come upright and move faster and more steadily. Still, they were silent as any other predator, circling like wolves to be sure the wind would not carry their scent. Naturally the men would not notice, but the horses and oxen might grow restless and thus give warning to guards who might be extra alert because of recent raids. In less than an hour they were on the low wooded hill that lay northwest of the armed encampment. The moon was just rising, but its light did not yet fall into the valley. For Simon and his men the time was perfect, the low moon providing even more disturbing shadows that flickered and shifted as the breeze drove clouds across the sky.

The field was also perfect, dotted with tall weeds, low bushes, and clumps of saplings. There was, Simon thought, cover for an army of Welsh. But there were guards in plenty too, not quite shoulder to shoulder but well within sight of each other. The little existing light gleamed fitfully on the ring-sewn leather armor they wore. Simon smiled. Such precautions surely indicated that Llewelyn's men had been at work.

Siorl, Simon's captain, and the other men knew what to do. They were now fading away into the open area one at a time. From his perch on the hill, Simon could see one guard and then another tense up and call softly to his neighbors. Most often all three would take a few steps forward and peer around. Simon did not see his men slip past and around the searching groups into the camp. He hoped none of them would be carried away by temptation and steal enough to wake anyone. He had said no killing— if possible—but made no limits against stealing. Some would have stolen anyway. If he punished them for it, there would have been resentment; if he did not, respect for his orders would have diminished. Leadership was mostly the art of the possible.

Finally there was only one man remaining. Echtor, the

underleader, and Simon slipped down the hill, hugging shadows, crouching beside bushes while they chose out another path. The light breeze shook the leaves on the bush beside which Simon had paused. Closer to the perimeter of the camp, another bush was more violently agitated and a low sound like a rising wind filled the air. Simon slid sideways, hesitated, and came upright behind two saplings. He stood perfectly still, knowing that even if a guard looked directly at him, he would not notice anything. The dappled coloring of his garments, broken by the thin trunks and branches and sparse leaves of the saplings, would convince the guard that he was looking between the young trees at the shade-mottled clearing behind.

Again the fitful breeze blew, and the bush off to the right became active again. Simon watched, turning only his eyes from one guard to another. Yes, now! The two nearest the bush were both watching it nervously, hefting their pikes. One started forward and the other fixed his eyes on his comrade to be sure nothing would jump at him out of the darkness. Simon laughed silently and pitched a stone well off in the opposite direction. He saw the head of the guard on the other side turn sharply as the stone hit the ground and Simon ran softly, softly around the guard's back into the camp.

Only a few steps back was an empty wagon, strategically placed for the guards to take shelter in case of an attack— more evidence that the Welsh raiders had been at work with their knives and longbows. It was also very convenient for Simon, who stopped in the deep shadow beside it to unfasten and unroll his cloak. This he donned, pulling the hood well over his head and down to conceal his blackened face. Then he strode out boldly, kicked awake the first man he saw, and asked where Lord Geoffrey FitzWilliam's men were quartered.

When he had found the area he needed, Simon strolled idly around the tents until he found Tostig, whom he shook awake, just dodging back in time to save himself a punctured throat but not quickly enough to prevent Tostig from seizing him by the ankle.

"Some welcome," he grumbled, a bit nettled at having been caught.

"Sir Simon," Tostig gasped, recognizing the voice. "Whatever are you doing here?"

Simon tensed. "Keep your voice down. What do you mean, what am I doing here? Is there some reason I should not be here? Damn and blast, did Henry learn I was with Richard and outlaw me?"

"No—that is, you have not been outlawed. As for the rest, I cannot say, but I heard my master tell the Earl of Cornwall that you had gone back to Wales."

"Well, we are in Wales," Simon said. "Is Geoffrey here?"

"Asleep in his tent. Sir Simon, it is the middle of the night!"

Simon grinned. "Yes, well, there are reasons I could not come calling by day."

"Yes, my lord." Tostig sighed. "Be careful you do not step on the boys. They sleep near the opening to protect my lord—for all that is worth. Both of them sleep like logs."

Simon laughed softly. He did not blame Geoffrey's squires if they did sleep heavily, although he guessed the remark was partly engendered by Tostig's anxiety for his master. Simon remembered his own campaigns when he served Lord William. It was a noble thing to be a squire to a great man, but it was hard, hard work. In addition to the same riding and fighting the men did, a squire had to run messages, oversee the care of his horse and his lord's, clean his lord's armor and weapons—and, of course, his own—see that meals were properly cooked for his lord and serve them with as much elegance as could be provided, attend to the comfort of visitors should there be any, keep an eye on the men-at-arms and report any gross mistreatment or neglect by the captains, set the pickets and make sure the guards were doing their duty—and do a million other one-time-only things either ordered by his lord or directed by his own common sense. And God help him if his common sense did not direct him and he missed doing something. It was no wonder that the boys slept hard.

Nonetheless, Simon spoke outside the tent before he entered and, although the boys did not seem to have awakened, he did not go too near Geoffrey's cot. His brother-by-marriage did not sleep heavily on campaign and was quicker and deadlier than anyone Simon knew. Adam might be stronger, but Geoffrey was as swift in striking as an adder.

"Geoffrey, it is Simon," he said softly once he was inside.

He was glad he had been careful. As he spoke, both squires came to their feet with swords bared. If he had gone closer to Geoffrey's cot, he might have been spitted before he was recognized.

Geoffrey sat up and laid aside his own bared sword, signaling the boys to lie down again. "Madman," he said, "what are you doing here?"

"Why?" Simon asked, throwing back his hood. "Am I accounted an enemy?"

"Not yet," Geoffrey responded dryly, turning to draw his bedrobe over his shoulders. Then he goggled at Simon's blackened face. "What is wrong with you?" he asked, jumping out of bed and coming closer.

"Nothing," Simon said, feeling much surprised until Geoffrey gingerly touched his face. Then he laughed. "Soot and grease, Brother, soot and grease. Did you expect me to walk through the lines in a white satin robe?"

"I did not expect you to walk through the lines at all. Is that how you came?" There was a note of relief in Geoffrey's voice.

"Of course. I do not intend anyone to know I am here. It would be unwise. I am with Richard at Usk."

"Fool! Why did you let yourself be trapped there?"

"I was not trapped," Simon replied indignantly, but Geoffrey had turned to reach for his traveling case of wine and the movement had brought the light of the night candle more clearly on his face. It was so haggard that Simon's heart smote him. "Is Papa well?" he asked anxiously.

Geoffrey waved him to a seat on a camp stool. "Yes . . . in his health, but . . . It was by God's gift that you left London when you did. A day later, or perhaps it was two days, when the news came to Henry that Richard had come and gone, he demanded hostages."

"From you?"

"Do not be a fool. My sons are already in his service. From Ian."

"From Papa?" Simon asked with amazement, then laughed. "But who?"

"Henry wanted you or Adam, but more you, I believe. Thank God William was serving wine in the room and heard the whole. He slipped out and warned Adam to be gone at once."

"But what did Papa say?"

"First he asked the king why hostages were needed from a man who had been faithful to his father. Everyone knows how John tried to have Ian killed and that he tried to take your mother. Still, Ian held to his oath. Then Ian said he would be his own hostage, give his men into my hand, and go into prison wherever Henry desired. You can imagine what happened. Ian is greatly beloved. Ferrars said that if Ian were doubted, then he could not be trusted either and he would go where Ian went. Then Cornwall pulled off his sword belt and threw it on the ground by Henry's feet. He said he would not violate his blood by rebellion, but he, too, would go into prison with Ian."

"And Winchester?" Simon growled.

"I thought the bishop would faint or burst with rage. There can be no doubt that he had not expected what happened. Perhaps he did not intend Henry to make his demand before the whole court. I cannot decide whether he intended that you should be confined secretly first and Ian told later, or that Ian should be asked privately to order you to give your parole to the king. I think the first. Winchester wanted a whip, I think, after that talk Ian had with him. But Henry wanted to show his power."

Simon snorted. "So he learned what little strength he has against an honest man. The king backed down, no doubt."

"Yes," Geoffrey sighed, "but that is nothing to be glad of. You know how Henry holds a hurt and remembers it. Still, no harm may come of it—I hope. I made it easy by pointing out that he already had two of Ian's grandsons in his service. Henry made a great to-do over that, clapping his hand to his forehead and calling himself a fool. He even came down and took Ian's hand and kissed him."

"Do you think he will try to hurt Papa some other time?"

For a moment Geoffrey's tired face lightened. "No, because Ian is Ian, thank God. He was not angry; he was hurt. You know he does not see Henry as a man, but loves him as he loved you—spoiled brat that you were. Henry saw the love. He is neither stupid nor unfeeling, only impulsive and unwise. The king cast a look at Winchester that really did my heart good."

"You mean he blamed Winchester for the trouble he had got himself into?" Hope made Simon's voice vibrant.

"Yes, but do not let yourself think that one mistake will do the bishop much harm. It took years of carelessness to rouse Henry against de Burgh."

Simon grimaced. "A few months more of Winchester and either the king or the realm will be destroyed." Geoffrey did not answer that remark but looked so grim and sad that Simon was sorry he had said it.

After a little silence, Geoffrey repeated, "What brought you here, Simon? Did you come to see your father? He is not here. He has gone north to keep that border quiet. I have his men in my care."

Guilt flicked Simon again. That was another reason Geoffrey looked so exhausted. In addition to his political worries, he was carrying the burden of Ian's troops as well as his own, and Geoffrey was one who always saw to everything himself. If Simon had not been opposed to the king, he would have been sharing Geoffrey's burden.

"No, I did not expect to see Papa. He worries too much about me. I thought you would tell him I am well. But that is not why I came. I have news. Richard really does not wish to come to blows with the king."

"That is scarcely news. However, he will have no choice," Geoffrey said dryly. "The king says he will take nothing but abject surrender. He says he will not even see Richard unless he comes naked with a halter around his neck."

"He will have a long wait for that," Simon replied. "Usk is victualed for half a year, and we could last another three to six months if necessary. The land is cleared and burnt for ten miles around also, and the people are fled or inside the keep. Can Henry pay his mercenaries for so long? And do these flatlanders know anything about fighting the Welsh?"

"As to the last—no," Geoffrey replied, smiling grimly. "I should not laugh, but I cannot help it. I warned both

Henry and Winchester, and they would not listen. The Flemish were badly hit by raids twice already and have lost half their supplies. The ballistas and mangonels were burnt—" Geoffrey stopped speaking abruptly and cocked an eye at Simon. "Now that is a strange thing," he went on. "I have never known a raiding party to bother with siege weapons unless the war was their own."

Simon lowered his eyes. "I am Llewelyn's man. Do not expect me to answer you."

That, of course, was the answer. Simon knew Geoffrey would understand. Geoffrey ran his hands through his hair. "What terms do you think Richard would take?" he asked.

If Llewelyn was involved, Geoffrey had much less hope for the successful outcome of the attack on Usk, as the question indicated. Simon was relieved to see that his brother-by-marriage was not at all depressed by this information. In fact, he seemed rather more cheerful.

"You must understand first that I have not discussed this with Richard at all, so I am not sure about anything. However, if any reasonable truce is offered, I do not think Richard will refuse. As to particular terms, I do not believe he will demand more than that a council be held to examine the merits of his case and Bassett's and that the king agree to give judgment only according to the decision of the council. Maybe he will also ask that the king's ministers be dismissed, but I do not think so."

"It will not be possible to prevent an attack on Usk," Geoffrey said thoughtfully, "but if the attack is resisted firmly, the king may become less adamant. He is not, as you know, patient or determined. If a thing does not fall into his hand like a ripe apple, he shakes the tree, then loses his temper and kicks the tree. Having hurt his foot, he blames for his pain the one who last mentioned apples to him and says he hates apples anyway."

"Blames the one who last mentioned apples, eh?" Simon repeated, smiling. "Now that would be a good thing for us and a bad thing for Winchester. If enough blame could be heaped up quickly . . . Hubert de Burgh made fewer mistakes and those further apart from each other, I think."

"You think quite correctly, Simon. I did not like

de Burgh. I am glad he was cast down, although I think it wrong he should be treated so harshly. However, I will say for de Burgh that, at his worst, he never drove the barons to rebellion. That mistake will come home to roost and lay the largest egg."

"God willing," Simon assented fervently.

CHAPTER 12

∗∶∗

Simon did not stay long after that exchange. Geoffrey saw him to the boundary of the camp and sent him off, the sentries assuming he was a spy in his brother-by-marriage's service. On the hillside at the edge of the woods, Simon's men were waiting for him, silently comparing their spoils. They came to their feet, stuffing away their ill-gotten gains, when Simon arrived and began the three-mile trek back to Usk. When they had come far enough so that no vagrant breeze could bring the sound of their voices back to the armed camp, each man in turn reported what he had seen to Simon.

All in all it was a most satisfactory venture. Simon had discovered not only what he wanted to know, but why Henry had stopped to offer battle in so inviting a place. It was not a trap in the usual sense, but the king's chances of defeating Pembroke in open battle were far better than his chances of breaking into Usk. Supplies were dangerously low, lower even than Geoffrey realized, and not only war machines but timber and leather to make new ones had been destroyed by the raiders.

The next morning Simon carried his information to Richard. "I have added up what the men told me," he said, "and they cannot take Usk."

"I did not think they could," Richard snapped testily. "If I had thought so, I would have chosen another keep in which to make a stand."

"Pardon, my lord, I said that ill. What I mean is they have not food enough to support the men while they re-build the siege machines and those they build will do them as much harm as us, I think, from being made of green wood. Nor can they obtain supplies from elsewhere. Bassett is in the south, and I do not think much will come to them from Hereford or Gloucester because Llewelyn's men will be lying in wait for the supply trains. They can try an assault or two, but I suspect there will be little enthusiasm for it from the English levies, and there are not enough mercenaries."

"They will not take Usk by assault," Richard said. "If they could batter down the walls . . . but that would take months. . . ."

"They have not supplies for three weeks. The Flemish leaders have been generous with provender to the troops while in England, so there would be no need for them to harass the local people. I suppose they were warned there would be no easy pickings in Wales, but they did not believe it. You know those mercenary captains always think the local lords are either fools or soft-hearted."

Richard smiled grimly. There were *no* pickings to be had around Usk. Men and animals were behind the walls. The crops had been harvested, the fruit picked from the trees—even what was not yet ripe—and the fields had been burned over so that there would be no grazing for the horses and oxen of Henry's army. It was too early for nuts. Perhaps there were a few berries. Those grew wild and could not have all been picked, but they would not sustain an army.

"Then they will try assault, and we will beat them back," Richard said. "Then what?"

The question was not addressed to Simon, of course. Richard might ask his advice about Prince Llewelyn, whom he did not really know, but he would not ask it about war or English affairs. Simon stood silent, waiting for the earl's mind to survey the possibilities. Finally his eyes fixed on his companion again.

"If I make truce with King Henry, will Lord Llewelyn feel I have betrayed him?"

"I cannot say for sure, but I think not. You did invite him to join you, but he made no answer. This may make him more cautious about committing himself in the future, should you ever desire such an alliance, but Prince Llewelyn respects a reasonable man."

Simon was rather relieved at the turn things had taken. If Henry had not brought matters to a head and he had been sent back to Llewelyn to negotiate a firm alliance, he would have had to warn his overlord that Richard was not really determined to prosecute the war and only wished to act defensively. Simon would have hated to do anything to increase Richard's troubles, but Llewelyn was his over-lord and his first duty must be to him. This way it was unlikely Simon would have to give any opinion; he would only need to relate facts.

At first the king's party made noises as if it would be war to the death. The insults Henry's herald flung at Richard when the army finally arrived at Usk two days later were disgusting. Many of Richard's men were incoherent with fury, but Richard himself only laughed. Such insults, he pointed out to his angry supporters, were designed to get them out of the keep so that they could be cut to pieces by a superior number of men.

To Henry's frustration, Richard replied gravely and sadly that he had no desire to contest at arms with his acknowledged overlord, that he would never attack his king but only defend himself against injustice, that he asked only for a trial before his peers so that they might judge his offense and Gilbert Bassett's. Since the outcome of such a trial would most certainly be in Richard's and Gilbert's favor, it was not a course that recommended it-self to the king. Henry was left to reiterate furiously that he and he alone was the judge of his vassals' rights and duties, which further angered and embittered those barons who had answered his summons.

No other course then remained but to besiege or attack. Teams of men were already busy building new siege engines, but it was clear that there would not be time enough to batter down the walls before the king's party starved—not to mention that it was not really possible to make satisfactory machines out of green wood. Raiding parties came back nearly empty-handed—if they came back at all. If Henry wanted Usk, he would have to take it by the crudest form of direct assault.

Simon watched the preparations with bright-eyed eager-ness, and Richard came across him on a dawn tour of inspection when it appeared that the assault was imminent. The earl examined Simon's preparations for repelling at-tack on his section of the wall and had no fault to find. He stood a moment looking out at the king's camp and then sighed.

"Do you not have kin in that army?" he asked.

"Yes," Simon agreed brightly, "and good friends too."

"Do you not care?" Richard asked, rather shocked at the young man's apparent hard-heartedness. "I mean, what if your brother came up the wall?"

"That is one worry I do *not* have, thank God," Simon answered. "Geoffrey cannot climb a scaling ladder. He was crippled at the Battle of Bouvines—oh, long ago. I was only a child then. It does not affect him fighting mounted or even on foot much, although he cannot run well and he cannot manage a ladder."

Richard's face relaxed a little. There was so much good-humored mischief in Simon's eyes that he guessed what was coming even as he asked, "And the others? The good friends?"

"They will not attempt this section of the wall," Simon said. "I sent a man over as soon as you told me where I would be. I hope you do not mind, my lord," he added with sudden doubt. "I thought it would be better that way. Thus we can honestly all fight our best. It is not like a battle on an open field, where we could see each other's colors and avoid. I do not think I could bear to cast over a ladder on which my mother's vassal stood. Those men, most of them, dandled me upon their knees."

"No, I do not mind," Richard said, smiling and feeling better suddenly.

The thought that tormented Richard most bitterly was that in a war of this kind, brother might fight brother and father fight son. Simon's insouciance reminded him that those who cared would probably find ways to avoid each other, and those who did not would have ended at each other's throats whether or not they had the excuse of war. He remembered, comfortingly, that his own father and elder brother had managed never to come to blows, even though William had rebelled against King John and had joined Prince Louis.

"Look!" Simon exclaimed, interrupting Richard's thoughts.

"I see," he responded, and took off around the wall at a trot, calling an alarm as he went.

It was hardly necessary. All along the wall men were shouting to their companions to come to attention. Simon's archers sprang to their feet and bent their bows against their arches to string them, plucking experimentally at the long piece of gut and listening to the music of the string. Here and there a man began to curse the wet South Welsh weather—as if it were different and drier in the north—and unstrung his bow to adjust it.

Simon found no fault with his own, but he was not the perfectionist about the bow that his men were. Although he was a fair shot and respected the bow and the bowmen from the bottom of his heart, Simon was still primarily a Norman knight. His weapons were the lance, sword, and mace, and it was there that his pride was fixed. That showed in his next move, which was to hook the bow over his shoulder so that it could not fall and loosen his sword in its scabbard. His shield, with its snarling black leopard on a silver ground—chosen to blend into the light and shadow of a Welsh forest—leaned against the merlon in front of him.

The sound of footsteps behind brought his head around. He nodded to Siorl, the leader of his troop, who was shepherding a number of serfs, each of whom carried a large wicker shield. One thing Usk did not lack was men. These churls could not fight, but they could protect the archers from the arrows of the opposing force. It was a most excellent idea, for the merlons of Usk were a little less than a man's height. Simon stood at a crenel opening roughly in the center of his troop. At the far end of his section of wall, Siorl divided his attention between the enemy, who were clearly forming to attack, and his master, who would give the word to shoot. At the other end, Echtor, the underleader, also watched the enemy and Simon, while smiling and running his hand as lovingly up and down the smooth, silken wood of his bow as he would over the side of a beloved woman.

The serfs chattered excitedly. They were not much afraid, knowing they would be behind the shields until the arrows stopped flying. If and when men came against the walls, they would be sent down—not to save them, but because they would be in the way. Then Simon bellowed for silence and the chatter stopped. He warned his men to look to their other weapons and to the thrusting poles with which the scaling ladders could be pushed over.

Simon's position would not be exposed to any dangerous assault machines. The siege towers he could see around to

find a chance to loose their own arrows. Simon himself was hit both times he stepped forward to shoot. His mail was superior to that of his men; one quarrel did not bite and the other slid along his upper arm, nicking the skin but doing no other damage.

Sheltered by the curtain of crossbow fire, the assault forces were busily laying their spanning devices over the brush, logs, and mud with which portions of the moat had been filled. Simon's men cursed and grew more daring, trying to pick off the crews who were working. Although they made a few hits, the cost in injuries to themselves was too high, and Simon shouted for them to let be and take care. Once the assaulters started to climb the ladders, the crossbowmen would have to stop shooting or they would hit their own men. Then Simon's men would have the advantage again.

More warily now, the archers continued picking off a man here and there, cleverly trying for those in charge of the working parties or men who were doing crucial tasks. The caution, coupled with the accuracy and deadliness of the great Welsh bows, paid well. Only one man was wounded badly enough so that Simon directed he be carried down. Many others were lightly hurt; with their injuries bound they were able to continue to fight.

Those among the attackers struck by the wide, barbed head of a longbow shaft were not so fortunate. The narrower head of a crossbow bolt could be drawn out with little further hurt; the longbow arrow had to be pushed through or cut out. If it was pulled out, the flesh was torn in a wide swath because the broad back-sloping barbs caught and held wherever they entered.

Despite the efforts of the archers on the walls, the spanning devices were set and ladders began to rise. Two out of three of Simon's men laid aside their bows, picked up stout, hooked poles, and began to try to push the ladders over. This was tricky work, since the crossbowmen shot as hard and fast as they could to prevent it. Fortunately, as the defenders bent low in the crenel openings, they exposed less of themselves as targets. Those who had retained their bows continued to shoot at the men trying to raise the ladders.

As rapidly as the ladders rose, they were tipped over.

Here and there one remained upright long enough for some men to mount. When they were about halfway up, the crossbowmen in that area began to slack their fire. That permitted more daring efforts to overturn the ladders, and Simon could hear the cries when the efforts were successful, the ladders tipped, and the men fell.

Now Simon could see that some of his men were deliberately waiting until the ladders were half-full. He weighed the danger and the profit and then shouted for the other teams to do the same. There was a chance that the men would misjudge their timing and so many would get up on the ladder that it would become too heavy to overturn; however, the few assaulters that could get up on the wall from one or two mistakes could be swiftly dispatched. On the other hand, dropping the men in the moat would eliminate most of them. If they fell on the blocked portions, they would break their bones; if they fell into the water on either side, burdened with their armor, they would drown.

Because the opposing army was large, discouragement did not come quickly. As fast as ladders were pushed over, others rose. Some were broken, but more were ready to replace those splintered. Eventually one remained upright in Simon's section and a captain swung through a crenel opening, thrusting with his sword and spitting an unwary Welshman. With a shout of joy, Simon snatched up his shield, drew his sword, and rushed forward to engage. This was his business, and he dispatched it well and swiftly, knocking aside the man's shield with his own and taking him in the neck with his sword.

One of Simon's men dragged the corpse out from under his master's feet and with the help of a companion tossed it over the battlement. Meanwhile, Simon had engaged the second man. While they traded blows, another of Simon's Welshmen leaned daringly from a crenel opening about ten feet away and began to pick off the climbers on the lower part of the ladder. Simon dispatched his second opponent, who was also tossed over. He was not dead and screamed as he fell.

More shrieks drifted up as others fell from the ladder. Several of the bowmen had taken cues from the one initially shooting at the climbers. A third man put his leg

over the crenel opening, thrusting his shield smartly out-
ward to push away a man-at-arms who struck at him with
his sword. This move was successful, but unfortunately
for him Simon was on the side and took his leg off at the
knee. He screamed and continued to do so as he, too,
was thrown over the wall. By then the load on the ladder
had been sufficiently lightened that the men with thrusting
poles could topple it.

Simon wiped his sword on his surcoat, no other cloth
being immediately available, and resheathed it after an
alert glance up and down his section of wall assured him
there was no further danger of anyone getting up from a
ladder. He was aware that the rain of crossbow bolts was
much diminished; quarrels must be running out. In fact,
it seemed that the attack as a whole was tapering off.
Almost as soon as Simon was aware of the thought, he
heard the blare of horns calling a retreat.

It was only then that Simon realized he was soaking wet
with sweat. That seemed odd, for mornings in September
were chilly enough, and aside from the little time he had
been engaged with those men who had reached the battle-
ments, he had not been exerting himself violently. Only
it was not morning. Simon looked stupidly at the sun
blazing down from the southwest. Two-thirds of the day
had passed, and he had not been aware of it.

Recalled to the anxiety that had occupied him just
before the attack began, Simon looked again toward the
southwest, but lower. The siege towers had been withdrawn to a safe distance. Simon sighed, thinking of the
captain who had led his men onto the wall and was now
dead. Geoffrey was always at the head of his men also.
Not Geoffrey, Simon prayed. Dear God, not Geoffrey. I
will never be able to go home again. How could I look
into Joanna's face? I should have been beside my brother,
not supporting those who opposed him and enjoying
myself.

With that fear, his own physical discomforts began to
press on him. He became aware that his mouth was dry
with thirst and his stomach ground with hunger. That was
nothing, but if he sent a man to have food and drink
brought up, he could also ask about Geoffrey. Before
he had a chance to act on this idea, he saw serfs running

from the kitchen quarters bearing loaves of bread and rounds of cheese. Others followed more slowly, lugging huge kettles of soup or stew and barrels of beer. Resignedly Simon sat down and rested his back against the wall. It was not likely, anyway, that anyone would have any sure word of Geoffrey for him.

They ate on the walls, watching the king's forces while the serfs ran back and forth bringing new arrows from the store of weapons, replacing any broken thrusting poles or dulled or damaged weapons for the smiths to start working on, and gathering the spent crossbow bolts to refill the quivers of their own crossbowmen. The leeches came around to wash and bandage the lightly wounded and direct the worst hurt to be taken down for treatment.

Simon had seen it all before, and after a while he stood and looked out toward the king's camp. There seemed to be a conference taking place there, but it was too far away for Simon to tell who attended it. All that was clear, then, was the result. The massed men broke up and drew away. Apparently there would not be another assault this day— or the defenders were supposed to believe that it would not be renewed.

But it was no device to deceive. Simon stayed until the clang of cooking pots and armorers came faintly from the camp, indicating that there really would be a period of quiet. He then chose a few men, all unhurt, and ordered them to watch closely for any hint of a surprise attack. The other men were to try to sleep, as it was quite likely the next attack would come at night. Those on guard could amuse themselves by firing burning, pitch-headed arrows at anything they hoped they could set afire.

Having done his duty, Simon went down and joined the other leaders in the hall. Richard was listening to reports and it was quite clear that they had sustained very little real damage. They were still in excellent condition to withstand anything the king could throw against them. As soon as he could, Simon made his way to Richard, waiting impatiently for him to be free of business for a moment. When he could, he asked about Geoffrey, naming his arms, but Richard had not see him at all. The siege tower he had faced had been commanded by the Earl of Ferrars.

"If you mean the demon with the lion and Danish ax on a green ground, bend sinister," Philip Bassett said, "I have this to thank him for." He pointed to an ugly bruise on his forehead. "But you need not worry. He is in the most excellent health, damn him."

"No, do not damn him," Simon protested, laughing with relief. "I am sorry for your bruise, but he is my brother."

"And you could not cozen him into joining us instead of opposing us?"

Simon blinked at the idea of cozening Geoffrey, who could think rings around anyone else he knew. Joanna might manage it, but no one else could. However, all he said was "He is the king's cousin, Salisbury's bastard."

It was easier to explain Geoffrey's attachment by a blood tie than to get involved in his belief that the friends of the king could eventually bring him to reason. Philip Bassett was of fiery temper and would not appreciate Geoffrey's desire to convince rather than force, but he would understand the bond of blood.

"Well, then, I will not wish him ill," Bassett agreed wryly, "since he is dear to you, but I hope he will be sent elsewhere—or that I will. He is not large, but he is a terror! He cost us more men than all the others put together and actually came across and held a piece of the wall for a time. There were moments when I thought he would win his way to the tower door. It was only the call to retreat that drove him off."

"I thank God he came to no harm," Richard said with a sigh. "Geoffrey FitzWilliam is a fine man." His mouth quivered and his eyes grew bitter. "God's curse and all the ill we are doing each other should fall on the Bishop of Winchester, who has brought us to this pass. May his body bear the pains of all the wounded, and his soul the weight of the sins and hate he has forced upon us all."

"Amen," Simon said, but the pain in Richard's face called to him and he said, "But there is no hate between me and Geoffrey. You must not think that. Where there is love, there is also understanding. We each honor the other that he holds to his principles."

"It is all the fault of the Bishop of Winchester," another

man said. "If the king had kept to his natural advisers—
we of the old barony—instead of turning to a man long
absent from this realm and steeped in foreign ways—"

"Yes, and that is what we must enforce upon Henry,"
Philip Bassett said hotly.

Because he was thinking of Geoffrey, Simon was in-
spired to unaccustomed tolerance and understanding. "It
would be better to convince the king softly than enforce,"
he said. "Henry has a long memory." An uncomfortable
silence followed this all-too-true remark, but Simon was
still thinking of Geoffrey and his last conversation with
him. "Yet we may all come scatheless out of this, if it can
be shown that what we have been saying a moment ago is
true—that the causer of the trouble is Winchester, that on
him the blame should fall, and when he is gone all men
will be at peace and return to their duty."

Richard could not help smiling at Simon, whose youthful face was so much in contrast to his sage advice. "It
is my purpose," he said. "I only wish you could tell me
how to bring it about."

Simon nodded. "But I can. Geoffrey gave me the
answer. He said to me that the king only likes apples that
drop into his hands. If they do not, first he kicks the tree
and then, having hurt his foot, he blames the last person
who mentioned apples to him—"

"What is this nonsense of apples and trees," Philip
asked irritably, taking literally what Simon said.

However, Richard was staring at Simon with deep interest. "Lord Geoffrey is a wise man," Richard said, "but it
will be a neat trick to know when the apple should drop
so that the blame does not swing back to the tree. It is,
after all, possible to fetch an ax to obtain apples."

Although it was pretty stupid to consider killing a tree
to get at its apples, Simon made no protest because he felt
it would be typical of Henry's behavior. He only shrugged
and nodded, adding Geoffrey's final caution. "Even if the
moment be right, it may not serve its purpose perfectly.
Henry is not so light-minded that one or two disappoint-
ments will make him change his opinion of a man he has
trusted from childhood."

"You are right about that too," Richard sighed. "However, all this is not to the point at this moment. First we

must be sure the apples are not shaken loose by kicking the tree."

"My lord, what apples? What tree?" Philip asked. "I swear there is not an apple left on any tree in all South Wales."

"We are the apples and Usk is the tree," Richard replied, smiling at Philip's confusion, "but Lord Geoffrey was doubtless speaking in a parable. Never mind that now. Let us consider how we can cause the greatest loss among our attackers at the least cost to ourselves."

"We can load the ballistas and catapults and fire them at the camp," Philip urged promptly. "They set up far too close, either trusting to your mercy—or contemptuous of your forbearance."

Simon tensed slightly. Philip Bassett might not recognize a parable until it was explained to him, but in matters of war he had keen good sense. Until now, Richard had made no move at all that could be called aggressive, but now his eyes were thoughtful as he considered Bassett's remark in the light of his earlier conversation with Simon.

In a moment, however, he had shaken his head. "Whether they be bold, trusting, or foolish, I will not attack my liege lord," Richard reiterated. "Some day I will need to answer for this to my peers, or, when I die, to God. Thus far, I hope, I have done nothing beyond my right."

"You take too strict a view. If the king has declared you outlaw, are you not freed from your oath in the sight of man and God?" Philip asked passionately.

"I do not wish to be free," Richard said, frowning. "I wish to be a loyal vassal, to be reconciled to my lord in such a way that there will be honor for him and safety for me and for us all."

"The Great Charter," Simon put in, it having been drummed into his head ever since he was a child, "must be upheld. Henry must understand that all men—kings also —must live within the law."

"And I agree to that with all my heart," Philip insisted, "but I believe it will be necessary to give the king a sharp lesson before he will come to the same understanding."

"Perhaps," Richard conceded, "but I will not affront

my lord yet. Let him see that even in war, even though he mocks me and tempts me, I will not move against him. Let us talk of our defense now—and before I forget, Philip, if Geoffrey FitzWilliam comes against you again, do him no hurt if that be in any way possible. If he can be taken prisoner, by all means do so. He is dear to the king and would make a most excellent ambassador to plead our cause. Pass that word, and I will also."

"Thank you, my lord," Simon exclaimed.

"I did not say it for your sake," Richard said, smiling nonetheless. "It will do us no good to harm those the king loves, and especially not those who, I believe, agree with our purpose in their hearts."

CHAPTER 13

❖��������������������❖

An attempt at a surprise attack that night failed miserably. Although it was difficult to tell, Simon thought the king's forces had taken more hurt than in the daylight. One siege tower had been burned to a charred skeleton by a flaming barrel of pitch that hit it just right, so that it exploded, spreading fire too widely to be quenched by sand or water or smothered by wet hides. It was not the tower Geoffrey had been on, but his position might have been changed, and Simon had something new to worry about.

A third assault followed the very next dawn. Aware of weariness, Simon felt some concern that Henry's huge force might be divided, one part resting while the other attacked. He soon realized, from the lack of enthusiasm of the attackers, that they were as weary as he and his men. They never even got ladders up this time, and the archers on the walls again took a heavy toll. For the first time Simon saw the men hanging back, needing to be urged and threatened by their captains.

This was an utter stupidity, Simon thought as he watched the troops retreat toward their camp. It was an act that the king would be likely to urge out of spite, but Simon could not understand how the great warlords, like Ferrars and Geoffrey, could have permitted Henry to have his own way—unless they did not wish any assault to succeed!

Simon was not alone in this opinion, and others, older and wiser, argued against Philip Bassett when he urged again and again that Richard ride out and attack the king's army now that they were in disarray. Richard would have resisted in any case, but it was easier for him because so many of his supporters now agreed with his passive role. So they sat and watched each other for four days. On the fifth, a mighty assault was made. New siege towers had been built and the king's forces flung themselves against the walls of Usk with a mad ferocity that spelled desperation.

After the attack was over, it reminded Simon of a great storm at Roselynde, when gigantic waves crashed against the cliffs below the walls, only to break in spray and fall back, helpless. Simon was sure that this was the beginning of the end, and he smiled grimly to himself and thought, *They are growing hungry.* Possibly they had used the four days for foraging as well as building, and had found nothing or even had been mauled by Welsh ambushes.

He was pleased and amused, thinking that Richard would soon know the worth of Prince Llewelyn's help, and he came off the walls rather smugly satisfied with himself and the situation. A few hours later, this mood changed abruptly when, as the last of the daylight faded, a single man rode to the walls under a flag of truce and begged that Richard send out Simon de Vipont, under safe conduct to come and go freely, so that he might speak with his brother, Lord Geoffrey.

The only thing Simon could think of was that Geoffrey was dying. He would listen to nothing, impatiently dismissing Richard's warnings that it might be a trap and ignoring his efforts to discover who the messenger was so he would be more secure as to Simon's safety. Simon could barely wait for his destrier to be saddled, flinging himself onto his mount and clattering across the drawbridge before it was properly down so that Ymlladd had to jump at the end. He was so frantic that he never noticed the expression on Tostig's face—the fact that Tostig had come confirmed Simon's conviction of disaster.

"Where is he?" Simon cried.

"In his tent, my lord."

"Quick, then, quick."

Tostig was well acquainted with Sir Simon and quite accustomed to his fits and starts. He regularly thanked God that he had been placed in the service of a man such as Lord Geoffrey, who was not given to sudden lunacies. However, if Sir Simon said "quick," it was not Tostig's place to dispute. Indeed, he would be in danger of a broken head if he did. Therefore, he obeyed Simon's order, wheeling his horse and clapping heels to its ribs with enough force to set it off at a gallop. This action, naturally enough, further increased Simon's fear that Geoffrey was at his last gasp.

It was thus a considerable shock to Simon, who arrived quite frantic and with his eyes half-blinded by tears, to find Geoffrey sitting at ease, with his feet up, comfortably sipping a cup of wine. He let out a bellow of mingled joy and rage that startled Geoffrey into dropping his cup and leaping to his feet with his hand on his sword.

"I will kill him," Simon roared, looking over his shoulder.

"Who? Who?" Geoffrey cried, drawing his own sword and limping forward, fearing that insult or treachery had been offered.

Had he not been so startled by Simon's shout, Geoffrey would have realized there was as much laughter as outrage in Simon's voice, but that became clear only a moment later when Simon ducked around his bared blade, seized him in his arms, and kissed him heartily.

"Your man Tostig," Simon chuckled, finally answering Geoffrey's question when he released him so that he could resheath his sword.

"What in the world did Tostig say to make you so angry?" Geoffrey asked, really amazed. Occasionally, like any longtime servant, Tostig offered his betters good advice—even when they did not want it or ask for it.

"Nothing!" Simon replied, still half-furious in reaction to his past fear. "That idiot did not say a word except that you were in your tent and left me to believe you were dying."

"Dying?" Geoffrey echoed. "But why should you think I was dying in the first place? What did Tostig say? I told him only to ask for you and to offer safe conduct."

"Well, that is all he did," Simon grumbled, watching Geoffrey pick up his cup, set another on the table, and pour wine into both. "But what did you expect me to think after a hard battle that went so ill for your side?"

Geoffrey's fair brows arched upward and his lips twitched. "I am old enough to take care of myself."

"Yes," Simon agreed, but with so little conviction that Geoffrey began to laugh aloud. Simon shrugged. "You do tend to run amok in battle."

"Coming from you——" Geoffrey began, then laughed

again. "Never mind. Sit down. I have something to suggest to you and I wish to hear what you think, but first a question. You told me the last time we spoke that Richard would make truce if one were offered. Is this still true, or has the attack on him changed his mind?"

"I am sure it is still true, but you must know that I am not the first of his advisers. Still, I am sure he does not wish to break his oath of fealty. And you must see this to be true. He has not used the catapults or ballistas or mangonels against the king's army and he has refused to ride out to attack, even after he saw that your men had been used too hard."

Geoffrey sighed with relief. "Good. That is very good. I hope that Henry is now willing to listen to reason, and I do not believe Winchester will oppose a truce. He is enough of a soldier himself to see that our situation is growing worse, not better. If a desirable arrangement can be devised, would Richard receive a delegation? I am afraid it will have to contain Winchester, but the Bishop of Saint David's and the Bishop of London will be there also, as will I."

"I am sure he will receive you, but whether he would agree with you as to what is desirable is a different matter. I think he is eager to make peace, but he has not changed his principles."

"I know that. I wish, however, to avoid making matters worse while I am trying to mend them. If Henry and Richard can come to terms before any real damage is done, it would be much better for everyone. It is possible to forget an injury, of course, but it is always better when there is nothing to forget."

Simon frowned. "Yes, but I fear things have already gone so far. . . . Do you really think the king, and more especially Winchester, will deal faithfully? However, you are right, I suppose. It is necessary to try. What do you want me to do?"

"Only to tell Richard what we have said to each other, and, of course, if he should have changed his mind to let me know as soon as possible. If we talk Henry around and Richard will not even receive us, that would be very bad."

"I do not think it," Simon assured him, "but if the other men should be so hot against it that Richard must yield to them, I will come to you myself or send Siorl. He can speak enough French to make himself understood. Before I go, tell me how everyone is at home."

"All well when I last heard. Ian is still in the north, just barely keeping his men from rushing down here and attacking our rear. Joanna is at Hemel. Your mother is riding the south holdings to keep them quiet, and—oh, I have a funny story for you. You know that old Sir Henry is too old for his duties, far too old. Naturally your mother would not turn him out, but there must be a new castellan. Lady Alinor chose Sir Harold, Giles of Iford's youngest son, to succeed at Kingsclere. He knew Sir Henry and will be kind enough to pretend deference and not hurt the old man. Unfortunately, Sir Harold is here with me, and it would cause Sir Henry great distress to put in a temporary castellan, so Sybelle is at Kingsclere. She is very clever at making her decisions look as though she were taking his advice."

Simon grinned at Geoffrey, who laughed back. Sir Henry was a total blockhead. He had been a strong fighter, was absolutely loyal and honest, but advice from him would be more likely to cause a disaster than to be of any help. Still, he had known how to defend his lady's lands, to recognize unauthorized encroachments, and to mete out simple justice. Now he was too old and too crippled to ride out, but his mistress had not forgotten his good service and was ready to do her best for him even at considerable inconvenience to herself.

"You remember," Geoffrey went on, "that the king disseisined Gilbert Bassett of Upavon—"

"Geoffrey," Simon protested, "do you think I am so addle-witted that I do not remember why I must come to speak to you under safe conduct?"

There was a brief, eloquent silence. Geoffrey's lips twitched, but he managed to remain grave and said, "No, of course not."

In fact, Geoffrey did not think Simon addle-witted at all, merely apolitical. Simon liked Richard Marshal and did not like the king. That would have been reason enough for him. He did not need the fact of Henry's offense to insinuate himself into a war.

"Anyway," Geoffrey continued, "Upavon is not much

more than twenty miles from Kingsclere, and Walter de
Clare has been raiding in that area so that the king would
get as little benefit as possible from having transferred
Bassett's property to Maulay. Some of Walter's men appear to have wandered a bit astray and have encroached
on a Kingsclere farm. Needless to say they were driven off
and soundly drubbed. They ran for their base camp
with—"

"Not Sybelle! No, that is too much. I will have to talk
seriously to that girl. She will never get a husband if she
takes to—"

"*You* will have to talk to her?" Geoffrey gasped. "Who
taught her to be such a hoyden?"

"Not I!" Simon exclaimed indignantly. "I always told
her she should not be so wild. Whenever she got so dirty
and her clothes in such a terrible state, I—"

Geoffrey burst out laughing. "Yes, you told her—*after*
leading her into the scrape in the first place. But this time
it really was not her fault—at least, I suppose she should
have ordered the men not to give chase or should have
gone back to the keep with a few while the others pursued
the raiders. In any case, she was with the troop when they
hit the camp, and she caught Walter de Clare with—as
the saying is—his chausses undone."

"You think that is funny?" Simon groaned.

"Do not you?" Geoffrey chortled. "You can imagine
what she said to him."

"I certainly can," Simon agreed sourly. "Well, there is
one marriage that will not be made."

"Are you so sure?" Geoffrey asked. Then he shrugged.
"If you are right, it was the wrong marriage to consider
anyway. A man needs to know what he is getting when he
takes one of the women of Roselynde to his bosom."

"Did you?" Simon asked interestedly.

Geoffrey eyed his brother-by-marriage for a moment
and then said softly, "Yes." His lips twitched. "I came to
Roselynde when your father married your mother. Joanna
was then nine years old. She was beautiful even then, and
very sweet and proper—until I crossed her will and she
hit me on the head with Beorn's quarterstaff. Yes, I knew."

"But I do not think Walter—" Simon began, and then
stopped. He did not find Rhiannon's aggressive ways dis-

tasteful. He found them exciting. Perhaps Walter would, too—after he recovered from how Sybelle expressed her disapproval of his management of his men—if he ever recovered. Simon sighed. "Where is he now?"

"In the same area, perhaps farther west, nearer Devizes. I think there is more to it than just raiding to make the king's adherents dissatisfied. I fear the end purpose has something to do with de Burgh. If you see or hear from Walter, Simon, bid him have no part in attempting to free de Burgh. Devizes is too strong, and any attempt will only increase the severity of the old man's imprisonment."

"I will," Simon said, but his voice was doubtful, and there was a question in his eyes.

"Do not be a fool." Geoffrey sighed. "I cannot write to him. If I know such a thing, I should warn the king of it—and that is the last thing I wish to do because it would bring about all the bad effects of such an attempt without achieving anything at all."

"But I do not believe I will go back to England when this siege is over, and I do not have a messenger I can trust to go anywhere but Roselynde, so—" Simon's voice broke off suddenly and he slapped himself on the forehead and grinned. "Oh, what a dunderhead I am," he laughed. "Of course. I will write to Sybelle. That will either set the fat in the fire or supply a miraculous cure—but she will not fail to send on your warning." Simon put down his empty wine cup and stood up. "Is there anything else?"

"No. Get back now, and hear what Richard says. If he is willing to parley, do nothing. Only send word if he will not receive us."

There was no question of that. Simon was told that Richard wished to speak to him as soon as he reentered Usk, and after he was assured that Simon's fears for Geoffrey had been groundless, he listened eagerly to Simon's news. Far from being reluctant, he was impatient to receive Henry's embassy and, when they came two days later, showed them all the courtesy in his power. Simon, of course, took no part in the negotiations. He was very junior both in status and in years to the others, and he was not even Richard's vassal. However, he was well informed by Geoffrey.

On the surface it was not an unreasonable proposal. To

save the king's pride, Richard was to yield Usk to him on the specific agreement that it would be returned intact and undamaged in fifteen days. In return, the king pledged himself to "make all necessary reformations in the kingdom." On the Sunday after Michaelmas, all the parties were to meet at Westminster to discuss what reformation was necessary and to take the proper steps toward it. The bishops and Geoffrey were securities for the king.

Richard was very happy. He felt that the yielding of his castle for two weeks was a small price to pay to achieve all his other objectives. He was prepared to bend his knee and say he was deeply sorry to have offended his overlord. It was true! He was sorry, and he had none of the false pride that would prohibit such an admission. He would not say his purpose was wrong; he still intended to achieve that purpose, but he would be very glad to do so by yielding and persuasion rather than by force.

The bishops were also happy. Theoretically the Church did not approve of war between Christians, although there were exceptions to this rule. In this case practical reasons reinforced theological doctrine. There could be no profit to the Church in the continuation of this conflict. Truthfully, few of the bishops liked Peter des Roches any better than the barons liked him, and they saw no advantage in his ascendancy over the king. It was their intention to support Richard's demand that the king reconstitute and consult a council of barons and bishops as required in the Great Charter.

Geoffrey was hopeful rather than happy. The eagerness with which Richard had responded and his willingness to agree to the king's terms had pleased Henry. The king was no longer talking about halters around his vassal's neck. Moreover, Henry had been quite sharp in his speech with the bishop these last days. Perhaps the wily Winchester would take warning from that and lean more toward moderation and conciliation. Geoffrey did not think Winchester had abandoned his purpose any more than Richard had abandoned his, but he believed that political intrigue was far less dangerous to the nation at large than open war.

Philip Bassett was furious. Although he, his brother, and all their adherents had been included in the truce and were to be parties in the conference on October ninth, he said openly that Richard was a fool to trust the king. Henry had no intention of returning Usk to Richard, he claimed. This truce was only a device to gain a better foothold in south Wales from which more devastating attacks could be launched, and anyone foolish enough to leave the protection of his own lands and appear at Westminster would soon find himself lodged in the Tower with no way out—if he did not find himself shorter by a head. Other of Richard's adherents hushed Bassett, pointing out that Richard was in no mood to listen, but the castellan of Usk looked very thoughtful.

The next day, when orders were given to vacate the keep so that Henry's men could take it over, Simon went to say farewell to the castellan's son, who had been a pleasant companion during idle hours. He could not find him. Fortunately, before he asked for him, Simon noticed that a number of the men in the castellan's troop did not know how to fasten their armor and that the weapons they bore were rusted and battered and broken. Simon shut his mouth hard and hastened away, telling his own troop to mingle with that of the castellan and help them and, if they could, hide the deficiencies of the serfs pretending to be men-at-arms.

Perhaps it was not honorable to the letter of the truce for the castellan to have left his son and most of the peacetime garrison of Usk in the keep disguised as servingmen. However, Simon was in perfect accord with him. If the king kept his word, no harm would be done. The castellan's son and his men-at-arms would hew wood, draw water, and have an unpleasant two or three weeks of hard labor. If the king broke his word, on the other hand, it would be *his* violation of the agreement that caused the harm. When Richard returned and attacked Usk to recover it, there would be no long siege or bloody battle. The castellan's son and his men would throw off their disguises, unearth their weapons, and open Usk to its rightful master.

Simon was delighted as he rode north with his men. He had lingered behind the others long enough to send off his letter to Sybelle and, incidentally, to be sure that the castellan's ruse was not discovered. Once he was on the road, he made the very best speed he could, expecting he would have to ride all the way to Aber or Caernavon. Hardly had he passed Abergavenny and plunged into the valley that ran west of Ysgyryd Fawr, however, than a messenger came leaping down the flank of the hill and hailed him. Prince Llewelyn was at Builth, he said, and bade him come there with his news. Simon was overjoyed.

It was rather late when they arrived at Builth, but Llewelyn was awake and waiting for him. News of the "surrender" of Usk had flown over the mountains and up the valleys by relays of swift runners, and the prince had guessed that Simon would not linger after Richard was gone. Although he had been in the saddle for hours, Simon gladly went to his overlord. He was eager to know what Llewelyn would make of the terms of the truce. Beside that, the sooner he had told the prince everything he knew, guessed, and even hoped, the sooner he would be free to go to Rhiannon.

Since the truce had been proposed, Simon's thoughts had turned from the arts of war to the arts of love. He had gone over and over that last day's happenings, from finding Rhiannon in the woods to the final, soft "Fare thee well." Unfortunately, the events showed him no clear path. He was puzzled and hurt by Rhiannon's doubt of him and of herself. In some ways Simon was very innocent despite his many sexual liaisons. Simplistically, he accounted all the women who yielded to him as bad. He acknowledged that, in many cases, their husbands did not deserve chaste or loving wives. Nonetheless, the woman who violated her vows was at fault—the Church said so, men said so, it must be so.

It was very easy for Simon to be positive on this subject. His mother had never violated her vows, nor had his sister Joanna, nor his sister-by-marriage, Gilliane—and the latter two were both superbly beautiful and he knew had been importuned by men in high places. He did not connect the behavior of the wives with the very obvious devotion of the husbands, although he knew that Ian, Geoffrey, and Adam had never taken a mistress and that the first two did not even use whores when they were separated from their wives. Probably, Simon thought, he would be like Adam, who relieved his sexual urge as he would relieve his bladder or bowels, but surely Rhiannon did not mean that—or did she?

Rhiannon was strange and did not think like other people. Still, he could not understand her doubts. To his mind, "everyone knew" that the men of Roselynde did not look elsewhere once their affections were fixed. Having achieved the goal of nearly fifteen years of longing, Ian truly had no desire for any woman other than Alinor. Geoffrey had been soured very young by a licentious court; he was no womanizer by nature and was too fascinated by the bright, exquisite "sun" of his life to think of deceiving Joanna. Adam loved his soft, seemingly submissive Gilliane, but he was no fool; he was aware of how often things went the way Gilliane desired rather than the way he had planned. He trusted his wife—yes—but he had no desire at all to give her a reason not to trust him. He had not forgotten that she had pushed her second husband out of a high window of Tarring keep.

What had begun quite naturally had hardened over the years into a fierce pride, partly as a result of ribald comment by other men and regretful admiration of women. The men of Roselynde might play in their youth, but once they chose a woman they were as faithful to the vows of matrimony as they were to their oaths of homage. Simon had been born into this atmosphere and had grown to manhood in it. He could not understand Rhiannon's doubts, and he wished he could talk over the problem with someone.

As he entered Llewelyn's presence, Simon wondered whether the prince could help him, but he remembered that Rhiannon's father had told him from the beginning that he did not understand his daughter. Simon hesitated and smiled. Rhiannon's father might not understand her, but her mother. . . . What a fool he had been. Perhaps he could find out from Kicva what was wrong.

"You bear good tidings?"

Llewelyn's voice snapped Simon back to the present, and he came forward quickly and bowed. "They are not ill, but whether good or not, I cannot say. I hope you will be better able to interpret them than I, my lord."

"I hope so too," Llewelyn said dryly. "It is not every day that a starving army, thrown back with heavy losses from an assault and plainly unable to maintain the siege or win the keep by attack, suddenly walks into it without a blow struck."

Simon grinned. "Put like that, it does sound odd, but there was reason in it." He then explained fully the terms of the truce, ending, "Do you think the king will keep his word, my lord?"

For some time Llewelyn did not answer. His bright dark eyes stared at nothing. Then he sighed. "I know men, and in a long life I have learned to judge them well, but I cannot answer your question, Simon. No matter what his years, Henry is not a man; he is still a child. Children have bright dreams of what they will be. For most, these dreams are limited by what they are. A serf child does not dream of being a king—but he can dream of being a man-at-arms or a freeholder of his land. A woman cannot dream of being a brave knight, but she can desire many children, or none, or to rule her husband by stealth or by beauty. But to a child-king's dreams, there are no limits."

"Do you mean that Henry has always desired to grind his barons into dust?"

"Not at all." Llewelyn looked sidelong at Simon and smiled a secret smile. "That is a baron's way of putting it," he said gently. "A king might call it being able to govern without being torn ten ways by different parties with different interests. However, if that *were* true. I could guess very well what Henry would do. No, that is not his dream."

"Then what does he desire?"

"A different wish each day or week or month. That is what I was starting to say to you. For most children one dream becomes fixed as the child grows into a man or a woman. It may sprout odd shoots, but those shoots are fixed to the first stem of the dream. Henry, alas, has never grown into a man. Sometimes he dreams of being a builder of beautiful things; sometimes he dreams of being a great conqueror and of winning back all that his father lost and more; sometimes he dreams of being as powerful as God, sometimes of being as merciful as Mary, good as a saint, bountiful and magnanimous so that all will love him."

Simon cocked his head. "My father always said that—I mean, that Henry desired to be loved because his mother and father did not love him."

"Ian is too soft to judge men well, but in this case he may be right. He may, indeed, be right. Nonetheless, it does not help, for at one moment Henry seeks to enforce love through power and the next seeks to win it by generosity, and—to the misfortune and confusion of his subjects—it is mostly impossible to guess which side of him will show." He shook his head. "We can only wait and see. At least his next move will not fall upon me. There will be time to prepare. So what will you do now, Simon?"

"With your leave, my lord, I will go to Angharad's Hall," Simon said eagerly.

Llewelyn smiled. "Still pursuing? You have not grown weary?"

"I will never grow weary. If I do not succeed, I will take no wife. There is no need. I have nephews enough to serve as heirs, and they are all good boys."

"You are set on this, Simon? Really set?" Llewelyn's smile was gone.

"I will give oath to you—in blood if you will."

"Hmmm. I had better write to your father, then, and to Kicva also. Do you wish to know with what I will dower her?"

"It is not needful, my lord. I am not such a fool as to say I do not care. I do care. But you know what lands I have, and I am sure it will be in your interest as well as in mine to dower Rhiannon with what will march well. I will leave it to your wisdom and your generosity, my lord."

Llewelyn burst out laughing. "Very clever. I especially like the inclusion of the words *wisdom* and *generosity*. They should certainly encourage me in the direction you want me to lean."

Simon laughed too. "But my lord, what do you want me to say? You have always been generous to me, and even your enemies say you are wise. I cannot help it if I sound like an idle flatterer. Would it be better to tell a lie rudely or be sullenly silent?"

"Go," Llewelyn said with raised brows. "You are incorrigible! Go to bed and then, if you will, to Angharad's Hall. But if you do not remain there for any reason, come back to me. There will be strong stirrings in Henry's court one way or another, and I might need ears or a mouth there."

CHAPTER 14

❖❖❖❖❖❖❖❖❖❖❖❖❖❖❖❖❖❖❖❖❖❖❖❖❖❖❖

Although it was late when Simon went to bed, he was among the first to stir in the morning. His mood was happy. From Llewelyn's last words, he thought that the war would be renewed—if not immediately, then soon enough. That provided a prospect of amusement and profit. Far more important, Llewelyn had, at last, recognized that his intention to have Rhiannon was fixed and serious—and would most likely succeed. Under no other circumstances would the prince write a proposal of marriage to Ian.

Simon could hardly believe his good fortune. Although Llewelyn had said more than once that he favored the match, Simon had always believed he was half-jesting and did not really believe Simon had much chance to win his wayward daughter. Even a natural-born daughter of a prince could look much higher for marriage than a younger son, no matter how rich and well connected his parents. But Simon did not miss the advantages for Llewelyn either. Rhiannon was obviously a special case. He thought of her married to a man who held a great court —and burst out laughing so that he was cursed sleepily by those around him who were not prepared to wake so early.

Just think of the wife of a man like Richard of Cornwall or one of the *ducs* of France running barefoot after game in the fields and woods with her hair all unbound, dressed only in a rough, dirt- and grass-stained kirtle. And Rhiannon was not one who could be forced into a pattern of behavior because it was considered correct. She would run away or might even kill a man who tried to enforce his will on her. In addition, there was the question of dower. For a great marriage, Llewelyn would need to find a large sum of money or a very substantial amount of property.

Without being told, Simon knew that Llewelyn was not willing to do that. Money was always a problem, for Wales

186

was dreadfully poor. Any of the great Marcher lords might be happy to take land, but Llewelyn was completely unwilling to increase the influence of any man whose primary loyalty must be to the king of England. Doubtless he knew that Simon would inherit his father's northern properties when Ian died, but with both a wife and the major portion of his lands in Wales—and his heart there also—Llewelyn had reason to trust that Simon would stand with the Welsh in any conflict of loyalties.

All the better, Simon thought, as he kicked Siorl awake and told him to get the men up. He would get a much smaller dower than a greater man, but Llewelyn would be aware of what he had saved and would be glad over the giving. But best of all was the fact that Llewelyn said he would write to Kicva. To tell Rhiannon he had made a serious proposal for her marriage would probably do nothing but enrage her. On the other hand, if Kicva approved, Simon knew he would have a strong ally, and one who could deal with Rhiannon.

The letter was waiting for him when he went to take his leave of his lord, and Simon flushed a little when he took it. It was large and official-looking, sealed with the seal of Gwynedd. It must be a formal proposal, he thought. He thanked Llewelyn passionately, and his lord looked at him with considerable amusement, but he only gave him leave to go without extraneous comment.

They went as far as Powys castle that night and slept soft and dry, for there was peace—at that moment—between its lord and Prince Llewelyn. The next day, Simon sent Siorl with most of the men to Krogen. Echtor and four others continued north and west with him. They camped on the shore of Llyn Tegid that night and then crept over the mountains, mostly leading their horses rather than riding them, to arrive at Angharad's Hall in time for dinner. Kicva did not seem surprised to see them, and Simon guessed they had been watched and their progress reported for many miles.

For the first time since he left Rhiannon at Aber, Simon's confidence was shaken. He had expected her to drop out of the hills any time since noon of that day, but she had not. And now she was not even present to greet him in her mother's house, where she had told him he would be welcome. However, his sinking heart was lifted by Kicva's smile.

"I have a letter for you from Prince Llewelyn," Simon said after greeting her, but his eyes asked, *Where is Rhiannon?*

Kicva took the letter and looked at the broad seal, which marked it as an official communication rather than as a friendly note. Then her eyes flicked to her loom, where a heavy roll of fabric lay beneath the portion on which she was still working. It was good, she thought, that she had not hesitated in her task. And then she had mercy on poor Simon, who was shifting from foot to foot with the impatience of a small child who cannot bear to wait but is afraid to speak.

"Out on the hill," she said, answering the question in his eyes, and began to ask whether Simon wished to eat before he went—but he was gone, and she laughed at her own silliness and opened Llewelyn's letter.

In spite of the official-looking seal, it *was* friendly in tone rather than imperative, and it contained some matters of considerable interest aside from the message Kicva had expected. Llewelyn had found over many years of difficult dealings with King John that the best unofficial ambassador is a woman. First of all, nine out of ten men dealing with a woman are at a grave disadvantage by thinking her stupid and of no account by nature. Then, when pleading is necessary, a woman would go down on her knees and rain tears without shame. Provided the woman was clever, she could obtain more information more quickly than most men—she would not be suspect; a man would. And most men, particularly King Henry, who had chivalric dreams, found it much harder to imprison, punish, or threaten a woman, even if she were taken as a hostage.

For many years Llewelyn had thus employed his wife Joan. Now that was impossible. What he had proposed to Kicva was to use Rhiannon instead. At first sight the idea was ludicrous. Rhiannon had no knowledge of a complex, corrupt court like that of Henry of England and had no connection with it. Joan had been King John's daughter and Henry's half-sister, but Rhiannon was no relative at all. Nor was she famous for tact or likely to become a favorite with the women of the court.

However, when taken in context with the proposal of marriage to Simon, the idea suddenly began to look possible, even promising. Llewelyn gave Kicva a brief summary of Simon's family. Kicva knew Ian; in fact she had considered him as a father for her child before she fixed on Llewelyn. It seemed as if the women would be the most likely of any to accept Rhiannon. And, for Llewelyn's purposes, the intimacy of Lord Geoffrey with the king was almost as valuable as Joan's blood tie.

Kicva smiled to herself when she thought how clever Llewelyn was, for the thing worked both ways. To couple the marriage with a most necessary duty to her father and to Gwynedd was to provide a perfect excuse for Rhiannon to back down from her refusal to marry. This would save her pride and make Simon very happy also. It was typical of Llewelyn and the key to his success as a ruler that he so often found a way to benefit his subjects—at no cost to himself—while they performed duties necessary to his purposes. Having read the letter a second time, Kicva settled before her loom while she considered how best to present the facts to Rhiannon. She worked quickly while she thought; there would not be many days to finish this piece of work before it was needed.

Hours earlier when the first message announcing the arrival of visitors was called across the valleys from hilltop to hilltop, Rhiannon knew it was Simon coming. Of course, each of the three warnings of a visitor over the past two weeks had, in her opinion, heralded Simon, but this time she was certain again. For a short time she sat still, fighting the urge to run out and meet him. It would be horrible, she knew, to meet under the eyes of all the people in the hall or the courtyards. Even in the garden, maids and men would peep, murmuring to each other that Lady Rhiannon had at last chosen a man. But it would be little better to meet surrounded by Simon's men, unable to touch him or ask the questions she wanted to ask.

Her mother was *not* looking at her. She had begun to make ready for the guests, telling the servants where to place the bed that would be set up for Simon's use and to which stable to take his horses, issuing instructions to the cooks for an extra dish or two to add festivity to the meal.

There was nothing in Kicva's voice, expression, or manner to show that she was even aware of her daughter. Nonetheless, Rhiannon felt the mingled amusement and sympathy. She controlled a desire to scream. It never paid to scream at Kicva, who merely looked at one with laughter or scorn in her quiet eyes.

Math stalked into the hall, his tail twitching from side to side. He crossed to where Rhiannon sat and looked up at her. There was no sympathy in his eyes and he was not offering the comfort of his roaring purr. Restraining a desire to kick Math, who was *not* laughing at her, Rhiannon rose to her feet with all the dignity she could muster and did what Math and Kicva—and all the others in the hall—were waiting for her to do.

"If you want me," she said to the open space of the hall, "I will be on the hill."

Simon did not need to ask Kicva which hill, and eagerness lent wings to his feet. Had Rhiannon intended to hide from him, she would have fled into the forest. This particular hill was one of her favorite spots when she wanted to be away from the bustle of the hall and yet still remain close by. It was some half-mile from the house up a steep rise where some fall of land or ancient excavation had created a cuplike hollow, bare of trees and facing south. The depression caught and held the heat of the sun so that from early spring until the deep snow fell it was warm enough to sit there and read or dream.

Never having ridden to the place when he had been at Angharad's Hall in the spring, Simon did not think of mounting Ymlladd. However, when he had gone to the hill with Rhiannon, he had not been burdened with mail and a heavy cloak. He was gasping for breath as he came up the final rise, but the sight of Rhiannon standing tensely waiting gave him one more burst of strength and he leapt the last ledge and ran toward her.

Rhiannon ran also. They met with such eagerness and so little caution that a most unromantic *ooff* was wrenched from both as they collided. They clung together, off balance, laughing.

"Are you whole, Simon?" Rhiannon asked when she could speak. "Are you safe and whole?"

"Yes, of course. How silly you are. You see me in excellent health."

"Then why are you breathing so hard?"

"If I had a speck of common sense, I would say that your beauty had rendered me breathless, but I am incurably truthful. I must confess it is because mail was not designed to be worn while climbing hills."

"Truthful!" Rhiannon exclaimed, laughing heartily. "You are a monster of deceit. You only tell the truth when you will profit by it."

"That is a gross injustice," Simon complained, dropping his cloak to the ground and fumbling at the lacing of his hood.

"Very well," Rhiannon conceded, pushing away his hands and loosening the ties for him. "Perhaps you also tell the truth when you know a lie would be easily found out." Before he could protest again, she asked. "Shall I take the hauberk off altogether?"

Simon hesitated, sensing some kind of game, but then agreed. He had to bend his knees to make himself short enough for Rhiannon to pull the mail shirt over his head. When he stood up again, the cool breeze of mid-September was like a shower of cold water. He breathed deeply with refreshment, watching Rhiannon fold the heavy steel rings of his mail into a long bundle that could be carried over his shoulder. Now the slight nip in the air became chilly rather than refreshing, and his sweat-wet woolen undertunic lay clammily against his body. Simon dropped to a squat beside Rhiannon where the wind could not be so free with him.

"I love you," he said softly. "You know what I desire before I know it myself. I gave no thought to our meeting. I was too taken up with eagerness to think. Yet if it had not been thus—perfect—it would have cast a shadow."

"Perfect? That we should run into each other like two oafs or wild children. . . ." Her voice faded, and when she spoke again the jesting sharpness had gone out of it. "I did give thought to it."

"Then I am of import to you?"

Rhiannon left the bundle of mail and lifted her eyes. "You know that. I have never tried to deny it."

"You do not care for me as—as a brother? A friend?"

"No, Simon. I desire you as a lover. This, too, you know. Why do you ask?"

"Do you dislike me, Rhiannon?"

She stared at him, utterly perplexed. "I am beginning to think you a little mad. Of course I do not dislike you. If I desire that you be my lover, how could I dislike you?"

"I have desired women that I disliked very much," Simon said. "The two things have little to do with each other."

"Not for me!" Rhiannon exclaimed distastefully.

"You must love where you desire?"

"It seems so—yes," she admitted.

"Then you love me," Simon insisted.

"Yes, but . . ."

"But what?" he asked eagerly. "Rhiannon, tell me."

She dropped her eyes. "I cannot bear to hurt you."

Simon sighed and sat down on the ground, stretching his long legs to ease the pinch of the mail hosen.

"Let me take those off also," Rhiannon suggested.

She reached for the ties that held the hosen up, but Simon caught her hands. "It is ridiculous to say you cannot bear to hurt me and yet refuse to marry me. What can hurt me more than that? Perhaps if you tell me why—"

"I *have* told you why."

"You do not trust me? Or yourself?"

"Both."

But Rhiannon's voice was uncertain. Over the month that Simon had been away, Rhiannon had looked closely into her own heart. She was no callow girl. Many men had paid court to her—for the sake of her beauty, her father's power, the dower he implied he would give with her, perhaps even for the strangeness that had attracted Simon. None had interested her until this man with the leopard's grace and swiftness had struck at her heart. Truth was that she did not think any other man could touch her while Simon lived. It was him she did not trust, not herself.

"Are you so light of purpose?" he asked. "I do not think so. Your father and mother do not think so. I have heard you accused by others of stubbornness, by yourself of carelessness—never of wavering purpose."

"It is so great a thing to hold a heart in one's hands,

not in jest or light words, but truly," Rhiannon murmured. "Even if my purpose never wavered, a moment's carelessness . . ."

"One is not careless about great things," Simon pointed out, "and I am not a fool. Do you think I would break my heart over a smile or a teasing look? I might well grow angry and let you feel my hand, but I would need to know that you loved me no longer before real hurt was done."

"Yes."

The simple admission told the tale completely. "Then it is I you do not trust," Simon went on. "Well, that is a relief."

"A relief?"

He smiled at her. "I can give sureties to you for myself, but how can I give sureties to you for you?" He released her hands and added, "Yes, take off the hosen. They pinch abominably when I bend my knees."

As Rhiannon leaned forward to undo the ties at the back, however, Simon caught her in his arms and kissed her passionately. At first, both ignored the awkward position they were in, but the discomfort grew more and more acute and finally Simon broke the kiss. When the metal leggings were neatly laid atop the folded hauberk, he spread his cloak on the ground and settled down again with Rhiannon leaning against him.

"We could be happy as lovers," she suggested.

Warmed by her kiss and the admissions he had drawn from her, Simon replied, "Perhaps I could be because I trust you. If you say to me you will be mine and mine only, then I will believe you and I will be content. But how would you be happy? I have already said I would be thine alone—and you call me a monster of deceit."

"That was in jest!"

"Then you do not think me a liar in general?"

"Only to women," Rhiannon sighed, and before he could speak again she went on, "I will say this to you, that I will be thine alone while you are mine alone—but no longer."

Simon pulled her closer and tipped her chin up. "With all my heart I will agree to those terms."

He lay back against the cloak, pulling her with him, and he was surprised at how warm it was. The wind still whispered through the trees above the hollow, but it seemed to pass right over them. The sun beat down like a feather-light comforter and the thick grass trapped under Simon's cloak made a resilient mattress. Rhiannon smelled of the sweet grass and the musky earth. Aware, too, of the acrid odor of his tunic. Simon sat up and pulled off the tunic and shirt. Rhiannon sat up too, her eyes wide. She had never seen his body bare.

Seeing her look, Simon was about to ask whether he had offended her, but she put out a hand and stroked his breast. Like his father, Simon was nearly hairless, except for a faint shadow that ran along his breastbone and down to the navel. A thicker shadow descended from below the navel to be lost in the pubic bush, but Rhiannon had not yet been attracted to that. She was examining the dark, satiny skin, distressed to see the lines of knotted white scar tissue here and there.

Simon laughed at her. There were not many marks. He was strong and swift—and lucky. Nonetheless, he was excited by the attention she paid him and by the breeze-soft touch of her fingers sliding over his shoulder. Hardly thinking, he undid her belt and unlaced the neck of her cotte. Rhiannon did nothing to impede him. She scarcely seemed aware of his actions, watching instead the path of her own fingers as they stroked his body. He captured one hand and undid the sleeve, then the other.

That seemed to make an impression. Rhiannon's eyes moved from Simon's body to her own loose sleeves, and she smiled and pulled at the string of his chausses so that the bow came undone. She was aware where they were going now, and raised her eyes to Simon's as she placed her hands on his hips to pull the chausses down. His face was a surprise to her—not the flush that had come up under the dark skin or the lips that were slightly fuller with the turgidity of passion, nor the knitted brows and rigid expression of desire. She had expected his eyes to be bemused, glazed. Instead they met hers fully, alert and demanding.

"Wholly mine, only mine, so long as I am solely thine," he said huskily.

"As you are faithful, so shall I be," she swore.

The oath was sealed by a kiss. If it was not quite the

passionless kiss of peace that usually seals a contract, it
served the purpose equally well. Rhiannon even managed
to slide Simon's chausses down over his narrow hips. He
had reached his cross garters and untied them so that a few
more contortions left him naked. He allowed Rhiannon
to stroke him and examine him while he caressed her face
and throat and hands. It would have been possible to lift
her skirts and deliver more intimate caresses, but it never
occurred to Simon to do so. Such behavior was for common hedge-whores or a serf girl in the fields. Those were
acts of physical relief in which the woman was not a partner but nearly an inanimate vessel.

Although most casual sexual encounters took place out
of doors, Simon had no association of those acts with
what he was doing with Rhiannon. One never bothered to
bare either body for a swift, impersonal coupling like that.
In any case, that was the smallest part of Simon's sexual
experience. He had a strong distaste for low whores and
stinking serf girls. Most of his associations with coupling
were in the dim light of a shuttered room or in the stuffy
darkness of a curtained bed.

To lie with a woman he cared for in the open light of
day was new and thrilling. To do so with Rhiannon was
somehow "right." She was a creature of field and forest;
hall or keep were only temporary shelters for her. Suddenly Simon was washed with urgency—not to take
Rhiannon, but to see her body white and bare, glinting in
the sunshine.

Simon broke the long kiss they had held and lifted
Rhiannon to her knees. Her hands clung to his body, slipping from shoulder to waist to thigh as he raised her more
upright. Gently he disengaged her skirt and lifted her
dress. She had been reluctant to change positions at first,
but now she understood what he wanted and rapidly
pulled off her gown and the simple shift she wore beneath
it. She had been barefoot when she left the house, so there
was nothing else. Simon drew a breath at the strong, lithe
perfection of her body framed by the green, waving brush
behind her.

Now he touched her, stroking berry-brown cheek,
smooth tanned throat, golden satin shoulder, and on down
to the white velvet breast with its warm brown nipple.

Rhiannon sighed, sat back on her heels to let Simon look at her. His admiration and growing eagerness were apparent, but she held back a moment to caress the entirety of his male magnificence with her eyes. While she looked, he cupped her breasts in his hands, stroking the aureola gently with his thumbs. Rhiannon shivered, and her nipples, already upright, thrust forward harder.

With any other woman, Simon would have pulled sharply to make her lie beside him. However, Rhiannon could not be driven or compelled. That knowledge wove through Simon's passion, became part of it, heightened it. He released one breast so that he could lever himself upward until his lips took the place of his fingers. Rhiannon sighed, and her eyes closed. Simon released the other breast and put that arm gently around her, and began to ease himself down again.

As he expected, Rhiannon leaned toward him, following the draw of his lips. When they lay together and he no longer needed to support her, he slid his hand from her waist across her belly and gently, very gently, between her thighs. Rhiannon moaned and twitched, pressed her lips against his hair; her hands fluttered distractedly over his body, seeking, but not certain what.

Simon made no attempt to guide her searching fingers to more erotic zones. Now, this first time for Rhiannon, Simon wanted no spur to his passion. It was impossible for him not to be excited by what he was doing, and Rhiannon's natural response was intensifying that excitement. He tried to draw his mind away, but each thing he fixed on only led back to the strong, silken body pressing itself more and more frantically against him.

A finger slipped between the nether lips. Rhiannon cried out softly and thrust forward. Simon judged her as ready as any virgin could be. For all her eagerness, it was not easy; Simon was a big man. It was very fortunate that he was not a green boy driven by his own desire. The many couplings he had experienced made him able to be slow and patient, penetrating, then pausing to reawaken the desire that pain diminished before he entered her farther. This coupling took a long time, but Simon was young and strong and able to endure—and his patience was rewarded. On the taking of her maidenhead, Rhiannon's lover had the joy of hearing her beautiful voice trill her infinite pleasure.

Simon had felt her climax coming, felt the tremors sweeping through her, her hands clawing blindly at his back. He dropped the walls in his mind to let in the images of her body, her writhing pleasure, his own actions, and he gained an ultimate success in bringing on his own climax so close after hers that he did not need to inflict further pain on her to achieve satisfaction.

Finished, Simon braced himself on his elbows so that his weight would not crush Rhiannon, and waited. Slowly the tilted green eyes opened, the fingers that had clawed at him now tenderly stroked his hair, his neck, drew his head down for a gentle kiss, infinitely sweet.

"I thank you," Rhiannon murmured. "You have given me a gift to treasure for my whole life."

Startled mute, Simon merely stared at her until she tilted her head and looked questioningly at him. Regaining his power of speech, he said, "I swear to you it grows easier and more pleasant each time—"

Rhiannon hugged him so suddenly that his arms gave way and he collapsed on her. She gasped with a mingling of laughter, having had the breath briefly squeezed out of her. "Oh, poor Simon," she exclaimed when she could speak, "did you think I meant I would never make love again? No, dear one, that would be a cruel reward for your gentleness and patience. I only meant that I would remember this for all time with joy. The other times will blend together—it cannot be otherwise—but this I will have forever."

He sighed with relief and slipped off her to the side. "I, too," he assured her.

Rhiannon laughed again. "You, too, what?" she asked. "Surely you do not mean this is your first time of having."

"Not by several thousand times," Simon replied merrily, "although I assure you I have kept no real count and only reckon by the years of such doing. No, you are the first maiden I have ever lain with and will be—God willing—the last."

Rhiannon was surprised. "Am I?"

"Yes, of course," he insisted. "Do you think I am a customary raper of babes or seducer of young girls? Where would I have come by a maiden?"

"Castellans and vassals have daughters," Rhiannon pointed out dryly, wondering why Simon should think her so innocent.

"We do not treat our liegemen so in my family," Simon said angrily. "One does not win loyalty by dishonoring a man's womenfolk."

"What dishonor?" Rhiannon asked, genuinely puzzled.

First Simon gaped, and then laughed. He had forgotten the Welsh custom whereby "the son of the handmaid shall be heir with the son of the free." In Wales there was no illegitimacy with respect to the inheritance of property, and it was reasonable that a vassal would not think it a dishonor if his daughter should be deflowered and conceive a child by his liege lord.

He said, "In England it is a dishonor," and explained.

Rhiannon was somewhat confused by the legal technicalities Simon described. Property rights did not loom very large in her life, for the people of the hills of Gwynedd were essentially hunters and herders rather than farmers. Their nebulous clan right to graze their cattle in a certain rather large area or hunt over several hundred square miles of trackless forest was all they knew. In the southern and eastern parts of Wales—where Norman influence had been strong for over a hundred years and where the terrain was not so difficult—agriculture was advancing and property right was better known. Even there, however, there was much confusion, and inheritance did not always go by primogeniture.

It did not matter that Rhiannon did not understand the actual conditions, however. What she did understand was that Simon did not look at the wives and daughters of his subordinates as potential bedmates. Her father had never forced unwilling women nor meddled with women whose menfolk would object to his action, but many men had thrust their daughters—and sometimes even their wives—at the Lord of Gwynedd. And, when he was younger, Llewelyn had taken freely the ones he fancied. Those women he bedded were acknowledged in his court and accorded honor there.

As Rhiannon thought over what Simon had said, she relaxed more against him and laid her head on his shoulder. Perhaps if he still desired marriage, she would consider it. If what he said was true, at least she would never need to smile and be courteous to her husband's mistresses. The confiding movement touched Simon, and he put his arm around her.

"Are you cold, love?" he whispered.

"No, not cold, but I think we must dress in a few minutes anyway."

"Must we? You are so beautiful and so . . . I do not know exactly how to say what I mean, but you belong here, naked and free." He sighed. "I have never done this before. I think it is much better to lie here under the sky than to be closed inside. You have given me something no other woman could give."

"Why?"

Simon smiled. There was no challenge in the question, only a pleased, slightly flattered curiosity. "Because with any other woman it would be false, an unnatural thing. They belong in their cushioned chairs and their pillowed, scented beds. Only you belong here, with the perfumes of of the warm earth, the crushed grass, and the sweet wind."

For a little while Rhiannon was silent. She was deeply pleased that Simon found something special about her, and she did not doubt his sincerity. Still, her irrepressible sense of mischief could not long be submerged. "But Simon," she said, "if you think it will be unnatural to make love to me in a bed, we are going to find it very inconvenient. You know how often it is rainy for days at a time here, and in the winter when it snows—*ugh*!"

The last guttural sound was not an expression of distaste for making love in the wet, cold snow but an involuntary grunt forced out when Simon flipped over and landed on top of her with a thud.

"Wood nymph!" he exclaimed triumphantly, without difficulty defeating her effort to cast him off. "That is the thing that was in the back of my mind. And it is true, too. You have no heart. Wood nymphs were said to have had no souls and to be very lecherous. That was the purpose of capturing them, I suppose."

This sounded very severe, but since the words were

interspersed with kisses, Rhiannon was scarcely crushed, except by Simon's weight. "Better call me a river nymph," she said in a rather muffled voice, "for if you do not get off me, I will be squashed flat as a rush."

Simon left off kissing her throat and nibbling her ear to murmur, "You do not deny the lechery?"

Ten seconds before, she would have done so. As wonderful as she had found her first mating, Rhiannon simply had not thought of repeating the experience immediately. Now warmth flowed through her from wherever Simon's lips touched, and when she felt the pressure of his hardening shaft against her thigh, a fury of desire seized her. Her breathing went all awry, and her arms went tight around her lover. She no longer felt crushed by his weight and only tightened her grip to hold him when he tried to ease up so he could get a hand to her breast.

Much as she wanted that, Rhiannon desired union more. She embraced Simon fiercely with her legs, a gesture at one and the same time so innocent and so sensual that Simon's practiced control deserted him. He thought no more of a long and delicate foreplay. Straining against the pressure of Rhiannon's embrace, he lifted himself enough to position his shaft and drove into her.

Rhiannon gasped, but when he thrust again she rose to meet him. In a way, Rhiannon was even more excited this time than after Simon's careful manipulation before their first coupling. Now she knew what her prize would be. She knew the rising pressure of pleasure inside her would burst in nearly intolerable spasms of joy. She could focus her attention on that pleasure, build it faster, higher. Her climax was an explosive convulsion that left her limp, hardly conscious of Simon driving toward his own release.

Rhiannon's first coherent thought was guilt for that. "I am sorry," she whispered. "I should not have gone so fast and left you."

Simon lifted his head, which had been resting beside hers while he gathered strength to withdraw from her. He chuckled. "Do not worry about that. A man can always content himself. It is when it happens the other way that it is a disaster."

"Is it not better for you if I . . . help?" Rhiannon asked rather shyly.

"Much better, beloved," Simon assured her, smiling.

He kissed her cheek, her forehead, her determined chin. She was perfect, completely, absolutely perfect. Simon was so much in love with Rhiannon's other qualities that he would have accepted some sexual failings. He had known she was not frigid from her response in the cove near Aber, but her eagerness was more than he had expected and her perception of his need was a real blessing. There would be nothing to teach her except the skills and refinements that prolonged joy.

"But do not trouble yourself about it," he went on. "You have done marvelous well for your first and second lessons. There will be time enough to learn the fine points."

"And I could not have a more experienced teacher, could I?" Rhiannon remarked a little sharply.

"No, you could not, so be properly grateful," Simon responded, laughing. Then he grew serious, sitting up so he could look into her face. "I have sworn I will be faithful in the future. There is no way to change the past. Moreover, you would be a fool to wish it changed. A man without experience always wonders whether there is something he has missed. For me, there have been so many women that I can never doubt I have finally found the *one*. I need seek no further, *eneit*."

Eneit, he had called her—his soul, his inner life—in the old language, and his eyes with their gold and green flecks were clear, hiding nothing. Rhiannon very nearly cried out that she would yield and be his wife, but she could not say the words. Thus far she had been the winner. Simon was her lover, and she had promised no more than she ever intended—to be faithful to him as long as he was faithful to her. But to be a wife. . . . A wife swore faith no matter what her husband did—and could be harshly punished, imprisoned, or killed, if she paid back his false coin with false coin of her own.

CHAPTER 15

For the moment, it was enough for Simon that Rhiannon had sworn to be faithful. It would not take long, he was sure, before her mother and father convinced her—without saying a word on the subject, perhaps—that she should marry him. It was possible she would hold out until she got with child, but then she would yield. She would not want any question to be raised about her child's right to the father's possessions, now that she knew the English law.

Sitting upright as he was, the wind caught him. He shivered and started to lie down, but Rhiannon shook her head and sat up also. "Get dressed," she said, handing him his shirt and tunic. "I am sorry to be so unromantic, Simon, but—forgive me, dear heart—I am hungry."

He sprang to his feet, laughing, then pulled her up and embraced her. "There are no sweeter words you could have said to me than those. There is a time for love words and they are food for the soul then, but when the belly calls it is a rare woman who has the courage to say so. I am hungry also. Your mother said something about eating, but at that time I had only a hunger to see you."

"And now that that is satisfied, the other calls more strongly."

Simon yanked his tunic down to look at her, but she was grinning like an imp. There had been no spite or blame in the remark, only a confirmation that she felt the same way. They finished dressing hastily and Simon hoisted his armor to his shoulder. It was a devil of a load, he grumbled, but Rhiannon only said heartlessly that he was lucky their way home led downhill, and it was not her fault he was such an idiot as to rush up the hill fully armed. This drew some sharp reminders from Simon about times when Rhiannon had not been very foresighted, so they arrived at the hall sparring with words and laughing as merrily as on Simon's first visit.

Kicva said only that those who came late to dinner could eat cold meat, standing. However, she would have kissed Simon's feet for making her daughter's entry into womanhood a warm blessing, had she been that kind of person. There was nothing in Rhiannon's railing words to betray her, but something in her voice and the glow of her eyes was proof enough to her mother, who knew her so well. Simon's look was more transparent. The line of his mouth, the sated droop of his eyelids. . . . Kicva laughed as he bowed and made a formal apology for being late to dinner. He looked like Math after a night out.

"Well, I will forgive you," Kicva said in reply to Simon's excuses, and she signaled a servant who brought forward a small table. Others carried in ready-laden trays and drew up chairs. Then in answer to Rhiannon's raised brows she said, "I am not abating my severity for this scapegrace's glib tongue but because he brought a letter from Llewelyn that needs consideration by all of us."

Simon blinked. He had not expected so direct an attack nor so soon. However, he realized instantly that Kicva had no choice but to mention the letter at once. He began to soak pieces of bread in a bowl of ragout and scoop it hungrily into his mouth. Rhiannon, he knew, had cast a suspicious glance at him, but he paid no attention. He would follow Kicva's lead.

She said, "Did Simon have a chance to tell you how the affair between Pembroke and the king was ended—if it has ended?"

Rhiannon blushed. Simon choked. There was not the slightest change of expression on Kicva's face, although she made a small gesture of the hand that implied her daughter and Simon should not be fools.

"Ah, well," she continued indulgently, "you are young. Stop stuffing your face for a moment, Simon, and tell us now."

"It will take more than a moment," Simon said indignantly, his mouth full of food.

"I do not desire a blow-by-blow description of each battle, only an overall picture of the terms of the truce."

Simon chewed and swallowed and embarked on a summary from which Kicva picked the salient points.

"Yes, indeed," she said, "I see very clearly why Llewelyn is so disturbed. If the king holds by his word with Pembroke, he can use the large force both have amassed to attack Wales."

"No!" Simon exclaimed, almost choking on a new mouthful of food. "Richard would never agree."

"He might argue against it," Kicva said, "but what could he do? Turn rebel again? He has sworn no oath to Llewelyn; they have no formal agreement that forbids the one to make peace without the other, or that forbids one to attack the other. What excuse could Pembroke make to refuse the king's demand?"

"You are right so far as that goes," Simon was forced to admit, "but if the king makes peace with Richard, there would be no reason to attack Wales."

"A reason could be found if it would make the barons forget why Pembroke had rebelled in the first place. Perhaps you do not realize, Simon, that once the raiders are loose it is most difficult to recall them. When the army withdraws, they may well turn their attentions to the border farms as is their custom. Would this not be an excuse?"

Simon hissed angrily between his teeth. He had foreseen any number of results of the truce, but not this one. After a moment, however, he shrugged. "It would not work; at least, I do not believe it would. Richard will most likely demand that Winchester and Rivaulx and Seagrave be dismissed before—"

"Before what?" Rhiannon interrupted. "You say Pembroke will have to be charged and cleared before a sitting of his peers. Then I suppose he would need to bring charges against Winchester and his friends. God knows how long that would take. Meanwhile, there is nothing to stop Winchester from convincing everyone that the most important business at hand is to curb the Welsh, since the king and his chief vassal are at peace. Is that impossible?"

Scowling, Simon was about to argue further, and then he saw the gleam of satisfaction and warning in Kicva's eyes. "I suppose it is not impossible," he said. "The Welsh and the Scots are often used as scapegoats. Agreed that there is raiding and that is a constant irritation, still it *is* often internal politics rather than any real fault in England's neighbors that begins a war."

"And even if it is not the first likelihood," Kicva put in, "Llewelyn does not wish to be caught unprepared. He would like to have an emissary—an unofficial emissary—who would plead his case."

First Simon felt betrayed. However, even as Kicva explained Llewelyn's notion that his daughter should serve this purpose, Simon saw the plan—neat, efficient, and accomplishing three purposes at once.

Rhiannon saw only half. Since she had no reason to think of the close tie Simon's family had with the king, she did not associate her father's wish that she be his ambassador with marriage. "But I have no way to reach the king," she protested, "and even if I did. . . ." A quick glance flashed at Simon and then away. "No, I cannot. I could cause more trouble than good. I cannot offer what most women who serve such a purpose provide, and I have no bond of blood to protect me from such a suggestion. If I should be asked and refuse—"

"Rhiannon!" Kicva exclaimed. "Your father is no panderer and, even if he was, he is not a fool. He knows well enough that tact is not your greatest virtue, and he has devised a way to protect you from the king and open a path to him at one and the same time. Simon's brother-by-marriage is cousin to the king—"

Kicva broke off as Rhiannon jumped to her feet with blazing eyes, but Simon had guessed what would happen and was also on his feet, holding up a hand.

"I did not know, I swear it," he said. "I did know Prince Llewelyn intended to write his approval of our union to your mother and propose it to my father, but I knew nothing of this other matter. There is no use being angry with *me,* Rhiannon. You have known that I desired marriage from our first meeting. I never lied to you, and I never changed."

"You still desire marriage?"

"You know that I do, and that I will strive forward toward that goal until I achieve it or I am dead."

Rhiannon's eyes met Simon's challengingly. It was entirely possible what he said was true, and all the more reason *not* to marry him. When he had gained his prize and she was his, the game, the purpose of being faithful would be ended. Simon's lips tightened at what he read in

Rhiannon's face, but Kicva's cool voice came between them.

"There is a middle way that will answer all purposes," she suggested. "Llewelyn would assume that Lord Ian will approve this proposal, yet it would be courteous and natural to show him the bride chosen for his son. It would thus be reasonable that you and Simon be betrothed and that he take you to see his parents."

"Yes, and that would be an easy door to the king also," Simon added. "I am not Henry's vassal and may marry in Wales without his yea-say, but my father *is* his vassal, and in England a son's marriage needs the king's approval. Henry would be very pleased if I brought my bride to him—"

"And if he took a fancy to her?" Rhiannon interrupted.

"Oh, no!" Simon was shocked and showed it. "Not Henry! There is nothing of King John in him in that way."

"He is free enough with his men's rights in other ways," Kicva remarked. "Why not in this? Does he not desire women?"

"He likes women well enough," Simon replied, "but he is no lecher. As to why he would not cast his eyes on Rhiannon, there are several reasons, but the most important is that family is sacred to Henry. Rhiannon will be Geoffrey's sister-by-marriage and as inviolate to Henry as his own sister, I assure you. Even if you were deliberately to try to provoke his lust, I do not think he would take you—unless he were too drunk to know what he was doing or otherwise out of his senses. He would be more likely to warn Geoffrey or myself of your lewd nature."

"Then you think this mad plan of my father's has worth? Or is it only a way of forcing me into a contract with you?"

"Do not be an idiot, Rhiannon," Simon said with exasperation. "Or, at least, credit that I am not one. The last way to convince you into marriage is by force." Then he frowned thoughtfully. "As to your father's plan, I do think it has worth. Prince Llewelyn knows Henry. They have met several times and your father is a keen reader of men. Anyhow, he would never force you into something to further my purpose; therefore, he believes you are the best emissary he could find."

This was too reasonable for Rhiannon to dispute. In fact, she realized as soon as the anger of suspicion dissipated that her father's encouragement of Simon's suit from the beginning was more political than affectionate. Surely Llewelyn would be glad if she and Simon were happy, but he was more interested in settling her cheaply with a man who could never use her blood as a threat.

Yes, Rhiannon could see all the reasons now, and the additional advantage of a new pathway to the king's ear would make the marriage very advantageous. But marriage had not been her intention, ever. Yet her father had always been kind, and if her marriage would aid Gwynedd. . . . She loved her people and her hills and forests. Perhaps her mother's way was a solution. A betrothal could last many years, not coming to fruition for this reason or that, and at worst it could be broken . . . and Simon was so eager for it.

Rhiannon put out her slender hand, and Simon grasped it so hard he hurt her fingers. "I will agree to a betrothal," she said, "if the contract is made here in Wales."

"Of course," Simon concurred. "It would not be fitting for you to travel with me to England without a betrothal, but it will also be a surety for you, *eneit*. If you find me not to your taste, I swear I will ask my father to discover some fault with the contract so that it may be broken."

Rhiannon laughed at him. "Oh, what a cocksure popinjay you are! It would serve you right if I demanded my freedom just to put you in your place."

"Of all idiocies, cutting off one's nose to spite one's face is the worst," Simon said complacently.

"I have heard more modest statements than that in my life," Kicva commented dryly.

"Is not honesty the best policy?" Simon rejoined provocatively.

Rhiannon held her head. "Is this what you wish me to marry, Mother? Do you really desire that I spend my whole life with a man who believes himself God's gift to womankind?"

"I have always known that to err brings punishment." Kicva shook her head and smiled as she rose to her feet. "It was a mistake to open my mouth and thrust myself between you two. I have been battered enough. Now, before this grain of wheat is ground to flour between the upper and nether millstones, I will slip away. I leave you to the fate you have sought, Simon, and you to the one you deserve, my dear daughter."

"She means," Simon said, opening his eyes wide to manufacture an expression of surprised wonder, "that both of us will be blessed by great happiness."

"I know her better," Rhiannon remarked. "She thinks the fool will gain a shrew to wife—which will not improve either of them."

But both knew better than they spoke, and Rhiannon did not draw her hand from Simon's. Nor did she even look doubtful when her mother bade a servant fetch her writing desk and set it on a stand by a window. Since it was clear that Kicva meant to write and tell Llewelyn his plan had succeeded so far as a betrothal, Simon was quite content. He leaned forward and kissed Rhiannon briefly, then released her hand. Without more ado, both began eating again.

After a few minutes and a glance at her mother, Rhiannon asked, "What is your family, Simon?"

Between bites Simon began to describe his relatives, but Rhiannon soon shook her head. She had asked a stupid question to begin with. No matter what Simon told her, she would not really know his family until she met them. She said this aloud and Simon smiled.

"True enough, and you will see them differently than I do, but one thing I can swear to you, Rhiannon. They love me and will desire to love you most eagerly. They will not look for faults in you, *eneit,* but only for good."

"I do not fear," Rhiannon said and smiled. "The worst that can befall is that they will oppose our marriage. Well, that will not displease me! They could not oppose it more than I. No one will care that you are my lover. I may be strange and uncouth, but I am well enough bred."

To her surprise, Simon did not look at all taken aback by this statement. His eyes glittered green and gold with laughter. If anything in the world could convince Rhiannon to marry him before the need to provide for a male child pushed her into it, the family at Roselynde would do it. He had many joys in her agreement to the betrothal, but a reason to get her to Roselynde was one of the greatest. Simon had infinite faith in the womenfolk of his family. He was quite certain that they would deliver his love to him, not only bound but content to stay so.

It would be unwise to say what he thought, but Simon knew Rhiannon had seen his impulse to laugh and he had to say something. "They will not find you uncouth, my love. Exotic, perhaps, but that will do you no harm. And if you can set one of your wild tales into French, my mother will think the sun rises and sets on you. She and Gilliane are great ones for a tale of romance."

"I will do it gladly." Rhiannon's eyes grew bright with pleasure. "Do you really think they will like my songs?"

"Eneit, they will take you away from me completely for the sake of those songs if I allow it. Geoffrey will want you to teach him every note. He is a fine player of the lute and sings most sweetly himself. My father will hang on every word, remembering the joys of his youth, and the children will keep you at it from dawn until they are driven to their beds. They are never done pestering my father to tell them tales of giants and magic in Wales."

However uncaring of disapproval a person may claim to be, it was pleasing and reassuring for Rhiannon to believe that she had a shield against criticism. Although she would never have admitted she wished to be liked and accepted by Simon's family, the key to their regard that he had given relaxed her. Roselynde ceased to loom so large in her mind that it obscured all else. She began to ask questions concerning the greater purpose behind their betrothal, questions about the king and the court.

It was a theme to which Rhiannon returned again and again. Simon, who had initially given little or no thought to what she could accomplish, began to recast his ideas. Over the next few days Rhiannon extracted from him a wealth of information that he did not even know he possessed and had designed several tentative plans to ingratiate herself with the king.

"You know," she said thoughtfully one afternoon as they lay together in the woods, "even if the peace is broken and my father makes common cause with Pembroke, Henry will probably not blame me—a mere woman. And if he likes me and I interest him—not as a woman, of course, but as an entertainer—I could be useful when the terms of peace are made even in future times."

Simon turned a little more toward her and pressed his face into the hollow of her throat. He did not wish her to see the amusement and delight in his eyes. Rhiannon knew that her presence in the English court presupposed a bond with his family, and, more and more, she spoke in the long term as if their being together was a natural thing. This had to mean marriage. Simon was far too wise to bring this to her attention yet. Let her mire herself in the quicksand farther. Then he would think of some good, pride-salving reason—and he would have her.

She stroked his head idly as he kissed her neck, not aroused by his caress because they had just finished making love a little while before; also, her attention was on a serious subject. Simon did not feel rejected. He was quite accustomed to women who regarded sex just as men did —a great joy and pleasure but only when more important matters did not supervene. He rolled to his back again, agreed with what she had said, and contemplated with extreme satisfaction the small forest glade in which they lay.

There was, of course, no way for them to be together inside the hall. Simon slept in the common room with all the men, and Rhiannon slept in the women's quarters, so they had not yet made love in a bed. There were plenty of other places, though, even when it rained, like the shepherd's hut where they had spent all of the preceding afternoon. The fleeces, with their sweet, oily odor, had made a softer bed than Simon's cloak over a heap of pine needles, but he still preferred the open, whether it was the hay-scented hillside in the sun or this odorous, mysterious hollow under the great, silent trees.

"How long will I have to make a friendship with the king if I can manage to do so?" Rhiannon askd after a few minutes of contemplative silence.

"The conference is called for the Sunday after Michaelmas. If anything is to be accomplished, it must be before then, of course, but—" He jerked upright. "I have been too much bemused by your sweetness, Rhiannon. The truth is that we have very little time indeed—if we are not already too late. Winchester would have begun at once to rave of the depredations of the Welsh and the need to bring us to heel if he intended to use that device. We should have had the contract written at once—but I did not know what to put in it. No, that is only an excuse. I thought only of being here with you."

Rhiannon sat up also, but she was smiling slightly. "I do not think your bemusement will have caused any delay. My father's wits are not so lightly beclouded, and I am sure he is as aware of the need for haste as you. Did you not notice how swiftly my mother went to reply to him?"

"I thought that was to keep you from changing your mind."

"I am not much given to changing my mind," Rhiannon said, but there was no sharpness in the words, and she leaned closer to kiss Simon's shoulder.

He did not need more invitation and soon they were coupled again, working more slowly and sweetly—as was usual for the second time—toward a rich flowering of satisfaction. Nonetheless, as soon as they had caught their breaths, Simon and Rhiannon rose and dressed. They knew the sweet idyll was ended. They would not enjoy their love less in the future, but in these few days the love had come first.

It was as if they had wandered over hillsides and forest-land, examining sections of the countryside to find those that would best serve as a backdrop for their passion. Henceforward other things would come first. Love would bring surcease from worry and tension, would sweeten life and make islands of joy, but they would no longer see the shape of the land only in terms of love.

After dressing they went back to Angharad's Hall. On the way they decided that it would be best to go to Llewelyn so that they would be ready for whatever he decided was best. Neither was very pleased with this notion. It would be difficult at best and impossible at worst to find any privacy for themselves, but each knew there was plenty of time for them to pleasure each other. The political problems in which they would be involved could not wait.

Just as they entered the gate, Math stalked up, spat viciously at Rhiannon, and ran his claws into Simon's leg. Both were too shocked to cry out, and stood staring, first at Math and then at each other, in blank amazement.

Rhiannon had wondered after she and Simon became lovers whether Math would be jealous. He had given no sign of it, seemingly as affectionate to Simon as ever.

But now Math had stalked ill-naturedly out toward the woods. Since standing and staring at each other could not produce any answer, they continued on into the hall. Here they found the solution. Kicva rose from her knees beside a long wicker traveling basket as they entered.

"So that was why!" Rhiannon cried, and burst out laughing.

"Why?" Simon echoed.

"Math saw Mother packing my things. He is always furious when I go away." She laughed up at Simon. "Somehow he must know it is something to do with you. That is why you were punished worse. Sometimes I wonder if that cat *is* altogether of this world. He has always ignored my other suitors. Could it be that he smelled I was attracted to you and thought you would keep me from leaving?"

"I see that we are going," Simon said, smiling at Kicva, "but I hope it is not any trespass that has decided you to drive us out."

Kicva laughed at him. There had been a faint note of inquiry under his jesting remark. Simon had been certain Kicva knew and approved of his relationship with Rhiannon, but seeing her packing her daughter's things had worried him because, until she had laughed at his remark, she had looked rather stern and sad.

"Only a need for haste. The betrothal contracts came from Llewelyn this morning, together with a gift for Henry and letters for you and me. Llewelyn is very eager for you to go to Roselynde with all speed. You had better read your letter and decide whether matters are so urgent that you should leave as soon as packing can be finished, or whether you can stay until morning."

Simon was cracking the seal as she spoke, and his eyes skimmed over greetings and formalities down into the meat of the message. In a few minutes he looked up. "There is no order here for me, only an explanation of some matters in the contracts and a message to my father, but if you are willing, Rhiannon, I would like to go as soon as you can be ready. I have a feeling that your father would not have sent the contracts here if he did not think that even one day might be of importance. If time were not of the essence, he would have bade us come to him."

"So do I think also," Kicva said gravely.

"Then I am ready now," Rhiannon stated.

"At least put on your riding boots, beloved," Simon suggested with a grin.

Rhiannon wrinkled her nose at him for his teasing, but did not delay to reply to it. She went to attend to her own packing, and Kicva began to assemble Simon's belongings while he returned to the courtyard to tell his men to bring in the horses and collect their gear. They ate an early meal and Simon donned his armor. But when Rhiannon was seeing to the loading of the pack animals, he went to say a private farewell to Kicva. He found her, for once idle, sitting empty-handed before her empty loom. Simon stopped short, staring in amazement.

To his memory it had always held a marvel of beauty, the leaf-green cloth with its interlacing trees on which perched a myriad of birds, all glittering so that they seemed to be in constant motion. He did not remember until that moment that the loom had been empty when he arrived for his first visit. Kicva had strung it the next day, and by the time he had taken Rhiannon to Dinas Emrys enough of the fabric had been woven to show the design.

"Where——" he began.

"It is for Rhiannon's wedding gown," Kicva said, looking past him. "It is packed in the basket." Then she brought her eyes to him and smiled. "I had the weaving of it. Let it be your mother, Simon, who has the cutting and sewing of it. Thus we will share in the decking of the bride."

"Will you not come to our wedding, Kicva?" Simon asked anxiously.

"Perhaps. That is as the future will decide. But it does not matter. I have seen your joining, and it was good. I am grateful to you, Simon."

"And I to you, Kicva, for you made—and I do not mean by breeding only—a daughter that could give meaning to the word woman and to my whole life."

CHAPTER 16

Math refused to go with them. He came out of the forest when Rhiannon called, but only to spit at her and stalk haughtily past his traveling basket. That meant he did not choose to go. Rhiannon would miss him; nonetheless, she was glad. He would not have been happy, she thought, on so long a journey with a host of unfamiliarities at the end of it.

They spent that night at Dinas Emrys. For reasons of her own, Rhiannon did not wish to share Simon's bed that night. She slept, if she slept at all, wrapped in her cloak on the walls. Simon watched beside her, dozing sometimes, while she listened to the voices in the wind. She never told him what she heard, but it was something that sent them forth before the dawn with increased urgency. Long after dark they came to Krogen, exhausted, the horses stumbling with weariness—except Ymlladd, of course, who bit the incautious groom for judging his condition by that of the other animals.

Simon and Rhiannon shared a bed that night, but they did not make love in it. Hardy as she was, Rhiannon was too quickly asleep to think of it, and Simon was tired enough himself that he was content just to have her beside him. The withdrawal at Dinas Emrys had frightened him at first, but later he understood that Rhiannon had made no attempt to exclude him from her communion with whatever lived there. He did not understand it as well as she, but he never felt personal threat from it, and Rhiannon seemed even more eager for the journey. Thus, he was content, not needing to claim and reclaim what was surely his.

They rode out of Krogen with a full troop, Siorl in command. When Rhiannon protested in surprise, Simon told her the tale of Sybelle and the raiders. He assured her he would try to avoid any area under contest, but such activity had a habit of spreading, and he did not wish to be caught unprepared. Although Simon was technically neutral in the quarrel between Pembroke and the king because his overlord was neutral, many things could happen to him—and more especially to Rhiannon—before that neutrality was established. Over the three days it took them to reach Roselynde, Rhiannon saw that Simon had been right. They had no trouble, but only because they were too strong to be attacked with impunity.

Rhiannon was stunned by the immensity of Roselynde keep. Some of her father's fortresses were very strong, but none were like Roselynde. "I will get lost," she cried.

Simon laughed at her. "It is very simple, really, but there will be guides enough—if you are not jesting."

"As to getting lost—yes," she answered, "but . . . it is too large, Simon. It has driven away the woods and the wild things, and the walls are steeped in blood. This is not a refuge but a threat to all who come this way. I could not live here."

"No, *eneit,* no. It does not come to me," he soothed as they rode up the steep path to the main gate. "The blood you sense is very old. The threat is only against those who come with hatred and evil in *their* hearts. There has been peace and love in Roselynde for near a hundred years."

She said no more, but her eyes were very large and her breath quicker than natural as they fronted the drawbridge. Ymlladd stepped on it without hesitation, but Rhiannon's graceful mare, Cyflym, balked and danced. Simon backed his horse and held out his hand. He knew the bridge was sound and steady as rock. It could only be Rhiannon's fear that caused her mount to refuse.

"Inside there is love," Simon said.

Rhiannon took his hand and they went forward together. At the first shouts of happy greeting from the men on the walls and the watchtowers, the tension in her fingers began to relax. She could not understand what they said, for they shouted in English and Simon replied in that tongue, but no one could mistake the tone. It was in the servants' voices too, in the grooms who came to take the horses, in the men and women who broke away from their tasks to welcome home a son of the house with whom they were not afraid to laugh and joke.

By the time Simon had greeted Knud, who had taken

Beorn's place as master-at-arms when the old man died, Rhiannon was standing at ease, looking curiously around at the activities of the inner bailey. It was not really so much different from the keeps in Wales. Here, too, the kitchens crouched against the wall of the inner keep close by the door of the forebuilding. She had noticed the grooms leading the horses around to the back, so there must be some stables there, although the pens for the cattle and other stables had been in the outer bailey. Off to the side, opposite the kitchen shed, were other sheds plainly used for storage.

Men and women moved about purposefully but without hurry. All seemed to be well fed, better fed, perhaps, than her father's servants. Their faces, although broad and fair instead of dark and narrow, had the same look about the eyes as her mother's servants. Simon had told the truth. Whatever threat Roselynde keep posed against intruders, those inside were, for the most part, content with their lot.

Knud had advanced on Siorl and began to discuss in broken French-English where to house Simon's men. Siorl replied in even more fractured French-Welsh. Simon grinned, but left them to solve the problem. "They are a little crowded," he explained to Rhiannon, "because everyone is here. We were wise to ride so hard. We have only just caught them before they left for Oxford. Usk is to be returned to Pembroke on the twenty-third. There has been a family conference on what to do if the king will not keep his word."

Rhiannon began to look a trifle apprehensive again, but Simon did not notice it in the joy of coming home. She was a step or two behind him when he was enveloped in a warm embrace by a man who came hurriedly out of the forebuilding. Rhiannon knew him at once, although many years had passed since she had seen him, and the lines of his face had blurred with age. This was Lord Ian.

"You cannot imagine my joy when I received Llewelyn's proposal," he said to his son. "I never imagined he would consider you for his daughter. I have written my approval, of course, and also a request that you should be sent home—but I did not expect you so soon. My messenger only went out the day before yesterday. But come in, Simon, come in."

"Are you well, Papa?" Simon asked.

They were the first words he had been permitted to say, and Rhiannon was startled at the intensity and anxiety in them. She looked more intently at Lord Ian. He was not young, but he had moved almost as gracefully as Simon. He was hard and fit and showed no sign of illness, except. . . . Perhaps the husky breathlessness of his voice was not all hurry. Nonetheless, he laughed at Simon's question and waved it away.

The gesture, taking his eyes from Simon for a moment, made him aware of Rhiannon. He stopped all movement and stared at her, his face softening into gentleness. "Forgive me," he said. "I was so surprised to see Simon that I did not notice you, my dear. You are Lady Rhiannon. I would never have known you. How good and kind of you to come. Be welcome. Be very welcome."

There was such warmth in him that the simple words were infused with deeper meaning. Without thinking, Rhiannon put her hand in Ian's and stepped forward to kiss him on the cheek. He circled her waist with his free arm and pressed his lips to her forehead, murmuring, "Be welcome, Daughter."

"I do not know how he does it," Simon cried laughing. "Papa, you should be ashamed. You are sixty years old, and still no woman can resist you."

"Hold your tongue, you impertinent boy," Ian said. "If she resists you, you deserve it."

"Indeed, he does," Rhiannon agreed, remaining comfortably in the circle of Ian's arm. "I am sure you never preened yourself like a cock on a dung heap, Lord Ian. You should hear your son."

"I would like to, but owing to our prior knowledge of him he is very modest with us." Ian looked at Simon with mock disfavor. "I do not doubt you speak the truth, Simon. I have never known you to lie. But your lack of wisdom shocks me. Is that how I taught you to woo a woman?"

"No, but it works quite well with a thistle," Simon said cheerfully. "When the thistle is heated, it unfolds, you know, and one can grasp its soft heart without being stung."

"I mark that match a draw and call a brief truce," Ian stated, holding his hand like a referee judging a bout of fencing. "Now let us go in before a new engagement begins. Your mother will be delighted, Simon. I could tell her nothing of Lady Rhiannon, only having seen her as a child. Alinor has been imagining that you took advantage of some poor, shy, innocent maiden who normally hid herself in the dark corners of the women's hall."

He led them in, retaining his grip on Rhiannon as if he realized that the clan gathered in Roselynde would be somewhat overwhelming to a stranger. As he introduced her around, her eyes grew larger and larger. Although she teased Simon about his lack of modesty, she was well aware that he was not nearly as vain as he might have been, considering his really astonishing beauty of face and form. Now she knew why.

Rhiannon was called a beauty, but here she felt like an ugly duckling. Alinor was old; nonetheless the bones of her face showed beautiful still, and her eyes were like Simon's, filled with dancing lights of gold and green. Gilliane, Joanna, and Sybelle were breathtaking, the first darkly glowing, the second a blazing flame, and the youngest golden and perfect as the sun.

Of the men, Simon was perhaps now the most beautiful because of Ian's age, but Adam was not far behind. He was more massive than Simon, like a great wall, except that he emanated the same feeling of leashed power. He was as handsome as Alinor must have been beautiful when she was young, and he, too, had her eyes. Rhiannon's gaze rested on Geoffrey, and she felt a marked sense of kinship. He was the only one who was not a model for some god. His lips twitched with amusement and understanding, and his eyes glowed golden.

"Do not let it trouble you," he murmured in her ear. "They do not even realize what they do to people all together like this."

But it was not only the beauty, it was the warmth of welcome that troubled Rhiannon. They were really overjoyed; she was thanked again and again for making so long and hard a journey so that her bethrothed's parents could come to know her. Color rose in Rhiannon's face. She had expected to be greeted politely, perhaps even with a slightly veiled hostility or with tepid approval. This open, eager, warm-hearted welcome was very pleasant but somewhat disconcerting. It made her feel guilty.

"But it was not for that I came," she blurted out. "My father wishes me to meet King Henry and, if there should be a threat to Gwynedd, to try to divert him from that purpose."

There was a moment of startled silence, broken by Simon's laughter. "She is not yet perfected in diplomacy," he chortled.

Rhiannon turned on him. "One is not double-tongued with those who offer love," she snapped. "I can say sweet enough words when there is falseness in the air."

"Thank you, my love," Simon rejoined with dancing eyes. "Now do I better understand why you lash me with your tongue."

"If she does it for love, you are more fortunate than you deserve," Alinor said, pleased by Rhiannon's honesty and totally delighted by Simon's obvious adoration. "Your father would never lay the rod on you as you merited. Perhaps Lady Rhiannon will tame you before you destroy yourself."

"Mama, if Papa had whipped me as I deserved, I would be dead," Simon teased.

"Certainly," Alinor agreed cordially, "but for once you seem to have done something right. Come, Lady Rhiannon, sit down beside me and explain what it is Lord Llewelyn fears."

"You do not need to call me 'lady.' Rhiannon alone is enough, Lady Alinor," Rhiannon said, coming forward and sitting on a stool hastily vacated by Joanna's youngest daughter.

She was immediately more comfortable because of Alinor's calm acceptance of and interest in what she had exposed. Beginning to explain, she was interrupted by eager questions. Some she answered, some she looked to Simon to answer. One at least, was unanswerable.

"So you do not know whether Llewelyn really has

reason to believe that Henry intends to make peace with Pembroke, or is only blocking every mousehole in his usual way," Geoffrey said.

"I think it must be the latter," Rhiannon replied. "Since the Earl of Chester died, he has no source really close to the king except Lord Ian."

"I agree," Simon said. "It was more likely that he just saw a way to solve several problems at once."

As he went on to explain how he had reasoned out Llewellyn's intentions, Rhiannon realized she had been accepted, absorbed—just as simply as that. She was now a part of this family. Simon was presently the focus of questions and attention, and there was time to watch the interactions. It was fascinating to her that the women were as interested and as involved in the discussion as the men. It was very different from her father's court. Lady Joan had been included in the political talk when relations with England were concerned, but that was an exception.

Of course, Rhiannon admitted to herself, she had never tried to be included. She had never had any interest in affairs of state, aside from discovering whether there would be any danger to Angharad's Hall. She wondered what her father's reaction would have been had she wished to be involved. But it did not matter. Rhiannon knew that her interest would fade again when the matter did not concern her directly. There was a more important aspect to it, however. These women who spoke and listened so eagerly might not run wild on the hills, but they were also free. It was in their voices and the bearing of their bodies and in the bright intelligence in their eyes. Then she saw the look Gilliane turned on her husband, and Rhiannon's throat tightened. They were not free, these women; they were enslaved as only a woman who had given her heart can be enslaved.

Adam had growled that it was a mistake to let the matter hang unsettled. "It is not enough that peace should be made between Pembroke and the king unless it is also made clear that Henry will no longer rule by decree. It would be better to continue the war, and I will say so and offer my support to Pembroke rather than see Henry discard Magna Carta."

Rhiannon saw terror flash in Gilliane's dark eyes, but

she lowered them to a small piece of work in her lap and her voice was clear, sweet, and steady. "But Adam, there are better ways to make a man see reason than by beating him to death. From what Papa Ian has told us, it is Winchester who is at the root of the trouble. If Henry can be convinced that Peter des Roches is leading him wrongly, he will mend his ways without adding to the bitterness between him and his barons."

"It took near twenty years to prove to him that de Burgh was wrong," Adam remarked impatiently. "I do not care to contemplate twenty years of Winchester's rule."

"That is not fair," Geoffrey pointed out. "I felt as most others did, that de Burgh had grown too mighty and that he dropped too much into his own purse. But mostly his rule was wise, and he certainly never bade the king cast aside the advice of his council."

"He worked in other ways," Alinor commented sardonically.

"Henry was furious with Winchester over the debacle at Usk," Joanna said thoughtfully. "But the bishop may have talked the king around already. It is unfortunate that Rhiannon and Simon were not here sooner."

"How could they have come sooner?" Ian protested, leaning forward to pat Rhiannon's shoulder protectively. "Simon needed to go to Llewelyn first. Then, it is slow traveling through the hills of Wales."

"I am not blaming Rhiannon, Ian," Joanna assured him, smiling. "It was the same as if I said, 'It is too bad it is raining.' But it *is* too bad. If we could have presented her sooner, she could have said this and that to remind Henry that Winchester led him wrong in Wales."

"Wait, now," Simon said. "I do not mind being a cat's-paw myself in a good cause, but I do not think I like the idea of Rhiannon incurring Henry's wrath—and I do not think that was what Prince Llewelyn intended."

"Nor is it what Joanna intended either." Gilliane's silken soothing voice somehow smothered Joanna's indignant retort. "To the contrary, Rhiannon's theme must have been of Llewelyn's regard for Henry—they are, after all, related by marriage—and of his regret that bad management and bad advice had caused the king's discomfiture. She could have said, with perfect truth, that foreign mercenaries are useless in Wales. It was Winchester who proposed the use of mercenaries, was it not, Adam?"

"Yes, it was." Adam's bright eyes fixed on Rhiannon.

"Yes, and I could say—also with perfect truth—that my father even dangled me as bait to keep the young bucks at court and prevent them from raiding. Only, of course, once Henry crossed onto Welsh lands, nothing would hold them back."

Alinor *tsked* with irritation. "You could have indeed, but it is too late. Winchester has had ten days and more to explain his failure and blame it elsewhere."

"Yes," Geoffrey sighed, "and I fear that Llewelyn is not so far off in his guesses as I would like. If the truce with Pembroke is allowed to stand, blame must be fixed elsewere. Still, all is not lost, and here, too, Llewelyn has seen most clearly. A girl like Rhiannon, speaking gently, is the most likely to make Winchester's advice less palatable if he tries to rouse Henry against the Welsh."

"There will be no trouble presenting her to the king, but she must be able to catch and hold his attention also," Joanna pointed out.

"She can do that," Simon said eagerly, "and just in the right way so that Henry will be often reminded she is Welsh but with no ill flavor. *Eneit,* where is your harp?"

"I packed it," Rhiannon assured him, "but where it is now I have no idea. The servants took the baggage in, I suppose—"

She broke off as Alinor rose to her feet with an exclamation. "Poor child," she went on, "you must think us monsters. We have not offered you even a cup of wine or a chance to take off those dusty clothes. You must forgive us. We are all so deep in this problem that we can think of nothing else. Come above with me, and we will find your clothing and anything else you want." Alinor gestured, and Joanna and Gilliane, who had also started to rise, sat back. Mama wishes to speak to Rhiannon alone, each thought.

In her concentration on the people she had met, Rhiannon had paid scant attention to her surroundings. It was only when she was led into the chamber that had been Joanna's, and now was Sybelle's, that she really saw the luxury with which those in Roselynde surrounded themselves. There was a rich carpet on the floor, tapestries kept the damp of the walls from invading the room, and beside the hearth stood chairs with backs and arms rather than stools or benches; what was more, every chair was richly cushioned. There were wall holders for torches, but the walls and tapestries near them were free of soot. Torches had not been used in a long time. The many-branched candle holders of intricate design showed that a better, cleaner kind of lighting was used here, regardless of the cost of candles.

"You will share with Sybelle—if you wish," Alinor said. She read the startled expression on Rhiannon's face and one question was answered. She had expected to sleep with Simon. Alinor smiled. "No one will stop you from walking down the stairs, my dear, but Simon is not welcome in the women's quarters. All I can spare for him is a small wall chamber while Adam and Geoffrey are with us. It will be more comfortable for you to dress and keep your clothing here. There is no need for you to be troubled," she went on in response to Rhiannon's expression. "I wished you to have a choice, but I understand that customs are different. And even in England, a betrothal—"

"You are so kind, madam," Rhiannon interrupted hastily. "It will be terrible to distress you all, but—but Simon and I may never marry."

"Do you mean that Simon—"

"Not Simon," Rhiannon said. "It is not Simon who is reluctant. It is I."

Rhiannon did not notice that Alinor had stopped speaking before she was interrupted. She had realized before Rhiannon said it that, if there was an impediment to the marriage, it was not of Simon's making. Although it was nearly inconceivable to Alinor that any woman would not leap at a chance to be Simon's wife, in this case it was true. Rhiannon did not wish to marry Simon. But that was ridiculous. She was already sharing Simon's bed; their fencing with words made it plain that they knew each other well and were companionable; both sets of parents agreed it was a good match. There were no impediments at all. What ailed the girl, then?

"Why?" Alinor asked flatly. She could be devious when

necessary, but this, she judged, was neither the time, the place, nor the person.

"Because I do not believe him capable of being faithful, and I am not a woman who can share a man."

"Neither am I," Alinor agreed, smiling slightly as she remembered the months of misery she had inflicted upon herself and her husband only because she thought he carried a dream of another woman in his heart.

"Then why should I marry?" Rhiannon asked heatedly. "He may wander as he pleases, but I will be constrained to keep my faith. I do not need his lands, nor his protection, nor the dower my father offers."

"You are fortunate in that," Alinor said, realizing that the girl must have lands of her own. "From whom do your lands come?" Alinor asked. Simon might have done even better by this marriage than they had thought, and they had been well satisfied with Llewelyn's offer alone.

"From whom? Who knows?" Rhiannon replied. "Perhaps they were gifted to my grandfather Gwydyon, or my grandmother Angharad, or they may have been his or hers by long descent. All I know is that there is Angharad's Hall and the flocks and servants and hunting rights. They are Kicva's now and will be mine."

Alinor did not like such a casual attitude toward property. Every foot of land that belonged to her was deeded and affirmed since the first patch had come to her remote ancestor when William the Bastard conquered England. However, she had learned through Ian's dealings with his Welsh lands that customs differed. Where little was under cultivation and population was low, ownership was less crucial. However, if Rhiannon's mother had the right to hunting and grazing, that was tantamount to ownership. She was also aware that neither Simon nor Rhiannon had her sense of possession. Still, land mattered, and the children would be well found between what Simon had and what Rhiannon would bring.

Although she and Ian had not thought of it, this was clearly the only marriage possible for Simon. They had offered enough English heiresses to him, God knew, and he had set his jaw and said he would never marry. In fact, despite their pleasure in Llewelyn's proposal, both had been a trifle hurt that their son was more obedient to his overlord than to them. Alinor had understood, as soon as she saw Ian come into the hall with one arm around Rhiannon and his face glowing with happiness, that the girl was Simon's choice and had not been forced on him. Now she barely restrained laughter. Simon certainly would get what he deserved: good properties and a woman who would never really surrender, so that all his life he would need to pursue her.

"Different lands, different customs," Alinor said, referring to Rhiannon's description of Kicva's ownership of her property, "and customs change with time also. My dear, we have enough to worry about in considering what foolishness Winchester may lead the king to do. Your father and my husband are agreed on the marriage. Let matters stand thus until we have time and peace to study private troubles more closely."

"I am very willing for that," Rhiannon replied with a sigh of relief.

She had feared that Simon's mother would be angry, would accuse her of using Simon to further her father's political purposes. Nonetheless, she could not bear to be so warmly welcomed on false pretenses. Now that she had told all the truth, she had the right to enjoy the interest and excitement offered by contact with the family of Roselynde keep.

It was all new and different. At Angharad's Hall, she and Kicva were usually in basic agreement. Even when she was opposed and angry, all the anger was her own. Most of the time, though, they were only two, and it was quiet talk that took place there. Rhiannon was also familiar with the crowd, color, and movement, the quick give-and-take of her father's court. However, there was no real unity at Llewelyn's court. One could feel, even among friends, the alert desire for advantage, the seeking for personal gain. In Roselynde, however, Rhiannon sensed the rapport she had with Kicva allied with the differences that provided the stimulation in Llewelyn's court. Quarrels there might be in Roselynde, loud and furious, but the purpose of the quarrel would always be to help, not to hurt or to profit.

Rhiannon was prepared for more searching questions,

but all Alinor asked was whether she had brought court dress. There was no offense implied. A girl coming to visit her betrothed's family would bring fine clothes but not necessarily clothing sumptuous enough for court. Then Alinor remembered that Llewelyn's purpose had been to send Rhiannon to court, and she began to apologize, but Rhiannon shook her head.

"Other lands, other customs," she said, smiling. "I have court dress, but whether it is fitting you must judge."

She laid out the garments while Alinor stepped out of the chamber to see why the maids were so slow about bringing the bath she had ordered. When she returned, Alinor's eyes opened wide in surprise.

"It is not in your style, I know," Rhiannon said, "but it is my purpose to catch the eye of the king. If you think it will give cause for mockery rather than attention, however, I have this." She displayed the cloth of birds. "Perhaps a gown can be made for me in time."

Alinor gasped. "Where had you this?" she asked in awe.

"It is of my mother's weaving. The birds are my sign. I am named after a princess in an old Welsh tale—Rhiannon of the Birds."

"This was no quick work," Alinor said, looking into Rhiannon's eyes.

"Sometimes my mother has foreseeings," Rhiannon admitted, a little uncomfortable but again driven to confession by Alinor's kindness. "She strung the loom soon after Simon first came to visit us. I—perhaps she had some premonition that I would need a grand dress different from those I usually wear."

Alinor struggled with herself briefly and then said with a calm gravity that concealed amusement, "Your mother has foreseeings, but you do not."

"Oh, no, never," Rhiannon assured her, eager to clear herself of that suspect skill.

Simon had warned her that it was better not to bring such things into the open, and after that dreadful experience with Madog, Rhiannon was in complete agreement with him. But Alinor had not given witchcraft a thought. She was only amused. Alinor was quite sure Kicva had not foreseen any need for court dress, only for a marriage gown—and that would not have taken much skill at foreseeing, considering Simon's behavior.

"There would not be time to make up a dress," Alinor said, "but there is nothing to fear. Among all of us, there will be clothing enough for you to borrow, if that is necessary."

The bath came in then, with its attendant train of men lugging water and maids carrying herbs and soap and drying cloths. Another maid carried a platter of cold meat and bread, since dinner was over and it would be some hours before the evening portions would be served. Alinor was much interested when, bathed and fed, Rhiannon assumed her full regalia. She had thought at first that it must be Rhiannon's resistance to him that had captivated Simon. Now she realized there was something much more important. There was a strangeness, a hint of the violent and barbaric past.

"There will be no mockery," Alinor said huskily. "The women of the court may be cruel out of envy, Rhiannon, but no one will laugh."

The dress Rhiannon chose that night was black, but so interwoven with threads of gold and silver and with sparkling stones that it was bright as a rainbow. It was not, like modern gowns, draped in graceful folds, but laced tight under the breasts and down the waist to the hips, where it widened greatly. The undertunic was a blue so pale it looked like silver under the wide black sleeves and where it showed at the throat. More stones decked the wrists and neckline of the tunic: polished onyx, yellow citrine, golden topaz, pale green chrysoprase, cloudy chrysolite, aquamarine, amethyst, ruby spinel, and carnelian. They were set in an intricate pattern that caught the eye so well that it was an effort to look away.

Then Rhiannon hung her ears with real precious stones, diamonds, emeralds, and sapphires. Last of all, she set a gold band around her forehead to keep her hair out of her face. From this band hung thin chains of gold fastened together into an open meshwork by horizontal chains, and fixed along the vertical strands were more jewels. They slipped in and out of Rhiannon's heavy mass of raven hair, twinkling.

"Did Llewelyn empty his treasury for you?" Alinor whispered, stunned.

Rhiannon laughed. To her the things were pretty and an aid in her art. She had no sense of their real value. "No," she replied, "these are mine. Kicva gave them to me. Her father, Gwydyon, brought them home from some far place. When he was young and desired Angharad, he traveled very widely seeking things that would please her. The more fool he. He won her with his own power, by singing. He was a great bard—the last, I think."

"If he won what you wear by singing, he was indeed a great bard," Alinor remarked cynically.

She was never ungenerous, but minstrels were paid in copper or very small silver in Roselynde, not in twenty yards of gold and gems. Later, however, she wondered whether her doubts had been just. Rhiannon struck her harp and sang to them a fantastic tale of grief and love and power. Alinor thought that, in the past, when men feared magic more than they did in this age, gifts of great value might have been given to propitiate one who could raise such images.

There was no praise when Rhiannon stopped singing. All were struck mute—even Simon, who was accustomed to her art. In Roselynde, where the practical and possible was a fine art, the magical and impossible had more power to shock, to stir deep-buried memories both ugly and beautiful, than in Llewelyn's court or at Dinas Emrys. But Rhiannon did not mistake the silence for indifference. She lowered her head and folded her hands in her lap over her harp, and waited.

Little by little, movement came back to the tense figures. Alinor's breath sighed out, Joanna's drew in deeply, Gilliane lifted a hand to wipe away the tears that had run unheeded down her cheeks. Ian smiled. He was the least affected; he had heard Gwydyon himself sing in Llewelyn's court, although the bard was very old then. Adam moved restlessly. If she had not been Simon's betrothed, he would have called Rhiannon a witch. Geoffrey was still transfixed; he was no mean performer himself, but Rhiannon's singing was far beyond his experience.

Simon turned to him as the most knowledgeable in the art. "She is a fine singer, is she not?"

Geoffrey started, as if he had been asleep, and cleared his throat. "She is beyond fine. Her singing is an ensorcelment." He smiled. "You do not need to worry about fixing Henry's attention or winning his heart. The king loves such things greatly. I only hope that Winchester does not decide to strike back by crying '*Witch.*'"

CHAPTER 17

❖•❖

The whole party rode north the next morning, and Rhiannon felt more and more at home. All the ladies bestrode their own mounts as she did. None, not even Alinor, who was old, traveled in a covered cart or sat pillion behind a man. Perhaps Joanna looked anxiously at her mother from time to time, but Rhiannon thought that was because of Joanna's nature rather than any real weakness in Alinor. They stayed at Kingsclere that night, and made much of old Sir Henry, who lost ten years off his age in his pride and pleasure.

On the day after, they came to Oxford. Geoffrey had a house there, the gift of the king, who often stayed at Oxford keep and wished his cousin to be near him. Henry would have preferred that Geoffrey remain permanently in his bachelor court, but he soon learned that Geoffrey would stay nowhere long without his enchanting wife. Henry would gladly have made room for Joanna also, but there was no female side to Henry's court. His mother had remarried in France and he had no wife as yet, although negotiations were under way. A house of his own for Geoffrey was the best solution.

Ian and Alinor had rented another house nearby, and it was easy enough to divide the party so that all would have comfortable accommodation. Because the servants had changed teams and traveled most of both nights, the baggage carts had almost kept pace with the riders. The men left the women to wait for the servants, the furniture, linens, and cooking vessels, and went off to see what had happened since they last had news.

Geoffrey went directly to the king, and Ian accompanied him. Adam and Simon asked around for Richard of Cornwall. They were not well pleased when they heard he was at his seat in Wallingford about fifteen miles away. Almost certainly that meant there had been another quarrel between the brothers, which boded ill for the truce with

230

Pembroke. However, guessing was useless. It *was* possible that Richard was simply taking care of the business of his property. It would be necessary to ride out to see him.

It did not take Geoffrey and Ian much longer to realize that all was not well. Simon's betrothal was a most convenient excuse to seek an audience with the king. The audience was granted—but only after they had stated their reason. This was a bad shock. Usually the king would welcome either of them without reservation, frequently coming out himself to escort them. In response to the rebuff, Geoffrey and Ian exchanged a single significant glance. Although neither permitted his expression to change, both were aware of sinking hearts. Geoffrey was one of the guarantors that Usk would be returned to Pembroke on September twenty-third. If Henry did not wish to speak to Geoffrey, it was probably because he was afraid Geoffrey would ask him to confirm that promise.

Since both knew that nothing would be gained by raising the question directly, they confined themselves to the subject of Simon's betrothal, praising the bride-to-be, and requesting permission to present her. Their forbearance had the excellent result of gaining Ian a quit-claim for his son's marriage without the customary fine for marrying whomsoever he chose. Nonetheless, Ian would gladly have paid the fine to escape seeing how Henry's eyes shifted when Geoffrey uttered a mild neutral hope that they would soon see the Earl of Pembroke at court.

They rode home with heavy hearts to discover that the womenfolk were equally uneasy. Without moving more than the few hundred yards between houses, all were aware of even worse news than their men had uncovered.

With the instinct of a bee attracted to honey, Walter de Clare had homed in on Sybelle's presence. He did not approach her directly—their last meeting was still too vivid in his mind—but he had spoken to Joanna. Her exclamation of distress had brought Gilliane and Sybelle. In view of the coming trouble, the past disagreement between Walter and Sybelle had been interred without even a hint of a funeral service. Naturally, Joanna brought her package of worry to Alinor, so Rhiannon had also heard.

Moreover, Alinor and Rhiannon had a message from Simon that he and Adam were riding to Wallingford to see Cornwall. The fact that this was necessary only seemed to confirm Walter's news: Henry would not give up Usk and intended, if Richard Marshal came to demand it in person, to seize him as a rebel and imprison him. This, of course, was Walter's dramatic version of the rumors that seethed and surged around Oxford. This was worse than Ian and Geoffrey had expected; they had assumed that Henry would hold out pardon for the ceding of Usk and future good behavior.

The worst was confirmed when Simon and Adam returned from Wallingford the next day. Cornwall had received them gladly, delighted with two new pairs of sympathetic ears into which to pour his rage and his frustration. He would have nothing more to do with his brother, he snarled, nothing. How could a man of honor live in such a situation, he asked. He was caught between the oath he had sworn to Henry—the blood bond that made the oath even more sacred—and the dishonor he felt at what Henry intended to do. He had not specifically been a party to the truce, but he could not bear to see his brother dishonor himself. Richard was so shamed, so furious, that if he came into Henry's presence again, he would put his hands around the king's neck and strangle him.

Even Simon and Adam blanched, although they knew it was temper rather than intention they heard. Everyone would have been more than happy to exchange Henry for Richard, but not with his brother's blood on his hands and conscience. There were many in the kingdom who prayed daily for the king's death from any well-known cause—except fratricide.

All in all, the visit had a good effect. Richard talked himself out, regained his temper, and asked his guests to spend the night. They agreed readily, even more eager to hear what Cornwall had to say when he was calm than when he was angry. A messenger rode off to Oxford to reassure the family that Simon and Adam were guests and would return to dinner the next day. Over breakfast, his temper spent, Richard discussed the matter more coherently, but, unfortunately, there was nothing new he could say. He had screamed at his brother and had pleaded on his knees, and both approaches had been futile. There was nothing else he could do to assist Pembroke actively. All he could do was to refuse absolutely to take part in any future action against him—no matter what Pembroke did.

"I am shamed," he said, his dark eyes glowing with resentment, "for Richard Marshal is a good man, and what he desires is just. But I cannot raise my hand against my brother—I cannot!"

"No, indeed!" Simon and Adam said in unison.

The political implications were awful enough, but both had actually responded emotionally, unconsciously drawing closer together so that they touched. The foundation of life was that a man could trust his own blood kin and that the bond of blood outweighed even the oath of fealty. It did not matter whether you loved or hated your blood kin. The men of Roselynde were fortunate in being tied in love as well as in blood, but love was not essential and hatred usually had no effect on loosening the tie.

Of course, there had always been those unnatural creatures who violated the bond of blood. The Plantagenets were infamous for it, the sons turning on the father and then, when they had destroyed him, attacking each other. The horrible example of a land torn constantly with war, of betrayals and counterbetrayals, of honest men driven to extremity by the need to choose between two oaths of fealty rose before Adam's and Simon's eyes. They, too, might pray for Henry's early demise, but neither would encourage Richard to use force to curb his brother.

"Winchester must be mad!" Ian exclaimed when he heard Adam's recounting of what had happened at Wallingford. "Geoffrey is one of the sureties for Pembroke's freedom and the return of Usk."

"Winchester is not mad," Alinor said, "just desperate. He is no fool. He knows how Henry's nature works. He intends, I think, to show the king he is his only friend, that all others are faithless. If Geoffrey, his own cousin, sides with the 'rebel' Pembroke, Winchester can say this proves that no man is trustworthy and Henry must rule alone."

Geoffrey sat still and silent, his quick mind momentarily frozen by this dilemma. Joanna was white as milk. Their sons were in the king's service, close under his hand. If Geoffrey fulfilled his oath to Pembroke, what would happen to the boys? Normally Henry was soft to them to a fault, and it was true that he probably could not bring himself to harm them, no matter how furious he was with their father. However, de Burgh had convinced Henry to put Cornwall's stepson, the child-Earl of Gloucester, into his care rather than leave him with his mother as Cornwall's ward. Could Winchester convince Henry to give him Geoffrey's sons?

"Now, wait," Simon said, looking at his sister's blanched face, "there is a way, easy enough. I can go to Richard and tell him what is planned. He need only go to Usk and knock on the gates on September twenty-third. If the keep is not yielded, the truce will have been broken and he will not need to come to the conference. Then he can be in no danger of imprisonment."

"He would have the right to call upon me to help him recover Usk," Geoffrey pointed out, but he no longer looked like a graven image. There was life in his eyes, and Joanna's color began to come back.

"He would not do that, even if he needed your help, and I happen to know he will not need it. No, do not look so surprised. Richard himself knows nothing about this little device. It was the doing of the castellan of Usk, who doubtless did not wish to face the danger of losing his position permanently—and I could not see that there was any dishonor in it." He told them briefly about the castellan's son and the men-at-arms still in Usk.

They were still laughing about this clever initiative and wondering how the castellan would explain what he had done to the very upright Richard when Walter came in. While the men recapitulated the conversation for his benefit, the women saw to the setting up of tables for dinner. Walter joined them with no more than a brief glance at Sybelle. She did not invite him, but she did not repulse him either, and he sat down, very much a part of the family.

When he had heard them out, he said, "You cannot go, Simon. You must take this opportunity to present Lady Rhiannon to the king. It would look too strange for Lord Geoffrey and Lord Ian to have craved such an audience and then for you not to bring her, even if there is no need for her services now, since Henry cannot plan to attack Wales. By the time this is over, any and all intermediaries will be welcome. I will go to Pembroke."

"Walter is right," Geoffrey stated, thinking with his usual clarity now that he had found his balance. "I will write the entire tale, and Walter will carry it to Richard. There will be no doubt in Richard's mind if the warning comes from me. Moreover, it is my right and duty as one of the guarantors of the king's action."

"Your right and duty, true," Ian warned, "but do not cut off your nose to spite *our* faces. You are our best lead to the king. If he hears of this . . ."

"Why should he?" Walter asked. "I will not speak of it, nor will anyone here. Pembroke will not, either."

"Just a minute," Adam said. "As soon as Pembroke takes back Usk, Henry will call a levy and begin the war anew."

"Yes, and at that time I will withdraw, as will we all. I do not think there will be many who support the king this time." Geoffrey paused; then his eyes narrowed. "May I be damned for a fool!"

"I have never known you to be a fool," Gilliane gasped, "and if you are thinking what has suddenly come into *my* mind—"

"Apurpose!" Sybelle's young voice was hard, and her face had set into lines that made Walter de Clare's eyes bulge. "Winchester *intended* to bring the barons to refuse their service."

"Child," Ian reproved, "you do not understand. There is sense in forcing the barons to obey, regardless of their desire, but—"

"No, beloved," Alinor interrupted, looking at Sybelle. Alinor's eyes glowed momentarily with satisfaction. Sybelle, this golden daughter of Joanna's, would be a worthy Lady of Roselynde when it came her time. "Sybelle has seen the truth."

"But there is no sense in it," Adam protested.

"Yes, there is," Gilliane insisted, the steel ringing clear in the velvet voice. "Listen to this case: All the barons will sit still, glowering but doing nothing since their oaths prevent them from attacking the king unless he attacks them first. Yet, because he has broken his oath to Pembroke, very few will come to his call, all saying the king broke the truce and has no right to their service. But Winchester has long prepared for this. The country is full of mercenary troops, and more come every day."

Geoffrey nodded agreement. "Yes, Ian. I thought, like you at first, that Winchester's purpose was to humble the barons into submission. I fear it is worse. He intends to destroy us utterly. If Pembroke can be beaten by the mercenary troops alone, it will be the first note of the mort for us all. He is the strongest. The heart will go out of many and they will submit. The king will then be maneuvered into picking a quarrel with another strong baron. When he is beaten, only fewer and weaker men will remain."

"I see it too," Joanna hissed furiously. "But the king will not call a levy. He will ask, instead, for scutage, and out of this he will pay his mercenaries."

"And they will have no land, no interest in this realm," Alinor said. "They will do as the king orders without thought for what is best for the people." Alinor's voice was like a knell of doom. She had cared for the land and the people on it so long and so fiercely that she was like a tree with deep, wide-spreading roots buried in the soil of Roselynde.

"In the long distance, only the king will have power," Geoffrey pointed out bleakly. "Most will not see the end to which this will lead and will pay the scutage gladly. You know that the cost of service is always more than the scutage, although it does not offer the compensation of loot. But I am sure Winchester will find a way to restrict the loot a knight may take. Knight service will die because those who persist in keeping their men armed will be always the target of the king's spite and attack. With the ending of knight service, our ability to resist the king's will or even to defend ourselves against our neighbors will die also. If a wrong is done us, we will need to cry to the king to send his mercenaries to protect us."

There was a silence while everyone contemplated this horror. Rhiannon alone was not affected. She looked from face to face with puzzlement. Knight service was not really the foundation of power in Wales, although Llewelyn had incorporated some of its concepts into his rule. Armies were still generated on a blood or clan basis, and, to a certain extent, these armies were all mercenary. They expected to be maintained and rewarded directly by the leader who had called them, either with loot from the enemy or with treasure from the leader's store.

The word *scutage*—payment in money instead of time of fighting service—did not even have meaning to Rhiannon; such a practice did not yet exist in her country. She had listened to the conversation very closely, although she said nothing. The high emotional content of what was said was clear even if she could not understand the cause. One thing, however, she did understand, and everyone seemed to have overlooked this obvious point.

"But," Rhiannon's voice was like a pure bell tone in the heavy silence, "you are all accounting a victory by the king's mercenaries a sure thing. How is this possible? They could not defeat Pembroke last month, even with the assistance of some of the barons and when the earl was not willing to attack."

Simon was the first to laugh, and the reaction spread swiftly from one to another around the table. Rhiannon's eyebrows rose, but Simon embraced her, crying, *"Eneit, eneit,* you are as wise as you are beautiful, and we are a gaggle of silly geese, sitting here afrighting ourselves by our own honking."

Geoffrey's smile diminished. "The case is not so desperate as I made out," he said, "but there is something to fear. Some twenty years ago Lord Llewelyn was defeated by our using his own tactics against him. King John ordered that all be burnt before and behind as we went. Each town and village was laid waste utterly, and the land and forest also. Winchester was close to John in those days. Perhaps he also remembers."

Now it was Rhiannon's turn to grow rigid with fear. She had been less than five years old the summer of that bitter defeat, but she remembered it as a time of horror. Llewelyn had fled to Angharad's Hall when all seemed hopeless. No army had followed him there, and they had not been attacked nor suffered directly. Nonetheless, for the first time in her happy life, Rhiannon had been surrounded by a pall of grief and bitterness and impotent rage. Sensitive as she was, she had never forgotten it.

Simon put an arm around her. "That must not happen, and I think it will not. This time Richard must have his craw full of insult and treachery. I believe he will be ready to attack as well as defend. I am almost sure, also, that Prince Llewelyn will make alliance with Richard."

"You must warn him, Simon," Rhiannon urged eagerly.

"Oh, I will, dear heart," Simon agreed, "but there is no hurry about it. For one thing, I am not sure your father needs telling. This may have been in his mind from the beginning. For another, the king cannot move against Richard until after October ninth, when the conference is set. Until then, he cannot be sure that Richard will not come in person to protest the failure to hold the conditions of the truce. Then he must send out his summons. Do not fret yourself, there will be time enough."

"Yes, and I think it very important that you engage the king's friendship," Geoffrey said.

A look of strong distaste passed over Rhiannon's face.

"Do not blame Henry too much for this, my dear," Alinor said. "He is easily led to unwise enthusiasms, I am afraid, but he is not evil. The blame really should rest on Winchester. He should know the men of this realm better."

"There I cannot agree with you," Joanna remarked dryly. "I fear that Winchester knows the barons of England very well indeed, and has devised this incredible lunacy because he despairs of ever bringing them to agree on *anything*."

"My dearling Joanna," Ian exclaimed, his expression changing from depression to surprise, "that is just what he said to me when I spoke to him in June—and I did not really listen! He is wrong, very wrong in what he is doing, but now I see he means well, not ill. It lay most heavily on my heart that a man I knew so long and respected should seem to change into a monster. He thinks that when the barons are powerless the realm will be at peace—yes! He said that also."

"And that is what he has convinced Henry to believe." Geoffrey also looked relieved. "He may even be right," Geoffrey added thoughtfully. "If there were no power in the land but the king's, it might bring peace."

"Graves are also peaceful," Adam growled, "but I have no particular wish to inhabit one."

Geoffrey smiled at this sardonic reminder. "Well, I agree to that, and Winchester must not be allowed to accomplish his purpose. But, Rhiannon, I assure you if we removed Winchester's influence, Henry would soon lose interest in the bishop's ideas. My cousin is not at all warlike at heart."

"No, he is not," Ian said. "He is a man of strong affections, which is why Winchester has had so easy a conquest. He was one of Henry's guardians when the king was a child. Partly owing to his close association with King John, he was not well liked and was pushed out as de Burgh gained ascendency. Naturally, when Henry began to resent de Burgh, he turned to Winchester."

"It will be worse soon," Walter said. "I have heard that Winchester seeks control of Devizes. That is what I came to tell you all before I was drawn into the other matter. I fear that if Peter des Roches becomes de Burgh's warder, de Burgh will die."

Geoffrey uttered an obscenity, which startled everyone because it was most unlike him to use such crudities. However, he made no direct comment on Walter's news except a warning glance at him. Instead, he looked at Rhiannon.

"We have not really strayed from the need to win Henry's friendship. As Lady Alinor said, the king is easily led; as Ian said, he is a man of strong emotions; as Walter implied, he is spiteful. If you can gain his affection and esteem, Rhiannon, it may be that you can turn aside his spite from your father and point it in the right direction—toward Winchester."

"I see it," Rhiannon sighed, "but I am the last person to be useful for such a purpose. Simon will tell you that I am not the softest-spoken woman in the world, nor the most tactful."

"Anyone who can deal with Math can deal with Henry," Simon said, grinning. "Fix it in your mind that the king is a two-legged Math with more self-love and less common sense, and all will go well."

Rhiannon burst out laughing while Simon explained Math to the others. There was only the most half-hearted protest from Geoffrey and Ian, but Gilliane did not join the others in their smiles and laughing objections.

"But Simon is perfectly right," Gilliane said seriously. "Henry is just like a cat. I never thought of it before, but it is so. He loves to be praised. He enjoys being stroked—when it is convenient for him. He loves to be kind—when it does not inconvenience him. He is quite clever about anything he desires and is deaf, dumb, and blind to anything he regards as unpleasant. And he can be quite vicious when he is displeased, even to those he loves."

Gilliane's serious analysis drew another round of laughter, but it was of enormous help to Rhiannon when she met Henry the next afternoon. Since she did not feel the same repugnance over a broken truce as did the others, her understanding of the king and her fear of making a misstep with him were, respectively, enhanced and reduced. To her eyes, the suggestion Gilliane had made was confirmed by sight of Henry. There was something cat-like in the way he lounged against the cushions of his chair—an inordinate love of physical comfort—and in the rather blank stare of his blue eyes, to which the drooping lid of one eye gave a measure of slyness.

By the time Rhiannon reached his chair of state, the king was no longer lounging. A pool of silence had moved with her and her escorts—Ian to her right and Simon to her left—as they came up the long room toward Henry. She wore the black dress and the jeweled mesh to hold back her hair, which hung loose to her knees, and she walked the long passage between the staring courtiers with the grace of a doe and the proud bearing of a queen.

"My lord king," Ian said formally when they reached Henry and Rhiannon sank into a deep curtsy, "in accordance with your gracious permission, I make bold to present you to my son Simon's betrothed wife, Rhiannon uerch Llewelyn."

"Goodness gracious," Henry exclaimed, smiling broadly, "had I known what Llewelyn was hiding, I would have come seeking it myself. You are a most fortunate man, Simon. Oh, rise, do rise, Lady Rhiannon. No need to hold that silly pose. Forgive me. I was so astonished at your loveliness."

Rhiannon stood upright and smiled. It was utterly impossible not to do so. What might have been an offensive leer was the simplest expression of surprised friendliness. The voice also was warm, unaffected, open. Rhiannon suddenly became aware why, after all the harsh things were said and all the hard plans were made to thwart him, nearly everyone who knew him defended the king. There was great sweetness, great charm in him.

Henry's admiration was as innocent as it was sincere. Obviously he was a man who could enjoy beauty for its own sake without desiring to touch or possess it. Had she been as exquisite as the moon or the sun, Rhiannon knew she would also have been as untouchable in Henry's mind.

"Thank you, my lord," she murmured. "My father assured me you would receive me kindly."

"Oh, did he?" Henry laughed. "Well, Lord Llewelyn knows I have a great admiration for beauty."

"So he does, my lord, and he sent to you two gifts, not of great worth, perhaps, but most curious."

With the words, Rhiannon handed over a broach for fastening a cloak, and a belt buckle, both of the same pattern. Each showed the lion and the lamb lying down together in peace. In terms of a gift from one ruler to another, the two pieces were of little value, there being no mass of gold or fine, large gems. But the work was very old, very cunningly wrought, the lion in gold, with a deeply carved curly mane and eyes of topaz, and the lamb of silver so delicately worked that one could almost swear the fleece was real.

Henry's eyes showed his appreciation of the beauty of the pieces. He handled the broach and buckle almost reverently. "I do not agree as to the little worth," he said. "These are precious things. The skill that made them does not come often to a man's hands. Two fine gifts, indeed."

"That is only one of the gifts," Rhiannon said. "The other needs some time to deliver. It is a song."

"There is time now," Henry replied instantly, with lively expectation. "Let us have the singer in at once."

"The singer is in, my lord." Rhiannon smiled at him. "I need only my harp and, if you will give me leave to sit, a stool, for I must hold the harp in my lap."

She sang a song of Culhwch and Olwen, whose tale

reached back into the mists of time when men drank the
sea, ran on the tips of grass without bending it, and held
their breaths for nine days and nine nights. It told of the
geas Culhwch's stepmother set upon him to marry Olwen,
daughter of Ysbaddaden, Chief Giant, and of the feats
of magic and mystery Culhwch and his companions performed to win her. There was grief and laughter in it and
great heroism, but Rhiannon had chosen it because Culhwch, who was obviously Welsh, was accepted by King
Arthur as his first cousin.

Rhiannon had considered her repertory very carefully,
and decided that *Culhwch and Olwen* was best. The song
started with a rather aggressive passage between Arthur
and Culhwch and ended in complete amity. Rhiannon
thought this song best conveyed the ideas she wanted
Henry to absorb.

Whether her performance would eventually produce
the desired effect, Rhiannon was not sure. The initial
success was overwhelming. Henry was so moved that he
rose from his chair to come down and kiss her, but that
appreciation was completely emotional and technical. He
had not really thought about the story or what it could
mean, only about the beauty of the sound.

As the afternoon wore away to evening, it became
apparent that Rhiannon's careful planning had been
wasted. She probably could have sung *Branwen, Daughter
of Llyr*, which had violent anti-English feeling, without
producing a political effect in the king. This both enchanted and annoyed her, for the artist in Henry had
totally supplanted the king. He did not think about the
meaning of anything, nor even about the fact that Llewelyn's daughter might well have business for her father in
hand. All Henry could think of was Rhiannon's art.

He wanted to know everything; when and where she
learned, where the songs came from, who had translated
them into French from the Welsh. He listened intently,
and her answers generated more questions. He examined
her harp minutely and reverently, recognizing at once its
great age and that it was a masterwork even finer than
the broach and buckle that Llewelyn had sent him.

The artist in Rhiannon responded enthusiastically,
charmed with Henry's delight, sincere interest, and man-

ner. However, the part of her that was daughter of a Welsh prince, who had come to England with a purpose other than singing songs, was thoroughly annoyed. More than once, with more tact than she knew she had, Rhiannon tried to turn the talk to the meaning of Culhwch's relationship with Arthur, to the forbearance King Arthur had shown his too-eager, too-quarrelsome cousin just because he was so much the stronger. As far as Rhiannon could tell, it all went right over Henry's head. The king responded quite naturally, but he praised the beauty of the lines that described the lofty sentiments. There seemed to be no connection at all in his mind between himself and English Arthur, and Llewelyn, a Welsh Culhwch.

When, almost by force, Henry was at last separated from Rhiannon to speak to more important people waiting for his attention, other listeners closed in on her. But Henry could not be kept away for long. He shook loose from his duty as soon as he saw Ian and Simon steering Rhiannon toward an exit, to ask how long a stay she would make. She opened her mouth to say it depended on whether or not he attacked Wales, but Ian was before her, smoothly regretting that this visit must be short, as she had been given no long leave from her father's court. Henry began to protest petulantly that Llewelyn had had her for years; why had she been hidden away?

"I was not hidden away," Rhiannon said, then laughed. "I only come to court after the harvest is in and the flocks are in winter pasture. When the snows come, there is nothing for me to do in Angharad's Hall, so I come to my father. Indeed, my lord, my father has not seen much more of me than you have—which is nothing—since early spring."

If that was not the precise truth this year, because of Rhiannon's unusual visit to Aber in July, it was true in general. Henry was somewhat placated, although he continued to grumble that Llewelyn should allow such a priceless gem to be buried in the Welsh hills.

"I would display you every day, like the best jewel in my crown," Henry exclaimed.

Suddenly Rhiannon became aware of how tense Simon had grown and of the anxiety in Ian's eyes. "But I love my hills," she cried, shrinking back into Simon's encircling arm. "And I am not so hard as a gem, my lord. I would soon wear out. The songs come out of the quiet days in the hills. Even Gwydyon could not always sing. He, too, returned to the hills to be renewed." Rhiannon's eyes were wide with fear.

"I did not mean to frighten you," Henry said, with unusual perceptiveness, "but I must hear you again. Surely you do not go so soon as to prohibit that."

"No, my lord." It was Simon who replied. "Unless there is some urgent reason to go, we will follow the court until October ninth, at least."

A black cloud passed over Henry's face, and he bowed stiffly to Rhiannon and moved away.

"Was that wise, Simon?" Ian murmured.

"Yes, because he thinks now that we do not yet know or believe what is planned for Richard. I gave no promise. We may leave tomorrow if we choose."

Rhiannon shook her head. She had recovered from the momentary sense of claustrophobia that had nearly choked her when she saw what seemed a threat of imprisonment. "I must sing for him again," she insisted, "and also promise to return to his court in the future. Otherwise he will be bitterly angry and hurt, and what good my father hoped I could do would be turned all to evil."

But Simon was angry still. "Jewel in his crown," he muttered, "you are none of his."

"Indeed I am not. He is an artist in his soul, but not a creator. He does not mean ill, only desires to draw into himself what he lacks. Yet, not being a creator, he cannot understand that to bind the art is to destroy it."

"Then perhaps it is not wise to tempt him?" Ian was uncertain. Would it be worse if Rhiannon left at once or sang again, as tacitly promised, and then openly refused to perform a third time? Henry had a horrible tendency to agree to something—like Rhiannon's leaving—and then keep putting it off from one day to another until it never happened.

"I am near certain I have an answer that will satisfy the king," Rhiannon offered. "Certainly it will not anger him more than departing without leave or farewell. Let me try."

CHAPTER 18

❖•❖•❖•❖•❖•❖•❖•❖•❖•❖•❖•❖•❖•❖•❖•❖•❖•❖•❖•❖

Ian had agreed at once, but Simon protested all the way back to the house. He was still angry while Rhiannon undressed him for bed. Ordinarily she would have told him sharply that she needed nothing from him and, if he did not like her behavior, he should cease to urge her to marry him. She was aware, however, that his reaction was her fault. If she had not panicked at the king's implication that he intended to keep her—which she had momentarily and irrationally connected with all the talk of de Burgh's imprisonment—Simon would not even have noticed the brief exchange.

Simon's anger also reflected his own guilt for bringing her to court and urging her to display her talent. Understanding this, Rhiannon curbed her impatience and uttered soothing murmurs that neither agreed to his way nor insisted on hers. This did not work. Simon glowered at her, his brilliant eyes dark.

"You need not treat me as if I were five years old," he said crossly.

Rhiannon bit her lip. She knew quite well that Simon expected her to reply, *Then do not act that way,* which would pave the path for a violent quarrel in which his tensions could be released. Unfortunately, Rhiannon did not feel she could give him the outlet he desired. The house Ian and Alinor had rented contained only the solar and the hall above the vaulted ground floor. Menservants and men-at-arms slept below, while the family and maids and some of Joanna's and Gilliane's children were distributed between the hall and solar above.

This was not the place for an argument, Rhiannon decided. Simon might not care who heard him, but Rhiannon was a private person. She simply could not quarrel where everyone could hear. A quarrel, however, was not the only way to relieve tensions. Rhiannon made her eyes large and allowed her lips to droop.

245

"You are trying to quarrel with me," she said tragically. "You really do think it would be unnatural to make love to me in a bed."

Simon had opened his mouth to say, quite furiously, that he had no intention of quarreling with her, but the second sentence struck him mute.

"You have avoided me altogether, ever since we came to Roselynde," Rhiannon went on dramatically.

This passionate statement was made with a total disregard for the real truth, although it was quite factual. They had not slept together after their last night on the road. However, it was Rhiannon's fault that they had not been together that first night at Roselynde. Although she had Alinor's permission, she found herself too shy to walk boldly down the stairs, across the hall where the men-servants slept, and into Simon's chamber. She knew quite well it was impossible for him to come to her. No man but Ian, except under very special circumstances, was permitted into the women's quarters of Roselynde keep. Simon had not been up those stairs since he left for fostering when he was nine years old. Probably he would not climb them again until his father or mother was dying.

As to the succeeding nights they had been apart, that was the fault of circumstance. Kingsclere was so small that all except Alinor and Ian, who shared the castellan's own bed, had slept on pallets, men in the hall and women in the solar. The following night Simon had been at Wallingford.

For a moment Simon was fooled by Rhiannon's pretense of hurt and her complaint that he had been avoiding her. "No!" he whispered. "No!" and stepped toward her with his arms outstretched.

Realization came before he embraced her, however, and instead of enfolding her gently in his arms, he grabbed her with one hand and slapped her briskly on the buttock with the other.

"Monster!" Rhiannon gasped, leaning heavily against him. "You do not love me any longer. Now you will beat me to death."

"I am more likely to eat you alive," Simon murmured,

applying his lips to her throat with an enthusiasm that gave a tinge of reality to the threat.

"You will have a hard time chewing this gown, I am afraid," Rhiannon murmured after a few minutes.

Simon bit her ear lobe gently. "I have good teeth," he chuckled, "but I think you are right. Perhaps it would be better if we took it off."

To that he got no reply but a soft sigh, since he had managed to undo one side of her bliaunt and slip his hand inside to stroke her back. However, after unlacing the other side, he drew off the gown with a briskness that was startling. Rhiannon stepped back silently to remove the rest of her clothing, assuming that Simon, now aroused, would wish to get on with the business quickly. During their travels his lovemaking had been rapid—but thorough.

This time, though, she could not have been more wrong. It was true Simon had been brief on the way from Wales to Roselynde, although he made sure she was both roused and contented. It had not occurred to Rhiannon that this was owing to his consideration for her fatigue and the cold and damp of the floor of the tent. Now, however, Simon had time to spare and all the comfort of a warm, curtained bed to play in. Haste was very far from his mind. Moreover, there was just a shade of truth in what Rhiannon had said. He did feel a sense of strangeness in making love to her in a bed. Not that he was unwilling, but the ordinary situation took on an exotic aura.

Having said he wished to eat her, Simon seemed to become fixated on the words. As Rhiannon stepped back, he seized one of her hands and raised it to his mouth. He nibbled the tips of her fingers, kissed her palm, tickled it with his tongue—all the while busily unbuttoning the sleeve of her tunic. His lips and tongue then proceeded to follow the path of the undone buttons, coming to rest in the hollow of her elbow. Then he worked the other sleeve.

Surprised at first, Rhiannon quickly slipped into a soft, sensual haze. At that moment she was not as hotly excited as Simon could make her by an assault on her lips, breasts, and thighs. Instead, she felt slightly unfocused in her thinking, while all the nerve endings in her body increased in sensitivity. It seemed that she could actually make out the shape of his mouth when he kissed her and feel the separate tiny ridges on the tips of his fingers.

Next to be undone was the neck of the tunic. Simon lipped the little hollow where the collarbones meet and nibbled his way down her chest, keeping carefully to the center of the cleft. Rhiannon stood passive, except that her hands made lazy circles and stroking movements on her lover's bare back. She could feel the muscles twitch very slightly in response to the caress.

As he bent lower to kiss the cleft between her breasts, Simon reached down and grabbed her tunic. It came up as he straightened, but he did not pull it over her head. Instead he maneuvered her through the curtains with kisses and love bites, drawing the tunic off as he laid her down on the bed. Now only the thin linen shift and shoes and stockings remained. The shoes were easy. Simon simply pushed them off with one hand as he untied Rhiannon's garters with the other. The stockings were more fun. He rolled them down an inch at a time, caressing the bared skin they disclosed.

Sometimes the kisses tickled Rhiannon almost unbearably, but that only heightened her all-over sensitivity. Having reached her toes, Simon began to work his way back up again, raising the shift as he went. Rhiannon's caresses became more urgent and her hands sought out the areas of Simon's body that woke the greatest response in him, like the inner thigh and the small of the back just where the buttocks divide. Strangely, although she was now growing very excited, Rhiannon did not reach for Simon's genitals. It did not seem necessary; all of him seemed peculiarly alive, as she herself was.

Neither had so far made a sound, aside from breathing rather more quickly than usual. There was a piquancy in their silent communication, for a hot glow of passion was now burning in each, and wordless demands were being made and satisfied, using only the instinct of mutual desire. At last Simon's mouth closed on Rhiannon's breast, and her hand went between his legs.

After so long a foreplay, their coupling was short and violent, culminating in an explosion that locked Rhiannon's powerful legs so hard around Simon's back that even his strong bones creaked. Mouth on mouth, they muffled the sounds they could not contain in climax. Replete, they slid apart and into sleep—another peculiarity, because usually they talked and fondled each other for a little while after their passion was spent. But both were too tired this time, partly because of the tension generated during their meeting with the king.

Although Rhiannon slept well, Simon's anxious dreams that night cast a pall over his awakening in the morning. Although he could not remember any specific event, the dreams intensified his resistance to Rhiannon's attending court again. He should have spoken about the matter directly and purged his system, but he did not wish to spoil Rhiannon's joyous morning mood. Then, immediately after they had broken their fast, he was called away to an urgent conference with Ian's and Geoffrey's friends, who wanted to know what Lord Llewelyn would do when —not if—the truce was broken.

Simon did not enjoy the conference. He never took pleasure as Geoffrey did in political maneuvering. He disliked intensely needing to watch and measure his words so that what Llewelyn had told him would come across clear and undistorted by his own desires and prejudices. Equally, he disliked needing to attend closely to what the others said, trying to judge the half-truths so that he could render to his overlord a good account of what he had learned.

All adjudged the situation dangerous to desperation, and to Simon's greater displeasure, it was decided that it would be best to include Richard of Cornwall in the discussion. Thus, the whole group rode out, but not as a group. To avoid bringing their intention too strongly to Winchester's notice, they went singly and in twos by different gates. As one of the youngest, Simon was sent out by the westward gate, which added several miles to his ride and a few degrees to the temperature of his temper.

This was not at all cooled by the knowledge that they would dine and spend the night at Wallingford. Nor did it help that he had to repeat nearly everything he had said before and have it thrashed out thoroughly for a third time. That night, deprived of Rhiannon's company, he awakened in the dark to the irrational fear that she had gone to court alone and had been seized and hidden away from him. One part of his mind knew perfectly well that this was ridiculous. His mother would never permit such a thing; also, Henry was not perfect, but he did not abduct women. The other part of his mind insisted the fear was an evil omen.

Perhaps if Simon could have ridden directly back to Oxford in the morning or could have discussed the matter with someone, the whole thing would have shrunk back to its real proportions. However, he was extremely aware of his father's haunted eyes, of Geoffrey's haggardness, of the fact that even Adam was deeply worried. There were those who had particular fears of or hatreds for the Welsh. They were his burden, and when a group of them asked him to join a hunting party, he could not refuse. He had, of course, shaken off the stupid notion that Henry would seize his betrothed, but he was left with an even stronger distaste for another court appearance.

The day was hot and the long hunt led them even farther from Oxford. Simon's companions elected to stop for dinner at—of all places—one of his mother's properties. Had it been anywhere else, Simon would have excused himself and ridden back alone, but he could not offer such a gratuitous insult—which might even be taken as a mark of dissatisfaction—to a faithful servant. By the time Simon was free to return to Oxford, he was half-mad with the frustration of needing to seem interested and absorbed in the problems of his companions, which in fact meant very little to him.

Over the period of separation, Rhiannon's mood had changed. Until this day, she had been busy every moment with movement and distracted by new experiences. After the menfolk left, however, a second stage of female activity began. At home, she would have ignored this. She would have run out into the woods and spent the day most happily luring wild creatures to her hand or shooting game for the pot or gathering herbs for her lotions and potions.

Instead she was wimpled and gowned with the most rigid propriety and dragged out on a round of visits with Joanna and Gilliane. Rhiannon understood that this was not an idle waste of time. She had displayed the romantic and barbaric aspect of Wales and now had to show that the Welsh could also be proper and civilized. There was information to be seeded and information to be gleaned, rumors to be picked up and those, more suitable to the purposes of Roselynde, to be spread. Rhiannon knew that Gilliane and Joanna were working as hard as their menfolk and toward the same purpose. She judged their efforts both necessary and useful, for she was no fool, and did what she could to assist them. Nonetheless, she found it weary, distasteful work.

Returning to the house tired and irritable, Rhiannon discovered that more of the same awaited her. Since Alinor had received a message from Ian to the effect that all the menfolk would neither dine nor sleep at home, she had invited various women to join her and her daughters. The ostensible purpose was to meet Rhiannon, newly betrothed to Alinor's youngest son—so Rhiannon had no choice but to attend. The real purpose was the same as before, to gain and disseminate information and opinion.

Unfortunately, in a larger group, it was not possible for the ladies of Roselynde to shield Rhiannon as effectively. Politics was not the only thing discussed, or, rather, politics was most often discussed from a personal angle. This resulted in Rhiannon's being innundated with information about who was sleeping with whom. Henry's court was not deliberately licentious the way John's had been; Henry himself was not a lecher. Nonetheless, he was a young, full-blooded man, no prude, and he would not think of troubling himself with moral regulations that were, in his opinion, the business of the Church and would make many of his dear friends miserable and resentful.

The gossip in itself was distasteful; Rhiannon was not in the least interested in the bed-hopping proclivities of people she did not know, but she was accustomed to such gossip. Her father's court was no different, though smaller. Where there are men and women there will be sexual games. The difference was that now, all too often, Rhiannon herself was the target of the tales. Although not all of the women had seen her performance, all knew of it, and many had carefully whetted knives with which to stab her. Thus she was the recipient of more than one broad tale of Simon's doings, delivered with every range of feeling from genuine concern to vicious venom.

At first Rhiannon was inclined to laugh, remembering how Simon had said that when she was warned against him the half of it would not be true at all and the other half, exaggerated. "Were I what is said of me," he complained, "I would need seven of everything a man uses to make love. . . ." But when she finally got into the empty bed that night, she began to wonder whether the bed Simon was sleeping in was also empty. It was quite difficult for a woman to be unfaithful to a man. Confined to a home and an area where she was known, it required effort and secrecy to take a lover. That so many women accomplished it was a tribute to female cleverness. A man, on the contrary, had no such problems. He rode where he liked, most often to places it was very unlikely his woman would ever go. How could she know, Rhiannon wondered, whether Simon was true to the oath he had sworn to her?

She told herself not to be a fool. It was ridiculous to think a man who professed love and had made love so eagerly and with such tenderness the preceding night would betray his vows on the next night. She knew that was true, yet she shook and burned, cold and hot with rage and grief and jealousy. Then, when Ian and Geoffrey and Adam came home the next day, saying that Simon had been invited to hunt and would return later, Rhiannon had to make herself busy so that no one would see her face. Choking on her anguish, she asked herself *what* Simon was hunting. Was he on the trail of a four-legged or a two-legged doe? And even if he truly was hunting deer, did that not show clearly that he preferred the company of his hunt companions to her? Well, and if so, he could have them. She would leave him to them for good and all.

Some time after she reached this resentful conclusion, a squire of the body to the king came with a special invitation and request that Lady Rhiannon come to sing for Henry and some special guests from Provence. Since the messenger came into the hall while Rhiannon was trying to calm herself by better fitting her French translations to her music, she could scarcely have found an excuse not to go. In her present mood, it never entered her mind to seek any excuse. She accepted the invitation at once, only requesting time to dress herself suitably.

No ease or hope had been discovered in the two days of discussions. Ian was tired and depressed. He did not wish to go to court and to put on a face of calm and goodwill. Naturally the squire's instructions did not forbid him to attend; in decency the invitation could not exclude the male kin of any woman invited to the court. However, the fact that they had not been specifically invited hinted that Henry would prefer their absence. Rhiannon's safety had been fully provided for. In addition to the squire, there was a full escort of men-at-arms and a promise of a full escort to bring her home safely when her performance was over.

A hurried conference resulted in Rhiannon setting off alone with the squire and her escort when she was ready. It was thought impolitic, almost insulting, to send for Geoffrey or Adam to accompany her. Ian had offered himself, but the sound of his breath rattling in his chest and the glances Alinor had cast at him made Rhiannon's decision very easy. By now she was sure that Henry had no intention of keeping her by force—which was absolutely true; the king had never thought of it at all—and her head was much fuller of a mingled desire to spite Simon and worry over Ian than of the king's intentions.

Simon returned not long after Rhiannon had gone. He could not fly into a rage with his father, whom he found surrounded by another group of men fearful over a new batch of rumors. Ian was already gray with worry and fatigue, and Alinor, who had excluded all the servants from the solar lest they hear more than they should, was serving her guests herself with set teeth and lips tight with anxiety. It would have been better if Simon had followed his first impulse and gone to Geoffrey's house to explode, but his second thought was that he must get to court before his precious prize was stolen from him.

Obviously, Simon could not rush to court in the dirty, dusty, bloodstained clothes in which he had hunted. Thus, it took a little time to wash his face and hands and get into decent garments. By the time he arrived, Rhiannon was nearly finished with her song. She had chosen a shorter piece this time, being less positive than the king that ancient tales of magic and adventure would interest sophisticated Provençals and Savoyards. In fact, the reception was so enthusiastic that Simon, a very junior person and not even a vassal of the king, could get nowhere near her.

The guests' sincere requests for another song, to which Rhiannon acceded with quiet pleasure, gave Simon a chance to work his way nearer. At the end of this second song Rhiannon respectfully begged not to sing again because she was tired. Simon tensed, but there was no need. Although the audience was regretful, not even the king insisted. However, he again came down from his chair of state to speak to Rhiannon. Simon could not quite get through the crowd to reach them, but he was quite close enough to see Henry give Rhiannon a beautiful ring from his own finger and hear him again try to convince her to join the court.

Rhiannon shook her head slowly, making her heavy, jewel-laden earrings swing and flash. "I could not, even if I so wished, my lord."

"You mean because Simon's lands are in Wales? But that is nothing. I can give him—"

"No, indeed," Rhiannon interrupted emphatically. "It is nothing to do with Simon. I love my father, but I could never abide even his court for very long. I need the empty space, the hills, and the forests. My lord, you may catch and cage a lark and it may live—but it will never sing. If you leave me free, I will return to you, often and gladly, for you love in your heart what I do. That is a sure lure and the mead I crave far more than this precious ring you have given me. I beg you, do not try to cage me."

"But if you go back to your hills, it will be very long before you come again, no matter how willingly."

"And that would be a very great loss to us all," the Bishop of Winchester added smoothly to Henry's protest. "We must find such inducements as will make our Welsh lark desire to nest in an English meadow. Larks fly high, but they do not stray from their nests. Thus, Lady Rhiannon may be free and we may still hear her sing."

Rhiannon would have stepped back, away from the black eyes that transfixed her, but a hard body blocked her move, and a hard hand encircled her arm. She uttered a soft, shocked cry, but before she could pull away from the restraint she feared, Simon's voice identified the man behind her.

"As I told my lord the king a day ago, there is no immediate need for any inducement. It is my intention to remain with the court."

The words were civil. They might have had a better effect if Simon's eyes were not brilliant with challenge. He had been able to come up to Rhiannon at last because as Winchester advanced, the people around her had fallen back, away from the bishop. The combined effect of the withdrawal and Simon's expression was not at all soothing to Winchester's feelings. Simon's look dried the saliva in Rhiannon's mouth, and she stepped sideways instinctively, although she could not flee with Simon's hand holding her arm like an iron band. The movement drew the king's eyes, but fortunately he misread the expression on her face.

"We have tired you," he said regretfully.

Rhiannon seized on his words as a drowning man clutches at a chance log floating by. "Yes, I am sorry," she whispered. "Will you give me leave, my lord, to go?"

"Yes, of course," Henry replied at once, and added contritely, "We should not have urged you to sing a second time. I shall take care in the future not to ask too much."

Winchester opened his mouth, possibly to protest or to offer a quiet chamber where Rhiannon could rest, but Simon was prepared and spoke first.

"There is no need to call her escort. I have my own men. I will see my wife home." He swept her away, hardly allowing her to curtsy to the king and bishop. As soon as they were out of earshot, he snarled, "Fool! Idiot! To come alone into their power. Have you no sense at all?"

Rhiannon made no reply because she had been far more frightened by Winchester than by the king. In retrospect, his smooth speech about an English meadow was terrifying. Rhiannon knew that the bishop had not been at all touched by her singing. He enjoyed it in a mild way, but if he was willing to offer inducements, it was to snare Llewelyn's daughter, who might be a useful hostage. He had no real desire to keep her for his pleasure. Nonetheless, as her fear receded a little, she grew angry. Simon had no right to insult her and call her a fool when he did not know the circumstances of her going.

"Did I not tell you not to go to sing for the king again?" Simon asked furiously when they were mounted and out of earshot of the guards at the door. "It is by God's Grace alone that I came there in time."

"You are a fool yourself," Rhiannon snapped. "I had no choice but to go. Ask your mother and father. They will tell you. And you are worse than I! You had no need almost to fling a glaive into Winchester's face."

"What would you have had me do? Should I have let him take you to a private chamber somewhere in the keep and tell the world that you found it so delightful that you wished to stay?"

"The king would not suffer it!" Rhiannon exclaimed.

"Why not? Oh, he might be angry at first, but after it was explained how fine a hostage he had in his hands, not only for your father but for me and my father and my brothers——"

"I did not say it was wrong to take me away," Rhiannon broke in hotly. "I said you were a fool to do it in such a way that Winchester understood your suspicions all too well. And you are more the fool because I could have got away on my own without making more bad feeling than there is already."

"Only an ignorant chit of a girl would think of such a stupidity," Simon snarled. "You might have left the hall, but you would never have arrived at home."

"And who would have given such an order to the king's squire of the body and the escort he led? Simon, you are ridiculous! Winchester would not take me by force, and you know it. Perhaps my father loves me, but he loves nothing so well as Gwynedd, and my life or death would not alter his purpose—except to make him put to death shamefully and cruelly ten or twenty or a hundred English knights to pay for my blood. Winchester must know this."

"I tell you, you know nothing about it," Simon raged. "You are ignorant of the ways of this court. In the future, simply obey me and do not cause me so much trouble."

"I will cause you none at all by my will," Rhiannon

hissed, "for I will have no more to do with you than I can help—and that will be little indeed."

At that inopportune moment they arrived at the house. Simon was appalled by the icy rage which gave force to Rhiannon's words. He reached for the bridle of her mare, to lead it on so that he would have time to take back what he had said and calm her, but she slipped from the saddle and ran past the gate, through the courtyard, and into the house. Simon was after her in moments, but it was too late. By the time he caught up, she was standing in front of the screen that shielded their bed.

"You are not welcome here," she said softly but very coldly.

"Be reasonable," Simon protested, also softly. "There is no other place for me."

"Go find yourself another woman's bed. There are plenty open to you, I hear. So skilled as you are, they should be far less trouble to you than I am."

"You hear aright, and it would be less trouble," Simon grated, infuriated past good sense, "but I am constrained by my oath and I will not so lightly release you from yours."

Rhiannon's lips drew back from her teeth, but not in a smile. "You think yourself irresistible? You have much to learn about me, Simon. We will see whose hunger conquers." She stepped aside. "Stay or go as you please then—but do not touch me."

She went about her business after that as if he were invisible, laying aside her jewels, undressing, and getting into the bed. After a stunned moment Simon followed her behind the screen and stood watching her, hardly believing what she seemed to mean.

"Rhiannon—" he said.

"Good night," she replied. "I beg you not to trouble me longer with talk. I am tired. Do not strain my forbearance."

Simon stood a moment longer, took an uncertain step toward the edge of the screen, and then stopped. The solar was dark except for the pale flicker of a night candle. That meant his father and mother were asleep. Even as he stood there, the oldest of the maids dropped the bars across the outside door and drew her pallet across in front of it. Another was snuffing the lights. Really, there *was* no place for Simon to go. He thought briefly of sleeping on the floor and resentment flooded him. Why should he?

Instead he threw off his clothes and climbed into the bed, dropping flat with an ill-natured thump. If he was not irresistible, he thought angrily, neither was she! In truth, Helen herself would not have been irresistible to Simon that night. He was bone tired, both physically and emotionally. Thus, in spite of the turmoil of resentment and remorse, he fell asleep very quickly.

His deep, even breathing was an additional insult to Rhiannon. Although the fury with which Simon had cited his oath to her as a bar to his seeking another woman's company had convinced her he had not yet betrayed that oath, she told herself angrily that it was only temporary. Next time he would. But she was uncomfortable even in her rage. There was a falseness in it and in the fuel she was using to feed it. Nonetheless, for some reason she could not bear to contemplate at all, she would not let it go.

Simon slept like a log and did not wake until he heard the tables being set up for breakfast. Then he remembered he had missed the evening meal the night before and was suddenly ravenous. He put out a hand to wake Rhiannon, but he remembered the quarrel of the preceding night before he touched her. Better to let her wake on her own. Simon's irritation with Rhiannon had evaporated with his exhaustion, but his memory of the scene with Winchester was more, rather than less, troubling. Grabbing a bedrobe, he went out and found his parents already eating.

To Simon's relief, his father looked quite normal this morning. His eyes were still worried, but the frightening gray tinge was gone from his skin, and Alinor's smile seemed quite natural. Thus, he was able to tell the whole tale of the none-too-subtle confrontation with Winchester. Ian was appalled, but Alinor shook her head at him.

"I do not say I would have taken the same path," she remarked, "but I can see a useful end to this one." A snap of the fingers summoned a servant, whom she sent to fetch Geoffrey. "Rhiannon must not come before the king again," she went on when she had finished the message to the servant. "At least, not while we are here in Oxford."

"I am glad you agree with me," Simon said.

"Yesterday I did not agree with you," Alinor pointed out. "Today is different because Rhiannon did go yesterday."

"I cannot believe Winchester ever intended such a thing," Ian protested. "He is devious, but not mad. Holding Rhiannon would never stop Llewelyn, but would only make him more ferocious."

"That was what Rhiannon said, but I am not sure Winchester realizes that Llewelyn would react that way," Simon insisted.

"It does not matter a pin what Winchester intended or understood. He may be innocent of all evil designs," Alinor snapped. "What does matter is that he has given into our hands another needle with his name on it to thrust into the king's hide."

Both her husband and her son stopped chewing to stare at her. "Well?" Ian prompted.

"Wait for Geoffrey," Alinor replied, smiling and taking a hearty bite from a slice of cheese. "I do not wish to have to say it all twice."

Simon and Ian looked at each other. They were never so much at one as in those times when they both wished to strangle Alinor. Fortunately for their pride and their tempers, Geoffrey and the others came in just then. A gesture made Simon recapitulate what he had just told them. Various expressions, some of approval and some of irritation, were cut off by Ian's shushing motions.

"Your mother," he remarked sardonically, "was delighted. She says she has a way to turn this stupidity to account, but it needs Geoffrey's concurrence."

Geoffrey immediately began to look very wary. Alinor was usually wise, but from time to time a really outrageous notion would occur to her. Since she was both clever and stubborn, it was very difficult either to prove her wrong or to divert her.

"You need not look as if I were about to hand you a live adder wrapped in rose leaves," Alinor said.

"But it is not unknown for you to do so, Mama," Gilliane pointed out gently, "and to say such a thing can only make poor Geoffrey wonder all the more."

Alinor laughed. "But do you not see it?" she asked.

"Henry is assuredly besotted on Rhiannon's singing. He noticed that she was frightened when he spoke of keeping her—you told me that, Ian. He cannot have failed to notice how disturbed she was at what Winchester said when she had just asked for assurances that she would not be caged."

"Come, Mama, spit it out," Adam said impatiently. "What are we to do?"

"You? Nothing! You are as bad as Simon for saying what you should not. What Simon will do is take Rhiannon to our house in London."

"Why London?" Simon asked. "I can see reason to take her home to Wales, but not to London. We will be even more vulnerable there."

"There is no question of vulnerability," Alinor replied. "You are letting your imagination run wild. No force will be used. Besides, you assured both Winchester and the king that you would remain with the court until the council." Then she turned her eyes to her son-by-marriage. "This is where Geoffrey's concurrence is needed. When the king asks for Rhiannon to sing again, as he will, Geoffrey must tell him that Winchester frightened her so much with his talk of nests in English meadows that she only wished to flee home last night."

Geoffrey's face cleared. "Yes, and you are quite right, this is not an adder wrapped in rose leaves—at least, not for me. I see the rest now. I can say that it took all our efforts to convince her not to go home but that nothing would make her remain here. Finally we managed to find a compromise. She would go to London and sing for the king, but only at Alinor's house or when Winchester was not at court. Then, when the king comes to London, I will remind him. Yes, yes, this is good."

"There is only one difficulty," Simon put in, rather red in the face. "I do not know whether Rhiannon will agree."

Every head turned to him. In the silence his flush grew deeper.

"Well?" Alinor urged sharply.

"We—er—quarreled over her going alone to court last night," Simon offered. "I was tired and said more than I should."

"You must have said a good deal more than was necessary," Alinor snapped.

"But it was *my* fault, Simon," Ian interrupted hastily. "Curse me! I should have gone with her. I knew it, but—"

"There is no sense in 'should haves' now," Alinor broke in. "I am sorry we could not explain to Simon how it came about that Rhiannon went alone. Who could believe that he would fix on this idea of abducting her? In any case, there will be plenty of time to explain to Rhiannon why it is necessary for her to go to London."

"Yes, because it will really forward Llewelyn's purpose more than ours," Geoffrey remarked. "Our point will be made even if she insists on going back to Wales."

"But I am not afraid that she will wish to go to Wales," Simon complained. "She is almost as enamored of the king's listening as he is of her singing."

"That is not true," Rhiannon said. Everyone had been so absorbed in the discussion that no one had noticed her come out from behind the bed curtains. She was standing quite near the table, her eyes angry. "Any singer is glad of those who listen with their hearts," she continued, "but a wise bird does not sit down on limed twigs just to obtain hearers."

Simon threw up his hands in disgust. "Everything I say is wrong these days."

To this no one bothered to reply. Alinor had done a quick survey of what had been said and decided with relief that nothing except Simon's last words could be thought of as critical of Rhiannon. This did not worry Alinor. She was quite confident of her son's ability to wriggle out of any stupidity he had fallen into with a girl who loved him. In fact, the best opportunity for him to redeem himself would occur when they were alone.

"Well, then," Alinor said, as if her son had not spoken, "are you willing to go with Simon to London and await the king's coming there?"

"Yes, I am," Rhiannon replied. "I may be ignorant— as some believe—but I am not too stupid to learn."

CHAPTER 19

To be sure they were not making any mistake, Geoffrey rode off to court while Simon took Rhiannon out into the countryside. That way, if Geoffrey were asked about her, he could say quite truthfully that he did not know where she was nor when she would return. As far as Geoffrey was concerned, however, that move was wasted. The court was in too great an uproar for anyone to think of a singer, no matter how fine.

As soon as Henry had come from his chamber after breaking his fast, a herald had delivered aloud and in public the Earl of Pembroke's demand that the terms of the truce be met. The earl begged in all duty and humility, the herald said, that the king's writ bidding his servants return Usk to Pembroke's men be sent at once. The herald offered to take the writ himself or to accompany the king's messenger if the king preferred to send one.

Behind his expressionless face, Geoffrey's thoughts flicked: Firstly, that Walter must have found Richard in good time. Secondly, that Richard had made a very clever move. Thirdly, that Winchester's first line of attack had certainly been checked. Doubtless the bishop had counted on Pembroke sending a deputy to Usk, since he was due at Westminster on October ninth. There had been no arrangement for any public announcement of the return of Usk. In fact, the expectation would be that it would be done as quietly and unobtrusively as possible to save face for the king. Winchester had hoped, Geoffrey assumed, that no one, including Richard, would know for certain that the terms of the truce had been broken until the date of the council.

If things had gone as Winchester desired, Pembroke's deputy would have been put off with some likely excuse—such as that the king's messenger had been delayed and Usk could not be handed over until the writ came. Two chances to one the deputy would have waited at least a week before sending a message to warn Richard that the king had broken his word and that Usk was still in his hands. But by then, Richard would have been at Westminster already, and if so, his protest could have been used as a reason to imprison him.

Instead, the king's perfidy was displayed to all the barons so openly that they could not ignore it even if they wished. Now the retaking of Usk could begin without delay, and, far more important, Pembroke was well removed from the king's power and safe on his own lands.

"You know what this means," Ferrars said heavily. "Henry will send out another summons to war."

"I cannot answer it," Geoffrey stated flatly. "I was one of the sureties that Usk would be returned."

Ferrars nodded. "I do not think Pembroke will hold you liable to fight against the king. I do not know what I will do." The earl's voice was suddenly old, broken. "I have never wavered in my faith, but this cause is foul! It stinks in all men's nostrils."

"There are many mercenaries in the land," Geoffrey remarked neutrally.

This was the second string to Winchester's bow, Geoffrey thought. No doubt the bishop would have preferred the easy way of taking Pembroke prisoner and quelling a rebellion that had no focal point. However, it was unlikely that he really believed things would be so easy. He must have half-expected that someone would warn Richard to stay away. But if the barons would not come to the summons and still Pembroke could be broken with the strength of the mercenaries, Winchester would have gained as much.

These dismal thoughts were broken by Ferrars's unmirthful bark of laughter. "Mercenaries will avail him nothing. Still, I wish I knew where this would end. It is Winchester—all Winchester—and just when there is no Archbishop of Canterbury. If only there were another man such as Stephen Langton to curb Peter des Roches. . . ."

Geoffrey doubted that even the Pope could curb Peter des Roches, but Ferrars's remark had given him another idea. The king's faith was really quite strong. Perhaps there was some way to involve the Church, although thus far the bishops had been reluctant to combine against Winchester. For some, this was owing to a lack of courage, but the best of the high churchmen had more than enough spirit. The trouble was that these men were also truly religious and most careful to obey the dictum that what was Caesar's must be rendered unto Caesar. They would not interfere in the political management of the kingdom, except by pleading as impartial persons for mercy and justice. Still, Geoffrey liked his idea so much that he took it home to Ian and Alinor.

"It is a good thought," Alinor remarked, pursing her lips. "Roger of London and Robert of Salisbury are strong enough and can carry with them many weaker vessels, but they will need a cause that touches the Church. There is no sense waiting for something to turn up. Perhaps—"

"No, Alinor," Ian said apprehensively, "for God's sake, let us not embroil ourselves with God's elect. Let us see what comes to light in this conference. The bishops will all be in London, and I promise I will sound them out. Then we will know better how to direct our efforts."

"Very well, I will do nothing until the conference," Alinor agreed, and her son-by-marriage and husband breathed more freely until, a moment later, she added, "But I will think about it," which made them groan gently.

Simon had been no more enthusiastic than Rhiannon when it was agreed that the safest thing to do was for him to take his betrothed out riding. She had gone with him as she was bid, but she was bristling like a cat about to spit, though Simon gave her no immediate cause to be angry. In silence he helped her into her saddle and in silence followed wherever she wandered, remaining a few paces behind her. Finally, after they had dismounted and Rhiannon had sat down on a fallen log, her irritation spilled over in speech.

"What do you accomplish by this?" she snapped.

"Nothing," Simon answered mildly. "Believe me, I would not be in your company if it was not necessary."

"I am very glad to hear that," Rhiannon interrupted caustically.

Simon shrugged. "It is true enough, but only because I know myself to be in the wrong, and I know you to be too angry to listen to my apology. For both of us it would be better to be apart. Since we are constrained to be in company, what can I do but hold my tongue?"

"So you are in the wrong?"

"Yes. I know now you had no choice but to go to the king. My father should have gone with you, but I can only thank you for not asking it of him. He was not well, I know. In any case, my choice of words and tone was uncivil. I was out of temper and tired, and I struck out at you."

There was a long silence after that. Rhiannon wandered away from the tree, drifting aimlessly here and there. Simon did not follow her, only turning so that he could keep her in sight. The horses, tethered to a low branch, nibbled at the leaves of bushes and at the thin blades of grass that straggled wherever a patch of sunlight fell. Eventually Rhiannon returned and resumed her seat on the log.

"Not all the fault was yours," she admitted quietly.

"It is ever so," Simon replied, equally quietly. "One cannot quarrel with a stone wall. But the initial fault was mine, and so it is for me to take the blame. It is sweeter and easier, Rhiannon, that you are willing to share with me."

"Blame, yes. My life, no."

It was said gently, sorrowfully. Simon breathed in as if he had been cut, but he did not speak for a few minutes. Finally he looked away from her face, which he had been watching.

"That seems a harsh punishment for a few hasty and unwise words."

She stood up and took his hand in hers. "You know I do not mean it so, Simon. I said as many hasty and unwise words. I knew you were tired and had only to hold my tongue and all would blow over. I am as much at fault as you—I have said that already. I am sorry to give you pain also, but I am trying in the only way I know to spare us both worse in the future. Dear Simon, it is not what you said to me or what I said to you that brought me to this decision. It is what caused me to answer you with such bitterness when there was no cause to do so."

"Rhiannon, if you think people who love each other do

not quarrel, you are truly an innocent. Roselynde, as you know, is a strong keep, but there were times when I thought that my mother and father would have it down around our ears by their violence. Yet surely you must see they love each other."

"You did not listen. It was not the quarrel that distressed me but what I felt before it. What did you hunt yesterday, Simon?"

He looked at her in considerable surprise but would not chance angering her again and answered simply, "A stag. We lost two before we finally killed. I could not divert those idiots no matter what I said. And then—"

"I was sure it was a doe."

"There is no harm in taking a doe in this season," Simon said with a slight frown of puzzlement. "Do you have some special feeling about it, my love? I will swear, if you like, to hold does sacred."

"A two-legged doe, Simon," Rhiannon said pointedly, with a bitter twist to her lips.

Simon stared at her, his mouth partly open on further words that were not relevant. Then he laughed. "You are ridiculous! How could you dream such a thing? I had you the night before. I could look forward to loving you the very next night. Even if I felt such a desire—which I assure you I did not; I am no satyr—you must think ill of me indeed if you believe I could not master myself for so short a time."

"I do not think ill of you. In my mind I knew every word you have just said—and knew the words were true. Nonetheless, Simon, I suffered as cruelly as if you had betrayed me."

"But Rhiannon—"

"I cannot bear it, Simon. I cannot! I absolve you of your oath. I do not wish to know or care—"

"You cannot absolve me of my oath. If you wish to withdraw yours, I cannot stop you. And if I have you, it must be with honor. If I cannot have you, then I will remain celibate as a priest until I am too old to care, but I will have no other woman, Rhiannon."

"Listen to me. Be reasonable," she begged. "Can you not see you are being cruel? I do not blame you in any way. I know you have been true. It is *my* mind, *my* heart that have failed. If I reach out to grasp you and hold you for my own, my fears and jealousy—whether real or unreal—will kill me."

Simon stared at her and then put his arm around her and drew her to him. "What do you want me to do, Rhiannon? I love you. I cannot force you to take me, but I will not give you up for a whim of jealousy. I could not, even if I wished it. I do not desire any other woman."

"Now. But if you put me out of your thoughts, in the years ahead—"

He laughed. "I may be dead in a few weeks in the next battle. It is ridiculous for me to think long years in the future."

Rhiannon was as still in his arm as a wild hare that mimics death, but inside she had been seized by a cold shuddering. Simon dead? How could he speak of his own death with such indifferent serenity? Simon's sidelong glance caught her loss of color, another confirmation, if any were needed, that she did love him. In a way it was very discouraging. Simon knew how to make a woman love him, but it seemed that the more Rhiannon loved him, the harder she struggled to be free. He really did not know what to do next.

She pulled free of him suddenly and ran away. Seeing that she was not keeping in sight as she had in her previous restless idling, Simon untied the horses and followed. He was really worried. This fleeing was symbolic of the inner emotion Rhiannon felt. When he thought back, he realized she had always done it. At Dinas Emrys, when she first realized she was beginning to love him, she had run away. And then she had tried to run into another man's arms, just to avoid his at Aber.

How far would she run this time—not in the wood but in her thoughts? How could he catch her again? No, he knew the answer to that. There were multitudinous snares that could be set to trap a woman into love or to demonstrate to her that she already loved, but that was the last thing he needed. Rhiannon would be taken in the snare easily enough, since she did love him; but she would tear herself apart—as a fox would chew off its own leg—to get free.

For the first time in his life Simon was truly and deeply

at a loss in how to handle a woman. When Rhiannon had sent him way the first time, he had been hurt and angered by the rejection; nonetheless, he knew the right moves to conquer her—or so he had thought. Now he was lost himself and did not even know to whom to turn for help. Ian could only tell him what he himself knew; not even Kicva could guarantee the future; and there was no sense in having a priest tell Rhiannon to trust in the all-encompassing mercy of Christ and His Mother. Rhiannon went to Mass and professed Christianity, but she still swore by Anu and Danu. The dark, merciless gods of a dim past had a strong hold on her.

Rhiannon ran until she could run no farther, then threw herself down to catch her breath. While she ran, there was relief. Her mind had been blank, her consciousness devoted solely to her physical effort. When her body was still, however, her mind began to move again. Tears flooded her eyes and then sank back. No one could run forever, or do any other task without rest and food. There was no way out by that door.

Simon was waiting at a respectful distance, not imposing himself. It was the right thing to do and, because of that, more wrong than anything else. Rhiannon came near to hating him for his gentleness and understanding. If only he would be angry; if only he would intrude so that she could find him coarse and unfeeling; if only he would even stare at her in silent misery so she could tell herself he was falsely demanding attention. There was not even self-pity in his face nor the determination that often showed when she had denied him in the past. He hardly looked sad; he seemed more thoughtful or puzzled. There would be no escape through Simon's unworthiness.

Although Rhiannon longed for her home and the freedom that she believed could bring her peace, she knew she could not leave England until she had at least one more meeting with the king. Somehow she needed to express clearly the idea for which she hoped she had laid the foundation: that she loved the king's appreciation of her music and would sing for him regardless of any enmity that might exist between her father and him—so long as she was free to come and go. Then, clearly, she could not even break the betrothal with Simon.

She was stiff and cold when she finally rose and came toward Simon, who also stood. "We must come to some terms, Simon."

In the hour and more that Rhiannon had wrestled with her fear and her conscience, Simon had done a good deal of thinking also. It had occurred to him, after he had struggled up out of a morass of hurt and self-pity, that this whole thing was a small pond stirred by a boy's stick rather than a great storm at sea. Rhiannon had been subjected to so many new and unusual experiences, all piled atop one another and all in a very short time. She was not used to so many strange people admiring and threatening, to the strain of an unaccustomed task for which she was unprepared and found distasteful, to the demands of a large family, all loving but nonetheless all pulling at her in different directions. Most of all, she was probably totally disoriented by the constant busyness and noise, which permitted no time for quiet.

As he had enumerated the pressures on Rhiannon to himself, Simon grew somewhat more cheerful. Perhaps she was, in her own controlled way, hysterical. Perhaps the period in London, away from the anxieties of dealing with his family and the court, would help. But then there would be another bad period when Henry moved to Westminster. It would be better to put no additional burden on her, Simon thought, while she had so many to bear already. He could wait. When she was home in Angharad's Hall, safe in her own place with her burdens dropped behind her, perhaps she would no longer fear to love.

Thus, he was better prepared for her appeal for terms than most lovers would have been. "I will not importune you," he assured her, "but I will not release you from your oath to me, either."

"No, I do not desire that. The betrothal must stand so long as I must deal with Henry, but you must understand it means nothing for the future. I will not marry you, Simon, nor do I any longer desire to hold you to your oath to me. You are free to do as you please with any woman you please."

"A worthless freedom, and one you *cannot* give me. I am not bound to you because of my oath. I gave my oath because I was already bound. But I have said already that I will force nothing on you. What else do you expect of me?"

"I do not know," Rhiannon admitted fretfully. "There is something about you that strokes me and whispers 'love' even when you are at the other end of a room looking elsewhere."

In spite of his worry, Simon burst out laughing. "My infamous charm! I swear I do not do it apurpose—at least not to you."

"Then it would be better, I think, if we were less often in the same place."

Simon regarded Rhiannon silently. He subdued a new feeling of hurt and was able to accept it. "We must live in the same house in London," he told her, "at least until the rest of the family arrives, but we can go separate ways. Before the court comes, you will be safe enough with a small escort. I will not need to accompany you to the markets or whatever other diversions you choose."

"And what will you do?"

The question pleased Simon. He had been afraid she would try to forget he was alive. "I will contrive to keep myself busy. I have friends I have not seen in some time —men friends."

She nodded acceptance and indicated she wished to mount. As they rode slowly back to Oxford, Rhiannon found she felt better. The settlement they had reached and her belief that she could cure herself of her love once she was home were helpful, but the lightening of Simon's mood was having a strong, if unrecognized, influence. Without thinking, Rhiannon asked a question about the river that wound lazily below them. Simon replied, and by the time they reached the house they were, outwardly at least, on easy terms.

Alinor sensed something very wrong, but she said nothing. Rhiannon was essentially beyond her experience. It was as if a wild doe had suddenly chosen to join a flock of sheep. One watched it with pleasure but did not try to herd it.

Besides, no one had much time to think about Simon and Rhiannon. When Geoffrey returned from court, he found more news at home than what he brought. Richard's herald had been accompanied by a small party for safety in traveling through the disturbed countryside, and one of that party had ridden aside to bring a letter from Walter. All were breathless when Ian read aloud by how narrow a margin they had averted disaster.

By God's Grace, Walter wrote, *I chose the road to Woodstock rather than to Burford on my way to Wales. Not a half-mile west of the town did I find Pembroke coming most innocently with only ten men and his two squires. By so slight a chance, the going on one road rather than another for only a few miles, was this enterprise saved.*

"I cannot believe it only chance," Gilliane breathed. Surely God was our help in this matter."

"God helped those who helped themselves by sending Walter out in the first place," Adam said cynically.

The whole family laughed. That God helped those who helped themselves was Alinor's favorite maxim and had been driven deep into her family's heads by repeated usage.

"Most certainly," Ian agreed. "Listen to this. Walter says that Richard did not wish to believe him. *So fixed was the earl's belief in the honor of those with whom he swore truce that had I not carried Lord Geoffrey's letter under his own seal, he would have clung to the conviction that I spoke wild rumor only and would have come to Oxford that very night to do courtesy by riding under the king's protection to Westminster.* I wonder . . . ." Ian looked up. "I wonder if that might have been better? The king would have been touched by such faith."

Adam snorted. "Yes, until the snake hissed in his ear again."

Ian made no reply to that, returning to the letter to read how Richard persisted in clinging to the hope that at the last minute Henry would not be able to break his word. *"He agreed so far as to return to Usk,* the letter continues, *and send a herald to the king, vowing he would not move until the king's own denial was delivered to him. There was a great anger held in check, however. I think when the truce is broken the earl will no longer hold himself back but will unleash his power and his fury."*

"I think so, too," Adam said with grim satisfaction. "I

am sorry his lands are so far from mine that I cannot offer the assistance of victualing or even of providing men, but I fear there will be many who will use the ill feeling against the king to raid here and there for their own profit."

"So I think also," Geoffrey agreed. "It will behoove us to keep our lands and—if we can—our neighbors quiet."

"But what if the king prevails?" Joanna asked.

"He will. He must." Geoffrey smiled wryly at the exclamations of horror that followed his statement, and added, "But I think Winchester will not. I do not think Winchester or Henry can lead any force effectively enough to hurt Pembroke. There are skilled captains among the mercenaries, but none strong enough to lead the whole group. I know. I have dealt with them. The king will be shamed worse than he was at Usk. At first he will be bitterer than ever against Pembroke, but when loss heaps on loss and he sees there is no path but reconciliation, he will abandon Winchester."

"Yes. Then Richard will gladly make submission, and all will be well," Ian said.

"After the blood and the death and the ravaging and the famine—oh, yes, then all will be well," Alinor remarked bitterly. "This nation is accursed, I swear it. First there was King Richard, who did not care. Then there was King John, who cared but had a wrongness in him that turned all to evil. And now we have King Henry, who—"

"Hush, my love." Ian kissed her silent. "He is young yet. He will learn."

Whether she would have remained quiet was doubtful, but just then Simon and Rhiannon came in, and the whole matter needed to be explained to them.

"Thank God Walter found him," Simon said. "Well, now what? I mean, do we go to London as planned, or back to Wales to bring this news to Prince Llewelyn?"

Geoffrey pulled the lobe of his ear in thought and then said, "To London. It is your belief that Llewelyn will join Pembroke against the king if Pembroke is firm to fight this time?" He accepted Simon's nod and went on, "I think so, too. Then all the more will there be a need for Rhiannon to serve as an unguent between Henry's too-sensitive feelings and Llewelyn's harsh acts."

A general murmur of approval from all preceded the decision that Simon and Rhiannon had better leave as soon as dinner was eaten. They were safe until then, but afterward there was the possibility that Henry would decide he needed Rhiannon's singing to calm his spirit after all his vexation. It would serve all purposes best if she were gone. This, too, found ready agreement, but going to Alinor's house in London was not as simple as packing one's clothing and leaving.

The house was only a shell. To make it livable, furniture, linen, pots and pans, and everything else must be carried. But Alinor's servants were accustomed to the procedure. While Rhiannon and Simon ate, maids and men scurried about dismantling and packing a selection of what had been brought to Oxford. Before the ladies and gentlemen had risen from the table, one cart was on its way with two maids, two men, and five of Simon's men-at-arms as a guard.

Although Simon and Rhiannon could easily have ridden the full distance to London, they went only as far as Wallingford to avoid outdistancing the baggage cart. Richard and Isabella made them very welcome, and the visit served a double purpose. It permitted the story of Rhiannon's fear of Winchester to be spread from another source. More important, in a personal way, was the other result of the visit. Isabella assumed without asking that Rhiannon would sleep in the women's quarters and Simon in a chamber off the hall. This provided an easy solution to the problem of whether or not they would make love if they slept together.

Alinor had sent to the London house only the one large bed Simon and Rhiannon had shared, but this posed no problem. Simon's traveling gear had been sent, since he expected to take Rhiannon directly back to Wales from London. Although his camp cot was not nearly as comfortable as the bed, he went to it with a sense of relief as well as of deprivation. Rhiannon was not the least shy. If she wanted him, she would tell him. Simon wished he was as sure of what the right response should be as he was that Rhiannon would not mind making the advances.

However, the question did not arise. Simon's relief diminished as his sense of deprivation increased, but he still did nothing. Rhiannon was growing more natural in her manner to him each day, and that seemed more important than reestablishing the sexual relationship. Every so often Simon wondered whether she still thought of that ugly challenge she had made the night they quarreled. But he did not dare dwell on it, and he did not need to.

He found plenty of occupation for himself with various young men to whom he had sent word that Simon de Vipont was in London and was seeking sparring and jousting partners. A group of young men rode in and made a merry company in the house. They fought each other singly, in pairs, and in various combinations that took into account the varying strengths of the combatants. Simon was very good, but he was sufficiently bruised and battered when pitted against two or three lesser opponents that he was quite content to seek his cot for sleep without thinking of love—at least, not too often.

Rhiannon was far less unhappy than she expected to be. She was no lover of cities, with their dirt and stench and disease and unnatural crowding together of people and houses until there seemed scarce room for a blade of grass to grow. Nonetheless, the places she knew were nothing—flyspecks—compared with the town of London. Protected by Simon's men-at-arms, she rode where she liked, alternately horrified and fascinated.

So, in spite of her distaste, in spite of the chills of horror that crawled over her when she thought of living in such a place, Rhiannon was aware that she might never see its like again. She wandered and poked and pried, bought seeds of strange herbs, bought silks as thin and as light as a mist. She had no money, but when she named Alinor's house, the merchants brought the goods with eager swiftness—and Simon paid. Rhiannon did not give the matter any thought. Kicva or Llewelyn would settle the debt, she supposed.

These pleasant few days ended on September twenty-ninth when, as dark fell, a tired messenger rode in with a brief note from Ian to inform Simon that Hubert de Burgh had escaped from his prison in Devizes and had taken refuge in a church. Since Rhiannon had heard de

Burgh's name often enough but knew virtually nothing about him, she and Simon were up half the night while he explained de Burgh's long and tumultuous career.

"Is he truly still dangerous?" she asked in the end.

Simon shrugged. "Impossible to say. He did many favors, but has virtually no blood kin, and you know how seldom favors make men grateful. But it also depends on the man himself. If he burns with hatred and resentment and cries aloud of his injuries demanding help from those he helped in their need, it is possible—considering the ill feeling against the king—that he could raise supporters. Then, too, he knows Henry. His advice might be of value to Henry's enemies."

"But if he is pent up in a church . . ."

Simon shrugged again. "Not for long. This is an act of final desperation. He must have heard that Henry was ready to give charge of Devizes to Winchester. That, he feared, would be his death warrant. Perhaps the gaolers feared it also and did not want the death to stain their hands, so they let him go. But it is six of one and half a dozen of the other. The king will set men to surround the church and prevent food and water from being carried to him. That is how he was taken last time. To save himself from starving he came out of sanctuary. Of course, last time he expected mercy. This time . . ."

But matters were not allowed to work themselves out in a natural way. Another messenger came pounding in to London the very next night with a much longer letter. Hubert's escape had not been the decision of the majority of his gaolers. Two young guards, William de Millers and Thomas the Chamberlain, had been stirred to pity by the broken old man. One had carried him, fetters and all, to the church. However, the master of Devizes, seeing ruin staring him in the face, sent out the whole garrison. They had found the fugitive and, instead of respecting the sanctuary, had beaten him and driven him back to Devizes, regardless of his clinging to the altar with a cross in his hands.

Simon grunted with excitement when he read this. It was a grave mistake, he thought, for the king was a religious man. Not only that, but the insult to the Church was just what his family had been trying to find that would rouse the bishops to combine against their fellow prelate. At present, Ian had written, Henry was so enraged that there was no approaching him, and he had ordered de Burgh strictly confined to the vault in which he had formerly been placed and fastened with three pairs of manacles; he was to have speech with no man whatsoever, including his guards. This, of course, was a further offense to the Church, that a man should be punished for seeking sanctuary. And, as Simon expected, the last of the letter directed him to take this news to the Bishop of London.

Early next morning Simon rode to the palace, where, to his relief, he heard that the bishop was in residence. His request for audience was granted. Simon prefaced his news by mentioning that his father did not believe in meddling with matters that belonged to the Church. This was quite true, although Simon had to pause a moment to control unwelcome mirth when he recalled certain actions his mother and Joanna had taken in the past against priests who differed with them.

The pause was quite effective, although Simon had not intended it as a dramatic device. The bishop urged him on, assuring him that he would not be considered officious or interfering. Properly cued, Simon told his tale, and Roger of London was suitably horrified. Although he said nothing to Simon about his intentions, there was a steely glitter in his eyes and a certain rigidity of his lips and jaw that indicated to Simon that his mission had been a success. Robert of Salisbury, the bishop in whose see the violation had occurred, would have to take the initiative, but the saintly Roger of London would be there to back him up—and London had already won one passage-at-arms with the king.

❖•❖

CHAPTER 20

A few days passed without further developments, and then Ian's letters began to come again. Robert of Salisbury had taken up the cudgels for Hubert de Burgh—or, rather, for the privilege of the Church. First he had gone to the castellan of Devizes and ordered him to send Hubert back to the church. The castellan had pleaded various reasons for the actions of his men and, when these were rejected, said flatly that they had rather Hubert be hanged than they. Robert of Salisbury, no more inclined to accept this reason than the others, promptly excommunicated all the offenders and set out for Oxford, where he remonstrated with the king with only slightly less vehemence.

The king, leaving the Bishop of Winchester to argue with his brother prelate, fled to Westminster. Simon and Rhiannon had warning of this and also that Geoffrey thought it would be a nice touch if Rhiannon presented herself voluntarily with an offer to sing, since Winchester was not at court. To Simon's delight—for a touch of jealousy had been roused in him by Rhiannon's response to the king's admiration—she was reluctant, although she admitted it would be the best thing to do. She felt more vulnerable in London, as if the wild countryside, which could shield her, was farther away and left her more at Henry's mercy. Simon, too, said he thought it would be best, but he did not urge her beyond that simple statement. In the end Rhiannon's conscience overrode her fear, and she agreed.

She hoped Henry would be too busy or too angry to accept the offer Simon delivered. The king, however, had a similarity to Rhiannon beyond his love of music; he also tried to run away from his problems. He was delighted with the suggestion and closed with it at once, sending the strongest assurances of his pleasure in her willingness to come to him. He greeted her with great kindness and even made a jesting reference to the necessary freedom of songbirds.

Nonetheless, Rhiannon felt choked and smothered, and she sang of the sorrows of the Rhiannon whose namesake she was, how the jealous women of her husband's court accused her of murdering her babe and smeared her with a pup's blood, and of the bitter sorrow and unmerited punishment she suffered until her husband's long faith in her was vindicated when the truth was exposed.

By chance the song fitted Henry's mood exactly, but for once he was as interested in the meaning under the tale as in the artistry with which it was told. "If Pwyll believed in her, he was a fool to yield to the demands of his barons," Henry said, after he had complimented Rhiannon on her singing.

"He did not do so," Rhiannon replied. "They bade him put her away, and he would not. It was for the sake of peace in the land and ease in the minds of his liegemen that he agreed to Rhiannon's penance—and, remember, she agreed with him and did the penance, if not gladly, willingly for the sake of peace."

"Peace is not everything," Henry said, starting to look black.

"I am a woman," Rhiannon murmured. "It is everything to me."

The frown cleared from Henry's face. "And that is as it should be. That is surely the woman's part, to make peace."

Rhiannon curtsied, as if in thanks for the king's approval, but it was a signal to Simon, who came to her side and asked solicitously whether she was tired. It had been planned between them and worked well; Henry took the hint quickly, excusing them graciously from further attendance. As Rhiannon curtsied again, he took her hand.

"You will not run away again if I just say I hope you will sing for me soon, Lady Rhiannon?"

"I will not run away from *you*, my lord," she assured him. "However, it is not a matter of my choice. My mother is alone. I must soon go home to make ready for the winter. It is a very hard time in the hills where we live. Sometimes the snow is so heavy that the hunters cannot go out and we are sealed into our dwellings. Much must be done in gathering stores to keep us over the worst months. But I promise I will come again, as soon as I can, and most gladly."

"All the way from Wales, just to sing for me?" Henry asked, raising his brows.

"Yes," Rhiannon said, "all the way from Wales to sing for you, my lord, for there are very few who listen as you do. You understand and appreciate my art. If you will receive me—disregarding how events may change in the future—I will come."

"I will receive you at any time. Between us, in the name of art, there will always be peace," Henry assured her, and it was quite plain that he understood her implications that there might be enmity between her father and himself. He had, almost openly, promised he would not blame her for what she had no power to change or control.

She and Simon got away after that, but Rhiannon's hand was tight on his wrist until they were clear of the hall. Outside, Simon put his arm around her as they waited for their horses, and she did not pull away.

"I am not cut out for this work," she sighed. "Gilliane was right. The king is like a wild cat. It may come to call and even let itself be gentled, but one cannot look away or trust it. With such a man, there must be strong bonds to hold him, for his own spirit is not master of itself."

"Your father said it was because he was king too young," Simon responded, but for the moment he was blessing Henry, whose erratic character had made Rhiannon willing to rest in his embrace.

"I want to go home," Rhiannon said pathetically.

"Then you shall, *eneit*," Simon agreed instantly. "I will write to my father tonight, and we will go tomorrow."

"No," she sighed. "It will not do. It would turn everything I said into a lie. We must stay until the Bishop of Winchester comes, at least. Simon, you should not yield so readily to anything I ask."

"I love you."

Whether she would have replied at all and what she would have said remained forever lost. The horses arrived at that moment, and Rhiannon pulled away from Simon and moved forward at once to mount. Simon was furious, but to punish the grooms would have offended

Rhiannon. It was better to let the opportunity go than to destroy by ill temper the good that had been accomplished already.

There was no need for Rhiannon to fear another summons from the king, for a powerful diversion was provided to turn Henry's mind from light entertainment. The Bishop of Salisbury, more knowing than Henry had hoped, did not stay to argue with Peter des Roches. Warned that Henry had left Oxford, he never went near his fellow prelate—who might not have been above laying hands upon him—but followed the king to London and was welcomed warmly by Roger of London. Reinforced by that saintly man's approval—and determination—he again fronted the king.

Henry squirmed and protested that what was done was his right. Restraining his temper, Robert of Salisbury reasoned gently but with total inflexibility; Hubert de Burgh must be returned to the church from which he was taken. Sanctuary was inviolable for *anyone*. Even the blackest criminal, the bloodiest murderer, was sacred when under the protection of the Church and could not be returned to prison or executed as long as he remained on holy ground.

That "even," implying as it did that de Burgh was less guilty than a criminal, grated on Henry. Unwisely, he exploded, saying that offending the king was a crime worse than murder. Robert of Salisbury, in turn, drew himself up and told Henry plainly, very plainly, that a man's soul belonged to God, whereas the pride of a king belonged to himself—and was a sin and an offense to God and might need humbling. When Henry became nearly incoherent with rage, the bishop withdrew, but not for long. His manner made it plain enough that this was only the first round, and he felt he had won it.

Henry would have been glad to flee again, hoping to wear out the older, frailer man, but he could not. The conference at which Winchester's next move was to be made was only two days away. A hasty message was sent to Peter des Roches, but he was already on his way. Alinor and Ian and Geoffrey and Joanna arrived very nearly on Winchester's heels. Adam and Gilliane had taken all the children, except Sybelle, and had gone to see to the provisioning and sealing of all the vast properties.

The king would get nothing from the men and women of the Roselynde blood. They would not rebel, but even Ian felt that Geoffrey's surety to Pembroke was a bond on all of them. If, in mercy, Richard did not call on Geoffrey to help him, the family must at the least refrain from giving any support to his enemy. It was not likely that the king would attack so powerful a clan when he already had one war on his hands, but others might use the family's passive resistance as an excuse to nibble at their rich holdings.

One personal problem was generated by the arrival of the family. Ian and Alinor would expect Simon and Rhiannon to share a bed as they had at Oxford. Neither of them was willing to do this, but neither was willing to explain why. By unspoken mutual consent a quarrel about nothing was generated, which ended with Simon complaining bitterly that Rhiannon changed her mind about everything just to spite him. This led Ian to take his son to task for his maladroitness, saying he had never known Simon to be so clumsy in the handling of a woman. Whereupon Simon, with a single flickering glance at Rhiannon, which left Alinor—who was the only one who noticed—mute with surprise, took the excuse to remove himself to Geoffrey's house some half a mile down the road.

Simon might have suffered from his half-sister's tongue had not his mother bade her daughter hold it. Alinor did not understand what was going on, but she had seen enough to tell her that Simon was not at fault. There was something wrong between the pair; Rhiannon was clearly oppressed and nervous, but for once in his life her self-centered son was sacrificing himself to another's need. Age had increased Alinor's patience—at least a little—and for once she decided not to meddle but to let nature take its course.

The course, however, was dreadfully painful for Rhiannon. She had said she would not marry Simon, yet in his family she had found the only women, aside from her mother, who were willing to accept her and be her friends. They did not fear her independence, and if they found her strange, that was only another attraction to their minds. She loved them all—men and women—and the more she loved them, the more some unnamable terror gripped her.

In Oxford Rhiannon had spent most of her time with the older women, but Alinor had realized that Rhiannon was not happy visiting and gossiping. Moreover, she knew that the wider society of London would only provide more jealous women to tell tales of Simon. Thus in London it was Sybelle who kept Rhiannon company. They soon found a common ground in their interest in the art of healing. Hours were spent in the carefully tended gardens, discussing the herbs and exchanging recipes for febrifuges and strengthening draughts, for pesticides and poisons. Sybelle knew the science of the cultivated herbs best, but Rhiannon knew more of the flora that grew wild in the forest, how to cull the mandrake so that its cry when torn from the earth would not drive one mad, and of those shy plants that grew only on the mossy banks of slowly trickling, deep-shaded brooks.

Less certainly, but with increasing confidence, they also exchanged views concerning men and marriage. Sybelle was much the younger in years but, because of her upbringing, was by far the more experienced and knowing on these subjects. As the putative chatelaine of the great lands of Roselynde, she needed to be able to hold her own against any man. Even though she would be protected by an adamantine marriage contract plus her brothers and other male relations who would take up arms in her defense if it was necessary, that would be a very undesirable way to solve differences of opinion with her husband.

Sybelle was mostly concerned with her own doubts about the wisdom of taking Walter de Clare in marriage. She was greatly attracted to him, more than to any other man she knew, and her father favored him because of the disposition of his estates. However, Sybelle was afraid that the passion and strength of Walter's nature, which attracted her so much, would be the cause of trouble between them.

While she was talking of Walter, Simon was continually mentioned in comparison and contrast. Sybelle knew Simon inside out, but the depth of her love by no means made her blind. Her innocent assumption that Rhiannon knew Simon as well as she did led her to speak with greater freedom than she might have in other circumstances. That freedom convinced Rhiannon that what she heard was no special pleading on Simon's behalf. Yet in all the talk Sybelle never once mentioned any fear that her husband's affections would stray. Rhiannon finally raised the point herself and her question was greeted by an astonished lift of Sybelle's brows.

"Our men do not do such things," she said distastefully, and then, seeing that Rhiannon was embarrassed, began to laugh. "Oh, please do not think you have spoken amiss and exposed an innocent maid to the horrid truth. I know that Simon has been between every pair of female legs that would open for him—and Walter probably is not far behind in this enterprise. Ian, I have heard, was near as bad, and Adam must have been worse, for he, if he saw something he wanted, would pursue even the unwilling. That is ended when they take a wife."

"I cannot believe it," Rhiannon said. "Why should the leopard change its spots?"

"I do not think they change their spots. They shed their baby fuzz and their playful ways for their true coats. One reason, of course, is that there is no marriage made among us except for true desire on both parts." Suddenly Sybelle looked at Rhiannon with frowning concern. "Surely you know the choice was free on Simon's part and had nothing to do with your father's desire."

"Yes, I know that, but—but you are saying that the men never change their minds. That is surely ridiculous—"

"Not at all," Sybelle interrupted. "Naturally, it is the part of the wife to make the marriage satisfying and interesting. If a woman loses interest in her man, he will soon begin to look elsewhere. But men are essentially simple creatures in matters of love. It is no burden to keep them anxious and eager."

Her lofty condescension made Rhiannon laugh. "I do not find Simon very simple," she confessed.

"That is because you are putting into him *your* thoughts and feelings," Sybelle remarked with clear-eyed perspicacity. "He is speaking the plain truth, and you will not hear it. Rhiannon, he has told me of his women since I was a child. Never, not once, did he speak of love until he spoke of you. There will be no other woman for Simon now. His honor is bound as well as his heart."

"I do not desire the grudging faith of honor," Rhiannon said hotly.

Sybelle *tsked* with irritation at her friend's obtuseness. "It will not be grudging unless you make it so by stupidity or cruelty. Why do you think so ill of yourself? You are beautiful. You have a—a strangeness that must entice any man. And Simon has already tasted all there is to taste in women. He has chosen you out of knowledge, not out of ignorance."

Rhiannon was silenced, bitterly regretting that she had let herself be drawn into this talk. She knew what Sybelle said was true; Simon had said the same thing and there was a basic logic in it that made disbelief impossible. But it did not make Rhiannon happy. It only added guilt to her desire, by tearing away a false cover from terrors she would not admit. And the more fiercely guilt and desire drove her toward Simon, the more terror she felt. All she knew was that the harder she loved, the more she would be hurt. She could not bear to think about it.

Fortunately, there was more than enough going on to thrust personal problems into the background. On the opening day of the council, the Bishop of Salisbury returned to the attack, with the Bishop of London in support. The king had gathered support also, but the king's creatures shrank into silence before Roger of London's pale eyes. His was truly a martyr's face, marked by asceticism and denial, and the gorgeous robes that testified to the majesty and magnificence of the Church covered a hair shirt, which rasped a body torn by self-flagellation, unwashed and stinking to remind the mighty Church prelate of his own mortality and sinfulness.

Only Winchester stood his ground, but elaborate explanations and close reasoning failed before the single-minded flame of London's faith. What was Caesar's was rendered to Caesar, but what was God's belonged to His Church.

"Sanctuary was violated," the Bishop of London said firmly. "No one denies this. Hubert de Burgh must be returned to the spot from which he was seized in the condition in which he was taken."

Twice Salisbury was nearly drawn into an argument that could only lead to a victory for Winchester's more adroit, more legalistic mind. Each time London stopped him with a touch and repeated his statement. There was something about Roger of London that shook the soul. Even in the violence of his rage and frustration, Henry was weakening. He had crossed wills with Roger of London before and had lost. He remembered that and had already begun to wonder whether the contest was worthwhile. Sensing this, Winchester urged him to say he would take the matter under advisement, thereby ending the audience. Salisbury looked as if he were about to protest, but London stopped him again.

"Yes," he said in his thin but carrying voice, "think about it. Think whether it is worth imperiling your immortal soul to spite an old, helpless, broken man."

Since Henry was truly, if not intelligently, religious, that might have won the case, if he had not been immediately distracted and prevented from thinking it over. No sooner had the bishops been silenced than the trouble with the barons began. By now, all had heard of the outcome of the truce with Pembroke. If Henry had had any delusions about the indifference of his other nobles to Richard Marshal's loss, he was very quickly brought back to reality.

The violation of that particular kind of agreement—the formal yielding and return of a keep—struck in each man a responsive, personal chord. Each saw the same kind of fate befalling him. It was common enough for any baron to yield a keep into the king's hands for a defined period of time and for a particular purpose—for example, as a hostage for behavior, as a surety for a debt, or for a special defensive or offensive purpose. Every man now saw himself conceivably defrauded in the same way by the whim of the king. Naturally, each remembered what had started this quarrel in the first place—that Henry had, without trial or public reason, disseisined Gilbert Bassett of Upavon.

The meeting grew so stormy that the bishops were moved to intervene. Even Winchester pleaded for less heated discussion. Then, since it was obvious that tempers were too furious for calm to be restored, the council was dismissed to reconvene the following day.

The whole proceeding was thrashed out for the women in Alinor's solar. Rhiannon was stunned to see that Alinor, Joanna, and Gilliane were even more excited than the men, even more adamant that tenure of land must be inviolate above every other cause, every other good and evil. She and Simon alone were relatively unmoved.

Both loved their homes—Simon, his four keeps, and Rhiannon, Angharad's Hall. Both would fight to preserve them. But the fanatic devotion to each stick, each shed, stalk of wheat, foot of ground, was not in them. Simon hunted the forests around his keeps, but if he found other huntsmen in them, he gaily asked them their luck and, if it was time for rest, would share his wine and food. Kicva's cattle grazed the pasturage that belonged by right to Angharad's Hall, but if there was enough grass, she had no objections to a neighbor's herd joining hers.

In times of scarcity, of course, attitudes were not so friendly. Then Simon might order poachers killed, and Kicva might order the slaughter of intruding cattle. That was understood by all, as it was understood that a request for help in bad times must be honored if it was at all possible to do so.

It was shocking to Rhiannon that these women, who loved their men both passionately and devotedly, would send them out to fight for a nearly worthless patch of wasteland if that patch was theirs. Alinor might wince each time her husband's breath caught or he coughed rackingly, but she firmed her lips and set her jaw when Rhiannon asked questions. But it was Sybelle who answered.

"It is because land is the basis of everything," Sybelle said. "On the land men live, and from land wealth comes. With men and wealth, one has power. Without power, one is a helpless victim, at the mercy of anyone. I will be the Lady of Roselynde. I will die. But Roselynde will remain, and my sons' and daughters' sons and daughters will be free and strong because the land is theirs."

It was a very clear answer, but it meant little to Rhiannon, and Simon grinned and drew her aside. "Now do you see why I thanked God that my mother's lands go to my sister and then to Sybelle? Oh, I do not mind fighting for the land, but anything to do with it is given the same weight with them. If a single field yields less one year than another, my mother is there asking questions, looking at the soil, examining the seed grains. Better Sybelle than I. I would rather eat chestnuts by the fire in winter than manchet bread, if to get the bread I must labor all the rest of the year harder than the serfs."

"I understand power," Rhiannon replied, "but it seems a high price to pay for it."

Simon shrugged. "Not to them. You may not believe it, but Sybelle takes *pleasure* in counting bushels of oats and barley and accounting this year against last year. It is only that you and I are different."

That was true, and it made him that much more precious. Rhiannon felt as if her whole being were a naked heart and that a pinprick on Simon would stab her so deeply that she would bleed to death. Terrified, she tried to withdraw into herself, to build a shell of uncaring, but Simon was the greatest hindrance. He seemed to have taken warning from what she said in Oxford about stroking and hinting of love; instead he was open-heartedly ready to be friends again, to laugh together over their bond of sympathy in their mutual lack of possessiveness.

Simon's nature was optimistic. He saw in the events of the next few days the culmination, both personal and political, that he desired: Henry's vassals would withdraw from him, the king would attack Pembroke with largely mercenary troops, Llewelyn would join Pembroke, and their forces would triumph. In any case, he saw that the council could not last long, which meant he would soon be free to take Rhiannon home. He told himself that, either on the way or once he had her in Wales, he would win her back.

Simon's first expectation seemed in a fair way to be satisfied. Henry used the urgent necessity of settling with his barons as an excuse to avoid further discussion of the violation of sanctuary. This did not rid him of the bishops, but it disclosed Roger of London's delicate perception of the rights and powers of the Church. Where he had demanded with burning eyes in the matter of violation of sanctuary, he now pleaded softly, begging the king to listen to and satisfy, if he could, the just demands of his barons.

Others were less moderate and less clear on the fact that a violation of sanctuary was Church business, whereas the king's relationship with his barons was not. They pointed out that the custom of the land had been violated, that those the king had outlawed and deprived of their property had never been tried by their peers. This brought a sneering Winchester to his feet. There were no peers in England, he said. They were all small men and not like the great, independent nobles of France. Therefore, the king of England had a right to banish or otherwise punish any person through the justiciaries he appointed.

This offended everyone so much that the bishops began to threaten to excommunicate all those who gave the king such evil advice. To speak the truth, Henry was himself offended. He liked the notion of being all-powerful, but he did not like the denigration of his men with respect to those of his old enemy of France. In fact, Henry was so annoyed that Winchester's snobbery might have won the barons' case for them had not the news that Pembroke had taken back Usk arrived that very evening.

The king was nearly hysterical. What he had not been able to do with a full army and siege train, Richard had accomplished in a few days with a third of the men. Henry's pride was lacerated. He would hear nothing further on the rights or wrongs of the question and stormed into the hall on the next day, demanding furiously that the bishops excommunicate Richard Marshal for his crime. None was willing, and their spokesman was Roger of London.

In the thin voice that pierced like a knife and was as impervious as steel, Roger ripped away Henry's pretensions. There was no sin, he said, in a man's taking back what was his own, what he had been deprived of unjustly and dishonorably by a king who violated his own oath and word of honor. More likely the Church would bless Pembroke than disown him, for he had been true, letter and spirit, to what he swore on the relics of the saints.

The cheers that followed this statement were so prolonged and so loud that the king was frightened out of his rage, at least temporarily. He abandoned his notion then and there of ordering a levy. He did not expect, nor even want, a positive response. He agreed now with Winchester that it was hopeless to expect to govern a country where each little lordling set himself up as the equal of the king. When the barons saw that the king had conquered Pembroke, their strongest, they would be less quick to cheer when the monarch was insulted. All murmurs against him would die. Then he would be able to be gentle and merciful, and all would come to admire and to love him.

It was not easy to cling to this conviction in the face of the roars of approval of London's statement—cruel and inaccurate, Henry thought it. No one would ever listen to his side, Henry thought. Resentment made him determined to force them to his will, but he was not fool enough to demand knight service at this moment. God knew what they would do; they might even threaten to seize him. Moreover, those most faithful in the past, Ferrars, Ian de Vipont, and his own cousin Geoffrey, were cheering. Henry rose and left.

But his troubles were not over. No sooner was it apparent that the political meeting had reached an irreconcilable impasse than the bishops returned to the attack on the question of the violation of sanctuary. For another day or two Henry resisted, but his heart was not in it, and when Roger of London's thin voice fulled to a deeper bell tone and began to thunder anathema, Henry began to think of ways to accomplish the same purpose without imperiling himself. The turning point came when the specter of the martyrdom of Thomas à Becket was raised.

"If Hubert de Burgh should die in prison," London warned, "you will be guilty of the murder of a man under the protection of the Church. Remember that all your grandfather's power was not enough to protect him. Remember how, to save his soul, he walked naked and barefoot and knelt to be beaten with rods in the full eye of all, crying *mea culpa* for his fault and his offense."

Henry shuddered. He was rather fond of going barefoot in his shirt to do penance for this fault and that. There was a delicious sense of contrition and uplift in it. But that was at *his* choice, and all who were invited to attend

were sympathetic and also uplifted by the purity and
humility of their king. What London was threatening was
different. Henry knew he would be an object of ridicule
and shame, and he knew the Church must win, for it was
God's special thing, and it would extract the harshest
penalty. There *had* to be another way.

When stimulated, Henry's mind was quick and agile.
He preserved his face by dismissing the bishops once more,
but this time with an assurance that they would have his
full answer the next day. By then he was ready. Once
before, de Burgh had sought sanctuary. That time he had
crawled out himself, begging Henry's mercy because the
sanctuary had been surrounded and no food could be
brought to him. Rather than starve, he had broken sanctuary himself. What had been done once could be done
again.

The next day, as he had promised, Henry gave his
judgment. He agreed that de Burgh would be returned
to the church near Devizes. Roger of London saw the
gleam in the king's eye, and he knelt down, soft-voiced,
to beg for mercy, to plead that de Burgh be allowed to
live in peace in that church. He would be no danger to
anyone there, the bishop pleaded; he was an old man and
broken. To this the king made no answer other than a
slight smile. The bishop sighed. He knew that Henry
would order the church surrounded so that de Burgh
could be starved out; however, that was outside the juris-
diction of the Church. Roger could plead for mercy as a
man, but he could not fight for it as a prelate.

The explosion that had taken place two days before
Henry released de Burgh was the signal that freed Simon
and Rhiannon; however, there was no particular urgency
about leaving. The news was important, but it would bear
no fruit for several weeks. There was plenty of time to
inform Llewelyn. Thus, time was spent in a round of farewell visits and in packing. Rhiannon found her baskets
far fuller than they had been when she came. Aside from
what she had purchased herself, Alinor and Joanna had
loaded her with gifts and there were even items from
Gilliane at Tarring.

Tearfully Rhiannon tried to tell them that she did not

expect to be married to Simon. All smiled on her and kissed her and assured her the gifts were for her in remembrance, not for Simon's wife. They all wished for the marriage and would pray for it, but their love was for Rhiannon herself whether she married Simon or not. Helplessly, Rhiannon did what she could, bestowing rings and necklets on each of the women she desired for sisters, except . . . . To Alinor she gave the length of cloth that Kicva had woven because Alinor had called it a wonder and Rhiannon felt it was the most precious thing she had that Alinor would be likely to use. She had feared that Simon's mother would protest, but she did not. Instead she had smiled and folded Rhiannon in her arms— a most unusual gesture, for Alinor saved her embraces for infants and for her husband.

"I know just what to do with it, my love," Alinor said. "You will be glad, very glad when you see it, and I am sure your mother will approve."

"My mother?" Rhiannon echoed.

"Yes, my love," Alinor laughed. "Be sure to tell Kicva that you have given me the cloth of birds and that I said when I took it that I would put it to the use for which she intended it."

"But—but how could you know the use? I am not sure that my mother had any special use in mind."

"Then do not bother your head about it. Perhaps your mother will explain. Now it is not important."

Rhiannon was annoyed. She was not a small child about whom adults spoke over her head as if she were not there or could not understand. Yet, without even being in the same country, without ever having met, Alinor acted as if she and Kicva were in complete communication and understanding. Rhiannon could not spoil a gift-giving with sharp words, but she told herself she would surely find out Kicva's intention for that cloth and prove to Alinor that she had guessed wrong.

CHAPTER 21

❖•❖

The small irritation with Alinor's seemingly superior knowledge was pushed into the back of Rhiannon's mind by the fact of starting home, which was by no means an unalloyed pleasure. Rhiannon desired her home and her freedom and told herself that, once there, she would be free of the mingled joy and pain of desiring Simon. It was a great surprise to her that this idea did not lift her spirits. Instead a pall so black settled over her that it made even the sunlight seem dim.

Simon did not notice Rhiannon's depression. He had a subject of absorbing interest to chew over in his mind. Just before they left, Ian had told him Hubert de Burgh would be returned to the church near Devizes keep. Then, seemingly dropping that subject, Ian had asked Simon to take a somewhat southerly route toward Wales, due west from London, so that they could stop at Kingsclere to see old Sir Henry. The old castellan was failing fast and had asked if "the young devil" would visit with him before he left England.

Simon knew from Walter that Gilbert Bassett and Richard Siward were raiding in the area around Devizes. He did not know what losses they had taken nor how widely their forces were spread. It was very likely that they would not have enough men to chance an attack on the guard the king would set to starve out de Burgh. The smallest alarm would bring out the entire garrison of Devizes.

Even if they could get de Burgh out, it was not likely they could get him away with that force following them. The man was old and weak from being harshly treated; he could not travel far or fast. To rescue de Burgh, only to have him recaptured, would serve the king's purpose. However, if he could be removed secretly, soon after the night guard came on duty, there would be a few—or with luck, many—hours before the escape was discovered. This would give the fugitive a good head start, and no one would know in which direction he had fled. The chances then would be quite good for a clean escape.

The trouble was that Simon did not think Bassett or Siward or any of their men would be capable of spiriting de Burgh away without raising an alarm. His Welsh could do it, but should he embroil himself in such an enterprise? Hubert de Burgh had been no favorite with his family in the past.

Ordinarily Simon would have thought a pox on the king *and* de Burgh, but his sense of honor and fair play was outraged. It seemed unfair and cruel to him to hound a helpless old man. If the king feared de Burgh, it was reasonable to keep him in gentlemanly confinement; that was what had originally been intended by the four earls who agreed to be his gaolers. To have abrogated that agreement and to have thrust him, loaded with chains, into a dungeon was too much. It was not the king, anyway, Simon told himself. Probably it was Winchester, who feared if de Burgh were freed he would work himself back into Henry's affection. Thus Winchester kept inflaming the king's mind against his old mentor and hoping cruel treatment would kill the old man and remove him permanently as a rival.

The whole subject would never have entered Simon's mind had they taken the shortest route back to Wales. They would have gone northwest toward Northampton and on through Coventry and Shrewsbury. However, Ian's request that they stop at Kingsclere changed that. On the northern road, they would have been too far from Devizes for de Burgh's plight to have any pertinence. But Kingsclere was only thirty miles as the crow flies from Devizes. There was some rough country between and no direct road, but that would be child's play compared with the trackless mountains of Wales.

There had been nothing in Ian's face to suggest any ulterior purpose in mentioning de Burgh's release just before he asked Simon to go to Kingsclere. The first was information Llewelyn would be interested to hear and Simon should know; the second was a personal matter entirely. Of course, Simon knew his father felt just as he did about de Burgh. Could he have meant. . . . No, Simon told himself, you cannot blame such a mad escapade on anyone. If you do it and get caught and get everyone into terrible trouble, you cannot tell yourself that Papa hinted . . . he did nothing of the sort. He would probably be horrified at the idea.

Still, the notion kept coming back. If he could find Bassett and obtain his agreement, the Welsh could rescue de Burgh from the church and deliver him to Bassett. Simon himself could then return over the hills to Kingsclere, and no one need ever know he had been involved. But it would not be fair to Rhiannon. Even if he left her at Kingsclere, she would be tarred with his black brush if he were caught, and all her effort to ingratiate herself with Henry would be wasted. In fact, probably the king would blame Llewelyn as well as Rhiannon for Simon's mischief.

All through the long ride to Kingsclere, the arguments flowed back and forth in Simon's mind. Rhiannon was herself agonized, mistaking his frowning absorption for unhappiness. A hundred times she opened her mouth to speak and closed it again, unable to offer comfort because she was still unwilling to offer herself as sacrifice.

It was an untold relief to arrive at the keep and be greeted with tearful gratitude by Sir Henry. The old man was in bad case. He was nearly paralyzed and often in pain. He was well cared for but terribly depressed by his helplessness and the boredom of sitting hour after hour unable to move and with nothing to do. Sir Harold did his best, but he had duties around the estate and his close attention was all the more necessary because he was new in his position.

Worse, Sir Harold did not yet have a wife. Until Alinor had fixed on him to be castellan at Kingsclere, he could not afford a wife unless an heiress could be found for him. Since there were many penniless younger sons and the parents or guardians of heiresses preferred men with something to add to the lady's estate, Sir Harold had never thought of marriage. Now his elder brother and Lady Alinor were both looking around for a suitable girl or young widow for him, but none had yet been found. Thus, there was no one to sit with old Sir Henry except the even older priest, who was also failing. There was no one to talk about subjects that would interest him, like hunting or fighting, or even to give him a game of chess.

Both Simon and Rhiannon were touched by the old man's joy in their coming and his tremulous fear that they would stay no longer than the one night. By common consent, without words, it was decided that they would extend the visit. Sir Harold was almost as grateful as Sir Henry. He felt dreadfully guilty about leaving the old man alone so much, but he did not dare neglect his duty. In addition, he had some problems he wanted to discuss with someone. Ordinarily he would have ridden down to Roselynde or to Iford for advice, but he felt he should not leave Sir Henry for the several days necessary.

Simon disclaimed any knowledge of the management of land, but the truth was that he had absorbed a great deal of information simply by living with Ian and Alinor. After Sir Harold described the problem, Simon began to think he might have something useful to offer. There really was no need to hurry back to Wales if Rhiannon was willing to stay.

Rarely had so simple, kind, and seemingly harmless a decision precipitated so much mischief. In the beginning, everything was innocent enough. Sir Henry was so flattered by Simon's bringing his betrothed to visit and so enlivened by Rhiannon's company that he took a new lease on life. Also, she suggested and taught a few new treatments to the maids who attended the old man, easing his pain. Seeing him so well, Sir Harold asked Simon if he would spend the night at a neighboring keep. A mild dispute over hunting in the forest west of Kingsclere had arisen. Sir Harold felt that the presence of his overlord's son might lend force to his claim. Rhiannon was agreeable, and it was decided that Sir Harold and Simon would go the next day.

There were times, after the king was forced to give orders to return de Burgh to the church, when the Bishop of Winchester wondered whether the task he had set himself was possible or worth doing. He had believed that when de Burgh was overthrown, little more would be necessary than to show Henry the way. He knew the king to be intelligent. He had not remembered, he now realized, that Henry was also less interested in governing than in music, art, and other amusements. He was controlled by his emotions, and of a weak and vacillating temperament made even more difficult by bouts of irrational and immovable stubbornness.

Still Winchester struggled on. Partly, he admitted it was because he loved power, but there was also a real desire to reform and improve what he considered a chaotic and unworkable form of government. He had expected resistance, but not so much—and most of it was Henry's fault. Like a child, the king seized an ideal envisioned for the future after years of slow preparation and expected it to work immediately. Then he reacted in fury when men objected to having their "rights" infringed on. He did not stop to think that he had not shown them first the great benefits that would ensue if they yielded to their king.

It was Henry's impatience and lack of restraint that had necessitated the use of force. Now they were committed to that path, which was the worst and most chancy. It was made even less certain because Henry was moved by odd impulses of chivalry—a total foolishness. One must use every weapon available.

That thought recurred to Winchester one afternoon as the king fretted over his injuries. At the moment he had no outlet for his frustration; he had already sent out the summonses for the levy to punish Pembroke, and his ordinary pursuits bored him. He mentioned pettishly that Winchester's presence even deprived him of his newest delight —the singing of Lady Rhiannon.

Instantly Winchester remembered that the girl was not only an entertainer but Lord Llewelyn's daughter and betrothed to Lord Ian's son. He cursed himself for forgetting her, but there had been so much haste and worry. . . . He was a fool for not laying hands on her at once, but Henry had been opposed to it—another chivalric idiocy. It would not have been necessary if they had been able to seize Pembroke. Now that that hope was gone, Lady Rhiannon might be very useful.

She would be a strong weapon in the armory with which he intended to threaten Llewelyn to keep him from joining Pembroke. Winchester was not much worried about the danger the ragtag Welsh would provide. He was sure his disciplined, well-trained mercenary forces would be victorious whether the Welsh joined Pembroke or not, but there was no sense in fighting both if it was not necessary. The Roselynde clan would be bitterly angry, but they could do nothing while he held the girl, and afterward they would do nothing either. After all, no harm would come to Lady Rhiannon; she would be kept in the greatest luxury. All she would lose was a few months of freedom, and she might even come to like it; many women did enjoy a life of idleness with no responsibility. In any case, Ian had withstood worse assaults from John without rebelling.

It had not occurred to anyone back in London that Simon and Rhiannon would spend more than one or two nights at Kingsclere. Therefore, when Roger de Cantelupe came from court two days after they left and asked that Rhiannon come to sing, Ian answered blandly that his son had taken his betrothed home. The messenger was clearly distressed, but that did not bother Ian. Which way had they gone, Sir Roger asked. Ian never lied and could see no reason to arouse animosity by refusing to answer, since he was sure Simon would have left the keep long before the messenger could get to it. To Kingsclere first, he replied, and after that he had no idea.

Had Ian known that Sir Roger came from Winchester rather than from the king, he would have said nothing; but the messenger had been intentionally deceitful—knowing how Winchester was regarded by most of the nobility—and Ian's nature was trusting. Winchester was furious when he heard the bird had flown. Then he reconsidered. It would be better this way. No one would know for some time that he had taken the girl and the youngest cub of the lioness of Roselynde, except Llewelyn and Simon's relatives. He would have *two* hostages and not need to trust to honor to keep Ian, Geoffrey, and Adam passive.

He sent out a strong enough force to overpower Simon's guard, but told Roger de Cantelupe on no account to show the troop at Kingsclere. Only Sir Roger himself was to enter there, and he was to discover which road Simon and Rhiannon had taken toward Wales. They should be easy enough to overtake. They would go slowly because of the woman, and they would have no suspicion that they were being followed. Every attempt should be made to convince them to return quietly. Any lie that would be useful would be absolved without penance, and any promise at all could be made in the king's name.

It was almost dark, but Sir Roger rode out anyway to satisfy the bishop's eagerness. It was some time before he discovered that they had taken the wrong road in the dark. Sir Roger sensibly told his men to stop and make camp. At dawn he found a village and asked directions, but Kingsclere was not an important keep. Some honestly said they did not know; others, either fearing punishment if they confessed ignorance or out of self-importance, made wild guesses so that Sir Roger's troop went even farther astray. About the time that Simon and Sir Harold were being welcomed with somewhat restrained cordiality at Highclere castle, Winchester's messenger, cursing futilely, was still trying to discover whether Kingsclere keep was north, south, east, or west of him.

Actually, Sir Roger was not completely lost. When they came to Henley they finally obtained directions Sir Roger felt he could trust. It was past dinnertime by then, and he and his troop had had no breakfast. Although he said nothing to his men, Sir Roger blamed Winchester. Had he not been so impatient, they would have waited until dawn to leave, and none of this would have happened. The resentment Sir Roger felt impelled him to give permission for his men to stop and rest, buy food, and eat. Winchester would never know, and he himself was hungry and thirsty. While he ate and refreshed himself with a few draughts of the best wine, he considered his information. They were north of their objective. They could go south crosscountry. . . . No, Sir Roger had had enough of that.

Sensitized by past experience, Sir Roger stopped often to ask the route, which further slowed their progress. It was not until the late afternoon that they reached Newbury. There, everyone knew Kingsclere keep, and Sir Roger was able to discover how far it was in nearly exact terms. They forded the Enborn, then followed its southern bank to a meadow surrounded by a small wood where the troop camped for the night. Sir Roger rode the last three miles alone, arriving just at dusk and thanking God that he could spend this night, at least, in a comfortable bed.

That cheerful thought flew right out of his head to be replaced by a burgeoning joy when he discovered that Rhiannon was actually still in Kingsclere and that Simon and the castellan were away. In moments his plan was revised. There would be no need to use force of any kind. If he could induce Rhiannon to come with him, he could send back a message that would bring Simon alone and unarmed right into his arms.

Success seemed to grow from good fortune. Although Rhiannon was clearly amazed and somewhat frightened when he first delivered his message—that she was urgently desired to return to the king, who wished her to carry messages to her father for him—his glib explanations about the change in the political situation seemed rapidly to dissipate her surprise and alarm. The matter was of grave importance, he said, and could not wait. It was unfortunate that Sir Simon should be away, but if she would trust herself to him with three or four men-at-arms from the castle for protection, Sir Simon could easily catch up with them before they reached London.

Rhiannon listened with downcast eyes, thinking quickly. It was possible that what Sir Roger said was true. Even though her last exchange with Henry implied that he did not regard her as a political person, that did not preclude the possibility of his wishing to send a message to Llewelyn by her. However, there were too many sour notes in Sir Roger's litany. One was the excessive need for speed. Why? Simon said it would be some weeks before an army could be assembled, and he was in no particular hurry to get back to Wales.

There was another false note. "How did the king know where to send you?" Rhiannon asked.

"Lord Ian told us you were going to Kingsclere."

"Lord Ian," Rhiannon echoed. If Ian knew, then it was certainly necessary for her to go, Rhiannon thought. "Yes, I will come," she said, "but it is ridiculous for Simon to follow us. He will be here tomorrow, and I can ride as fast as any man."

"But we must start at once," Sir Roger insisted.

"No!" Sir Henry cried. "It is dark. You cannot ride all night, my dear. You will be cold and wet. It is raining. Wait for Simon. He knows these lands and can take you crosscountry to save time."

"You know nothing of the king's needs, old man," Sir Roger snapped harshly. "Hold your tongue!"

Rhiannon had almost been swept away by the man's urgency, but the way Sir Henry shrank from the lash in his voice enraged her. Then two realizations occurred to her simultaneously. The first was that what Sir Henry said was true. Simon could save them more time than could be gained by riding on a black, wet night. The second was that she had not the slightest interest in preventing her father from joining forces with Pembroke. It was what Simon wanted him to do, and, from all she had learned, it was probably the best thing for him to do. Regardless of the king's hurry, then, she was in *no* hurry. She patted Sir Henry's hand.

"No, I will not go tonight. I have no intention of stumbling around in the dark when it rains and there is not even a moon to guide us."

"The king will be ill-pleased by this delay," Sir Roger said threateningly.

Rhiannon's large eyes, clear as glass and as hard, fixed on him. "He is not *my* king," she said succinctly. "He is asking a service of me, not I of him. I will do it when I choose, or not at all."

Realizing he had trod amiss, Sir Roger began to apologize and excuse himself, trying to induce her to go by saying he would be blamed if they delayed. It was doubtful that Rhiannon would have been moved, even if she heard a word he said, but she did not. Although her eyes remained fixed on him, another discrepancy had occurred to her. If Ian knew a messenger had been sent to her from the king, he would surely have written a letter either to her or to Simon urging her to go—if he had wanted her to go. Then, either it was a lie that Ian had told Sir Roger where to find them, or, more likely, Ian did *not* want her to go. Something began to stink to high heaven. Still, Rhiannon was not sufficiently sure of herself to refuse outright.

"I am very sorry," she said, vaguely aware of the self-pitying arguments Sir Roger was urging on her. "None-theless, I will not go tonight."

From the corner of her eye, Rhiannon saw that Sir Henry was very much upset. The old man was trembling and plucking uneasily at his tunic with his crippled fingers. Rhiannon wished to calm him, but the pestiferous Sir Roger was talking again. Apparently he had given up on the notion of leaving that night. Now he was insisting that they go at dawn. Rhiannon was tempted to tell him that if he did not shut his mouth, she would not go at all, when she suddenly bethought herself that she could shut his mouth without his knowing anything about it.

"Yes, yes," she agreed smiling blandly, "we will go as soon as you are ready tomorrow. Now allow me to fetch you some wine to refresh you while we wait for the evening meal to be brought."

Enormously relieved, Sir Roger thanked her fulsomely. They would be well away, he thought, long before Simon returned from the visit he was making. And once Rhiannon was a hostage among his men, the time factor was no longer important. He was so satisfied with his accomplishment that he did not stop to wonder why Lady Rhiannon should fetch wine for him herself rather than signal for a maid to bring it.

As she poured sufficient sleeping draught into the cup to lay out a horse and laced it with usquebaugh to hide the taste, Rhiannon also smiled with satisfaction. This was much better. She could blame any delay on Sir Roger himself, and she certainly would not leave before Simon came. Since it was his family that would suffer if she did the wrong thing, he must make the decision.

Sir Henry was very much surprised, and quite pleased, when the offensive messenger dropped asleep right in the middle of a lofty sentence before supper was served. Rhi-annon said, with twitching lips, that he must have been very tired from his long ride. She summoned two hefty menservants and instructed them to carry Sir Roger to bed in one of the wall chambers. When he was gone, Sir Henry commented that Sir Roger must be an idle popin-jay to be so tired from a little ride. Then he became embarrassed and said he imagined Rhiannon must be sorry.

"I am sure you would rather listen to his talk of the court—"

"I certainly would not!" she exclaimed. "I prefer greatly to listen to you."

"That is very kind, my dear, very kind, even if I know it is not true. I was never very—very clever at talk."

"Sir Henry, if you were mute as a wooden board, I would prefer to sit with you in silence than to listen to that self-important fool."

The old man smiled. "Is he? I thought so, but. . . . So much the more I wish you would not go with him without Simon, even if the king is not pleased."

"Oh, I am sure that will not be necessary. He is so tired, you see. I only said I would go when he was ready. He will sleep long tomorrow. We will not allow anyone to disturb him. Simon will be here before he wakes."

"How clever you are, my dear. Yes, yes. Bid the men close the door. It will be so dark in that wall chamber, he will never know night from day, and no sound will wake him either. How clever you are."

Rhiannon thought so too, and they laughed together in amity and played a pleasant game of draughts with much silliness and little skill on either side. She felt even cleverer midmorning of the next day when Simon and Sir Harold arrived, breathless with anxiety, with their horses all in a lather. Having settled the hunting problem to everyone's satisfaction, they had ridden up to the priory south of Newbury to discuss obtaining a chaplain for Kingsclere. Sir Harold had been reluctant to make the arrangement on his own for fear of hurting Sir Henry. The old chaplain wished very much to return to the monastery for his remaining years, and Sir Harold felt he needed a younger man, but neither had wished to tell Sir Henry. Simon agreed that Rhiannon would probably be able to break this news gently.

On their way back to Kingsclere, they had seen signs of the passage of a large troop of men. Careful investigation had brought them to the camp where Sir Roger's men waited. The master-at-arms knew of no reason to conceal from Sir Harold the little bit he had been told and said they were waiting to accompany Sir Roger de Cantelupe, who had been sent on an errand by the Bishop of Winchester. Sir Roger had ridden ahead to Kingsclere, and that was all the master-at-arms knew.

Since the camp and men were orderly, Sir Harold made no objection to their remaining where they were. He rode back to where Simon was waiting—to bring help in case the troop was hostile—thanking God that he did not have to deal with whatever Winchester's messenger wanted by himself. It was not until he saw the horror on Simon's face that he guessed Sir Roger might have a purpose connected with his guests rather than with himself or his keep.

Simon's mind moved swiftly, and although they rode at full gallop, the three miles to Kingsclere seemed the longest distance Simon had even ridden. He had started by thinking of rape and murder and imagined other, ever-increasing horrors, which even a whole army would have had difficulty accomplishing in one night, before they arrived. The smiling, casual greetings of guards and servants restored his perspective, and he realized he should have trusted Rhiannon not to do anything hasty or foolish. Thus, he came into the hall with an expression of bland interest and welcome, but only Rhiannon rose to greet him from her chair beside Sir Henry's.

Simon looked around, and Rhiannon hurried forward. "You know we have a guest?" she asked.

"Where is he?" Simon wanted to know.

Rhiannon laughed. "Asleep. And he will stay that way until we decide what our answer to him should be."

"Answer to what?"

"He says the king desires me to carry messages to my father—"

"The king! There is a small army a few miles up the road whose master-at-arms told Sir Harold that Sir Roger is on an errand for the Bishop of Winchester."

Rhiannon's eyes opened wide with amazement. "Oh, the clever liar!" she breathed. "He bade me take three or four men-at-arms from the keep for protection and ride away with him at once. I almost believed him because he said your father had told him where we were."

"My father!" Simon was shocked, but then realized that Ian would not have expected them to stay so long, particularly if he had hinted about de Burgh. . . . But that was not important now. Simon dismissed it from his mind as he considered the present problem. He tried several interpretations but only one seemed at all reasonable.

"Winchester did mean to take you hostage, Rhiannon," he said finally. "The troop he sent is large enough—to his mind anyway—to overpower my Welsh. Probably he intended to take me, too, and make Mama and Papa and the others dance on a string to his tugging. I wonder whether the king knows of this."

"I do not think so, Simon," Rhiannon said slowly. "Partly it is because he—he is an artist and respects that in me. Truly, he would not wish to still my song by confinement. But also, I think King Henry knows my father too well to believe holding me would do any good. He knows Llewelyn would only turn vicious. Winchester thinks like—like—"

"An ignorant Frenchman. Yes. Very likely you are right, but it does not help, really. If the king does not know, Winchester will keep the secret as long as he can and then convince Henry that letting us go would be more dangerous than holding us longer." Rhiannon shuddered, and he put his arm around her. "They would do us no harm. I am sure of that."

Her eyes had a wild look when they turned up to his. "To be caged like an animal would do me no harm? I would go mad!"

"I would not like it much either," Simon agreed. "But since there is no longer any chance of such a happening, do not think of it and frighten yourself with shadows. All I need to decide is how we can leave behind the greatest amount of confusion in Sir Roger's mind and the least amount of blame for Sir Harold."

"Sir Harold knows nothing about this—do you, Sir Harold?" Rhiannon asked, smiling sweetly.

"Certainly not!" Sir Harold replied promptly.

"When Sir Roger wakes, which should be around dinnertime, you may tell him that I could not get him up in the morning, that he bade me go away." This was the truth. Rhiannon had stirred Sir Roger just enough to pour some more sleeping draught down his throat. He had certainly told her to go away. "Since he had made so great a point of the king's hurry, as soon as Simon returned we—we left to go to Westminster."

Simon burst out laughing and clapped Rhiannon on the back so heartily that she staggered forward a few steps. Then he caught her and hugged her. "I am sorry, my love, I did not mean to hit you so hard, but what a thought! What a beautiful thought!"

"Is it safe?" Sir Harold asked, and then when Simon opened his mouth to explain, he held up his hand. "I am no good as a liar. Tell me no more, I beg you, but if you wish to stay here, you are very welcome. Sir Roger could be put out, and no one would dare use open force to take you."

"I am not so sure of that," Simon remarked. "There may soon be no law aside from the king's word—or perhaps Winchester's. But that is not all my reason. If we go, you and my father and my mother are innocent. When it is possible to accomplish the same end without them, insult and defiance should be avoided," he ended sententiously.

Rhiannon looked at him in such patent amazement and disbelief that both men laughed.

"Besides," Simon went on, his eyes gleaming, "it is much more fun this way."

"For you," Sir Harold said dryly, "but it will be too much exertion for Lady Rhiannon. If you go, I can say she went also. That much lying I will contrive to do. She can stay safe and quiet in the women's quarters until—"

Both Simon and Rhiannon interrupted him with laughter. She put her hand on his arm. "I thank you for your consideration, but I can ride as long and hard as Simon, and can outrun him also."

"You cannot!" Simon exclaimed. "On the flat I outdistance you two times out of three. It is only when leaping up mountains like a goat that you outpace me. We are a match!"

Rhiannon's breath caught. They were a match! But if she yielded to what Simon desired, they would become one. Half an apple could not live without the other half. Desperate not to answer, Rhiannon's eyes went past Simon and saw Sir Henry watching them with pitiful anxiety.

"I must explain to the old man," she said softly. "He knows we must go. I have explained that already, but this long conference is frightening him."

"Yes, of course. I will go see to the men and to the horses while you start the packing and explain to him. Then I will come back and say farewell before we leave. Oh, and Rhiannon, could you tell him gently that a new chaplain is coming? Brother Michael is too old and not well. He is to return to the priory."

"Good. That will divert his mind from our leaving and give him something to look forward to. You told the abbot, I hope, that whoever comes must be ready to spend much time comforting an old man—and not affright him with hell and damnation, either."

"I will see to it," Sir Harold promised, his face lightening. He had not realized that his responsibility to Sir Henry's loneliness would be solved so easily.

As they were crossing the drawbridge several hours later, Rhiannon said, "That was most fortunate. Sir Henry is so eager to tell the new chaplain just how things are to be done and who is pious and who a sinner that he was easily reconciled to our leaving. He is sorry to lose Brother Michael, but. . . . What is it, Simon? Is there more danger than you wished to mention in Sir Harold's presence?"

"No. I am just trying to decide which way to go. Naturally, I do not wish to pass Sir Roger's men, but that is easy enough to avoid." He paused and his lips tightened. "I am really very annoyed with Winchester—and with the king, too, if he is a party to this. They need their hands sharply slapped for reaching out to grasp that to which they have no right. Yet if I bring you home to Wales first, it may be too late."

"What are you talking about?"

"That I would like to spite Winchester, and the king, too, by snatching Hubert de Burgh out of the church where he is, no doubt, slowly starving to death."

Rhiannon's green eyes opened wide. Then she giggled. "I think we should. My father might not agree. I do not believe he has forgiven de Burgh for that execution of hostages two years ago, but he will be even angrier at Winchester when he hears there was a plan to seize me.

Or we could say nothing about it to him." Then she frowned. "But can we do it, Simon?"

"We?" he repeated.

She shrugged. "There is no place to leave me, and as you said, he will be back in prison or dead if you ride into Wales first. What I meant was, where will you take him when we have him out? I do not think he would be welcome on my father's lands."

"No, Pembroke would take him gladly, I think. Anyway, that would not be our problem. I am not fool enough to involve Prince Llewelyn in such a matter without his permission." He explained about handing de Burgh over to Gilbert Bassett. "But where to find Bassett is beyond me. He should be in the neighborhood of Devizes, hoping for a chance to get at de Burgh, but I cannot go around openly asking the whereabouts of a rebel and an outlaw."

But Simon was making a problem where there was none. In the end, Gilbert Bassett found him. Simon should have realized the rebel leader would not long remain unaware of a large, armed group traveling furtively crosscountry. They avoided villages, climbing the forested, desolate hills and camping in a fold of the downs about ten miles from Devizes.

There had been game on the way, brought down by the quick Welsh bowmen, and they ate well. Sleeping, however, was another matter. Although neither had mentioned it, and it had been covered by the talk of rescuing de Burgh, both Simon and Rhiannon were hungry for each other. As it grew dark, flickering glances crossed, but did not meet. Rhiannon was aware that she could not accept Simon's lovemaking without reiterating that the question of marriage was closed. To invite Simon to take her without a clear statement of the situation would be a deliberate deception. Yet to make the statement must force Simon back into his original position: no hope of marriage, no physical love.

In this case, Rhiannon had misunderstood Simon. His mind was moving on another track completely. He had assumed that Rhiannon's growing silence and stiffness were owing to unwillingness. As soon as she began to withdraw into herself, he had remembered the bitter challenge she had flung at him in Oxford: *We will see whose hunger conquers.* He was hungry—very; but a man has his pride. He did not wish to humble Rhiannon. He wanted to think of some device that could bring them to a mutual yielding, which would be equally a mutual conquest.

Unfortunately, the ache in his loins blurred his mind and the ache in his throat blurred his eyes. Eventually, stiff and silent, Rhiannon rose and went into Simon's tent. If he had not been so wrapped in his misery and his need, he could have risen at the same time and taken her hand. A single pressure of the fingers would have solved the problem. But the opportunity passed. Simon sat on by the fire, talking desultorily with Siorl. Then he went to bed—but not to sleep.

Both rose heavy-eyed and silent, miserable, seeking hopelessly for a way to explain. But the more eager each was to mend the rift, the wider the chasm looked. Suddenly, as the men ate the cold meat with which they were breaking their fast, a rush of bird whistles burst out from north and west. Simon leapt to his feet and began to issue low-voiced commands to his captains. Armed parties were approaching from two directions.

CHAPTER 22

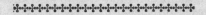

The bird calls diminished slowly, retreating southward and eastward in a most natural manner. By the time the armed troops converged on Simon's campsite, there was nothing to be seen there except the cookfires burning away cheerfully and the trodden earth. Many tracks—horses' and men's—led into a small wooded area just behind the open field. The armed troops moved forward quickly, then the leader pulled his horse to a stop just inside the trees as a singing voice called something he could not understand from above.

"As I live and breathe," Simon said, stepping out from behind the trees, "I have been wondering for a full day how I would find you, and you have found me. I am Simon de Vipont. You are Gilbert Bassett from your arms, are you not?"

The leader pushed back his helmet. "De Vipont! What the devil are you doing sneaking through the woods, and where are your men?"

Simon laughed. "Around and above. Half of you would be dead already if I wished you ill. You have a look of your brother."

Bassett had stiffened at Simon's warning, then relaxed and smiled. "Ah, yes. Philip has written about your Welshmen, but you do not say what you do here so secretly or why."

"A long story. Will you trust me and bid your men dismount? And by the by, how did you find us? I thought we came quietly enough."

After an eye blink's hesitation, Bassett ordered most of his troop to retreat and be at rest. The others rode back to the campsite and also dismounted, although they cast nervous glances at the woods around them.

"As to how I knew where you were," Bassett said to Simon as he came down from his horse, "you passed by the grazing meadows of Upavon and a shepherd saw you.

The king may disseisin me, but he cannot change the
hearts of my people."

"That is true. I am glad you are so well served." Then
Simon turned and cheerfully called out to someone hiding
on the branch of a large tree. The branches parted and
Siorl dropped to the ground lightly. His bow was strung,
but the nocked arrow now drooped negligently from his
hand. He replied shortly and sharply to Simon's remark,
which made Simon laugh. "I asked him how come we
were seen," Simon explained to Bassett. "Siorl prides himself on not being seen."

"Shepherds have long sight and are accustomed to
watching for stealthy movement," Bassett suggested.

"No, that was not Siorl's excuse. He said there is no
way to hide fifty-two horses."

Reminded, Bassett looked around, but there was neither
sight nor, what was far more puzzling, sound of a horse.
It was a small wood. Bassett did not think it possible to
keep fifty horses so quiet that they could not be heard.

"But it seems you have done it," he remarked.

"Not I," Simon said, grinning. "That is Lady Rhiannon's skill."

Simon called another command and shadows began
to drop from the trees and slide out of the brush. A long
bird call trilled into the distance. Bassett watched with
hard eyes, accepting the fact that he had ridden into a
trap and his troop could have taken heavy losses without
ever having even seen their enemies. It was something to
remember. But what startled him most was when Rhiannon came through the trees, her skirt looped up to mid
thigh for running and her hand on Ymlladd's neck. Unbound, the other horses followed, all silent except for the
sound of their hooves on the earth. Gilbert Bassett's
mouth dropped open.

"This is my betrothed wife, Lady Rhiannon uerch
Llewelyn," Simon said.

Lovely as she was, Rhiannon scarcely looked like an
elegant, high-bred lady. However, she came forward, gave
Ymlladd's rein to Simon, and extended her hand in regal
greeting without the slightest self-consciousness about her
naked legs or the leaves and twigs in her hair, which she

had not yet wimpled for riding. Bassett swallowed. When she moved away from them, the horses began to nod and blow with nervousness, and the men led them away. He recalled that Simon had said Lady Rhiannon had kept the horses quiet, but he had thought that some kind of private joke.

"Sir Gilbert?" Rhiannon said, in a perfectly normal, pleasant voice, marked by a faint puzzlement at his immobility.

Recalled to himself, Bassett bowed over Rhiannon's hand with grace, and then what Simon had said penetrated his shock and assumed greater importance than the behavior of some horses. "Uerch Llewelyn?" he echoed. "Are you daughter to the Lord of Gwynedd? But I—ah, a natural daughter."

Rhiannon inclined her head.

"And betrothed to Simon de Vipont?"

"Why not, Sir Gilbert?" Simon asked. "Prince Llewelyn is my overlord and my father is his clan brother. That is part of the reason we are moving so quietly rather than riding the roads, but what you should have remembered about me is that I was squire to William, Earl of Pembroke, and my family has been close-tied in love to the Marshals for many years."

For the first time Bassett relaxed completely. "Yes, I should have remembered. Are you in flight to Richard?"

"Not exactly in flight. I am not proscribed, but apparently it came into Winchester's mind that Lady Rhiannon would make a prime hostage for her father's behavior. It is not true, but Winchester does not understand the Welsh."

"He does not understand *anything*," Bassett snarled.

"I think you are right. Nonetheless, he has offended me, and it is in my mind that I can use his ignorance to increase his problems and to have my revenge. The Bishop of Winchester, for some reason, fears Hubert de Burgh, and I would like to see him free."

There was a long moment of silence. Then Bassett said, "Are you offering to join your troop to ours in an attempt to rescue him? I would be more than happy to accept and would be very grateful, but I must warn you

that our hopes of success are small. The garrison of Devizes will be down on us before we can hope to take the
Earl of Kent away."

Simon noted that Bassett, who was indebted to him,
gave de Burgh his title as Earl of Kent, but he did not
comment on that. All he said was, "Not if they do not
know he is gone."

"The church is close-guarded day and night," Bassett
remarked with a touch of contempt at the foolishness of
a young man. "I have friends who watch and send me
word. Believe me, there is no way to reach him without
raising an alarm."

"Perhaps not," Simon agreed, "but I think there may
be. If you will tell me whatever you know about the way
the guards are stationed and relieved, I think my men can
slip through and bring de—I mean, Kent—and his companions out."

There was another silence while Bassett absorbed this.
His expression, unguarded now, wavered between enthusiasm and disbelief. Then a certain look of cunning came
into his eyes. If only Simon's men were involved, he would
have lost nothing, even if the effort failed. He would do
what he could to help, even what he could to support and
protect any who escaped, but his own force would be
untouched and ready to try again if such a possibility
arose. One other problem had to be brought to Simon's
attention, however.

"We think Kent is weak and sick," Bassett said.

"So I guessed from his age and the treatment he has
had," Simon acknowledged. "Also I assume he has been
starved since entering the church. But that does not make
much difference," Simon assured him. "He could not slip
out softly enough, even if he were whole and strong. We
will have to quiet the guards on the side of the church
where we come out. I will need men to replace them.
Mine cannot speak English at all or French well enough
to fool anyone."

Bassett blinked. Simon sounded so sure that he was
beginning to believe this himself. "This is not a forest,"
he said after a moment.

Simon turned his head and translated Bassett's warning to Siorl. The Welsh master-at-arms answered with a

brief, contemptuous sentence. Simon did not translate it specifically, he only said that Siorl was sure it could be done. Bassett was not completely convinced, but he had already decided that he had little to lose in the attempt. He put out his hand.

"I am more grateful than I can say," Bassett remarked. "If there is any way in which I can return this favor in the future, it will be done. For now, would you like to come into my camp? We have a secure place closer to our goal, and I think Lady Rhiannon will be more comfortable there."

He looked around and did not see her. Bassett had been so concentrated on what Simon was offering that he had not heard Rhiannon move away. Now he had a moment of anxiety, wondering whether the men in his camp would take her for a new drab that had arrived. He wondered whether he dared tell Simon to hint that she had better be careful of her dress, but when Simon called and she came out of his tent, Bassett breathed a sigh of relief. Her skirt was down, her hair bound in a tight net, and her look was that of a perfect lady.

Indeed, Rhiannon's manner was so ordinary that Bassett began to find all sorts of reasons for the brief vision he had had of her as something different. In fact, he almost forgot about her entirely because she was so quiet the entire time the details of the rescue were being discussed. Simon's men and those who would pretend to be guards were chosen. The mechanics of entering the church, searching out the three prisoners, and convincing them it was not a trap were outlined. This last had involved Bassett personally in the business. He did not hesitate to offer himself. By now he was convinced there was a good chance of success, and Richard Siward would lead his men until his brother could take them over if the mission failed. All was smooth as silk until the escape was planned.

"It comes to this," Bassett said. "Is it less dangerous to send enough men to carry all three a substantial distance or to have the horses close enough?"

"Why should it be dangerous to have the horses close so long as they are out of sight?" Rhiannon asked.

Bassett smiled indulgently at so innocent a question. His mind had already rationalized the brief, impossible vision of Rhiannon with her hand on the great, vicious destrier's neck and a whole troop of horses following docilely as sheep.

"Because a single snort or whinny would warn the guards as clearly as seeing a troop of men."

"The horses will make no sound," Rhiannon said. "I will be with them."

There was a silence. Bassett was stunned. He did not wish to remember what he had seen; it was unhealthy to think evil of Llewelyn ap Iowerth's daughter or the betrothed of the youngest son of the Roselynde clan, but if he could not allow that thought, then he must be enraged by the woman's silliness. Simon was simply considering the suggestion. It had not occurred to him to bring Rhiannon along, but now that she had suggested it, his mind was busy with the possibilities generated.

"How many can you keep quiet?" Simon asked.

Bassett turned purple and made a peculiar sound, but neither Simon nor Rhiannon paid any attention.

"That depends on how quiet you want them. This morning I found a drop in the ground, so it was only necessary to keep them together and I could speak to them softly. If you mean they must not snort or stamp and I must keep silence, then I need to be close enough to touch each often. Ten or perhaps twelve, I could manage. But Simon, the Welsh can go back on foot. They will even be safer that way, I think."

"You are right," Simon agreed. "I should have thought of that myself. "Good." He turned to Bassett. "Three of my men, myself, you, Lady Rhiannon, and four of yours to take the place of guards. That makes ten. Is there something wrong, Sir Gilbert?"

"With me?" Bassett exploded. "No! But I think you must have lost your mind."

"Why? I assure you it will take no more than three of my men and myself to dispose of the guards. Two could—"

"Sir Simon, I am not talking about the men." Bassett's voice rose to a roar. "You cannot bring a woman along on such an enterprise."

"Why not?" Simon asked. "Rhiannon *can* control the

horses, and I will be there to protect her. No one expects her to fight."

"I could bring my bow," Rhiannon suggested innocently, teasing.

"No," Simon objected. "I do not want anyone killed if it is possible to avoid it. You will get carried away and shoot too straight."

Bassett choked again. "You are insane. She will scream or start to chatter at the wrong moment, or—"

"No, indeed I will not," Rhiannon protested. "My brother David has often taken me on raids—"

She broke off suddenly and put her hand over her mouth. Llewelyn did not control her, but he did control David. It was true Llewelyn would not hesitate to thrust his daughter into danger if he thought it would benefit Gwynedd, but he would never expose her on a petty raid merely so that more goods and/or men could be carried away. That was not why David and Rhiannon had done it originally—he was mischievous and she, curious—but the mercenary motive had induced them to repeat the adventure. If Llewelyn discovered what David had done, he would be punished.

Looking at her stricken expression, Simon thought she realized that going raiding with her half-brother had been unwise. However, David was not the wisest or most scrupulous of men. He often reached for immediate profit without considering the long-term effects of his actions. Then Simon grinned self-consciously. He was not much better himself, and he was planning to make use of the effect of David's inconsiderate actions. Under the circumstances he uttered no reproof.

This, combined with his smile, convinced Rhiannon not only that Simon would not betray David to her father, which was quite true, but that he did not disapprove of her ventures, which was not true at all. It convinced Bassett, too, and unlocked the memory of Ymlladd biting and kicking at the grooms in the camp in contrast with the stallion walking gentle as a lamb by Rhiannon's side. He withdrew his objections, but he looked sidelong at Rhiannon and had a tendency to try to stay on the opposite side of the group when they rode out of camp that night.

They left as soon as it was dark. Every hour extra that de Burgh was imprisoned would further weaken him with hunger and thirst. Thirty of Bassett's men and all of Simon's rode together to within a mile north of the town, clinging to the wooded slopes of Roundway Hill. All arms and harnesses had been padded and dirtied so that there would be no jingle or gleam of warning. About a half-mile to the west was the road to Chippenham and Malmsbury. If the rescue was successful and there was no alarm, Bassett's men would take de Burgh along that road.

When Simon's master-at-arms felt that the men and horses were as well concealed as possible, the small group of rescuers remounted. It was not the best night for such an enterprise. Simon had prayed for rain, a steady, miserable drizzle, but his prayers had not been answered. Still, it was not the worst night, either. The moon was only one-quarter full, and there was a sharp, cold breeze, which sent clouds scurrying across its face. Shadows flickered and skipped across any open space. Simon hoped that a few more shadows would not be alarming.

Bassett had been dumbfound at the preparations Simon and his men made—the blackening of their faces and hands with soot, the mottling of plain leather tunics which replaced Simon's mail and his men's plate-sewn jerkins, the laying aside of all weapons except long poniards and strangling cords, and the smearing of any solid-colored horse with light and dark blotches.

There was to be no killing, Simon had ordered. The men grumbled a little because the silence of the dead was assured; that of the living had to be ascertained by effort. But the grumbles were smiling ones; they were accustomed to their lord's softness, and they made ready cloths for gagging and thongs for binding. Then Siorl and Echtor set out on foot to do a little spying. Silence lay heavy. The orders had been uncompromising. Any man who made a sound louder than soft breathing would get his throat slit—and Simon's soft-footed Welsh prowled round and about so that no one dared to whisper lest the shadow behind him take note and report. Rhiannon also moved about, stroking and murmuring to the ten horses that were to go. If someone leaned close, he might hear her voice. A foot away it could not be distinguished from the breeze moving the bushes and leaves.

In half an hour, without sign or sound, Siorl and Echtor reappeared. They made two brief gestures, and Simon nodded to Bassett. Everything was as he had expected it to be, and the Welshmen had removed two men who were patrolling the periphery of the area. The ten chosen remounted and rode south and then a little west, picking their way around farms and through coppices so that they would not alarm the dogs. There was one bad section, where open land had to be crossed to reach the sanctuary of the small grove of trees that surrounded the church-yard.

Eventually they were all in the shelter of the trees again, not a secure shelter because the grove was thin, many of the leaves fallen. Still, the trunks of the trees and the brush with the few leaves that remained moved fret-fully in the erratic breeze; these broke the lines of horse and man and turned them into something unrecognizable, part of the shifting shadows.

One by one the men dismounted. As each did, Rhian-non touched his horse, uttering a faint cooing sound of reassurance. When all were afoot they moved away cau-tiously until they were opposite the side of the church where the cemetery lay. The animals stood like rocks. Looking back over his shoulder, Simon nodded with satisfaction. Following his glance, Bassett had to restrain a gasp of surprise. Even though he knew where they were, the horses had disappeared. He could not even hear them breathing, let alone the normal stamping and blowing of an idle horse.

That was not the last of his surprises, but self-discipline kept him quiet even when Simon and his three Welsh stepped out into the graveyard and also disappeared. He had been so sure that, because he knew where they were, he would be able to follow their progress. Frustrated, he turned his eyes to the guards, whom he could see as darker shadows moving against the solid bulk of the church. There were two, and both seemed at ease, un-aware of what was approaching. Then one moved slightly forward and began to stare fixedly into the graveyard.

For the first few seconds, Bassett was tense, expecting the man to cry an alarm. He was sure the guard had seen him, but the tableau remained fixed. Then Bassett suffered that irrational impulse to leap out and dance and scream which affects any person who lies hidden when a watcher's eyes seem to fix on his place of concealment; instead, Bassett gritted his teeth and prayed that the men with him would not yield to the urge he felt. He tore his eyes away.

Horses are nervous beasts, but these were accustomed to men, and it took little effort to put them into a state near sleeping. Rhiannon had prepared them well. All were fully fed and contented. A touch and a murmur sent them off into whatever state it was that permitted them to remain on their feet when they were completely at rest. All ten responded immediately, so that Rhiannon had time to turn and watch Simon and his men disappear into the graveyard. She was able, in fact, to follow Simon's movements, which were not quite as smooth and practiced as those of the others.

Nonetheless, Rhiannon was intensely proud of him, and she suddenly realized she was not afraid. What Simon was doing was very dangerous, yet she felt no fear. It was odd. She should be afraid. She was excited, yes, but the sensation was intensely pleasurable, nearly sexual in its effect. She had not felt that when she went with David, although she had enjoyed those ventures also. Was that because she cared less for David?

She lost sight of Simon, but the excitement did not diminish. It had little to do with the persons involved—except herself, she soon discovered. The excitement was generated by the danger. It was more acute, sensually thrilling, because of her own closeness. When she had quieted horses for David, she had always been well away from the immediate scene of action. The horses were brought forward to carry loot and the men led or rode them to the scene of action only after the attack was already successful. This time Rhiannon could see the surprise itself, and whatever would happen would happen to her also. It was a revelation to her. For the first time in her life she understood why many men loved war more than they loved women. There was a kind of sense in it. Rhiannon could understand how a man might come to crave the pounding excitement that pulsed in her—especially when a man could get rich at the same time. It was no wonder that men could not be weaned from war.

As he slipped forward among the tombstones, Simon warned himself never to set up anything in or near a church. The graveyard was an open invitation to ambush. He could have brought an army across it. It was even better than a forest because the grass was scythed close and raked. There was no chance of stepping on a twig or brittle leaf and having the snap or crackle warn a wary enemy. In any case, these enemies were watching for a surprise attack in force, not for a few men slipping through the dark.

Simon reached the last tall standing stone and waited. Off to the side, there was a faint scratching. He wondered whether a neighborhood cat was cooperating with them, then smiled to himself. More likely it was Siorl. The guard's head turned and he took a single step forward, staring hard. Simon did not grin for fear his teeth would gleam, but he was laughing inside as he slipped from the stone, crouched low, and scuttled quickly into the dark area right against the wall of the church. Two steps, three . . . the strangling cord was ready in his hands.

To the anxious watchers it seemed that the guard had momentarily stepped back into the deeper shadows near the wall. Almost simultaneously the second guard did the same, but the first was already coming forward. Bassett was obscurely disappointed. When the guards had disappeared into the dark like that, he had thought they had been taken. It was too soon, he told himself. Waiting always made time seem long, and such invisible movement must be slower than normal.

Even as he braced himself for more waiting, a hand touched his arm. Bassett barely restrained a cry. Despite knowing, he had been startled by the near-invisibility of the mottled clothing and blackened face and hand. He was being beckoned forward, drawn from shadow to shadow. But the guards . . .

Only the guards were Simon and Echtor, wearing the

helmets of the men they had strangled into unconsciousness. Siorl fetched two of Bassett's men-at-arms and prodded them into taking the places of Simon and Echtor while Simon led Bassett forward and helped him lift the bar that locked the back door. All the fittings had already been liberally coated with goose grease, and the two men, raising the bar straight up, freed the door with no more than the faintest of creaks. Simon lifted the latch and opened the door minutely, then more, then more, less than an inch at a time, feeling gently for sticky spots on the hinges that would squeal or squeak. When he had it opened sufficiently for Bassett to pass through, he took no further chance.

Siorl had come back and was standing behind him, so Simon knew all was secure. He followed Bassett into the church and Siorl closed the door quietly. It was dark inside. Since no one was allowed to enter, there were no candles burning to the saints. Simon began to wonder how they would find their men, but that, too, was easy. One of the men snored like a hive of demented bees. He and Sir Gilbert picked their way carefully in the direction of the sound.

There was no need to worry about low voices. Hunger must often keep the three men awake, and presumably they talked or prayed. However, he hoped that waking the men and the explanations would not take long. In fact, there was no hesitation. As soon as de Burgh recognized Bassett, he began to weep silently and raise his hands in thanks. Since they had nothing to take—they had been brought back to the church with barely enough clothing for decency and surely not enough for warmth —they had only to rise and follow Simon to the back of the church. Here he said one soft word in Welsh and the door began to open. When they were out, the bar was replaced.

There could be no question of de Burgh's running through the churchyard. He had barely made it to the door. Without discussion, Simon lifted him to Bassett's shoulders. Echtor had drawn William de Miller's arm over his shoulder, and Simon did the same with Thomas the Chamberlain's. Siorl followed the group, stepping backward and watching for any sign of alarm.

The silence was not so absolute now. Twice Simon had to put a hand over Thomas's mouth, and de Burgh was sobbing softly. When they reached the trees, Bassett set his burden down.

"He is too weak—" de Millers began.

"There are horses," Simon replied, removing the hand with which he had stemmed Thomas's speech. Now he realized what it was that the two young men had been so eager to say. "Be quiet," he added. "Sound travels in the quiet of the night."

His voice did not travel far, but Rhiannon heard. She came stepping softly through and around the brush by a path she had marked out earlier, and behind her, one at a time, as if they were ensorceled, the horses followed, not even switching their tails. She touched Simon when she came near. It was only meant as a greeting, but both their breaths caught. It was as if a hot spark of lightning jumped between them carrying bold spices and bright colors that assaulted every sense.

Bassett had looked, and then looked away, as the horses filed along behind Rhiannon. She had one hand still on Ymlladd's forehead and had placed her other hand on Sir Gilbert's own stallion's neck. Now she ran her hands down to the horses' noses and pressed lightly. Simon rose into the saddle of his mount and Bassett lifted de Burgh and then, while a man held him, got up behind. Then Rhiannon drew forward one of the men-at-arms' horses. Simon signaled to William de Millers, and one of the Welshmen helped him into the saddle. When they were all mounted, the Welshmen started back at a steady lope.

The silence was as deep now as when they had arrived. It was like a thick, wet blanket and had taken so firm a hold on the rescued men that even de Burgh's sobbing was stilled. Simon began to pick his way out of the thin patch of trees. His eyes were on the ground, choosing a path where the fallen leaves were thick and would muffle the sound of the hooves. Nonetheless, he could see Rhiannon quite clearly, her green eyes alight, her lips full and hard as if he had been kissing them. She knows, he thought, and his own excitement multiplied until he feared he would have a physical reaction.

He could not permit himself to submit to that luscious tide of sensation nor even to think what effect Rhiannon's new understanding might have on their relationship. Now he had to concentrate on bringing them back to the main group at the foot of Roundway Hill. There was the one open area. Simon gestured to Bassett, who was holding de Burgh, to go first. De Millers and Thomas the Chamberlain followed with Siorl, then Rhiannon. Simon and the others brought up the rear. In case there was an alarm, they would have been ready to silence it. The maneuver was successful, however, and the rest was easier. Soon they were safe in the woods of Roundway Hill.

Bassett and his men did not dismount. Hardly waiting for his troop to get to their horses, he started west toward the Chippenham road. There was no need for farewells or thanks; each knew what had been accomplished and what it was worth. Simon had no idea where they would go, but he did not want to know. Now that the adventure was over, he was extremely glad to be separated from it. During the ride from the church back to the main troop, while he was filling his mind to avoid thinking of Rhiannon, Simon had imagined the disaster he might have created for his family if he had been caught. He was eager to go, to get out of the area altogether so it would be impossible to associate him with the escape.

As they withdrew from the danger, Rhiannon's excitement faded. The glance she had exchanged with Simon had been the last flicker of it. Now it was over, and she was aware of a sense of loss, of flatness and depression. Before she realized what she was doing, she began casting about in her mind for a new adventure. The desire brought another revelation to enforce the first. One could become addicted to danger, she thought. Simon in the meantime was shifting impatiently in the saddle, waiting for the two men who had given up their horses to de Millers and Chamberlain to get back to them. The slight movement drew Rhiannon's attention. She wondered whether Simon was also feeling the letdown that afflicted her. It was better to make love, she thought suddenly. When that pleasure had passed, there was peace and contentment.

The two for whom they waited appeared, took the horses held for them, and the troop moved off. Simon went east instead of west around the base of Roundway Hill. One reason was that he wished to divorce himself as much as possible from Bassett's group. Also, from Marlborough there was a road to Cirencester and Gloucester where the Severn became fordable. West of Gloucester, the king's power was greatly diminished. There were some loyal barons, but most would look the other way when a fugitive from the king rode by, and some were outright rebels who would help.

They did not go as far as the town, since Simon did not wish to approach any inhabited place from the west. Instead, they camped south of it. This was not entirely safe but was better than riding into a town at this time of night or riding around it in the dark. That would seem furtive and be certain to draw notice. As soon as they found a stream, Simon ordered that a camp be set up and patrols be sent out to warn them of any approaching troop. Then he went down to the water to wash the greasy soot from his face and hands. It occurred to him that Rhiannon had been unusually silent during the ride, and then, vividly, he recalled her expression when he had returned with de Burgh. Fatigue evaporated under a wave of desire—but would she be willing? And if he made the advance and she yielded, would she consider that some form of victory? Did he care?

The answer to the last question clarified everything. The truth was that Simon did not care. So long as Rhiannon was willing, she could win every battle; Simon knew he would still win the war. There was only one danger. Although Rhiannon was sensual and plainly enjoyed lovemaking, she had a will as strong as tempered steel. She might still refuse him! Simon flicked the cold drops from fingers and face and hurried back to the camp. He was a fool. He should have sent the men ahead and taken her while she was still aroused by danger.

There was no sign of her when he arrived at the camp. Simon gritted his teeth and hurried toward his tent. If she was already abed, his problem would be enormously increased. He threw back the tent flap and rushed in, only to be brought up short by the sight of Rhiannon sitting quietly on a stool waiting for him.

"What is it?" she asked tensely, jumping to her feet in response to his precipitous entrance.

"Only my impatience to be with you," Simon replied.

She put out a hand to him, at the same time beginning to say, "Simon, I must—"

But she never finished. The extended hand was sufficient invitation. Simon pulled her close and kissed her, finding himself trembling with eagerness as if he were a green boy with his first woman. Rhiannon responded immediately. Simon could feel her press forward against him, and her mouth opened to draw in his tongue. Yet, even while her desire made her draw him closer, tightening her arms around him, her head moved slightly as if she felt she should draw away.

Simon tried to slip a hand between them to untie the neck of her tunic so that he could kiss her throat and eventually her breasts, but the moment he relaxed the pressure of his embrace, she freed her mouth.

"I must tell you," she gasped.

"Not now, for sweet Mary's sake," Simon groaned. "Later. Tell me later."

He pulled her closer again, and she did not resist, only whispered in a troubled way, "But Simon—"

"I am afire," he pleaded. "I do not care."

He muted her again with kisses, and this time when he eased his grip to loosen her clothing Rhiannon did not try to speak but slid her hands down to his buttocks to pull his pelvis tighter against hers. She had tried three times to warn him that the yielding of her body did not imply any change in her mind. She would be glad to appease her hunger and his; it was Simon who had always insisted that the intention of marriage and permanent union accompany lovemaking. Rhiannon felt a little guilty. She knew she had not tried very hard to tell him, but she wanted him so much.

As Simon untied her tunic, she slid her hands forward and fumbled for the knot of his chausses string. One hand touched his swollen shaft, and Simon gasped. Rhiannon was distracted. When she touched him and felt his reaction, that stimulated her own pulsing pleasure and she wished to touch him again. But if she served that desire, she could not undress him, which was the direct path to even greater joy.

Simon was similarly distracted between two goals. He hated to make love in a half-clothed scramble. There was something ugly about taking a woman with her skirts turned up over her face and his own chausses down and undone, binding his knees or ankles. He wanted to take off Rhiannon's clothes and his own and couple decently, cushioned by his cloak and covered by hers. However, for the first time in many, many years Simon was too eager, too excited to wait. Rhiannon's touch had raised his desire to a pitch that was painful. He also wanted to fling her down and drive into her to still her aching craving and his own. Torn between desire and desire, he hesitated, shaking with passion.

"Pendeuic! Penn Emrys!" Siorl's voice was nearly a scream, and he beat on the fabric of the tent so that it vibrated around them.

Simon jumped. He realized that for several minutes he had been blocking noises he did not want to hear from the camp outside. Still, he could not bear to release Rhiannon. "What?" he called hoarsely, more for the sake of clinging to her yielding warmth for another second or two than because he did not know the answer.

"There are many men, a hundred or more, riding a sweep pattern. They cannot fail to find us. Do you wish to run, stay, or fight, my lord?"

There was another brief hesitation. Simon knew what was right, but it went sorely against his training and the grain of his own disposition. When he had released her lips, Rhiannon had laid her head against his breast for a moment. Now she pulled away gently, and he let her go.

"Run," he answered, and stalked out of the tent.

Rhiannon was already on her knees packing the few things she had taken out of the traveling baskets. Tears of frustration ran down her cheeks, and she cursed the oncoming forces with every ill she knew by the old gods and the new. There would not be another chance like this. Now she would have to tell him before he took her, see the pain in his eyes, and deal with his gentle but irrevocable withdrawal. This had been her last chance to touch him and love him. Once back in Angharad's Hall, Rhiannon knew she would have to end the relationship completely. If she did not, she would feel every pain for him a thousand times when he was not even hurt.

The pain of parting would be terrible, but it would end if she did not see Simon again. It would be like a twin-trunked tree, riven by lightning. It took long, but the scar would heal over and the standing tree would live. If she could not endure now, she would be smitten with worse pain later, and it would never heal. It would grow worse and worse as her love deepened and she grew more dependent on it with the years. But she had wanted him one more time.

For the first time in her life Rhiannon cursed her womanhood. Many women did so from the day they understood what it meant, but not Angharad's descendants. They were proud and free—as Rhiannon had been, until she had loved Simon.

CHAPTER 23

It was clear as soon as Simon stepped out of the tent that he had managed to ignore more than a few dim noises. Siorl must have called him more than once, but the master-at-arms made no comment on his lord's most unusual inattention. Siorl had been at Dinas Emrys when Rhiannon sang with the winds, and Simon's flushed face and suffused eyes were excuse enough. Siorl was only glad the witch had let him go in time.

Quite unaware of his man's conclusions, Simon gave his complete attention to his duty and was relieved to see that his desire for Rhiannon had not caused a disaster. In case Simon decided to stay, Siorl had taken the preliminary steps for fighting or running without disrupting the overall appearance of the camp.

Final orders were given now and fires were killed with earth, the readied pack animals were loaded, and the tent was rolled up around Rhiannon as she finished strapping the baskets. Then the men came in and took apart cots, table, and stools, and rolled up the bedding. By the time Rhiannon's mare was brought to her, there was no sign of the tent, aside from a flattened section of grass and weeds that would soon spring upright again. Similarly, there was no sign of past passion or tears on Rhiannon's face.

Simon's heart sank as he looked at her. He knew now, without words, what she had been trying to tell him— that she had been willing, but it would be the last time. He tried to think of something to say, something that would change her mind or at least make her suspend her decision, before the intention became fixed. But there was no time to think. The need to escape precluded argument. All he managed to say was her name.

"Do not," she whispered. "Let me be. I will die, Simon. I will die."

There was a thin, tense quality to her voice that was

more frightening, more eloquent of the disaster she skirted, than screams and tears. Simon surveyed his men again, saw they were ready, and gave the order to ride forward. He could do nothing now about Rhiannon. He told himself that the hills would cure her, that when she was safe and could run free again, she would accept him. But there was a sickness of disbelief in him. It was not fear of being captured or any other fear that had driven Rhiannon to reject him completely. It was something to do with him, and her eagerness for lovemaking had been the final, deciding factor in her mind, he feared.

All personal emotions were dulled as Simon led the troop out. They did not go too quickly at first. The fore-riders of the searching groups were not very far away, and it would never do for them to hear a large group thundering off. As soon as a rise of land behind them formed a baffle, they picked up speed as well as they could in the dark, hoping that the slow sweep behind them would give them a good lead. They gained their end and did slip away from that searching troop, but it did little good. It seemed as if every keep loyal to the king in the area had been warned and had sent out its garrison to search. Simon could only curse the unfortunate circumstance that Hubert de Burgh's own lands and closest allies were east, in Kent, whereas his greatest possibility of safety lay west in South Wales. Thus, the king's forces were searching with equal assiduousness in *every* direction.

On foot and without the baggage, Simon, Rhiannon, and the men could have scattered and disappeared into the dark. But Simon was not willing to lose a troop of horses, including his own fine destrier by which it might be possible to identify him. In addition, there was all the clothing and jewelry, his camping equipment, the food, and other supplies that would have to be abandoned. If Simon had to, he would rather identify himself and give one of the excuses he had been concocting for wandering around in the middle of the night; he would even rather fight than lose his horses and goods.

In fact, Simon's temper was disintegrating so rapidly under the mingled effects of anxiety, distaste for running away, and sexual frustration that he would have loved to have someone pick a fight with him. Unfortunately, every force his scouts noted was stronger than his own. This meant attacking from ambush, which was really unjustifiable, or taking too great a chance of defeat. Simon's light-armed bowmen were not really the equals of a superior, heavy-armed force in open combat.

So they dodged and zigzagged from one wooded area to another, barely avoiding some troops, running hard ahead of others. Simon tried to keep them headed north, but they were driven east several times. In the end, this was an advantage because they stumbled upon a main road, which Simon figured had to be the Winchester-Cirencester road. Here, Simon decided to stop and outface any searching troop if necessary. It was nearly dawn anyway. Even at first light it would be reasonable enough to be traveling along a road—so long as no one noticed the blown and lathered horses.

That was the deciding factor. The horses had to be rested in any case, and it would be best to rest them before fording the river Kennet. Simon did not know any ford except the one at Marlborough. Since the ford would surely be guarded, they could neither cross it at this time of night nor take the chance that the condition of the horses would be noticed. The only reason not to stop was that Simon had come to the conclusion that he did not want to talk to Rhiannon for a while. The reason was scarcely tactically sound, and Simon was forced to put it aside.

They moved sufficiently off the road to be screened by trees and brush, watered the horses at a small streamlet, and fed them. No scouts were sent out. Simon had decided to run no farther. He did not think there would be any searches on or near the road. It led south to a town loyal to the king and north only to the ford at Marlborough. In either direction there was no escape for any fugitive, so there was no real point in patrolling the road. Simon's expectation was correct. No one moved on the road until the ordinary traffic of the morning began.

When he had set the watch, Simon came back with some reluctance to where Rhiannon lay. It had occurred to him, somewhere in the muddled night, that if she did not say aloud that she did not wish to see or speak to him again after this journey was over, there would be a greater chance she would relent. Commitments spoken aloud are very hard to forget. Again Simon wondered whether she had thought of the bitter challenge about whose hunger would triumph. He thought it was a draw, but Rhiannon might consider herself shamed. She had first held out her hand. But he had kissed her. . . . Simon's eyes closed, and he swallowed.

Mercifully Rhiannon was already asleep—or pretending to be asleep. Simon lay down softly a few feet away. It was cold, but he was accustomed to it. He noticed that Rhiannon, practiced camper that she was, had provided herself with blankets from the horses and would be warm enough. It was marvelous to be with a woman for whom you never had to feel concerned. She could go anywhere. She needed no watching or tending. Then grief choked him. What had he done that had changed her mind? Yet she had said it was not his fault. Had the threat of confinement somehow connected itself in her mind with marriage?

If so, it was all the more important to be patient and not to press her. When she was calmed by safety and soothed by freedom, he could approach her again with promises never to take her from Wales, even from her own home, unless she desired to go. He must do everything in his power to keep her from speaking to him about the future. There were reasons enough now to make haste to Llewelyn's court. He could leave her there; her father would send her on to Angharad's Hall with a small escort. Simon intended to ask permission to return to Richard, and he thought Llewelyn would give it, even if he decided to pretend he did not know what his vassal was doing. The tension that had prevented Simon from sleeping eased; he smiled slightly, and his eyes closed. Women were very tender toward a man away at war.

Simon allowed his men to rest until midmorning. Then, when the road was empty for a time, they came out into it and rode openly to Marlborough. Although Simon was questioned minutely and each man in his troop was carefully scrutinized—especially the wrists and ankles, for all three prisoners had been manacled and would have sores there that were impossible to hide—no other problem arose.

Rhiannon asked no questions about their sudden haste. Simon could not help wondering whether this was because she understood that Llewelyn must have news of de Burgh's escape at once, or whether she was so eager to be free of him that she did not care to ask why. One moment Simon was in a pit of despair, then a quick glance or a turn of her head would give him hope. Perhaps, he told himself, Rhiannon was eager to be at home so that she could think before she said more than she meant to say.

The truth was that Rhiannon did not know either. One moment she wished passionately to be away from the dark, beautiful face and lithe body that aroused her; the next she had all she could do to keep from weeping at the thought that she would never see him again. She was sufficiently absorbed in her own troubles not to realize that Simon was avoiding her deliberately. He seemed busy with his men and the details of traveling, and when it would have seemed unnatural not to speak, she was not surprised that he concentrated on the political situation and how the freeing of de Burgh would affect it.

When they crossed into Wales, Simon began to ask for news of Prince Llewelyn. They learned, to Simon's relief, that he was at Ruthin and made for the keep with all speed, arriving very late, long after the gates had been locked for the night. However, the guards opened readily enough when Simon and Rhiannon had been recognized. Rhiannon went to the women's quarters at once, and Simon breathed a sigh of relief. If he caught Llewelyn at first waking, he could be away before she came down to break her fast.

Late as it was, Simon spent some time composing a letter to be given to her, reaffirming his faith and his love. He would come to Angharad's Hall when he could, he promised. He could not tell her where he would be, he added cleverly, because he did not know. He thought her father would want him to act as liaison between him and Richard, and the Earl of Pembroke would doubtless be traveling from one stronghold to another to make all ready for war.

This letter was handed to Llewelyn to use as he thought fit. Simon had concealed nothing from Rhiannon's father, who knew he was hearing the story from Simon's point of view—but his sympathy was with Simon in any case. Prince Llewelyn had long thought Rhiannon quite mad. As long as this madness did not interfere with his plans, he was willing for her to go her own way. Now that he had found a use for her, however, he was determined that she would serve his purpose. To act as intermediary between himself and King Henry, Rhiannon had to be married to Simon, and married she would be by hook or by crook.

Previously there had been some doubt, but now Llewelyn was sure there would be need for an intermediary. He foresaw that there would be handsome profits in the war that was inevitable between Pembroke and the king. If he allied with Pembroke, there was no way a mercenary army, totally unprepared for the kind of warfare that would be waged, could win. And a mercenary army meant pay chests as well as the valuable supplies that any army carried. Llewelyn grinned wolfishly. If they were beaten badly enough, the whole western border would be undefended. And Chester was dead. Llewelyn licked his lips. There was no longer any oath of friendship to hold him back. The cities would be open to looting—not Chester itself; Llewelyn's spirit shrank from that, but Shrewsbury was just as good. Yes, they would take Shrewsbury.

A double profit would be gleaned from that. The taking of Shrewsbury would surely shock even King Henry and bring home to him the stupidity of what he was doing. Yes, but after that an intermediary would be needed. For a long time, Henry would be too furious to talk reason with any man. But a woman, in no way associated with anything military, truly grieved over the animosity between her father and the king who appreciated her art—yes. It would be of particular value that the songbird the king admired so much had been frightened away from Henry by the threats of the Bishop of Winchester. Llewelyn began to grin again as he thought the story through. Yes, Rhiannon would have returned in spite of her fears to plead for peace between her favorite listener and her father. How touching!

But first there was the question of getting her married. His eyes narrowed and he tapped Simon's letter, which he had read before it was sealed in his presence, against his fingertips. He could not say too much. There was no forcing Rhiannon. She would run away, even kill herself if the pressure became too extreme. But there were ways to make a person apply pressure to herself. Llewelyn beckoned a maidservant and told her to carry Simon's letter to Rhiannon. As he expected, it brought her down to the hall a few minutes later, so soon that her hair was uncombed and her gown undone.

Seeing her father, she cried, "Is he gone?"

"Some hours," Llewelyn replied gravely. "Does it matter? I had proposals to make to Pembroke, and Simon was fittest to make them."

"Where is Pembroke? I will send a messenger."

"As to where Pembroke is—I have no idea. Simon will have to track him by rumor and possibly follow him from place to place. Just now the earl's friends are peculiarly unwilling to speak freely of his whereabouts, even to me. And why, Rhiannon? What is of such importance to say to Simon that you must send a man after him?"

"I do not wish him to come to Angharad's Hall," Rhiannon said bleakly.

"And the letter says he will come?" Llewelyn asked, to establish the untrue fact that he had not read it.

Rhiannon nodded. Llewelyn looked at her, waiting for her to say something, but she did not speak.

"I saw that Simon was not happy," he continued. "How has he offended you, Rhiannon? Were his mother and sisters unkind?"

"No. I was welcomed most warmly." Her voice dropped. "They will be disappointed that we do not marry."

"Do you not? Why not?"

"I cannot." Rhiannon stared glassily at nothing.

"I guessed as much from Simon's face, although he would say nothing." Simon might tell only the truth, but Llewelyn was not in the least averse to a big thumping lie in a good cause. "It is not sufficient to say 'cannot,' Rhiannon. I ask again, how has Simon offended you?"

"Not at all," Rhiannon cried, grasping her hair and

holding on as if it were a rope and she dangling from a cliff. "It is nothing to do with Simon."

"You have found him unlovable? He no longer attracts you?"

"No . . . Father . . . I love him too much."

Llewelyn reached out and drew Rhiannon to him and put his arm around her. She never called him Father. The word was a cry for help. For an instant Llewelyn's resolution wavered, then firmed even harder. Silly chit, it was the best thing for her, and she simply did not know it. She had come too late to desire and was frightened by it—or thought it would restrict her freedom. So it would. And about time, too!

"That is unreasonable, Daughter," he said gravely. He was about to say that if she knew she could never learn to love the man, a woman might resist marriage, but the other way around was ridiculous. However, Rhiannon cut him off.

"It is not unreasonable," she rejoined hotly, pulling away, and forthwith described her terror and her pain, ending, "He will be hurt for a little time and then he will find another woman to assuage his pain and—and to take my place." Her voice stumbled a little over those last words.

Llewelyn had to hide a smile, but he only said, rather flatly, "I do not think so. I knew Simon's father when we were both barely men. I was seventeen and Ian the same age. He was in love with Lady Alinor then—I heard enough about her to choke a horse. She married his lord and best friend, Sir Simon Lemagne. Ian never touched her nor even looked at her—in the sense of being a woman —but he loved her still. Oh, there were other women to warm his bed, but not one warmed his heart and he never married until Simon Lemagne died. Then he took her for whom he had longed for—what? Near twenty years, it had been."

Rhiannon had stepped away and was staring at him with wide eyes. She had accepted the fact that Simon would be faithful to her if he became her husband because he had chosen, as Sybelle said, out of knowledge and not out of ignorance. It had never occurred to her that he might have told the truth when he averred he would be faithful whether or not she accepted him. Yet his father had done just that, and without any hope of satisfaction for his love from the beginning.

"You are not by nature cruel, Rhiannon," Llewelyn said into the silence that fell after his last words. "Perhaps you have not looked at the matter from both sides. Consider whether to ease your own fears it is right to inflict a life of loneliness and childlessness and sadness on a man who loves you. His constant nature is not by his will or sheer stubbornness but something with which he was born."

"Then I must be the sacrifice," Rhiannon exclaimed bitterly.

"Only you can judge that. If it is truly a sacrifice—a laying down of your life—then perhaps Simon, who will live because he has duties and obligations that he cannot slough off, must live with his endless longing." He reached out and pulled her close again. "My love, there is time enough for you to consider these things peacefully and at leisure. Pembroke will surely fight now, and Simon will be with him. He will be too busy and too tired to think of women." He smiled. "Go and make your dress decent, Daughter, and then come back and tell me how you fared at Henry's court."

He had heard that from Simon, too, but pretended he had not and listened eagerly to Rhiannon's version. That both tales were so nearly identical was a good sign for the future. Inexperienced as she was, she had learned more than he had expected. Yes, indeed, Rhiannon would be *very* useful to him once she was Simon's wife. Nonetheless, he did not mention that subject again, and when Rhiannon asked if she could go back to Angharad's Hall he agreed readily, admitting that he would be busy gathering his men for a proposed campaign in conjunction with the Earl of Pembroke's forces.

From the corner of his sly eyes, Llewelyn noted that his daughter had become paler. Since he was sure her fear was not for his sake, he rightly assumed she had followed his statement to its logical conclusion. Simon would very soon be physically at war whether he remained with Pembroke or came back to Llewelyn.

Rhiannon left the next morning carrying the burden of that knowledge and the understanding that she might be condemning Simon to great and lasting unhappiness. A less subtle man might have tried to conceal the fact that Simon would be fighting, in the hope that Rhiannon would fear for him less, feel less pain, and be more inclined to marry. Llewelyn knew better. Let the fear peak now.

Perhaps Kicva would see it and soothe her daughter, although Llewelyn was never sure of what Kicva would do or say. Even if she chose to ignore Rhiannon's distress, no emotion can long remain at fever pitch. In a few months the fighting would probably be over, at least during the worst months of winter. Simon would go to Rhiannon as he had promised. By then the pain would have become dulled by long familiarity, whereas the joy and lust aroused by seeing him again would be fresh and new. In any case, Kicva would know what to do if Rhiannon changed her mind, whatever the cause. The escort who went with Rhiannon carried a letter to be given to Kicva in secret.

The weather was unusually benign as Rhiannon traveled home, as if the countryside had set out to make her welcome. The days were warm, the nights crisp and just cold enough to make a fire a true pleasure. The hills were breathtakingly beautiful, each tree flaming or glowing in gold, orange, red, or maroon. A multicolored carpet of shifting patterns, all lovely, padded the roads and the pathways through the forests. Rhiannon was too sensitive to be unaware, but the awareness only caused her more pain, for she saw the beauty and could take no joy in it. Worse, the nearer she came to home, where she expected to find peace, the stronger grew her compulsion to turn about and hurry back. If she were with Llewelyn, at least she would hear news of Simon.

The impulse was so imperative that she would have yielded if she had not known she would be unwelcome. Llewelyn did not carry his womenfolk around with him when he was going to or preparing for war. If she went back, he would promptly send her home again. She cursed and wept, and when she arrived at Angharad's Hall she barely greeted her mother before she ran out on the hills. But even this last comfort failed her, and when she tried to call some wolf cubs to her, they retreated into their den.

Rhiannon called herself a fool for that. She knew she

could not "call" when she was angry or hurt, and the hills could give no comfort when each favorite spot reflected an image of Simon. There could be no quick cure, she admitted, having known it all along. She would have to endure from day to day, not even aware of the healing, until one day she would be quite well. It would be easy to know, she thought, as she plodded wearily back to the hall. When she could think of Simon with the same calm pleasure she felt on thinking of Llewelyn, she would be cured of love.

Simon's troop was not well pleased when they were ordered out of Ruthin before they had caught up on their sleep or had eaten a decent meal. Simon, however, was eager to be on the move, to be doing something that would dull both his hopes and his fears. Llewelyn had increased both by his reception of Simon's report. There was no doubt of his pleasure over the political news. He had unlooped a heavy gold chain from his neck and placed it around Simon's.

The prince had been somewhat less forthcoming on Simon's description of his personal problem: that instead of leaning more toward marriage, Rhiannon had barely been prevented from formally breaking the betrothal. Llewelyn had listened without comment, but his eyes and his lips narrowed. Simon knew that Llewelyn favored the marriage, especially after hearing that Rhiannon had made so strong an impression on Henry. Therefore, Simon assumed that Llewelyn's expression of determination meant he intended to see that the marriage took place.

In a sense, that gave Simon confidence. He could not remember anything Llewelyn undertook that he did not eventually achieve. Rhiannon had to marry Simon reasonably soon, however, or Llewelyn's purpose of using her as an emissary could not be fulfilled. What increased Simon's fears was that Rhiannon's father might push her too hard and she would be driven to some desperate action.

Simon found Richard Marshal at Usk by the twenty-sixth of October and was welcomed warmly both for himself and for the news he brought. On the thirtieth, Gilbert Bassett appeared with Hubert de Burgh. Surprisingly, the Earl of Kent was not at all desirous of being revenged or of unseating the king, nor did he desire any part of his power be restored. He wished, he said, only to be permitted to live in peace on the diminished estates still permitted to him. He was reluctant to engage in any action against Henry, but when pressed gave his opinion that war could not be avoided. He would not approve a treaty with Llewelyn, despite his gratitude to Simon, although Richard's own good sense and his other advisers insisted that such an alliance was a necessity. Simon did not fail to remind them of the benefits that had come from Chester's long friendship with the Lord of Gwynedd. There had been peace on the border for many years, Simon pointed out.

This caused a burst of merriment. "What peace?" Richard asked sarcastically. "Those Welsh thieves come out every summer and autumn like a plague of locusts and mice."

"That is nothing," Simon protested, laughing, "only a little playful raiding. The Welsh are poor. That is not war."

His point was acknowledged, and it was soon agreed that Richard and a few others would meet with Llewelyn at the Welsh leader's stronghold at Builth.

"Circumstances being what they are," Richard said bleakly, "I will be in less danger in Llewelyn's keep than in one of my own."

With great rejoicing, Simon sent word of this decision to Builth, as instructed. Either Llewelyn would be there, or word would be sent on to him. His overt mission accomplished, Simon lingered at Usk, greeting old friends and arguing war and politics with them. He had nothing else to do, since his compliment of men was already with him and he did not dare go near Rhiannon. Besides, Llewelyn had suggested Simon should stay if he was welcome. He had suspected that there was still a possibility of Henry's making new truce proposals to which Richard, ever hopeful of peace with his overlord, might agree.

Simon was very willing. Richard found him useful, and the duties and male company kept him occupied. He had a good deal to suffer from his young friends, who could not understand his sudden and unnatural chastity, but he found that the jesting at his expense honed his pride and made it easier to resist his physical urges. What was most painful to him was the kindly weather, which prevailed over South as well as North Wales. He constantly saw Rhiannon running the hills like a wild doe and remembered the joy of being her stag.

However, Simon was wrong in imagining Rhiannon tasting this free joy. After the first abortive attempt to do just that, she did not go out to play and dream in the usual way. She busied herself with practical matters—the end of the harvest and the work of storing the hall against the lean months of winter. She practiced her music and made a round of the far-flung dwellings to treat the sick, both man and beast. Yet each day her longing for Simon grew rather than diminished, and her fear and pain increased. There was something else that frightened her even more. Math was avoiding her.

She could not understand that, but she was afraid even to think about it. Instead, she wondered why time was not performing its usual service of healing her wounds. At last she realized that her increasing fear for Simon was a result of uncertainty. It was far worse, she decided, not to know what was going on than to know the hour and day of a battle. This way she felt a death stroke every minute when, in truth, it was far more likely that Simon was talking and laughing with his friends or hunting or drinking or playing some game.

When the realization came upon her, Rhiannon and Kicva were sitting beside the fire, Kicva spinning and Rhiannon grinding an aromatic herb in a mortar held in her lap. Rhiannon uttered a gasp of frustration, and Kicva looked up.

"Ah, have you worked out the puzzle at last?" she asked.

"Puzzle?" Rhiannon snapped. "Do you think I am playing a game?"

"Not every puzzle is a game. Some are matters of life and death," Kicva replied placidly.

Rhiannon was silent, ashamed at having lashed out at her mother without cause. "There is no answer to this puzzle, I fear," she said at last. "I do not wish to love Simon, but I cannot cure myself."

"Why should you wish to do so?"

Kicva was not the least surprised by Rhiannon's statement. Llewelyn's letter had been very explicit and had
given, as accurately as he could—for he knew better than
to lie to Kicva—both sides of the story as he had heard
them from Simon and Rhiannon. Interestingly, the letter
had ended with a request for Kicva to send her news to
Builth keep when she had any.

This was as close as Llewelyn dared come to saying to
Kicva that he wanted Rhiannon to marry Simon. To give
orders to Kicva could easily produce a result opposite from
what he desired, so he gave none. In this case, however,
Llewelyn and Kicva were in total agreement. Rhiannon
needed to be married. Her nature was not at all like that
of her mother. Kicva regretted this but accepted it. She
thought it very unfortunate that Rhiannon could not find
a man to suit her when she was younger, before she had
built so comfortable a pattern of life. It would have been
much better if Rhiannon had married seven or eight years
past, but no man attracted her; worse, there had been no
man who would permit her to remain Rhiannon, until
Simon.

Rhiannon again poured out the tale, ending with the
passionate avowal that it was lunacy for a woman to love
any man.

"So I have always thought," Kicva agreed with a faint
smile, "but it seems you are too late to worry about that.
It is quite clear that you already love Simon."

"I *will* cure myself," Rhiannon cried angrily.

Kicva stared at her and then laid down her spindle.
"You know it is not my practice to tell people about
themselves. It does no good. But I will say this because
I am disappointed in you, Rhiannon. You are acting like
a fool."

Rhiannon dropped her eyes. "You also think I am
being cruel to Simon, and it is better for me to suffer than
for him to suffer?"

"Have you lost your sense and reason completely?"
Kicva asked. "How could I prefer Simon's well-being to
yours? You are my daughter, flesh of my flesh, bone of
my bone. For you I groaned with the pain of bearing and
sighed with the pleasure of suckling. I will not say I am
indifferent to Simon. I like him as well as I have ever

liked any man, but he is nothing to me compared with you."

"Then why are you disappointed in me?" Rhiannon raised her eyes.

Her mother made a brief, impatient sound. "You have passed twenty-two summers, Rhiannon, and since you were six or seven it has taken no more than one or two questions for you to examine your own heart and find the truth. From the time you met Simon, you have gone back to being a kicking, screaming infant. Why do you lie to yourself, Daughter?"

This, of course, was why Rhiannon had not brought her troubles to her mother in the first place. There was never any sympathy to be had from Kicva, except for injuries like a scraped knee or a bee sting. To complain of misery only brought questions, which delineated the cause so clearly that an obvious solution always appeared. Unfortunately, the solution was seldom easy or flattering.

"This is not your first attempt to cure yourself," Kicva continued. "When you first met Simon, you sent him away. Did it help? You were even ready to believe yourself a heifer lowing in her heat for any bull. Did that help? Do you really believe there is a cure for your love?"

"There must be! What if Simon were dead or did not want me?"

"If he had never wanted you, I doubt you would have loved him. To love, one must know a man. To see a handsome face from afar and be stirred by self-induced longings is not love. The fact that he did seek you ends that, even if he should change his mind owing to your stupidity—men grow tired of women who cut off their noses to spite their faces—yes, I know that is Simon's phrase, but it is very apt. If he were dead . . . Silly child, do you think I love Gwydyon less because he is dead?"

"But you suffered when he died, suffered greatly."

"That is quite true, Rhiannon. And I suffer still—if that means that I miss his physical presence. It is more than ten years and I am not cured. To speak the truth, I do not wish to be cured. My love for Gwydyon gives me great pleasure. If a little pain is mingled in—well, that is life. Do you really wish to spend ten or twenty years trying to cure yourself of a great pleasure?"

"It will not take so long. It is different for me; I *do* wish to be cured."

For the first time, Kicva looked really worried and leaned forward to see Rhiannon's face better. "What has made you hate yourself, Rhiannon? Daughter, why are you punishing yourself?"

"Hate myself?" Rhiannon's voice scaled upward. "I am not trying to punish myself. I am trying to save myself from pain."

"How? By inflicting unending torment upon yourself? It is true that anyone who loves also fears and that fear is painful. But there are compensations. The fear is brief and not frequent, while the pleasure endures always. It even mingles with the pain and—"

"Makes it sharper and crueler," Rhiannon spat angrily.

"More poignant—yes—but sweeter, too, for it is shared."

"I do not wish to share," Rhiannon cried, springing to her feet. She was so overwrought that she did not even notice the mortar falling to the floor and spilling its contents far and wide. "Why should my life be tied by so many threads? Why should my heart check when Lord Ian's breath rattles in his breast? Why should I ache when Lady Gilliane fears for her husband? Why should I worry about whether Sybelle has chosen the right man? I need to be free!"

"Now I know why you hate yourself, my daughter," Kicva said.

She then lifted her spindle and began to spin again. Panting with shock and rage at what her mother had said, Rhiannon kicked the mortar out of her way and ran from the room. Only then did Kicva permit herself to smile. The problem was all but solved. Soon Rhiannon would understand what she herself had said. Another day or two of bitter struggle and she would accept the burden. Kicva's eyes grew sad and distant. It had never been in her, the ability to feel what others felt. She knew and understood what they felt, often more clearly than they did themselves, but she did not feel it. It was her art to hear the cause underneath the word, but neither cause nor word touched her—not even for her own daughter.

Then she shrugged. Each person was as God devised.

Briskly, she put aside her work and took her writing desk out of the chest where it was stored. She sharpened a quill, unstoppered a horn of ink, and wrote: *To Prince Llewelyn from Kicva, greetings. I hope you are well as I am. So, too, now is Rhiannon, or she soon will be. If it is possible that she and Simon be brought together quickly, that would be best, as it is not impossible that he will be driven to do something foolish by her silliness. Even if he does not, the more time she has to consider what she has done will make her ill at ease and increase the awkwardness of the reconciliation. Thus, if a reason can be found to send her where Simon is, find it. Written this last day of October at Angharad's Hall.*

Later, when one of the hunters came in, Kicva gave him the letter and told him to take it to Prince Llewelyn at Builth as fast as he could go.

Rhiannon fled from the hall out across the courtyard. The night air was cold and bit her fire-warmed flesh. Instinctively she turned toward the stable where the big bodies of the horses warmed the air. But horses were too restless for her mood. There were six half-grown lambs penned in a corner. Rhiannon did not know the reason they were penned there rather than out on the pasture, but she ran in among them, grateful for the warmth of their fleece and the placidity of their natures. They would not react, as the horses would, to her inner turmoil.

Hate herself! Was her mother mad? Rhiannon clung to her fury and to her sense of hurt as tightly as she could. To let go of the rage would open the way to an everlasting prison. All her life she had been free to work or to play, to dress as she liked, to say what she wanted to whomever she wished to speak. Was she to yield this freedom? Was she always to need to think whether what she said, did, dressed would affect others? How dare Kicva say she knew why Rhiannon hated herself? Was that freedom not the life Kicva had chosen for herself?

But had she chosen it? Did Kicva have any more freedom of choice than Rhiannon herself had? The question sent chills up and down Rhiannon as she understood it. She would never know whether Kicva's choice had been made freely—the Christian faith said there was free will for man—but she realized finally that she herself had no choice. Whether or not she hid herself from Simon, she *cared* what happened to him—and not only to him, but to all of them. She was already caught in the spiderweb of love relationships, and there was no way to break free. She could die struggling, hating herself for trying to avoid all bonds of love, or she could accept her silken prison together with its comforts and its joys and the occasional pains of its manacles.

The lambs stirred gently, baaed sleepily; their fleeces smelled oily-sweet. The last time Rhiannon had pillowed her head on unwashed fleeces with so strong an odor was in the shepherd's hut where she and Simon had taken refuge to make love on a rainy day. Desire washed over Rhiannon, and a storm of violent tears swept her into exhausted sleep when she had cried herself out.

Math was snuggled to her side when she woke. She met his large passionless eyes, so like her own in appearance but much closer to her mother's in expression. Math did not need her, she knew. He hunted for himself and found warmth enough. Yet he went with her to places he did not like in a conveyance he loathed because he loved her. With that, he was also free—sometimes. Her lips twitched.

"So you have forgiven me, Math, have you? Well, I am glad. I have forgiven myself also. Now, since you are so wise, how will I explain this to Simon and manage to keep a rag of my pride? I cannot, after all, simply appear curled up in his bed. He will ask why, and I cannot just stare coldly at him as you do at me."

CHAPTER 24

❖⊹❖⊹❖⊹❖⊹❖⊹❖⊹❖⊹❖⊹❖⊹❖⊹❖⊹❖⊹❖⊹❖⊹❖⊹❖⊹❖⊹❖

Kicva's messenger was in Builth on November third, but
Llewelyn had not yet arrived. He came on the fourth, only
there was such a press of business that he could not worry
about the peculiarities of his daughter. On the fifth, the
Earl of Pembroke arrived, and Llewelyn was still busier
so that he completely forgot Kicva's letter. That evening,
when he called Simon over for a few words, he noticed
that the young man was looking rather fine-drawn. That
reminded him, but he said nothing to Simon in case Kicva's
news was bad.

When he was free, he read the letter and cursed luridly.
If he had read it when he first saw it, he could have sent
for Rhiannon to entertain the earl while Pembroke was a
guest at Builth. In truth, he doubted that Pembroke would
care for or understand Rhiannon's singing. The earl was
not given to the arts, except those of war, and what he
knew of singing were delicate ditties in the French mode.
However, it would have been an excellent excuse.

Llewelyn tapped his teeth with a finger. Why should
he feel it was too late? It was still an excellent excuse. It
was perfectly logical that, having now met Pembroke
personally and liking him for himself, Llewelyn would
offer to him the greatest delicacy he had—his daughter
Rhiannon's singing. Yes, and it could do no harm if
Pembroke thought he was not perceptive enough to realize
that Welsh folk tales would not be the most appropriate
entertainment to offer a French-oriented Marcher lord.
The choice would underline Llewelyn's intense pride in his
heritage as well as imply that he did not understand his
guest very well. Good!

The letter to Kicva was written before Llewelyn sought
his bed, and the messenger was sent out with instructions
that it be delivered with more than usual haste. Then
Llewelyn dismissed both Simon and Rhiannon from his
mind. He had more serious matters to consider than a

love affair, particularly since he now had good reason to assume it would come to the conclusion he desired.

Reports came in every day. Henry and his army were still at Gloucester. As long as they remained there, Pembroke could afford to stay at Builth, discussing what moves he was willing to make and what he could provide for offense and defense. Llewelyn could put forward his proposals and detail what he would do to support them. The Welsh prince was inwardly irritated by Pembroke's excessive sense of honor; he called it not knowing on which side of the bread the butter lay. However, it had its advantages, too. Once bound, Richard would stay that way; so Llewelyn concealed his impatience with this exaggerated nicety and spoke of many plans as contingent when he was certain from long experience that they would have to be used.

On the ninth of November, news came that Henry and his army had begun moving north. Pembroke sent out word that his men should assemble at Abergavenny, which would put him sixteen miles from Monmouth—a royal stronghold—and twenty-four miles from Hereford—another keep and town loyal to Henry—or, at least, not openly rebels. Both passages were easy, a day's travel or less for Pembroke's troops so that they could counter any move westward the king might make.

Llewelyn assured Pembroke there was no need for him to leave to join his army yet. Welsh scouts would bring in news of Henry's movements every few hours. Although he would not *admit* that he did not trust the wily Welsh leader, Richard could not eliminate all his doubts. He found a solution to his dilemma by asking that Simon be in charge of the scouting parties. Despite the fact that Simon was Llewelyn's vassal, Richard was certain his dead brother's squire would do nothing to harm him.

It did not take much perception for Llewelyn to understand the request. He was mildly irritated again because he had wanted Simon to be at Builth when Rhiannon came. However, that was certainly not important enough to increase or confirm Pembroke's suspicions. Rhiannon would simply have to wait. She would be perfectly safe at Builth until this action was over. Llewelyn not only sent Simon out but asked Pembroke to give him his instructions, since only Pembroke knew how much warning he would need to join his men and get them in action.

Simon was delighted to go. He still knew nothing about Kicva's letter or Llewelyn's answer to it. In Llewelyn's opinion, to expect a reconciliation with one's love from moment to moment was no way to make that reconciliation proceed smoothly. Rhiannon would come; Kicva was never wrong, but whether she would come flashing down from the mountain like a bird or ride slowly over the roads with an escort and baggage, Llewelyn could not guess. He wanted Simon's mind on what he was doing, which was mixing with Pembroke's men so that Llewelyn could know what Richard's supporters thought and how close their ties were to Pembroke.

There had been nothing new to learn on that score, however. Simon had told Llewelyn all he could days before, and he was bored with trying to keep the peace between the northern and southern Welsh and the English-Norman contingents. He had not been sleeping well, and although he had twice wandered through the section where the camp followers plied their trade, he had come away without relieving his needs. And his feelings about Rhiannon still seesawed from hope to despair and back again. Llewelyn's order and Pembroke's instructions were the answers to his prayers. Simon had gathered his men and was away before anyone could change his mind.

Kicva's hunter returned to Angharad's Hall with Llewelyn's letter just after breakfast, about two hours before Simon set off to watch the movements of the king's army. He apologized for being slow. The fine weather had broken with a heavy fall of rain, which had overfilled several small rivers, making the usual fords useless. Kicva smiled. She knew about the fall of rain. It had imprisoned Rhiannon in the house, so that instead of examining her fears in the soft melancholy of the autumn forest and healing herself in silence, Rhiannon had worked them out on her harp. She had produced her first original song, not a translation or a distillation of an old story or her grandfather's work, but her own tale and melody—and it was good, the equal, Kicva thought, to Gwydyon's work. When she had played it through complete, Rhiannon had looked at her mother in dazed amazement. "That is my pain," she whispered, "and it is beautiful."

"Yes, Daughter. Did you think the songs Gwydyon wove came from a dead, untouched heart? They, too, were leached out of blood and agony. It changes, too, you know. Not now, perhaps not even soon, but it will breed more songs."

Less rebellious than she had been for nearly a year, Rhiannon accepted that. She did not strain to make more music and only used her harp for her customary practice. She was not ill-humored, but she was restless. It was not only that she wished to go to Simon so that she could think of him as happy rather than hurt and wondering, nor that she wanted to know what he was doing so that her anxiety would pinch and prick her less. Those just added to her general sense that she must be up and doing something—anything.

Needless to say, Llewelyn's command was greeted with cries of enthusiasm. Rhiannon did cast one single suspicious glance at her mother as she went to pack, but then she told herself severely that she did not care whether Kicva and Llewelyn had planned this to manage her. She wanted to go. She would *not* cut off her nose to spite her face. Her laughter trilled like bird song when she thought of "Simon's words," and Math came and rubbed against her legs. Then to her blank amazement he went and sat beside the padded basket in which he traveled.

Rhiannon paused in her packing, sat back on her heels, and stared at him. "I do not think you should go," she said. "We will be in a keep, and you hate that. Also, we may have to move several times."

There were occasions when Rhiannon almost expected to get an answer from Math. She never did—except in the way things worked out. All he did was stare back at her with his clear, pale eyes, the pupils down to slits. Rhiannon thought briefly of trying to imprison him when they left. Unlike dogs, cats hunted by eye and could not follow a trail. Then she shrugged. If Math wanted to go, why should he not? She would be glad to have him when the men moved on while she had to wait to know where they would stop before she could follow.

A faint chill washed over her as she focused on her own

thought. For the first time she understood what she intended to do. Not that *she* was shocked by the idea that she intended to follow Simon wherever he went, but Simon might be. Then another thrill passed up and down her spine. How had Math known she did not intend to return to Angharad's Hall until Simon came with her? Rhiannon shook the thought away. If Math was more than a large, beautiful cat, he meant well for her and for Simon. It was as unwise to look too closely into the kindly doings of the old gods as it was to look at the teeth of a gift-horse.

An hour after the messenger arrived, Rhiannon was mounted and ready to leave. Four men—strong, devoted, clever, and fierce—rode with her, and in spite of the horses they did not take the roads. Still, even as a bird flies, it was more than seventy miles from Angharad's Hall to Builth, and birds do not have to backtrack to avoid chasms or to ford rivers or to pick their way along goat trails over precipitous mountains. Rhiannon might have ridden through the night if the ground was reasonable, but even she was not so eager as to try to ford an overfull river that sounded angry in the dark.

Simon settled down to catch some sleep at just about the same time Rhiannon did. He had had a pleasant and satisfactory day. He had established most of his troop and all the horses on Orcop Hill while small detachments, including himself, scouted west and south on foot. Pembroke had told the truth when he said there was nothing left for the king's army around Clifford and southeast of Hereford. You could tell which lands were beholden to which side. Pembroke's were stripped bare, but neatly and cleanly. Hereford's were blackened, and one could smell the dead serfs as one passed.

There had been no sign of the king's army yet, except one patrol, and they had seemed more interested in forage than in the terrain. That was an interesting piece of information; it might mean that Gloucester had not been very generous with provender. The men beholden to Gloucester could not be open rebels; their youthful overlord was now with his stepfather, Richard of Cornwall, and his mother—who was Pembroke's sister. They could, however, do their best not to help, by concealing their stock, by pleading the effect of a murrain or a bad harvest. They could also say that Henry had already levied on them in August, and they had no more to give.

If that was true, the king's army was already short of supplies. Henry could not, then, strike due west because he already knew that Usk and the surrounding area was naked as a newborn babe. But the scouts would tell him that there was nothing around Hereford either. It could mean that Henry would do nothing until supplies could be gathered from England. That did not please Simon, and he turned restlessly and then rerolled himself in his blanket and cloak. As warmth seeped into him, he smiled. Henry was in a terrible rage, and patience had never been one of his virtues, even when he was not angry.

On that pleasant thought Simon slept. He woke easily at a touch some hours later. The troop ate pressed cakes of flaked, dried meat, dried fruit, and meal, passed around a small wineskin that one of the men had been carrying, and set out again. They found the army before dawn. Henry's force was camped amid the burned-out farms midway between Gloucester and Hereford. As the sun came up, the army began to stir. Simon and his men squatted in the cover of a grove of trees and watched, finishing their sleep by turns.

The sights and sounds were familiar: men waking each other, crying out for one reason or another, cooking pots clanging, grooms shouting and cursing at their charges as they fed them or prepared to lead them to water. After a while, the camp quieted somewhat while the men ate. Then the bedlam began again and even increased. Simon breathed a sigh of relief. The army was going to move. He watched a little longer, until he saw some handsomely caparisoned horses being led toward the largest tent on the field. Then he gestured Echtor closer.

"I will take four men and follow the royal party. You follow the army with the rest of the men—three for the head, three for the rear guard. When they settle for the night, we will meet at Orcop Hill. If they should not stop but strike west toward Wales, send two men to Builth—or to the nearest of Prince Llewelyn's men they can find—with as much information as you can glean about their intentions."

The next few hours were quite exhausting. There was no keeping up with the horses, of course, but Simon and his men found where Henry and his companions had turned off the road and were then able to follow their trail, which led due west to the Wye. They had ridden along the river, apparently having the escort test places that looked fordable. The heavy rains of the preceding week had filled the river, however. A man might swim it, as could horses, but for the baggage wains there was no passage except the one near Hereford.

Simon rejoiced at the persistence in looking for a crossing. Apparently Henry intended to move his army west, which could only mean he planned an attack. Owing to the care with which the river had been examined, Simon had caught up with the party just before they reached Hereford. He saw Henry and the leaders enter the town while the escort turned back. Simon did not bother to wait for the royal party to emerge or to follow the escort. He returned to the camp on Orcop Hill and sent out Siorl and six of the men, who had lounged away the two days watching an empty pass, to watch instead the roads leading north and west from Hereford.

At midafternoon Echtor sent a messenger to say that the vanguard of the army had reached Hereford, crossed the Wye, and turned south again. Simon found this very interesting and went north himself with the man Echtor had sent. By the time he arrived, it was certain that the group turning south was no mere work party or scavenging expedition. Simon clicked his tongue against his teeth in disapproval. If the king and his mercenary leaders had learned anything from their experiences in August, it was not much. There were a few outriders at the front of the column to give warning in case a large body of enemy should appear, but that was all. They would be as easy to rout as ants.

The baggage train was not yet in sight, but in his mind Simon was already counting its worth. He told Echtor to wait for it and send him word of how it was guarded and whatever he could determine of its contents. As they were speaking, the king and his nobles and mercenary captains rode down through the marching men and on toward the south. Simon sent two men after them, but without much hope. If they remained on the road, they would soon outdistance their followers, and there would be no way to tell which side road they turned off on, if they turned off at all. However, Simon was not much worried. Presumably the army would end up wherever the royal party was going.

He did not have to wait that long to find out, however. By evening one of the men was back with the news that the king and his party had entered Grosmount. He had struck it lucky on a shortcut he had taken, coming up on a rise of land quite a distance behind but not so far he could not recognize the colors of the men entering the keep.

This was news of real moment. The area around Grosmount had not been attacked by Pembroke. There was a concentration of castles from Monmouth in the south to Grosmount in the north, all in the control of Poitevins. It had made the area too dangerous for Pembroke to raid seriously, and there were probably supplies for the army there. Simon did not think Henry had pressed the Poitevins hard during the preceding campaign. Now they would have to victual his army—and that would mean a stay of a day or two, surely time enough for Llewelyn to mount a surprise attack that might be very profitable indeed. Simon went to watch Grosmount himself, taking his horse.

To Ymlladd, twenty miles was nothing. As soon as Simon was sure the army was settling down in the fields surrounding the keep at Grosmount, he set out for Builth. Shortly after compline he was reporting to Pembroke and Llewelyn. Fortunately, neither of them had yet been asleep, and those other leaders who were, were roused as soon as the significance of Simon's news was understood. There was an avaricious glitter in Llewelyn's eyes and trouble in Pembroke's by the time Simon had emptied his budget.

"I do not wish to attack without provocation," Pembroke began.

"I do." Llewelyn's voice cut off any further protest. "This is an opportunity to do us much good and the king's forces much harm with little bloodshed. If you will not come in your own person, so be it. Let the blame fall on me. However, you have just made an agreement to prosecute a war—"

"Only to fight if attacked. For the king to march his army here and there is no attack."

"My lord," Gilbert Bassett put in, "I know that much of your trouble is on my account, and I should be accepting of your rule in gratitude, but the king's intention is clear. Really, you go too far in patience."

"The king in his own person is there," Richard said.

There was a soft sound, almost like a pack of beasts snarling. Richard sighed. It was all too obvious that no one agreed with him, that all had abandoned hope of any settlement outside of force, and that the king's presence at Grosmount was an inducement rather than a detraction to the idea of attack. It was also obvious that every man who was not directly his vassal intended to follow Llewelyn. To withhold his own men, then, would merely increase the danger for his allies without preventing the action. And most probably they were right after all. Nonetheless, Richard could not bring himself personally to lead a surprise attack on the king.

"I will go back to Abergavenny," he said, "and send my men out under Bassett's command. I am sorry, but I cannot lead them myself. I—"

"If God had sent me such vassals as you," Llewelyn interrupted, "I would be prince of the Garden of Eden." Then he laughed. "I do not know whether that would be entirely to my taste. So much peace and justice and mutual respect. . . . No, I cannot imagine it." He put out his hand to Richard. "But one or two like you, Pembroke, would be the greatest gift God could give a ruler. What a fool Henry is."

While this talk had progressed, Simon was shifting impatiently from one foot to the other. Now Llewelyn turned his head toward him and raised his brows sardonically. "And another vassal like you," he said affectionately, "would make me inquire why my men never bathed. If you itch, Simon, then scratch. Do not stand there wriggling."

"I do not itch," Simon protested, "except to go at once.

If we do not move at once, they may victual and be away before we arrive. It would be impossible to hide all traces, and . . ."

Half a dozen pairs of eyes fixed on him with varying degrees of amusement and irritation. Simon swallowed. It was rather foolish for him to be instructing a group of old war dogs, one of whom, at least, had been staging successful surprise attacks for nearly forty years. Yet Llewelyn was least annoyed and only said firmly that Simon should get a few hours of sleep, assuring him that if he would stay out of the way, they would be at Grosmount and ready to attack at the proper time.

At first light they did, indeed, set out. For his sins, Simon was put in charge of the baggage animals, not wagons and oxen but sure-footed asses that could climb the mountain trails that lay between Grosmount and Builth. He cursed and laughed at the same time, recognizing that the punishment surely fit the crime. It was not so bad, either. He arrived at Llewelyn's camp only an hour after the main body of the troops, well in time to join the others for a late dinner. Llewelyn was not there. He had ridden with Pembroke and Bassett to Abergavenny.

Scouts went out and returned to say there was plenty of activity in the camp but no sign the army would move. The troops settled down to give a last look to their weapons or to sleep, but Simon remounted Ymlladd to bring in his own men from the camp on Orcop Hill. They were not needed, but it would be a shame for them to miss the fun and what individual pieces of loot they could pick up. By the time he got back to the main camp, Simon was beginning to feel tired, but he went at once to join the conference that was planning the attack. He had more news that would be of interest. His men had discovered that all the leaders of the army, the king, Winchester, Seagrave, Peter of Rivaulx, and nearly all the mercenary captains were inside the keep. Only lesser men were with the army.

Rhiannon had reached Builth just before terce to find that the keep was all but empty. The old knight whom Llewelyn had left in charge of the skeleton garrison told her willingly enough where the troops and her father had gone, and assured her that they expected to return to Builth and that the women in the keep were ready to receive her. Rhiannon had all she could do not to burst into tears of frustration. At that moment, for all she knew, Simon might be fighting, and her selfishness had deprived her of saying farewell to him.

Cursing herself, she climbed to the women's quarters, but the questions and greetings that met her drove her nearly to distraction, and she fled down to speak to the old knight again. She soon understood that no attack would take place until that night and that the troops could not even have arrived at Grosmount yet. At first this frustrated her even more because she knew she would have to wait that much longer before she had news of the result of the battle, but she could not leave the subject alone. Pressing for this detail and that, she finally realized she had extracted directions for getting to Grosmount and a good knowledge of the surrounding area.

At this point, the crazy notion of riding to join her father's army took hold of her. She knew it was crazy; she knew Simon and her father would be fit to murder her just for thinking such a scheme. She put the idea away— for all of five minutes. Each time it recurred, it became more irresistible, and she could not see that it could really do any harm. Excusing herself abruptly, she went down to speak to her four men, nearly tripping over Math, who had been following her like a striped shadow ever since he had been released from his traveling basket. This was most unusual. Math's normal behavior was to explore any new place with extreme thoroughness, reducing all the other domestic animals to subjection and ignoring his mistress until he was in full command.

Rhiannon broached her idea to her men, half-expecting that they would threaten to tie her down as a madwoman or say that Kicva had specifically ordered them on no account to permit her to do such lunacy. Instead, a light of avarice and adventure lit all four pairs of eyes.

"Do you know the way, mistress?" Twm asked. "This is far from our lands and we could easily go astray."

"I think I do," Rhiannon said with confidence, in complete ignorance of the fact that the old knight had described the paths taken by merchants and other travelers, not the route the army would follow. "We must go along the Wye to Clifford keep and then go south until we find the river Dore. It runs, the old man says, in a deep valley, so if we keep to the low land as we go south, we should find it without fail. There will be no danger in asking if we lose our way, either. That land is all Welsh or the Earl of Pembroke's, and the people should be friendly."

"Well, then, mistress, it is for you to say. There will be rich pickings there." Twm's eyes glittered. "You can ride with the best of us if we should need to flee."

Math nudged Rhiannon's leg, and she looked at him. "Go get his basket," she said, "and make the horses ready."

Her final talk with the old knight was less agreeable than her previous ones. Even though she did not tell the truth and only said she would follow her father to Abergavenny, he protested. First he was amused, then outraged, arguing that he did not know whether there were any suitable women for company there and that her father would not want her mingling with so many Saesones. Finally, grudgingly, he let her go, although he was by no means happy.

Everything went according to plan, which made Rhiannon forget for a while the lunacy of what she was doing. There were good roads running along the Wye, and they made excellent time, skirting south of Clifford and steering easily by the sun, which was intermittently visible near the midpoint of the sky but low to the south, as was normal for the season.

Finding the Dore was not quite as easy as Rhiannon had expected. At the point they met it, it was close to its source and little more than a stream. They wasted several hours following streamlets that meandered purposelessly, and Rhiannon began to have serious doubts about the sanity of her enterprise. Just as she was thinking of giving up, the stream they were following ran into a larger one. This engendered enough hope to keep her from ordering a return, and she was soon rewarded by the stream's turning south, again joining a larger tributary, and running into what they knew must be the Dore. There was a well-marked track beside the river—not a road but a passage for cattle and packtrains. Again Rhiannon and her escort began to move with confidence, unaware of the fact that they were on the wrong side of the river. She had asked how to get to Grosmount, and the knight had told her, but Llewelyn's camp was some miles to the west.

The next check to their progress came late in the afternoon. Rhiannon believed that they must be quite near their goal by then, and they rode along in momentary expectation of seeing signs of the army or being hailed by one of her father's scouting patrols. Doubts entered Rhiannon's mind when they came first to a confluence of several streams the old knight had not mentioned. They were not difficult to ford, the confusion of currents having swirled rocks and sand together and spread the waters wide and shallow; however, on the other side was a well-worn road marked by the imperishable stones set by the Romans. This, too, the old knight had failed to mention.

"Either the old man's memory is failing," Rhiannon said, "or we followed the wrong river after the ford. There is a little wood." She pointed about half a mile south to where the land started to rise toward a low mountain. "Sion and Twm will come with me. You others go, one west and one south, to find our people if you can."

This was a sensible plan and was carried out without delay. As soon as Rhiannon and her men found what they felt was a suitably sheltered spot, they dismounted. The wood was utterly silent, for there were no insect sounds and the birds that had not flown south were mostly in the fields. It was cold, too, and Rhiannon, the men, and the horses were all tired. The men loosened the horses' girths and put out a little grain for them to eat. Rhiannon shared out what food she had and let Math out of his basket for a while. She was not yet frightened—except about what her father and Simon would say. They would have been furious enough if she had reached the safety of their camp before the attack. If she missed them . . .

She put aside the thought, though her worries were not lessened when Math voluntarily got back into his basket and sat there. However, there was nothing more she could do, so she wrapped herself in her cloak and determinedly closed her eyes. She had been even more of a fool than usual, but it was too late to worry. They could not have gone far astray. When the battle began, they would be able to orient themselves on the sound and make for the camp where the servants and other noncombatants would wait.

The sun was just above the horizon when faint bird calls reached Rhiannon's guards. It might be only crows that had discovered a dead animal, but Twm promptly set out to see. Sion looked at his mistress's daughter, who was sleeping soundly, and decided not to wake her yet. When Twm came back would be soon enough. But then Sion heard what might be horses, and Twm had not returned. He had begun to tighten the girths of the mounts when Twm burst through the trees.

"A hundred or more," he gasped, "and they are ranging the wood, beating for game."

Shaken awake, Rhiannon was half-dazed. They mounted and rode southwest as quickly as possible. It was the only direction they could go. The river was northwest, and they did not know whether it was fordable; east was all king's country. At first they thought they would make good their escape. The hunting party was making so much noise of their own that the sound of their horses would be insignificant. There was no pursuit, and they drove their mounts harder as they came out of the trees into more open land.

This was a grave mistake. The thunder of their own horses' hooves and the sun full in their eyes masked sights and sounds they would have noticed had their progress been more careful. Suddenly, cries rang out from ahead, a challenge in French and English. They could not answer. Rhiannon's men spoke neither French nor English, and a woman's voice would be no way to reduce curiosity and obtain freedom. Desperate, they wheeled east, but it was too late. Warnings were sounding before, behind, all over. Sion and Twm reached for their bows.

"No!" Rhiannon cried. "You cannot fight an army."

"Welsh! Spies! Have a care!" rang from every side.

Several men-at-arms rose with crossbows ready out of a screen of bushes along the side of a stream about twenty feet away. Rhiannon reined in her horse.

"I am no spy," she said in French. "I am a Welsh gentlewoman, and my men and I are lost."

The cultured language and the quality of the horses and their trappings saved Rhiannon and her men from excessively rough handling. There were some Welsh gentlemen who, from violent opposition to anything Prince Llewelyn did, were attached to the king's cause, and the leaders of the men on patrol and scavenging expeditions knew better than to take the chance of offending any of their women-folk. They also had strict instructions that any Welsh person caught must be brought to an officer for questioning. It seemed impossible that any woman should be a spy, but if she were brought politely to their commander, they would have obeyed both orders.

Excusing himself but nonetheless firmly, the captain of the patrol relieved Sion and Twm of everything that could conceivably be a weapon and bound their feet beneath their horses' bellies and their hands to the saddles. This indignity was not forced upon Rhiannon, but she was as securely bound as her men because, in spite of their urging that she escape, she would not leave them.

Until Rhiannon saw the keep itself, she had been uselessly castigating herself for her lunacy in leaving Builth, but she had not been personally afraid. As soon as she identified herself, she knew she would be treated with the utmost courtesy. When she saw Grosmount, however, she realized that, respect or no respect, she would be asked what she was doing in the area. And even if she told them nothing, her very presence would proclaim that her father must be somewhere near.

Not only that, she would be a prisoner and would remain one until the war was over. Simon might be brought to heel by her predicament, and he would love her no better for placing him in such a position. And if the king tried to use her as a bargaining counter, her father would be so angry that he would probably plead with Henry to drop her down the deepest castle well that could be found. Better, far better, to suffer whatever indignity was necessary now. It could not be long before the attack took place. Surely during that confusion she would be able to escape.

"Twm, tell them I am Rhiannon, wife of Pwyll, if they ask," she called out in Welsh, "and that my husband put me away because I am barren. You were taking me home to my father, Heffydd Hen. You know the place and the rest of the tale."

"What are you saying? What are you saying?" the captain of the guard demanded angrily.

"I told them to tell the truth if they are questioned, that we have nothing to hide. I am Rhiannon, wife of Pwyll of Dyfedd, and I am going home to my father, Heffydd the Old."

"What was there in that to laugh about?" the man insisted suspiciously.

Obviously Rhiannon could not admit that her men were amused because she had adapted an old fairy tale to fit her needs. "That I will not tell you," she said with dignity. "It is personal to me, and I love them less for they laugh at my shame."

This answer scarcely satisfied him, but he did not wish to take responsibility for more than telling her firmly not to address her men in their own language again. This Rhiannon readily promised, for the details of the old fairy tale were so well known that she was sure her story and her men's would fit together perfectly. They soon came to the camp where the officer in charge was as puzzled as the patrol leader had been as to what to do with a Welshwoman of good class—he knew well enough what to do with the others.

His first move was to ask whether she knew anyone in the king's entourage who would vouch for her. Naturally enough she denied vehemently that she had any connection of any kind at all with the Saeson or those who loved the Saeson. She reiterated that she was no spy, that the officer should allow her and her men to pass on in peace. Since this was impossible, she was passed up the chain of command, arriving at last in the tent of Baldwin de Guisnes, the castellan of Monmouth keep, and the most important man—and best soldier—in the camp.

By then it was completely dark. The men were already quieting for the night. About half of them had only reached the camp that morning and had spent the afternoon putting up tents. Those who had come in the day before had either been out on patrol, had been scavenging, or had been collecting and distributing supplies under the eyes of their officers. De Guisnes, however, was not tired. His activities had been confined to riding the distance the men-at-arms had walked and then riding around the camp on a tour of inspection. He had just been considering whether he should go up to the keep for a little male companionship or send his squire out to procure a woman for him when Rhiannon was brought to his tent.

He listened to her story with creased brows. "Take the men away and get an interpreter to question them. No torture yet. And you, my lady, get down from that horse."

Rhiannon did so without comment, only turning to unlash Math's basket before the horse could be led away. Hands grabbed the basket from her and fastened on the lid. "No! Do not!" she cried. So, naturally, the lid was pulled off at once. Math's yowl and the shriek of the man who had opened the basket mingled and were loud enough to drown the single choke of laughter she could not restrain.

"I told you not to open it," she said, still choking and hoping her mirth would be mistaken for grief. "Now my cat is lost."

"Cat?" de Guisnes repeated, looking at the slashes which had torn the unwise man-at-arm's forehead, nose, and jaw so that blood was pouring down his face. "That looks like the work of a lion."

Then he transferred his eyes to Rhiannon's face, which he could see more clearly now that she had dismounted. In a moment all thought of riding up to the keep or using a camp follower disappeared from his mind. He reviewed the story he had heard. No claim of influential friends or relatives. Who did she say her husband was? Pwyll of Dyfedd? He had never heard that name—or had he? It was vaguely familiar. But the father's name, Heffydd Hen, he had never heard that. No male relative he need worry about offending. She was a nobody—but a very pretty nobody.

"I do not understand how you came to be so conveniently lost right here," de Guisnes said. "It is not common for a woman to act the spy—but it is not impossible. You had better explain yourself more clearly."

"There is nothing to explain," Rhiannon insisted, but she entered the tent without protest when he gestured her inside.

He dropped the tent flap, but there was no reason to tie it. His eyes were on Rhiannon, whose beauty, although a little marred by dust and fatigue, was quite striking in the better light provided by candles. Thus, he did not notice the gray shadow that slipped under the flap and then melted away under his bed. Rhiannon's eyes flicked to it and away. The sidelong glance was unintentionally provocative, for she had just been replying to the question of why her men had laughed.

De Guisnes seized on that, called it a lie, and insisted on an answer. But he neither wanted nor expected one; he simply needed an excuse to punish Rhiannon. The questioning continued for almost half an hour, with Rhiannon pretending to weep but refusing to answer "for shame." Then, feeling he had justification in case the Pwyll she had mentioned was more important than he thought, he began to threaten her. Rhiannon realized she would have to offer something new, and admitted with more false tears that her husband had put her away for being barren. The men he had sent to escort her back to her father's house had laughed at her in mockery.

This was better than de Guisnes had expected. The name Pwyll of Dyfedd had seemed familiar to him—which was not surprising since the story of Pwyll was one of the commonest legends in Wales—and de Guisnes had felt a touch of uneasiness about raping the wife of a man who might be important. But if he had rejected the woman already, there could be no harm in it. De Guisnes cocked his head as some faint sounds in the distance caught his ear. Then, someone closer cried a challenge. An authoritative voice answered in cultured French. De Guisnes dismissed the matter from his mind, grasped Rhiannon's wrist, and drew her toward him.

"I think your husband was a great fool," he said.

CHAPTER 25

❖•❖

The commanders at Grosmount were no more intelligent about patrols after they camped than on the march. Some men did ride around, but they went no farther than the banks of the Dore two miles away. Not a quarter of a mile west of the bank, most of Prince Llewelyn's army had slept away the hours between dinnertime and dusk. By then sufficient places had been found in the river that could be used as fords with a line slung from bank to bank to prevent men from being swept away and drowned.

A few advance posts had also been set up by the mercenary captains, but these were on the road. It was quite fixed in the minds of continental mercenaries that armies carried huge siege trains and supply wagons and, therefore, traveled on roads. By dusk the advance posts were gone and the strangled bodies quietly removed. Before it was completely dark, Prince Llewelyn's army was across both road and river and advancing quietly on the main camp behind a fan of scouts who cleaned up the few men wandering out of the camp for one reason or another.

Just beyond the perimeter of the fields several hundred chosen men waited, watching the activity die down and the fires burn low. There were guards, but not very many. Soon shadows began to flit across the fields and there were fewer guards, then fewer still. Then the whole open area seemed to darken and crawl and heave. Prince Llewelyn's army was on the move. They were not aimed toward the rows of tents where the men-at-arms slept, but toward the area closest to the keep, where the draught animals were tethered and the baggage wains lay. It was not completely silent; it was impossible that so many men should not make some noise, but the camp was not completely silent either, and the invaders did not raise any alarms.

Simon and his troop were in the second wave, although the best of his men had worked with the scouts. When it came to actual battle, Simon preferred to be in mail and on horseback. There were already a few cries in the distance as Simon rode across the fields toward the camp. Here and there a groom or a guard of the supply train could not be silenced quickly enough. It would not be long before the whole camp was stirring.

Even as he thought it, a voice cried a sleepy challenge. Simon could see well enough to make out a face peering from a tent. He answered with an autocratic snap. The mail-clad form, shield on shoulder and sword sheathed, together with the tone and the cultured voice and accent, were enough. The sentries had not called any alarm; it was not the business of a common man to question a knight riding through the camp with a few men on his tail. No one would bother to inform a common soldier about any duty but his own.

Simon went on, laughing silently. He was nearly to the center of the camp. Pembroke's forces must by now be poised at the edge of the woods to come down the moment action started. His business, and that of others like him, was to cause enough disturbance to prevent the men-at-arms from going to the assistance of those guarding the baggage when the inevitable alarm came. Then Pembroke's men could come in and sweep up the remains. Simon was beginning to wonder whether he would have to begin the disturbance himself, when a violent outcry broke out almost simultaneously in the supply area and at the southern end of the camp.

He had just time to notice that he was close to the largest and most luxurious tent he had yet seen when there were shouts of alarm right behind him. He swung his shield onto his arm, drew his sword—and almost dropped it in shock. The most appalling squall he had ever heard burst from the tent just ahead of him, followed by a man's hoarse scream of pain, and then the single word, "Math!" coming from the last voice Simon expected to hear. All around him now men began to cry out warnings and alarms. His troop spread out, shouting at the top of their lungs, cutting tent cords, knocking down lean-to supports, striking men with the flats of their swords, and in general creating the maximum amount of terror and confusion.

A male shout of rage had followed the scream of pain

and the woman's cry of protest just before the chaos began, but the man's third yell, of surprise as much as pain, was almost drowned by the rising noise. Then the tent flap billowed, emitting first a squalling fury of a cat and then— *Rhiannon*. The whole thing took only five seconds, but Simon felt as if he had been sitting mute and paralyzed for an hour. When the man burst from the tent behind Rhiannon, Simon was at last galvanized into action and urged Ymlladd forward, shouting a challenge.

He hoped for one moment in which to come close enough to strike Rhiannon's pursuer down. If the man rushed back into his tent, it would be more difficult to deal with him. Either Simon's shout or the sights and sounds that met his eyes when he came out had just that effect. De Guisnes stopped, his mouth and eyes distended. The flat of Simon's sword caught him on the side of the head hard enough to knock him two feet to the left.

As the blow fell, Simon could not help but feel sorry for the man. He had had enough to stun him, apparently, before he came out of his tent. His face and neck were covered with blood, as was the sleeve of his left arm. Simon knew what had happened, and he did not have time to wonder why it had happened. That would come later.

"Rhiannon!" he bellowed.

It never occurred to him that she might have run away in terror, and indeed she had not. She slipped back around the side of the tent instantly, crying out happily, "Oh, Simon, how fortunate! I came to find you."

This statement, not unnaturally, had almost the effect on Simon that his sword had had on de Guisnes. His stunned speechlessness gave Rhiannon time to add, "My men are prisoners somewhere here—Twm and Sion. Will you pass the word to look for them? And I must get Math's basket."

On the words she nipped back into the tent. Simon let out another bellow, this time of rage. At once Siorl was at his elbow. "Get—" Simon began, just as Rhiannon stepped out of the tent, calling for Math. Siorl's eyes nearly popped out of his head. He had heard Simon shout Rhiannon's name just after he struck down the owner of the tent, but he had been busy at the moment and had assumed it was a war cry. It might be an odd one, but it would identify Simon as attached to the Welsh party, and it was not unreasonable in Siorl's mind that his master would call his witch-woman's name as a talisman. However, Siorl had hardly expected the appearance of the witch herself in answer.

"Get her a horse, and get her out of here!" Simon roared.

"What about my men?" Rhiannon cried.

"Any Welsh prisoner will be freed," Simon replied, then turned to order Echtor to strip de Guisnes's tent and found Rhiannon was gone. "Rhiannon!" he bellowed.

"I am getting Math," she shouted back.

She was not far, but he could hardly hear her. The whole camp was a bedlam as Bassett with Pembroke's troops poured into it. The confusion was indescribable, for Henry's whole army had been caught sleeping, unarmed and unprepared, and was now in a state of total panic. Here and there a captain would try to organize his men to resist, but by specific instructions he would be struck down as the first target. The few knights and barons were being immobilized by the simple expedient of cutting their tents down around them, extracting them half-smothered, and rendering them unconscious.

The common men-at-arms were being rounded up and put to work at loading everything movable on carts and pack animals and driving them out. Welsh guards with arrows nocked to their bows patrolled up and down the line of carts. The pack animals were fastened together in long trains, each led by a single trustworthy man.

As Rhiannon came back around the side of the tent, Ewyn came up with a cart, and Echtor drove forward some dazed, bloodied, and half-naked Flemish mercenaries, who promptly fell on their knees, thinking they had been brought before Simon for judging. They could not, of course, understand a word Echtor said to them.

"Get up," Simon said in French, "and load the goods into the cart. No more harm will befall you than already has."

Their relief was so great that they worked with more enthusiasm than could have been expected. The tent was down and rolled, its contents stowed away by the time Siorl returned with a great black brute of a stallion that was kicking and plunging. Simon called his captain several improbable things, but Siorl shouted back that the stallion was the only horse he could find. Nothing but oxen were left. The stallion remained because he was too wild to handle.

"Not in this noise," Rhiannon cried. "I cannot quiet him in the middle of this chaos."

"Take Ymlladd," Simon yelled.

Rhiannon ran to the horse's head and stroked him. He, too, was nervous and snorting, eager to rear and fight as the smell of blood excited him more and more. Still, he did not attempt to savage Rhiannon, and she went to the side and up into the saddle before Simon came down. It would not do in the midst of such turmoil to leave the stallion with an empty saddle.

As it was, when Simon came down, Ymlladd plunged and reared, fighting the lessening of the weight he was accustomed to bearing until he realized there were still firm hands on the reins and a voice he knew well in his ears. It took time to strap Math's carrying basket on behind the saddle, as even Simon was cautious about approaching the horse where he could not see and Math was yowling like a banshee.

Then came the question of mounting the black destrier. Shouts brought men to hang on the bridle so he could not rear, and at least he was not as bad as Ymlladd and did not try to bite. Simon sprang into the saddle, tore the reins from Siorl's hands, and checked the horse as hard as he could. The black rose, pawing the air; Simon roweled him hard.

"Go," he bellowed. "Siorl, take her to Llewelyn before Ymlladd starts to fight."

The noise, which had lessened around them, began to swell again. Groups of men who had run out of the camp in panic had been gathered by some of the captains who had escaped. Once their shock diminished, so did their terror. They began to realize that the army attacking them was far inferior in numbers to their own. They had found weapons and scraps of armor and began to return to try to drive the invaders away. Partly it was a matter of pride, but an even stronger inducement was their own need for the supplies that were being stolen. If they did not fight back, there would be no food for them, no money, no tents, no shoes, no blankets—nothing. Some had gathered loot in past battles. That was being taken, too, and they did not want to lose it.

Where these groups were fighting their way back into the camp, the sounds were different—curses and cries of pain but no screams of unreasoning terror. Rhiannon turned her head to listen and knew she must go. Her eyes were blazing like emeralds even in the dim light.

"Give me a bow, and I will guard the wagon," she cried.

Simon was battling with his new stallion and had no attention to give to anything else. Siorl, who had listened to Rhiannon sing to the voices in the wind around Dinas Emrys, would never question the orders of the witch. He set up a cry for a light bow, and a man came running up with a boy's weapon as the wagon was started forward. Rhiannon swung the quiver over her shoulder and then grasped the bow.

"Have a care, Simon," she shouted back as she kicked Ymlladd into forward motion, which finally stopped his dancing and plunging. "I will marry you where and when you will, so have a care to yourself."

Simon heard and for a moment his control of the black destrier faltered. He started to rise and tip in the saddle, but his knees gripped hard and he pulled back the rein until the animal's mouth was forced open. Then, as the wagon and its escort disappeared into the dark, he wrenched his mount around to the direction from which the sounds of battle rather than rout were coming, relaxed the rein, and roweled the beast hard again. The horse sprang forward. In moments they were among the fighters. Simon called warnings in Welsh and then let his half-crazed mount attack:

That group broke soon, but there was more legitimate prey on the way. Once the noise of the initial rout began, it was inevitable that the keep should be warned. It had taken a little time for those within to understand what was happening. Now the few nobles and the mercenary captains who had been with the king inside Grosmount were leading out the garrison of the keep in an attempt to drive away the attackers.

Before the defenders from the keep could reach the

camp and interfere with the systematic looting that was going on, they were met by both Bassetts, Siward, Simon, and half a dozen others plus their mounted men-at-arms. The black destrier now had his fill of work, and the strange, cruel hands became kind and steadying. Spurs no longer raked his sides but touched him gently, directing him here and there. The unfamiliar scent began to mingle with the familiar and grow acceptable. His energy and fury could be directed at opposing horses and men.

The clash was sharp, and half an hour of hard fighting ensued, but those who had come out of Grosmount were driven back in. Several were unhorsed and their animals caught and led away, but no attempt was made to capture anyone, even after he became easy prey on foot. They were simply prevented from coming anywhere near the camp where they might rally the men and prevent the removal of every stick, shred, and crumb that might be useful for any purpose at all.

Another sally from the keep was met and thrust back, and now the sounds of battle within the camp were dying down as well. The defeated were thoroughly cowed, and there was very little left to fight over. As the last of the wagons and packtrains rolled out of the camp, Gilbert Bassett rode back and ordered his men to begin an ordered retreat that would prevent any attack to recover the loot. The Welsh were already gone. Organization was not a strong point of their fighting style.

For half an hour more, Simon, Philip Bassett, and their men held the land between the keep and the camp. A final blast of horns told them that all the allied forces were out. Then they turned and galloped away. They assumed that as soon as they were gone, those in the keep would rush down and try to organize a counterattack, but no one was worried. The men were so demoralized that they would not respond well to orders, and there was hardly a weapon or a piece of armor left in the camp. The garrison of the keep had been somewhat mauled already, and they were far inferior in numbers to the rearguard Gilbert Bassett had set up.

The rearguard action was maintained all the way to Abergavenny, but no one expected it to be necessary, and it was not. Having fought hard twice and having had an energetic gallop with a proper load on him, the black stallion had settled into a model of obedience. Naturally, the moment Simon's mind was free of the need to concentrate on keeping alive, it turned to Rhiannon. First, equally naturally, he was so consumed by outrage that he gasped for breath and felt as if he would burst.

What the devil had she meant when she said she had come to find him in the tent of an officer of an enemy camp? Idiot woman, imagine wandering around in the middle of a battle looking for a cat! And how dare she scream aloud that she would marry him where and when he desired and make that an afterthought to demanding a bow?

At this point, Simon began to laugh. No one would believe this, no one! He was not sure he would have believed it himself if he were not riding a strange black horse instead of Ymlladd. Then, as soon as he thought of his destrier, he began to worry about whether the wagon had been attacked by one of the organized bands and, if so, whether Rhiannon had been able to manage the stallion. Fear for her woke anger again, and he fretted and fumed until the ridiculous aspects of the situation struck him anew.

Between this seesaw of emotion, he wondered how the devil he was going to find Rhiannon in the madhouse that Abergavenny keep must be, with loads of loot of all kinds coming in and ten times the number of men the keep was designed to hold accompanying it. Actually, Simon should have known better than to worry about such matters when both the Earl of Pembroke and Prince Llewelyn had remained at Abergavenny. By the time the rearguard reached the keep, everything was completely organized. As each man entered, he was asked his name and the name of his leader and directed to where his group was resting and reorganizing. Simon's name made the guard look up.

"You are most urgently wanted in the hall, my lord. Your men will be quartered and word sent to you."

Such a summons to a very junior member of the army could only have to do with Rhiannon, so Simon was not surprised to find her sitting with Llewelyn, Pembroke, and Gilbert Bassett. Although Simon's predominant emotion was outrage as he threaded his way through the bailey

and entered the keep, the expressions on the four faces—
no, five, for Math was sitting in his mistress's lap—when
they saw him struck Simon so funny that he whooped with
laughter and could barely walk straight.

Llewelyn's face became rigid as wood and his eyes were
suffused. To Simon it was clear his overlord would have
been laughing too, if he were not afraid of offending his
companions. Bassett was seated as far from Rhiannon as
possible. One could not call the daughter of a major ally
a witch, but . . . Pembroke, staring at her, simply looked
stunned. And Rhiannon . . . Simon choked. Rhiannon
and Math both wore the same smug, self-satisfied look of
contentment.

Llewelyn signaled a servant to bring another stool. "Sit
before you fall down," he said to Simon. "We must settle
this quickly. There are more important matters in hand
than the behavior of my idiotic daughter, but I must be
rid of her before I can deal with them. Simon, I will have
you locked up! What the devil are you laughing at?"

"She—she—do you know what she did?" Simon
hiccuped. "She—in the middle of the battle she shrieked
at me that she was willing to marry me where and when
I chose. The—the whole army . . . *both* whole armies are
witness. *Eneit,* you do not do things by halves, I will say
that for you."

Rhiannon shrugged. "It was no one's business but ours,
and there is nothing shameful in agreeing to a marriage.
Of course, you *are* a Saeson, but not so many in the army
know that," she teased.

"Rhiannon!" Llewelyn roared.

She went silent and lowered her eyes—she had not
meant to say anything offensive to Bassett and Pembroke
but had just forgotten they were there—but Math made
a rude noise, a weird mixture of a hiss and a belch.
Llewelyn looked at the large cat with marked disfavor
and then looked up. Bassett's eyes were going from
Rhiannon to the cat and back, and Llewelyn did not like
the look. Other men were looking around at the group
impatiently. There was no more time to be spent on this
minor matter.

"I gather from what you have said that you are still
willing to have her. Is this true, Simon?"

"Yes, but—"

"No buts. If you are willing to have her, take her now. And you are responsible for her. Keep her off the battlefield and away—from—these—gentlemen. I do not care how you do it, just do it. And do not present yourself to me again until you stop laughing."

Simon did his best to swallow his unseemly mirth, which was, of course, compounded of lack of sleep, overexertion, too much tension, and a great and sudden relief. He seized Rhiannon firmly by the wrist and retreated hastily, ignoring the fact that Math had fallen from her lap when he jerked her upright. In the back of his mind, he was surprised that Math had not scratched him nor had Rhiannon protested; she went willingly right to the edge of the hall. Here she pulled back a little.

"Wait, Simon, where are we going? The keep is packed like a cask of herrings."

Simon paused and looked into her eyes. His half-hysterical laughter had ended as soon as he gripped her. When his fingers closed on her arm, it was like taking hold of some great source of strength. Warmth and refreshment flowed into him, and it was like being back in the tent after freeing de Burgh. Rhiannon's eyes had the same deep luminescence, and he had the same aching need. His face went rigid with desire.

"I do not think my father is really angry," Rhiannon said, seeing the change in his expression and misreading it.

"No, and I do not care if he is," Simon replied through stiff lips.

Then she understood, and fire coursed through her also. She turned her hand so that she could grip Simon's wrist while he still held hers. They stared at each other. They could not go outside the keep. Not only was it dangerous, but it was too cold in the middle of a November night. Inside, even the lice would feel crowded, so close were the pallets packed together. Then Simon called to mind the stone storage sheds where bins of grain and roots were kept in Roselynde. If Abergavenny had them too. . . . He started off again and Rhiannon followed, with Math at her heels like a dog.

Even starved as they both were for each other, the

crowded conditions and organized bedlam of the courtyards began to quell their desire. If Simon had not already
been so tired, he would have suggested that they ride to
his mother's keep at Clyro. He began to consider the idea
seriously while they struggled across the bailey, but the
sheds were there. He chose the nearest, even though it was
small and low-roofed, and prepared to break the lock—
only the door was not locked; it opened easily to Simon's
pull.

The odor of sheepskins in the shed was too strong to
be pleasant, yet both Simon's and Rhiannon's eyes lighted
and their smiles were unstrained and full of remembered
gladness. The shed had been left open so that anyone who
was cold could take a fleece. They were too large to steal
easily and of little value in any case. Simon laughed and
jammed the door shut. Whoever was cold would have to
wait until tomorrow or find some other source of warmth.

It was black as pitch inside, but when they tripped over
a skin they fell soft on a pile of fleeces and lay kissing.
The shed walls were thick so that only a muted noise
drifted in through the air vents under the roof. They were
separated from the crush and excitement in the bailey
outside, and the feel and smell of the sheepskins—not so
overpowering now that they were accustomed to it—
carried them back in memory to the open hills and the
shepherd's quiet hut.

They began to undress each other, fumbling and laughing in the dark, but the tension and passion of the raid were
still in them. Simon's teeth left bruises on Rhiannon's
breasts, and her nails scored his back and buttocks. She
was so aroused—by abstinence, by the excitement of
being captured and the battle that followed, by their
strange yet familiar situation—that she came to climax
almost as soon as Simon entered her. He was not ready.
Near bursting but still reluctant to let his pleasure end, he
held off, kissing and caressing until Rhiannon began to
moan again, and he brought her with him to a second
fulfillment.

They slept at once, both of them, like mallet-struck
oxen, snuggled into the fleeces and covered by their
doubled cloaks, until a cat's yowl and a man's cry of pain

and curse woke them. A faint light was coming in through the air vents under the eaves. Simon lifted himself on one elbow to call a warning, but it was not necessary.

"Leave it alone," a hoarse voice shouted. "That is the witch-woman's familiar. She will curse you—if you need cursing after the cat has done with you."

"Damn Math," Rhiannon said faintly, "he is giving me a dreadful reputation."

"And undeserved?" Simon teased. "Bassett is sure you are a witch. He would accuse you to the Church, only he does not wish to offend your father. And you have Pembroke badly worried, although not about witchcraft. What on earth did you say to them?"

"I? I said nothing, as a modest maiden should," Rhiannon exclaimed, but she started to laugh. "It was that silly man you sent with me and the wagon—Siorl. We had a little trouble because there was fighting near the road. We shot two or three, and then a few charged us. Ymlladd —perhaps by accident I gave the signal, or he knew what to do himself—he rose to fight. That must have frightened Math, and he let out a yowl that even startled me. I do not know what those stupid men thought it was, but they turned and ran. I suppose Siorl thought I had told my familiar to drive them away."

Simon had to laugh, too. He knew Siorl had regarded Rhiannon with awe ever since the stay at Dinas Emrys. After a minute he frowned. "It is funny and not funny. We will have to think of a way for you to redeem yourself. Someday this war will be over and Bassett and Pembroke will be reestablished. We cannot have word spread in England that you are a witch. But what I want to know is what you were doing in that camp in the first place?"

She told him the whole story, from Llewelyn's letter through her capture. Simon laughed again at the Pwyll's wife fabrication and Math's defense of her when she resisted de Guisnes, but despite his amusement his eyes were troubled.

"You need not tell me it was foolish and dangerous," Rhiannon said seriously. "I will not do it again. I would have waited at Builth, or come here perhaps, only—only I was happy, and I wanted you to be happy, too, Simon. But I will never be so foolish again. I know I could have become a chain to bind you. What happened in the camp after I left?"

"We cleaned them out. They are naked as babes, and we are rich. We have everything, even the pay chests and the king's tent and some of his plate and jewelry which, for some reason, were not taken to the keep. They have no horses, except the few that were in Grosmount, no oxen, no food, no tents for the men, no armor, no weapons. And we tried not to kill if we could avoid it, but they know we could have slit their throats in the dark."

"Is the war over, then?" she asked hopefully.

"Not yet, but I do not think it will be long. The king will be hysterical after this. First he will blame Richard and make all sorts of useless threats that he cannot fulfill. Then, after another defeat or two, when he realizes he is helpless and is being beaten, he will turn his hatred on those who put him into this case."

"But until then you will be at war?" Her voice was tight with fear.

Simon hesitated, but he said, at last, "Yes, Rhiannon. It is my duty."

"I will not try to turn you from it," she assured him. "I am not that foolish. But I must be near, Simon. I cannot stay at Angharad's Hall or Dinas Emrys. I must be near. I will stay where you tell me and will not add to your danger—so long as it be close enough that you can come to me—or I to you—when the battle is over, soon after the battle is over."

Simon burst out laughing. "Soon enough that I still desire to couple? Am I so worthless at other times?"

"Simon, it is no jest. When I am near, I am not afraid."

"I understand, *eneit,* believe me, I understand," he assured her, still smiling. "I will take you with me whenever I can, right into the camp. Was it that? Was that why you turned away from me? Or was it something I did? I must know, lest I drive you away again."

"No, that will never happen. I told you so many times that it was not you, but I who was at fault. You see, I never loved anyone except my mother and father and I—I only loved them as a child loves."

"I do not understand."

"It is so hard to make plain," she sighed. "A child

thinks its elders are invulnerable. A child does not believe in death. When Gwydyon, my grandfather, died and I saw my mother's heart torn, I must have learned a dreadful fear, so dreadful that I closed off my own heart."

"I see. But then you agreed. What changed your mind after that?"

"I never really agreed. I was pretending to myself that if we did not marry, I would feel less. It is stupid to lie to oneself, but fear makes one stupid. As for what frightened me away altogether—I met your family."

"But they loved you, Rhiannon."

"I know it. I felt it. That was what frightened me so much. You see, they were all real people, not like my mother and father, whom I still saw with my child's eye and therefore never thought of as growing old or susceptible to any danger. I heard your father's harsh breathing—" She stopped because Simon winced, and she kissed him softly.

"Now I see better what you mean," he said grimly. "I prefer to think of Papa as invulnerable, too."

"Yes, but I could not. And I saw how Gilliane fears for Adam—"

"Which is about as sensible as fearing Roselynde will be washed away in the rain. Adam is a bull."

"Yes, I saw that, too, but her fear hurt me. And I worried about Sybelle and Walter. . . . Everything hurt me. When I began to love you, my shell was forced open, and I was all soft inside. All I could think of was to run away."

"Poor love," Simon crooned, stroking her and laughing softly. "And then you found you could not run away from love."

"Yes, but how did you know?"

"I have tried it too, of course, but I always go back to Roselynde—and run away again."

"I made a song. When we go home to Dinas Emrys, I will sing it to you."

Those were beautiful words, *home to Dinas Emrys*. They would visit the other keeps, but Dinas Emrys above the Vale of Waters with the voice-laden winds was the right home for the witch-woman and her lover.

AUTHOR'S NOTE

❖∙❖

I wish to apologize to my readers for the use of feudal terminology in discussing political and social relationships in thirteenth-century Wales. I am well aware that feudal relationships were only beginning to appear among the Welsh at that time (except, of course, in the English- or, rather, Norman-dominated areas). However, I felt that a satisfactory explanation of the political operation of clan and blood ties could not be given without impeding the story; after all, this is a historical novel, not a textbook. Thus, I chose deliberately to use a terminology with which my readers have become familiar, and I hope I will be pardoned for the anachronism.

Again, as usual, Simon and Rhiannon and their families (except for Prince Llewelyn ap Iowerth) and servants are fictional, as are the individual adventures in which the fictional characters are involved. However, any major event in which the historical characters, such as Prince Llewelyn, Hubert de Burgh, or Richard Marshal, Earl of Pembroke, take part is a real historical event. These I have described as accurately as possible, even if the description is given through the eyes of a fictional character.

To the best of my ability I have also presented living conditions in the period realistically. However, this necessitates a peculiar balancing act. In actuality thirteenth-century living conditions were unclean and uncomfortable. For example, all people, including the nobility, who bathed when convenient, were afflicted with fleas and lice. Sanitary conditions were appalling. It was not unusual to throw unwanted bits of food such as bone or gristle on the floor where cats, dogs, rats, and mice, along with an incredible variety of insects, scavenged the remains. Much woolen clothing was worn, and this might be washed only once or twice in a year, although the linen might be done more frequently or special circumstances might produce an extra scouring.

Yet, to the people who lived in these conditions, there was nothing extraordinary about them. They did not consider themselves dirty or uncomfortable, except in unusual circumstances. Therefore, to make a point of the discomfort of medieval life in comparison with our own is to falsify the conditions more surely than to ignore them or mention them lightly and in passing. Thus, I do not dwell on the dreadful fact that 60 percent of all children born died before they were two years of age, mostly of typhus or typhoid, and nearly 30 percent of all women died in childbirth. Nor do I emphasize the minor dismaying differences, such as the chilblains everyone, high and low, suffered in winter, or that human as well as animal excrement was carefully collected to be used as fertilizer, or the myriad other habits that would horrify a modern person.

If man survives into the future without any of the catastrophes that now threaten us actually overtaking us, our descendants may well feel the same horror when they look back on the primitive conditions in which we live. As we are not aware of what we lack, neither were medieval people. They were happy or sad as extraordinary circumstances affected them—good and bad masters, love and hate, war and peace—and I have tried to show them as nearly as possible as they were.

Roberta Gellis
Roslyn Heights, NY
January 1982

GLOSSARY

BALLISTA: a gigantic crossbow which hurled huge arrows.

BARON: a man who held land in exchange for doing military service to the king or another superior noble; in medieval times the term was general and applied to the greatest as well as to minor noblemen.

BETROTHAL: the engagement of a man or woman in a contract of marriage; a legal condition far more binding than a modern "engagement."

BLIAUNT: a low-necked gown, usually laced on the sides to fit the body, and worn over a tunic; in summer it would be sleeveless and in winter it would have wide sleeves that showed the tight-fitting sleeves of the tunic.

CASTELLAN: the governor or constable of a castle, assigned at the will of the "holder" of the castle and liable to removal at the holder's will. There were some cases of hereditary castellanships.

CHAUSSES: a garment much like modern pantyhose, except that chausses were sewn, not knitted, and therefore were not form-fitting; they were tied at the waist with a drawstring and fitted to the legs with cross garters.

COMPLINE: approximately 9:00 to 10:00 P.M.

CRENEL: an indentation in an embattled parapet; the opening, about knee height, in a battlement through which archers could shoot.

CROSS GARTERS: long, thin strips of cloth or leather that were wrapped crosswise around the leg and tied below the knee to prevent the chausses from bagging excessively.

CYFLYM: "swift" in Welsh; the name of Rhiannon's mare.

CYMRY: the Welsh people; this is what the Welsh called themselves in their own language.

DESTRIER: a war horse, a highly bred and highly trained animal.

DISSEISE: to put out of possession; to dispossess a person from his estates in such a way that his legal heirs were also disqualified from inheriting; the term was usually used when the dispossession was wrongful.

FEBRIFUGE: a medication to reduce fever.

FOREBUILDING: an addition to a keep that sheltered the stairs which went up to the entrance. For reasons of defense, no keep had an entrance on the ground floor.

GEAS: a fate, combined with an unbreakable compulsion to seek that fate.

HAUBERK: armor; the mail shirt made up of linked rings or chains of metal; it had a hood that went over the head and could be laced at the neck and extended a little below the knee, being split in the middle, front and back, almost to the crotch so that a man could mount and ride a horse.

HOSEN: dialectic plural of *hose*. In this book specifically, the mail leggings worn to protect the legs in battle.

KEEP: technically the innermost, strongest structure or central tower of a medieval castle, the place that served as a last defense; in general used to mean the whole castle.

MANGONEL: an engine of war; a military machine for casting large stones.

MEINIE: a household guard; the group of men-at-arms employed by a nobleman.

MERLON: the part of an embattled parapet between two embrasures (crenels); a higher portion of wall behind which archers or men-at-arms could be protected.

NATURAL SON, DAUGHTER: a child born out of wedlock; an illegitimate child.

THE NORMANS: technically, descendants of the men who had come to England with William the Bastard (the Conqueror) but expanded to include later arrivals from all parts of France.

PROVENDER: food, especially dried or preserved food, like wheat or salt meat and fish.

ROWEL: to use a spur, a moderately sharp metal spike attached to the heels, to prick or stab a horse so that it would run faster.

SAESON: an English person; the word in medieval times was used in a derogatory sense.

SEE: the abode of a bishop or the diocese he controls.

SOLAR: a withdrawing room, usually better lit than the great hall, reserved for the use of the lord and lady and their invited guests.

TERCE: approximately 9:00 A.M.

WAIN: a large open vehicle, usually four-wheeled, drawn by horses or oxen and used for heavy loads.

WIMPLE: a veil of linen or silk worn by women and so folded as to envelop the head, hair, chin, sides of the face, and neck.

WITCH'S FAMILIAR: the animal through which magic—usually evil—was performed; most often the familiar was a cat, but it might be anything at all.